SLASHER GIRLS & MONSTER BOYS

SLASHER GIRLS & MONSTER BOYS

Stories selected by APRIL GENEVIEVE TUCHOLKE

DIAL BOOKS
an imprint of Penguin Group (USA) LLC

DIAL BOOKS
Published by the Penguin Group
Penguin Group (USA) LLC
375 Hudson Street
New York, New York 10014

USA/Canada/UK/Ireland/Australia/New Zealand/India/South Africa/China

penguin.com
A Penguin Random House Company

Library of Congress Cataloging-in-Publication Data

Slasher girls and monster boys / edited by April Genevieve Tucholke.
pages cm
ISBN 978-0-8037-4173-7 (hardback)
1. Horror tales, American. 2. Short stories, American.
[1. Horror stories. 2. Short stories.] I. Tucholke, April Genevieve.
PZ5.S629 2015
[Fic]—dc23   2015003730

Printed in the United States of America

3 5 7 9 10 8 6 4 2

Designed by Maya Tatsukawa
Text set in Sabon MT Std

For everyone who read Stephen King
when they were way too young.
–A. G. T.

CONTENTS

THE BIRDS OF AZALEA STREET

Nova Ren Suma

When the police questioned me—same as they questioned Paisley and Katie-Marie—they didn't want to hear about the birds. They weren't paying attention. None of the adults around here ever did. Even when the body bag was carted out, on wheels, and the wheels got caught in a gopher hole in the lawn, and the stretcher knocked into the tree, and the sudden motion caused a whole host of birds to burst out of the branches, exploding into the blue over our subdivision, and I looked up after them, and the EMTs guiding the stretcher stopped and looked up, and all my neighbors who'd gathered to see what the commotion was about looked up, heavenward, into the sky, even then they thought it meant nothing. "So that's where the birds have been hiding," one of my neighbors said. Not one adult could connect it to the fact that Leonard was now dead.

I knew the birds were no longer hungry—they'd feasted and had their fill, and now they took off, every last one of them, satisfied. But the adults of Azalea Street, curious about the murder, seeing as it was the first since our subdivision was founded, gathered in knots on our landscaped sidewalk corners to talk. They were hungry for information and gory details. They should have looked out of their windows sooner. They should have been watching. We were.

Truth is, we'd been watching out for our neighbor Leonard for years. Since we hit puberty, and for some of us, that was way early. Since forever and always, it felt like. Before we saw him bring that girl home in the dead of night, all we knew was that he'd been trying to get his hands on us.

My house on Azalea Street was next door to his house, so I'd say I got the worst of it, what with my parents always feeling sorry for him and inviting him for dinner on Sundays. The three of them would sip watery pre-dinner drinks out back by the bug zapper, and somehow my parents would miss how, when he apologized for his stomach growling, the object he had his eyes hooked on wasn't the cheese plate. It was me.

He said things to me sometimes, in the hallway while heading for the guest bathroom. Did I have a boyfriend yet? Did I ever happen to try the kind of kissing that used tongue? Then he'd shuffle away, fast, making me question what I'd heard. When I caught him looking at me later, over the pear tart he'd brought from next door, or over the sugar-dusted strudel, I saw his round black glasses go dim with sweat and fog.

Other girls had run-ins with him too. Some of our fathers and stepfathers used to work with Leonard at the plant, before he got downsized and they got to keep their jobs, so they said we had to be civil. Even kind. Our mothers and stepmothers appreciated how he'd bring something fresh-baked for potlucks and fund-raisers, like a Bundt cake or a still-warm pie. None of our parents saw what we could see, which had us decide that growing up into adulthood must mean going blind.

Teenage girls know more than we're given credit for. We sense danger even when everyone's telling us it's fine, he's a perfectly nice man, an upstanding member of our community, have you *tasted* his sugar-cream pie?

When Leonard's gaudy lawn came into view, we knew it was time to cross the street. Ever since he lost his job, he liked to feed the birds, and he hung lots of birdhouses, spilled lots of seed.

It seemed innocent from the outside, maybe. But out back, from over the white picket fence that separated Leonard's house from mine, I could swear I heard the shots. Little pops in the air. I was never sure of it, never positive. But one time there was a squawk and a feathered eruption as a bird went down.

I can't prove he shot it, but I did see him hunching over it, kicking it with his enormous shoe. Other times I suspected he used poison in the feeders. This was slower and left them stiff, so when they fell from their perches they dropped to the ground like rocks. I found one over the fence on our side of the lawn once—red-bellied and dark-feathered, its beak open mid-bite—and I buried it in an orange shoebox, the most cheerful I could find, near where we made the cairn for Buster.

When the birds stopped coming—not just to Leonard's house, but to my house and to the Willards' house across the street, to Aggie's house a few doors down, to any house I passed on the way to the bus stop and back, all our trees birdless, all our patches of sky clean—I guess he turned to other hobbies. That must have been when he bought the camera.

We'd catch him standing on his porch, fancy long-lensed camera trained outward like he was waiting for a finch or a woodpecker. But with all feathery creatures avoiding his feeders, he couldn't have been aiming for the birds. His telephoto lens was as long as an arm and seemed suspiciously trained at the sidewalk. When Katie-Marie went past in her field hockey skirt, on the way to my house from her house so my mom could drive us to practice, she swore she could hear his camera snapping. She took off in a run.

The last time one of us was alone with him, it was Paisley. She said he cornered her in his kitchen and forced her to bake bread. Her mom had sent her on an errand, wanting one of Leonard's recipes, and when Paisley knocked on his back door, she found him elbow-deep in flour, prepping sticky coils of corpse-pale dough.

"Why, hello there," he said in his deep baritone. His lips were pink and plushy and we didn't like to look at them when he shaped words.

Paisley told us she could sense the hunger coming off of him, like she was plump and roasting and he hadn't eaten for a week.

She heard a faint titter behind her, a lone bird that had lost its way in the treetops over our subdivision and drifted to the wrong set of branches over the wrong house. Or maybe it wasn't lost and that was a warning call. Maybe it knew what was about to be set in motion.

Paisley stepped inside his house.

"What're you doing?" Paisley had said. I would have asked for the recipe without going in, I would have told my mom to just get Leonard to e-mail it, but Paisley pressed her whole body into his kitchen and let the door shut behind her. She leaned forward on the counter, letting her long hair fall and her split ends dance. She took a finger. With it, she traced a word in the flour dusting the counter for him to see. It said *hi*. She was testing him. She was testing herself.

Leonard lit up. We imagined it wasn't often a teenage girl started a conversation with him voluntarily. He was pink in the face usually, but at that point he was bright red.

He began talking. He kind of couldn't shut up. He was explaining his method for baking braided bread, and then it became very important, essential even, to teach Paisley how to properly knead the dough in order to do it herself. She had to put effort into it, use all her strength and not hold back. It's just that she had such small hands.

On the windowsill, while this was going on, the bird was perched, black-eyed and unblinking. Paisley only thought it was weird later. Leonard was behind Paisley, very close, so close, she couldn't back up and get around him. She felt the bird watching. She smelled Leonard's yeasty breath.

We know our parents wouldn't believe us if we told them. Leonard was only *instructing* her. He was only being a *kind neighbor*, which in these times was a dying breed. That's what they would have said. They wanted us to have skills beyond phone-scrolling and one-finger texting, like knowing how to bake edible food in the oven and feed ourselves if they suddenly were dead.

But we believed Paisley right away. We knew he was too close. We knew how he pressed his front up against her to adjust her technique and how he breathed heavy, shaggy breaths against the nape of her neck. We knew how much he was enjoying this.

"Knead," he told her in a low, careful voice. "Go on, yes, like that. Knead."

He meant the slick mush in her hands, but Paisley had had enough. Out of all of us, she was the strongest, and that went far beyond her arm-wrestling skills against her brothers and the thick runner's muscles in her legs. She told us she'd only wanted to prove he was a perv, prove it once and for all so there was no longer any question, and with this little bakery demonstration, she had won.

She elbowed him in the stomach and whipped a braid of wet dough at his rosy, stubbly face. She dodged him and was heading for the door before the dough was even on the baking sheet, before the baking sheet was even in the blazing oven, before the bread had risen, before it had browned. She was breathing fast. The bird outside the window flapped its wings in a frantic slap and took off.

Behind Paisley, there was a strange sound. A faint, high-pitched whimper. In a moment of weakness, Paisley paused and turned back.

He was talking, but his voice was different now. Smaller in his throat. Pathetic.

He only wanted to teach somebody something, he called after her. He was sorry, he said, he didn't mean to scare her, it's just that he led such a lonely life.

The door was open. The sky bare and blank.

Paisley held still in the entryway. She was questioning herself, having a peculiar moment of compassion. Sometimes she could be so very live-and-let-live.

"Maybe . . ." Paisley started.

Leonard pinkened—or else he was standing in direct range of the oven light.

"Maybe you should get a dog," she said at last. "So you're not so lonely."

He looked down the length of his giant legs to his giant feet. No dogs, he said. Animals didn't like him for some reason. He shrugged.

Paisley smirked. She had a dark streak. "Then you should buy a blow-up doll online and make her your wife," she said. "I can send you a link." At this, his mouth gaping open, his cheeks full of flames, she took off. She'd gotten what she came for: Leonard's sugar-cream pie recipe for her mother was already secured in hand.

But so was the thought of Leonard getting himself a girl.

It was Paisley, we've agreed, who gave him the idea. He couldn't have her, and he couldn't have any of the rest of us, but his hunger was still there, eating at him.

It was days later when we heard his car pull into his driveway in

NOVA REN SUMA

the middle of the night. His house was one of the smaller designs in our subdivision and didn't have a garage, so we could see everything from my bedroom window. There was nowhere he could hide.

Usually his car held only him and sometimes a tripod or some grocery bags. That night we noted the questionable shadow in his passenger seat. It was taller than usual. It had a distinctly human-size head.

Had he listened to Paisley and bought himself a companion? No. Our illusion was shattered when he circled the car to open the passenger-side door, and the shadow moved on its own and stepped out.

What he came home with that night couldn't be brought to life with a tire pump. She was already alive and breathing. We would have sworn she was real.

She wore a dark hood, and around it was a haze of fur, like she'd just landed in our subdivision from the North Pole and didn't realize that, down here, it was spring.

The problem with the hood was that it hid her face. And her puffy coat hid the rest of her, though it did stop at her hips, and her legs could be made out beneath it. Even from my bedroom window next door, with a picket fence between us and the dark having fallen and the motion sensors not responding to the motion as she walked past where we swore they were. Even with all that, I could see her legs. Her legs were in black stockings, the kind with seams. At the end of her legs were little pointed blades that took to the pavement like ice picks. When she touched grass, her heels sunk in and she stopped and the light from the car door showed us one leg bent to retrieve the shoe. I wanted a leg like that. I wanted to grow up and look like that and have two.

Paisley was sleeping over. So was Katie-Marie.

"Leonard has a new friend," Paisley announced. "A *lady* friend.

Did you know about this, Tasha? You knew, and didn't tell us?"

I shook my head, unable to keep my eyes off the lady in the night. She'd retrieved her shoe, slipped it back on. She was now standing still on the lawn while he was closing the car door. The fur trim on her coat rippled in the wind like a layer of black feathers. Her legs didn't fidget or pace or shake, showing no hint of nerves. Leonard was right there. He was *right there,* and she didn't run.

"I've never seen her before," I said. I would have remembered.

But there was something about the way she moved. She didn't seem surprised by the clutter of ugly, vacant dollhouses meant to entice the nonexistent birds. She wove around the mazelike lawn as if she'd been here before.

"Is she tied up in the trunk?" Katie-Marie called out from across the room. "Is she bound and gagged?"

Katie-Marie couldn't see the scene outside. She was lying on my bed, an arm draped over her eyes. Before we heard Leonard's car, we'd been trying to psychically impress boys we liked into becoming our boyfriends by thinking about them with pointed intention and hoping, somehow, across the airwaves, they heard. Paisley had long given up on Georges, and I only halfheartedly tried to psychically seduce Takeshi because I was pretty sure he liked me already and I figured I didn't have to try so hard. But Katie-Marie really wanted Mike, and her forehead was all scrunched up with effort.

The power of the mind was something we experimented with on Friday night sleepovers. Also light-as-a-feather-stiff-as-a-board, and the Ouija, before Katie-Marie's dad burned it in her backyard. We also tried texting boys alluring emoticons and, on one brave night, posted photos of our faceless boobs to a message board, but then took them down fast when the comments got scary and promised among us that we'd never show the photos to anyone, not even Georges or Takeshi or Mike.

After Paisley's visit to Leonard's house, we had wished harm on him and tried out our psychic impressions to make that happen. We realized it would be easiest if he just went away, so we wished him gone, like to Florida. Then he showed up for Sunday dinner like always, my father sharing a cigar with him in the garage, where he thought we couldn't smell the stink, and I had to admit our magical thinking wasn't making any magic. Leonard was still here.

All that seemed so juvenile now. Leonard had real live company, and we couldn't see who it was.

"Leonard's friend is walking on her own two feet," I narrated for Katie-Marie. "Leonard's friend's nails are painted"—I waited for it as she reached up to touch one of his gaudy hanging birdhouses, then recoiled like it stung—"ooh, black."

"No," Paisley corrected me. "Purple."

She was right. His lady friend had dark, deep-purple-painted nails, and they were long and curling, almost like claws. The hand seemed to lift up and out. It seemed to face us, to be motioning our way, like it was . . . waving. Then the sleeve dropped and hid her hand from view.

I blinked.

"She has very nice legs," Paisley said.

Katie-Marie finally opened her eyes and crawled over to join us by the window. "I hope he doesn't bake her in his oven like he tried to do with you, Pais," she whispered.

Paisley nodded solemnly.

We lost the will to make jokes or even talk. We watched as Leonard unlocked the front door and his friend entered his house. We knew the layout because there were only five different kinds of architecturally approved homes for the subdivision, and his was the one with the front porch and the sunken living room and the two bedrooms that had windows like eyes on the second floor. She must have gone down to the living room, because we didn't see a light come on.

Leonard came out once more and headed for the trunk. He seemed so eager. We watched him lift something out, and at first we assumed it must have been a suitcase, but then we noticed the odd, bulky shape and the way he had to circle it with his long arms. The birdcage was round and empty, as far as we could tell from this distance, and it had a latched and gated entrance that flapped in the wind. He carried it toward the house and didn't return for more luggage.

Her legs had told us one thing. Her lack of suitcase another. But it was the quivering smile on Leonard's face when he walked under the porch light that told us so much more.

The first night there were no birds, as usual. The first night was dark and quiet. The first night was long.

The second night, Paisley and Katie-Marie stayed at my place again, even though Katie-Marie's house had satellite TV and all the premium channels, and we perched at my Leonard-facing windows. We'd skipped dinner. We were worried for his lady friend and had lost our appetites. She hadn't come outside all day, which meant we hadn't seen her leave. We discussed ways of sending over a warning, like slipped in the mail slot, or left on the welcome mat to tell her she should not feel so welcome, but we knew he'd see it before she did. We tried looking up his number and couldn't find it, so we couldn't call and feign wrong number if he picked up. We were deep in discussion when she appeared at the window across the way.

The light came on, a bright spot in the darkness, and we ran to the window, huddling under the sill. One by one, we popped a head up.

Paisley said she was prettier than she thought she'd be—a high nine to Leonard's withering two—but to me, her face was exactly how I'd pictured it, as if I'd selected her from a catalog. Or conjured her up from the *Vogue*-glossy pages of my imagination and sent her here. In a way it felt like I had.

She was all mystery. She had dark, low-lidded eyes and a small, subtle mouth that did not seem capable of making a smile. Her cheekbones reflected stabs of light. Her hair was purple-black, much like her nails. It was wild, ragged, coasting into her eyes. I wanted to get close enough to see her eyes.

"Do you think she goes to our school?" Katie-Marie said.

We were getting bothered by how young she looked. She wasn't so much a lady as a girl like we were. The age difference couldn't have been much. Chop off a couple, and she could have been us.

"No," I said. "No way she goes to our school." She didn't look like she lived around here—she didn't look like any girl we knew.

"We should go in there," Paisley said. "Tasha, your parents made you water his plants when he was away on vacation that one time, didn't they? We need a key to his house."

I knew where the hide-a-key was kept—it looked like a rock under the fifth shrub. But should we break in right then, in the middle of the night? Should we barge in, guns blazing? The only weapons we had were a field hockey stick and a bottle of slick, sticky leave-in conditioner to aim at the eyes.

"We can't go in there!" Katie-Marie said. "We have to talk to her from here."

I nodded.

She was in the bathroom window, at the sink. We could tell by the way she bent down, and how when she came up, her face was dripping wet. Cleaned of makeup, she looked even younger. She didn't see us through the curtain at first, but then our waving must have gotten her attention. She parted his ugly curtains and she put her pretty face to the screen. It pressed against her skin and waffle-ironed her cheeks.

She was watching us as we'd spent the weekend watching her.

"Tell her to run," Katie-Marie said. "Tell her to get out of the house right now."

"We can't yell that," Paisley said. "He'll hear."

"Tell her she can come over here," Katie-Marie said. "You have that extra sleeping bag, Tasha. Tell her."

I hesitated.

"We can just yell fire?" Katie-Marie suggested. "Then she'll know it's an emergency and come out?"

"They both will then," Paisley said. "And Tasha's parents and brother will wake up too. And they'll be like, Where's the fire? And we'll have to say there isn't one."

"Let's write her a note," I said.

We started off with a simple message. I used my special notepad with the lavender paper and the pink lines, so she wouldn't be scared, and used marker to write in the biggest letters that could fit on the page so she could see from across the way.

WHO, I wrote, ARE YOU?

She cocked her head in the frame of the window, eyeing our words. She made no reply.

I held my arms as far out the window as I could, waving our sign, but still . . . nothing.

"Do you think she doesn't speak English maybe?" Katie-Marie asked. "Do you think she's from another country?"

"Oh, *everyone* speaks English," Paisley said. "Tell her our names. She's probably just shy."

PAISLEY, I wrote, with an arrow, and held the sign under the face of Paisley. *KATIE-MARIE*, for Katie-Marie. Then I shoved my body out of my window and showed her: *TASHA, I LIVE NEXT DOOR, HELLO.*

No change in expression. She bent down once more and came up with a wet face again. She dried her face with a towel. She barely blinked.

We offered her my cell number. We asked if she was in danger. We said, *Do you need help? Should we call 911?*

There wasn't any hint she understood.

We stopped, frustrated.

Then she made a movement. Sudden, like time skipping. There'd been a screen in the window, but she must have popped it out. Her bare arm, purple-taloned and catching the moonlight, came thrusting out into the open air. In her fist was something white and balled-up, like a hunk of tissues, but when she opened her hand, the white thing cascaded into one long, light expanse and caught the wind and fluttered down and down. I thought for a moment that she was performing a trick—a gasp of supernatural, like that time our few fingers lifted Paisley's body a whole inch above the carpet and when we removed our fingers, she stayed aloft from our concentrated energy alone. At least it felt like she did.

But no. The girl in the window had only thrown something white-colored out through the frame and it landed in a heap over the fence and on my side of the lawn.

A bedsheet? No, not a sheet from a bed. A veil.

The kind a bride would wear on her big day. Why was she showing this to us? Was this some kind of clue?

The veil drifted languidly in the faint wind, and understanding came over me.

"That's his wife," I said. The word turned my stomach. "He found some girl to marry him and he brought her home."

"No," Paisley said in horror.

The girl in the window watched us watching her. She did not scream. She didn't have to.

"Oh my freaking god," Katie-Marie said, and the dread in her voice made our hearts seize and our fear spike. "Do you think he made her marry him? Do you think he stole her passport? Do you think her parents know where she is? Do you think she's a prisoner?"

What did we know? Only that we had suspicions. We had to assume she was here on false pretenses, because who would marry Leonard by actual choice? We suspected we were the only ones alive who were aware she was here on Azalea Street, inside that house. He could have gotten her from anywhere. Maybe he found her in a parking lot. Maybe he picked her up on the side of the road and offered her a ride. Maybe he bought her off the Internet, like Paisley had innocently suggested. Maybe the girl came from nowhere we could name, and would fly off to nowhere we could pinpoint on a map, and maybe, ever after, we would remember her and think about where she could have ended up.

She replaced the screen in the window and turned off the light. We couldn't see where she went in the darkness, but we felt her there, right next door. Our subdivision vibrated with the sense of her, this stranger among us, this caged girl.

We didn't suspect then that she had come as if we'd called for her, as if our magical thinking on the night Paisley still smelled like yeasty-wet dough had come to fruition, rising up like the browned loaf of bread before it turned charcoal and burned.

"We have to help her," I said.

We tried to stay up all night, making plans that became all the more impossible, until Katie-Marie crashed on one side of my bed and Paisley crashed on the other and there was no room for me to sandwich in between, so I had to take the sleeping bag on the floor.

I curled up on the carpet, near the window. Just as I was about to drift to sleep, I sensed stirring over the fence. Something pulled on me, forced me to sit up.

I rubbed the sleep from my eyes. I was right: She'd come outside. I spied the girl through the window. There she was, his new bride, in the backyard of his house. His lawn actually touched our lawn—the same grass grew—but the white wooden fence stood between. Still, seeing her bare feet in the dewy-green blades of grass, mashing her toes in, like she wanted to wake the ants and gather up all the mud, it felt like she was walking *my* patch of green grass, wandering my backyard.

Where was Leonard? Sleeping. The light in his bedroom was off.

The girl was out there alone, in her fur-lined coat. Nothing on her feet and nothing holding back her hair. Without the makeup and the stockings, she looked smaller than before. She looked skinned.

She turned her face up, and then up some more, and at first I thought she was counting the stars above our subdivision, seeing if the stars here were the same ones she remembered from there, wherever she came from.

All this I could see through the window of my bedroom.

Then I noticed the sag in her cheeks and the shift-shaping of her mouth and realized she wasn't doing what I thought she was. She wasn't stargazing. She was searching the tree branches. I don't know why. Each one she came to was empty.

She reached the farthest tree. She put one hand, palm out, onto the rough bark and pressed it in, like she wanted the ridges imprinted on her skin. Then she pressed her other hand into a nearby spot. Then she pressed her face, the whole side of her face, cheek and chin and eye-bone and nose bridge and nostril, into the bark of the tree and stayed that way for some time.

The sounds of the neighborhood filtered through. I could hear them faintly: Mrs. Abernathy had her car alarm set too sensitive again and the acorns dropping kept setting it off. The Willards across the street were up way too late watching a sports game of some kind, I could tell by the cheers. A dog barked—the Ruiz dog. Another dog barked—that mini screechy one that belonged to the McCoys. A car pulled up, quiet, and a door opened, a giggle emerged, and then so silently like it was lined with cotton, the door closed. That was Aggie home from the party with her boyfriend; her mom would kill her if she knew she'd stayed out till three.

All around, the usual things were going on, and down there in Leonard's yard was the girl we thought could be his child bride, hugging a gnarly tree instead of sleeping in bed with him. It was the saddest thing I'd seen all year, even worse than the time Miranda from school showed us her suicide notes and asked us to pick the best-written one so she could impress her dad.

The girl stood still. She looked up in her dark coat at the branches. The clouds moved to cover the stars and not even an owl hooted, but far away, down the street, Mrs. Abernathy's car alarm sounded again like a sudden, lonely song.

I closed my eyes. I told myself to get up, get to my feet, put on

NOVA REN SUMA

some jeans, they didn't have to be clean jeans, go outside. Go help that girl.

When I opened my eyes, the sky was filled with them. It was night, and they never came out at night, but there they were, a ferocious fog of winged creatures, covering her coat and coating her hair and seeming to beat all around her, to drone a cyclone around her body, to buzz. The birds had come back.

I couldn't have said for how long this went on. A few minutes at least, maybe more. I really had to pee, so it seemed much longer.

Then the flock of birds lifted, and the black sky was full of static like a dream had already been long going, and I was asleep and didn't come to again until sunrise.

We decided to knock on Leonard's door in the morning. We couldn't wait. We'd considered calling the police and leaving an anonymous tip to check his house for a missing girl, but then Paisley said we should see her in person first. How many times had we said Leonard squicked us out and our parents responded by saying we were exaggerating, making fun of the poor man, being cruel? If we saw the girl in daylight—better yet, if we could speak to her, face-to-face, if we could introduce ourselves and say a proper hello—then we'd know for sure if she needed saving.

It was Paisley's idea to bring the empty bag of sugar and ask if we could borrow some (we dumped it out in the garbage so it would look like it needed filling), and it was Katie-Marie's idea to invent a baking project we were doing to raise money for field hockey. We'd noticed how he paid extra-careful attention to us whenever we wore the plaid skirts home from practice.

We did look for it in the grass, walking all up and down the white picket fence trying to find it, but it wasn't there. The bridal veil. The wind must have blown it away in the night, or else the birds must have snatched it.

When we entered his yard through the fence divider, that's when we noticed them. Birds on the branches above us. Birds all along the bushes and on every shrub. Birds clamoring at his feeders and lining the sloping arc of his roof. Birds on the gutters. Birds perched on the roof of his car. There were so many. Silent. Pointy beaks aimed down on us, following our path to the back door, beady eyes on our every move.

Paisley knocked.

When he came to the door, he didn't open it all the way. Through the crack, the Sunday sunlight showed us his pink-tinged face, and his mouth, so fat, it looked swollen.

I held up the empty sugar bag but swallowed my words too fast. Katie-Marie grabbed on to my shirt from behind, pulling the neck tight and practically strangling me.

"Hi, Leonard. Good afternoon. I mean good morning. Um. We were hoping we could borrow some sugar?" Paisley said, taking over. She talked fast. Bake-sale, she was saying. To raise money for the team. He didn't need to know that the season was over or that not all of us were on the team.

"What are you making?" he asked, and his words jolted us, because we'd forgotten to determine what it was we were pretending to make before we walked over.

"Cookies," Katie-Marie said from behind me while at the same time I said, "Cupcakes," and Paisley said, "Cake pops."

We shot glances at one another, alarmed.

"You'll need a lot of sugar, then," Leonard said. "It's early, so I'm not decent yet. Wait here."

He closed the screen and then the door behind it. Paisley had her body pressed up against the screen, and it practically scraped off the tip of her nose. She rested an ear to it, trying hard to listen. But she shook her head: nothing. We strained our ears in case the girl was crying for help, and we wondered from where she'd be calling—from the basement? From the broom closet beneath the stairs? The windows were shuttered. The walls were warm.

"We need to go in there," Katie-Marie said.

My hand reached out and there was this brave bolt of energy in my body that made me turn the knob. The screen door came open and then there was one more door to open and in seconds we were inside.

Leonard was in a pair of boxer shorts and a stretched-out V-neck shirt that horrified us with its display of chest hair. He held a large ceramic container that said SUGAR on one side. His glasses were crooked on his nose. "I told you to stay outside," he said. What—who—was he hiding?

"It's cold, we were cold," Katie-Marie started, but Paisley had had it with the lies.

"Where is she?" she said.

"Who?" Leonard said. He was holding the sugar container in front of his crotch, but believe us, we were already averting our eyes.

"The girl. The girl with the purple hair. The girl with the fur coat. The girl we saw you bring inside. Where's the girl!"

He set the sugar down. Outside a bird shrieked. Another followed, and another. The room was very hot, and his oven wasn't even on.

Katie-Marie was so shaken, she'd begun to cry. Paisley was on alert, hands in fists. I held the empty bag up like a weapon and a few grains of sugar rattled inside. We were not prepared.

"What girl?" Leonard said. We watched his pink lips. How carefully he said it, how slow and with a drawl, like he believed that because we were girls ourselves we could be fooled.

"We *saw* her, Leonard," Paisley said. "We saw her come in."

"There isn't any girl," Leonard said. "Apart from you three."

Once he said that, it happened. The sound of rustling from another room.

His neck snapped toward the noise, knowing he was caught, then trying to hide it. But he couldn't hide her.

"What's that!" Paisley shrieked, pointing wildly, vindicated and foaming at the mouth practically, and we kicked open the door and converged on the next room. We expected to find her there, cowering. The girl. She'd be in her coat, pulled up to hide her face. "It's us," we'd tell her. "It's us." At first she wouldn't know we'd come to rescue her.

But when we landed in the room, it was a room with no other doors out and only the way we'd come in. It was a room with shuttered windows, hiding the view of the neighbors' houses and all trace of sun. It was a room meant to be the dining room, maybe, but the table was covered with papers, so no one could eat a meal on it, and up above the table, like a centerpiece, was an object hung from a hook in the ceiling, swinging ever so slightly like someone had been here to give it a push. It was a cage built for a bird, the same one he'd carried out of the trunk. The cage was empty.

The room was empty too, except for the girls. There were girls everywhere. Girls on every surface. Girls splayed out on the table and girls spilled over the chairs. Girls pinned up against the walls and girls pasted to the back of the closet door. Girls propped up against the shuttered windows. Girls on the floor, some facedown and some faceup staring blankly at the ceiling. As we stood shocked in the doorway, a few girls skittered through the air as if from the sky itself, like a burst of bad weather, and Katie-Marie startled and stepped on one.

We were the girls. These were our photographs. It had been Leonard's hobby these past months to take pictures of us, from his porch or from his bedroom window, and he must have spent hours printing them all out to collect them—to collect *us*—together in this room.

There was Katie-Marie, bent over on the sidewalk picking up something she'd dropped. The camera focused on what was under her skirt. There was Paisley, in the hammock in my backyard, legs stretched out. The camera looked down her shirt and centered in on her crotch. There were girls I knew from down the street, and girls I knew from across the way, and the girl in the house behind mine, Aggie, slipping a bare leg out of a car in the dark night.

There were also photos of me, a great many—as if of all his targets, I was most wanted, I was the star. In some, I was sleeping. In others, I was on my lawn, or on my porch, or in my bedroom, getting undressed. Sometimes I was looking out my window, like he was looking into mine.

Leonard's photography hobby was worse than we'd guessed. What would he do now that he had us all inside his house, in real life?

We backed away and got jostled in panic. Paisley bumped into me, and I knocked into Katie-Marie. When we untangled and shot out of the room, Leonard was there, blocking the way through the hallway. None of us wanted to get near enough to touch him.

"The three of you," he said, in wonder. Like we'd fallen from the heavens into his cupped and waiting hand.

There were three of us, and one of him. We outnumbered him. We had strong legs from field hockey and track. We had sharp fingernails, painted in bright colors. We had knees and elbows and teeth.

But something held us back. It was all too real, all of a sudden. We'd suspected. We'd told tales. We'd heightened our stories into gross and grandiose lies. And even with all of that, we never really thought we were in danger.

The slithery smile on his face sent us into a tailspin. Until we looked past him. Until we saw what was there. Who was.

She was behind him. The black-eyed girl. Right there drinking at his ear, and somehow he didn't sense her hovering.

Then he must have caught something on our faces because he turned. How innocently he turned around to look.

She was strong. She grabbed his neck and dragged him back into the kitchen, and we followed the blur.

It was hard to keep focus. She was purple-black and without hard edges, like a cloud of static, a mass of feathered fury and fright. She didn't voice anything to us in any human language, but we heard it all the same. A high-pitched shriek. Something terrible and terribly right.

Paisley was shaking—since she'd seen the photographs, she hadn't stopped. But Katie-Marie was animated. "Get him!" she was crying, drowning out the wails. "Get him, get him!" We were surrounding him on the linoleum, but all we had to do was watch. The sugar container was knocked over and there was white powder everywhere, covering him but also sifting into the air so it got in our eyes, our noses, our mouths, studding our tongues. How sweet it was.

She came at him, it looked like with her mouth. The sounds in the room were squishy and made of wet smacks. She was stabbing him, but she didn't have a weapon, not that we could see. Still, something was leaving punctures. Something was bulleting him with small holes.

Then quiet through the white haze. Dead calm.

Katie-Marie lifted her head. Paisley hiccupped uncontrollably, breaking the silence. We looked down and down. He was quite tall, and his legs took up a lot of space on the floor, so I had to step over him to get a view from a better angle.

It seemed like he'd been pecked to death, like from the knife beaks of a horde of birds. None of us could look at where his face had been. None of us wanted to remember his plushy lips, or his certain kind of smile.

"I—" Katie-Marie started, and said nothing else. Paisley was hiccupping and shaking.

The girl in the black-furred coat seemed fine, though. Black hides blood, so she looked clean, she looked calm.

"She—" Katie-Marie tried to say, and said nothing.

Through hiccups, Paisley spoke for all of us. "You," she told the girl. "Killed him." The way she said the words, it was almost a question.

"You have to go," I said to the girl. She stared me down and made no move. "Can you understand what I'm saying? You have to get yourself out of here. Do you get that?"

She only wrapped the coat tighter around herself. Her legs were bare underneath, and she didn't have shoes.

I turned to Paisley, I turned to Katie-Marie. "We have to get her out of here. She has to go."

"How?" Paisley said, and her voice was the smallest I'd heard it. "None of us can drive."

Katie-Marie was holding her nose and trying not to retch in the sink. Then she did retch, and I turned to the girl. Her eyes were perfectly black, swallowed by pupils. She didn't blink. "Who are you?" I said. That had been our first question.

She cocked her head to one side, like she was saying didn't I know already? Hadn't I known all along?

Katie-Marie was hunched over the sink, and Paisley was stunned into an un-Paisley-like silence as if she'd bitten off her own tongue. Only the hiccups shook her. I was the single coherent one left. I led a path through the red-spattered sugar. The back door was open. We'd forgotten to close it when we came in.

"Go," I said.

The girl stared at me, black eyes unblinking. Her mouth was covered in blood.

"Run," I said.

She must have heard me. But she didn't run. She didn't have to.

There was a point when she was still in the kitchen with us, the air heavy and sickly sweet with what she'd done to him, and then there was the point when her feet were lifted in the air and her legs, her beautiful legs, shrunk in and shifted. Her coat became a part of her body, or maybe it always was. Her arms—what was left of them—opened wide. A dark streak took off from the back steps and the sky caught it and it was a bird, it was always a bird, she was, and the bird soared up into the clouds, a rapid retreat of wings, until it was a speck, a small seed, a dot, a blink, a memory.

I wanted to give her a head start, so I waited a good while before calling my mother to say we'd come over to borrow some sugar and found Leonard stabbed to death on his kitchen floor. I said "stabbed" because we didn't know what else to call it. My mother was the one who called 911.

NOVA REN SUMA

When the police questioned me—same as they questioned Paisley and Katie-Marie—they wanted to know only certain things. Their questions were so ordinary. Why did we knock on our neighbor's door so early on a Sunday morning? Where exactly did we find his body? What did we do next, after Paisley froze and started hiccupping and Katie-Marie puked in the sink?

They didn't mention the photographs, and we weren't sure if they were protecting us because they thought we couldn't handle it, or if they were waiting for us to say it first.

I didn't say, and Katie-Marie didn't say. Paisley didn't say either. We didn't want to give ourselves any motive, now that the girl was long gone. We'd all agreed on that ahead of time.

Besides, they couldn't pin anything on us. No witnesses, no fingerprints that matched ours on the body. No connection, except my house was right next door and my sugar bag was covered in blood on the floor. It was all I could do not to wave my arm up at the blank blue sky and tell them to search there for answers. Except that would have given her away.

Then the police had one last question, and it was here that I sat up straight and felt the heart in the cage of my chest pounding.

Could I describe the girl who was in his house the night before?

I didn't know who let that piece of information loose, Paisley or Katie-Marie, but to me this question had only one answer. "What girl?"

It was easy to deny her. Even as I remembered the blacks of her eyes, and the painted points on the ends of her fingers. That was only my mind making her into what I thought she should be.

"So there wasn't ever any girl," the police said, they made me say, they made me write in some kind of official statement and sign while my parents watched, and I had to do it. I don't know what Paisley said, and I don't know what Katie-Marie said. But I said we were mistaken. It's what we owed her. We thought we saw a girl, but it was dark. It was dark outside and confusing and we were wrong.

"So you're sure?" they said.

"I'm sure," I told them. "I never saw any girl."

Because, could a girl be so terrible? Could a girl tear a man's face out and could a girl litter his body with holes from the sharpest parts of her red mouth? Could a girl do something so perfect, and then vanish into the clouds?

Could a girl come at the exact moment we needed her? Could she come only to protect other girls?

I wasn't lying when I said that to the police. In the end, she wasn't even anymore a girl.

For Leonard's wake—closed-casket; no one would have been able to stomach it otherwise—my mother made me help her bake his signature sugar-cream pie. His murder would be unsolved for some weeks, and then I guess it fell off the police's radar, because summer was coming, and the softball tournament was approaching, and we were fund-raising for the dying oak trees now, and at some point our parents said it was safe to canvass the neighborhood and knock on every door.

Before his house sold, I ducked under the crime-scene tape and went onto his lawn. I swiped one of his bird feeders and put it on our side of the picket fence, and robins and little swallows started to flock to it. I fed them seeds from my trail-mix packs and sometimes bits of sugar-coated breakfast crunch. Sometimes I'd go outside under the bright beautiful blue and all I'd hear were these little titters, like the birds were trying to tell me something in a language I couldn't understand.

I tried to tell them I knew. I tried to say thanks. I spent a lot of time in the backyard, searching the sky.

Inspired by the 1954 film *Rear Window* and the 1963 film *The Birds*

In the Forest Dark and Deep

CARRIE RYAN

Seven Years Old

When Cassidy Evans was seven years old, she found the clearing in the forest. It was far enough past the edge of her backyard to feel dangerous, but not so far as to be technically out of bounds of where she was allowed to roam. She wasn't the first to discover the place—there were several cut stumps of wood scattered about. But she was the first in a while, as most of them had been turned to their sides and had long since sprouted thickets of slickly pale mushrooms.

The first afternoon, she touched nothing. Instead she chose to wander and crouch and peer closely at the stumps and the ground surrounding them. The grass grew long enough that a recent footstep would have been visible. Seeing none after careful investigation, Cassidy smiled and slapped a foot on top of a loose stump. "I declare myself queen of this realm," she announced, raising a fist high into the air the way a conquering hero might.

Hearing no objection, she set about making plans.

First, she righted all the stumps and arranged them in a circle. In the middle she laid out an old tablecloth she'd snatched from the bottom of her mother's corner cupboard. Day by day through the summer, she smuggled things to the clearing. A cracked saucer here, a chipped mug there. The kinds of things no one would notice missing.

But then something strange happened. She arrived at the clearing one afternoon to find a table sitting in the middle. Hesitating at the edge of the forest, she scanned the underbrush, eyes sharp and stomach squelching in disappointment that she might now have to share her private kingdom.

"Hello?" she called.

No one answered. She walked slowly toward the table. It was rough-hewn, the edges raw with gaps between a few of the boards. Pushing at it, she was surprised to find it sturdy and solid. She looked again over her shoulder. The forest was empty.

Frowning, she backed from the clearing before turning and running for home. For days, nothing else changed. And then it rained for a week straight.

Once she was finally free again, she tripped her way through the forest to the clearing, only to be brought up short. This time the table had been set. The smuggled tablecloth stretched the length of it, each place set with an assortment of unmatched odds and ends. Some of it the familiar cracked china from home, but most of it unfamiliar.

She approached the table slowly, warily. The mugs were all filled with murky water, the same with the plates and saucers, and as she neared, she could smell the moldering of the damp tablecloth. It must have all been set out before the rain.

But by who?

"Hello?" She craned her neck, listening. There was only the sound of stray raindrops falling through sun-slicked leaves, the call and response of birds, the damp rustle of squirrels foraging.

Cassidy had been warned enough through her life about strangers offering candy or other treats to lure her away, but she couldn't quite figure how this situation fit into that. There was no candy. There were no strangers.

On further exploration, Cassidy found three unexpected objects at the far end of the table. The first was an old top hat that had seen better days. Its brim was ragged, its top lopsided, and it sported a dent on one side.

Next to it sat a pillow with a pinecone on it. Two sprigs of long brown pine needles arched from each side of the narrow end, and two red berries perched above them. Trailing from the thicker end was a length of browned rope.

And third was a white apron, neatly folded. A wide blue ruffle traced the edges of it. Cassidy couldn't help but smile and laugh. "The Mad Hatter," she said, tapping the top of the hat. "The Dormouse." She carefully petted its bristly back. "And Alice!" She slipped the apron over her head, admiring the way it fell, just the way Alice's had in her favorite cartoon.

She scanned the other seats. "I guess the March Hare is running late again," she whispered behind her hand to the Dormouse. Then she giggled. "But what would you know since you're always asleep!"

Any trepidation or hesitation now gone, Cassidy set about enjoying her unexpected tea party. She was a girl well-known for her imagination and had no trouble carrying the conversations for all of them. It was the most fun she'd had all summer. So much so that it wasn't until gloaming had wrapped tight around the clearing that she realized how late it had grown.

"Now I'm the one late!" she cried, jumping from her stump. She dashed from the clearing and was halfway home before she realized she still wore the apron. Stopping, she bit her lip and looked back over her shoulder.

She already knew she'd be in trouble for staying out so late, and she wasn't sure how to explain where the apron had come from. What if her parents forbade her from returning to the clearing? She'd be stuck playing with her neighbor Jack and his little brother, Tommy, all summer. No, thank you!

She hastily drew the apron over her head and started back toward the clearing. It wasn't until she'd burst from the cover of forest that she saw him.

The March Hare.

When trying to decide whether to tell the police about him later, Cassidy couldn't figure out how to describe the white rabbit. He was the size of a man, that was for sure, and he had the proportions of a man as well—long legs and arms. But he wasn't dressed as a man. He didn't *look* like a man.

What stood out to Cassidy most were the ears. They were a shock of brilliant white against the gathering darkness of night. Everything else about him seemed to recede from memory until that's all he ever was to Cassidy: ears in the shadows.

The first time she saw him, he stood just past the first row of brambles on the far side of the clearing. Had she not been so startled, she might have ducked and hidden. Watched him for a while. But it was too late, she was already too loud, each step a crash against old dead leaves and broken sticks.

He froze at the sound of her, face jerking in her direction. It was darker where he was, back under the cover of leaves. Too dark to see him clearly, except for those ears.

Cassidy opened her mouth but no sound came out. She flung her apron at him, as though that could do anything to deter him. It only fluttered, caught on the air, and drifted slowly to the ground. No matter. Cassidy ran.

The entire way home he chased after her. His breath hot on the back of her neck. She felt sure she heard the thump of his heart between the skittering beats of her own. But when she reached her backyard and allowed herself a glimpse over her shoulder, she found the forest empty.

She waited one moment and then another, eyes narrowed in fierce concentration as she scoured the dim underbrush for a hint of those ears. Chillbumps started at her toes, overtaking the rest of her body in a slow wave.

It was broken by the sound of the screen door slamming. "Cassidy Evans," her mother called from the porch, "where have you been?"

Hands trembling, Cassidy shook her head, walking backward toward the comfort of her mother's voice. "Nowhere, Mama," she mumbled.

By the time she went to bed that night, she'd convinced herself she'd just imagined the March Hare. But every time she closed her eyes, she'd see him, until eventually the thought of it boiled through her veins, and she knew beyond doubt that he was there, watching her.

She'd open her eyes to find her room empty, but that wasn't enough. Her heart wouldn't settle until she'd slipped from the bed and stolen to the window. Telling herself how ridiculous she was being, she'd tent back the edge of her curtain to reveal a sliver of night, and she'd scour the darkness for a dash of white that never appeared.

Seventeen Years Old

The side of the table bit into Cassidy's hips and she pressed her palms against it, feeling the cut and swirl of wood grain as she lifted herself to sit. Jack took advantage of the new position, stepping between her legs. Lazily he slipped free the top button of her shirt and she leaned back, hands flat behind her, watching as he made his way down her abdomen, one finger trailing along her skin in his wake.

Around them the thicket of forest hummed and sang of night: crickets with their sharpened legs, cicada wings buzzing, wind through pulp-heavy branches. The sound of their breaths tangled with it, became a part of it.

When Jack pressed his lips to the base of her throat, Cassidy arched her back, watching the moon splay across her bare skin. Jack leaned over her then, hand firm between her shoulder blades as he pulled her to him. She went willingly, arms around his neck.

With her chin on Jack's shoulder, Cassidy could see behind him. Watch the starstorm of lightning bugs. The figure seemed to materialize out of nothing, all at once. A thickened shadow, well hidden except for the ears.

She gasped, but Jack just took it as a sound of pleasure and he used the opportunity to dip his head lower. Giving her a full view of the March Hare and him a full view of her.

It was her hands she didn't quite know what to do with. In the end she held a forearm ineffectually across her chest, the fingers of her other hand reaching for the collar of Jack's unbuttoned shirt. "Let's get out of here," she murmured to him.

The March Hare circled silently just beyond the edge of the clearing. It seemed to Cassidy that his ears were duller now, the edges of them grungy and well worn. She couldn't see his eyes, they receded too far into the darkness of the underbrush, but she felt them on her.

Her throat tightened, breathing labored as though it were ten years ago and his hands still circled her neck, claws raking against the column of her throat. Each time she closed her eyes, she remembered the sight of the other girls arranged around the table, their rotting bodies so bloated under the early fall heat that their skin threatened to split.

Jack continued to work on unbuckling her belt and she shoved her knee against his torso, knocking him off balance. "I said let's go."

His fingers hesitated, but he didn't release her. "Come on, Cassidy," he said. "It's still early."

She shook her head. In the periphery of her vision, she tracked the March Hare. Though she'd been back to the clearing a handful of times after she was rescued and the bodies were found a decade ago, she'd never seen the March Hare again. Not until tonight. She didn't know what had changed—what was different—but the familiar wash of chills began its slow wave up from her toes.

Jack blew out a frustrated breath. "I thought you were cool with this," he said, and Cassidy wasn't sure which part of *this* he meant: the fact that he was three years older than her and interested in nothing more than hooking up, or the fact that he'd brought her here because it would make a great story for him to tell his friends later.

And maybe she *had* been cool with it all, despite what that said about her feelings of self-worth, but the addition of the March Hare changed things. "Yeah, well . . ." She grabbed the edges of her shirt, pulling them together as she pushed off from the table.

Jack's fingers closed around her forearm. "Cassidy—"

She looked down at where he held her. The scars cutting around her wrists glowed white against the rest of her skin. In the darkness of the clearing it almost appeared as though fishing wire still bound her, causing her fingertips to burn.

From the tree line she sensed movement, and when she glanced over she saw that the March Hare had taken a step closer. Perhaps Jack would have noticed as well, but he was too busy staring at her wrist. Whether he felt the force of her pulse, flashing in a warning, or whether he simply didn't like the visceral reminder of her past, she didn't know. Either way, he let go of her.

Instead he danced the tips of his fingers under the edge of her shirt, up over her hip. He curled his touch, trying to bring her closer. "I'll keep you safe," he said, the words deep and low with a lift to the corner of his mouth.

He didn't seem to notice the irony that, of all the dangers in the clearing, *he* was the one she most likely needed protection from. There was a lot that Cassidy was willing to put up with in the guys she allowed to touch her: fumbling hands, impure motives, a subtle sort of pressure that bordered on uncomfortable. But stupidity was something she didn't tolerate well.

Rolling her eyes, she twisted away from his reach and stalked into the woods. "I'm going home."

Jack called after her. "Come on Cassidy, don't be such a—"

She whirled and glared at him, daring him to finish. Smartly, he swallowed whatever he was about to say next, but he did nothing to shutter his obvious irritation. He was someone not used to being turned down, especially by girls, and he remained in the middle of the clearing, obviously expecting her to return.

Behind him, the March Hare stood at the edge of the tree line, like a ghostly echo of Jack hovering in the darkest shadows. They both watched her, waiting to see what she'd do.

Though her estimation of Jack had taken a serious nose dive, he was still her neighbor and he deserved a warning. "Go home, Jack," she told him.

Now that she was no longer willing to put out, he was apparently done with her. "Screw you." He flung his hands at her in dismissal before reaching into the crumpled paper bag at his feet and pulling out a beer. Popping it open, he hoisted himself up on the table.

"Jack," she warned. "It's not safe."

In response, he raised the can toward her, as though in a toast. It was such a mockery that it caused a tremor to roll through her. Everyone knew about the way the bodies were found—the way *she* was found: posed like dolls with teacups tied to their fingers, hands lifted to mimic a toast.

Hate and disgust spilled into her blood. She spun on her heel leaving Jack Marshall to whatever monsters roamed the forest.

Seven Years Old

Cassidy spent most of the next afternoon standing at the edge of her backyard, trying to find the courage to go farther. The crack of a stick snapping nearby caused her to jump and she whirled to find Tommy Marshall hopping the low fence that separated their houses. He was more than a year younger and a grade below her at school, but because they were neighbors and their parents were friends, he always seemed to be around.

That didn't mean she liked him. The girls down the street had taken to making fun of her whenever they saw her with him. Since then, she'd made it her mission to avoid him as much as possible.

"You've been standing out here for ages," he said.

Cassidy placed her hands on her hips. "So?"

He came up beside her and stared into the forest. "What are you looking at?"

"Nothing." She bit the word out.

He crouched, poking through the grass until he found a slender stick. He bent it, testing how far it could go before breaking. "You wanna ride bikes?"

"No."

Frowning, he bent the stick farther. "We could jump on the trampoline."

Cassidy let out a snort.

"Or go down to the park and see if the ice cream truck is there."

Rolling her eyes, she scowled down at him. "I'm not hanging out with you, Tommy, and that's that." Then she stomped off into the forest.

"Hey," he called after her. "Where are you going?"

She didn't even bother looking back. "Somewhere you're not invited!"

But as she ventured deeper, her bluster began to fizzle until she flat-out regretted not allowing Tommy to come with her. He was a slower runner, she knew. If he were with her when they found the March Hare, he'd be taken first if they had to make a quick escape.

The thought of him still sitting there at the edge of her yard, along with the memories of the girls down the street taunting her, propelled her to the edge of the clearing. There, she hesitated.

"Hello?" It came out more a whisper than a shout. Her hands trembled and she shoved them into her pockets. But that just felt weird, so she took them out again. Swallowing, she stepped beyond the barrier of trees. Beneath her feet the grass bent without sound, dewy soft and plump from the recent rains.

When she reached the table, she found the apron neatly folded as it had been before. The hat was also there, in addition to the Dormouse. The cups and saucers appeared to have been wiped clean. She found it difficult to breathe, ears straining for any unusual noise.

She knew that if she ran then, she'd spend her whole life running. She had to prove to herself that she could control her mind. That it couldn't throw dark thoughts at her and expect her to believe them as truth.

Carefully, she took the apron and slipped it over her head. She ignored the tears in her eyes as she sank onto the stump at the head of the table. There she sat, trying to think of something to say.

"Good day to you both," she finally managed to squeak out. Neither the Mad Hatter nor the Dormouse responded. "Do either of you happen to have a story or a riddle perhaps?" she tried.

Nothing. "Exactly so," she finally sighed. She dropped her eyes to her hands, noticing that she'd been gripping fistfuls of her apron. Forcing her fingers to relax, she smoothed her palms over the material, now wrinkled and damp with sweat.

When she looked up again, the March Hare was there. Inside, Cassidy felt like the whump of an atom bomb hitting the ground. Outside, every square inch of her skin tingled as though a million nerves had just sparked awake. Her legs twitched, wanting to run, but she forced herself to stay.

As before, the March Hare hovered beyond the clearing's edge, still shrouded by tree trunks and underbrush. He didn't move toward her, nor did he back away. He merely stood there, fully visible. His hands hung limply by his sides, empty.

"Good day." She tried to put sound behind the words, but it wouldn't come. He must have heard anyway, because he nodded, slender white ears bending forward and curling at the tips and then snapping upright again as he lifted his head.

For the rest of the afternoon, he came no closer and she said nothing more. As evening hinted across the sky, she carefully lifted the apron over her head and folded it. Standing, she set it on her stump. For lack of anything else to say, she told him "Good day" again. Except this time there was force behind her voice.

The March Hare raised a hand as if to wave. As calmly as possible, Cassidy turned and strode from the clearing. But with her back turned to him, the dark beat of her fears won out, and she was only a few trees deep into the forest before she turned to look back. He still stood there, hand raised, watching.

That same wave of chills broke over her, and she ran all the way home.

Seventeen Years Old

Cassidy woke that night to someone tapping at her window. Through the billowing curtains, it was impossible to tell the shape of the figure outside, and her body went rigid with panic.

The March Hare, she thought wildly, her heart skittering beyond control.

But he'd never come to her house before—never stepped beyond the boundary of the forest. And when he did move, he was silent.

She escaped from her sweat-soaked sheets and tore aside the curtain. Tommy hovered just outside, balanced on top of the trellis that covered the back porch.

He gestured for her to open the window. Frowning, she complied.

"I've been texting you," he hissed.

She glanced toward her desk, where the face of her phone glowed with a series of alerts. "My phone's on mute. What do you want?"

"I'm looking for my brother."

Instantly, her cheeks flushed. She hadn't realized Tommy knew about them. It made her uncomfortable and she crossed her arms. "How should I know where Jack is?"

He let out a frustrated sigh and for a moment she could see his brother in him—that same sense of disappointment with her. She ground her teeth.

"He hasn't come home yet," he said. "And since you were . . ." He sort of moved his hand in the air, as if embarrassed to say it out loud. It was obvious he knew what kind of person his brother was—what Jack wanted, and got, from the girls he pursued. And it was also obvious he'd never expected Cassidy to be one of those girls.

She looked over his shoulder to the woods, dark and tangled in the deep of night. She thought of Jack sitting on the table, lifting his beer to her in a toast, the March Hare in the forest behind him, and cursed.

"Meet me at the edge of the yard," she told him. Dropping the curtain, she pulled on jeans under her nightgown and grabbed the closest pair of shoes. Silently she slid her bare feet across the hardwood floors, easing down the stairs and out through the back door.

Tommy waited for her by the woods. She was already running by the time she reached him, and she didn't slow. He chased after her. "Wait, what were you doing out in the forest?"

It was a stupid question and so she didn't answer him. Though it was night, the moon was full and she knew these woods well. She weaved through the tree trunks, skirting and dodging brambles. Tommy didn't fare as well, cursing and grunting as he tripped his way after her.

When she neared the clearing, she stopped, pressing her hand against his chest to keep him from plunging forward. His heart raced.

The sounds of the night had dimmed somewhat, nocturnal creatures buttoned up against their threat.

"Shhh," she whispered. He nodded, eyes wide. "Wait here." She crept forward, feet soft against the ground. The clearing bowed open ahead of her, a wash of moon-dampened grass. There was no sign of Jack nor of the March Hare.

She let out a trembling breath.

Tommy brushed past her, breaking from the trees. She trailed after him toward the table. "Jack!" he called up to the sky through cupped hands. He spun, scanning the woods and calling his brother's name again.

Jack's beers had been arranged around the table, one at each place. Four of them were empty, Cassidy noted, the other two unopened.

Tommy had his fingers locked on top of his head, frustrated and concerned. "Is this where you saw him last?"

She nodded. "A couple of hours ago."

"And you left him out here?"

Whether there was accusation in his voice or not, it made Cassidy defensive. She crossed her arms. "I told him it wasn't safe."

Tommy tensed. "Did Jack . . ." He hesitated. "Did he do something to you?"

"Other than be a complete asshole?" She shook her head. "No."

"It's not like you didn't know that about him," Tommy grumbled.

The words sent fire down her spine, anger seeping out through her pores like sweat. But before she could reply, a flash of movement caught her eye. Two slender bands of white, curving into tips shifting in the darkness. It was the March Hare. Deep in the forest. He nodded to her, ears dipping forward.

Cassidy cursed and took off running. By the time she reached the spot where he'd been standing, he'd disappeared. But it didn't matter. She'd found Jack. He lay crumpled at the base of a tree, one side of his face already mottled with a bruise and dashed with cuts. His eyes fluttered, but didn't open.

"Jesus, Jack!" Tommy shouted, falling to his knees beside his brother. He reached for his shoulder, to turn him onto his back, but Cassidy stopped him.

"Careful," she said, gesturing to his leg. It was twisted at a horrible angle, something sharp pressing against the inside of his jeans. His foot was lodged in a hole, and she could feel shards of bone shifting under her touch as she worked to free him.

Jack's breathing, already rapid, increased in volume from the pain. "It's okay, Jack, we're here." Tommy cupped the uninjured side of his brother's face.

Together, Tommy and Cassidy were able to pull Jack up, one of his arms over each of their shoulders, and start for home. "He must have tripped and fallen against the tree," Tommy said, glancing back at where they'd found his brother. "Maybe he got lost trying to get home."

Cassidy pressed her lips together for a moment before finally answering, "Exactly so."

Seven Years Old

Again and again she returned to the clearing to throw wild imaginary tea parties, but the March Hare never stepped from the tree line.

He never came closer and he never uttered a word. But he was always there, watching.

Thus began her renewed obsession with all things *Alice in Wonderland*. On rainy days, it was the only movie she clamored to watch.

At the library, it was the only book she'd check out. And so it was unsurprising when, at the end of the summer, her mother suggested an Alice in Wonderland tea party for her eighth birthday.

Cassidy thought about asking to hold it in the clearing in the woods, but then reconsidered. The clearing was a place that belonged only to her and the March Hare. She didn't like the idea of others intruding.

With great care she set up the picnic table in the backyard, smuggling some of the cups and saucers back out of the woods. Earlier in the week, her mom had taken her to a vintage clothing shop to pick out a variety of ridiculous hats for everyone, and she even found an old velvet pillow she could use for the Dormouse (her cat's slightly used toy mouse).

The morning of her birthday, she donned her blue dress and white apron before returning to the clearing. It had rained the night before and the teacups were once again filled with murky water. The pinecone Dormouse's whiskers had been washed away, and one of its eyes had begun to rot. A puddle collected in the sunken dome of the top hat.

When she and her mother had been writing out the invitations, Cassidy had intentionally messed one up and later smuggled it to her room, where she'd carefully addressed it to the March Hare. Now she set that invitation on the table, leaning it against a cracked teapot.

"I know you probably won't come," she said to the empty woods. "But it didn't seem right to host a tea party without inviting you."

Of course it was Cassidy's luck that her neighbor Tommy was first to arrive at the party. She'd begged her mom not to invite him but had been informed quite crisply that not doing so would be rude. Cassidy tried scowling at him, hoping he'd get the hint and go home before anyone else arrived, but she had a difficult time maintaining her ire as he tried on hat after ridiculous hat, making up voices and characters for each one.

Which is how she ended up clutching her stomach and braying with laughter the moment the girls from down the street stepped into the backyard. Completely lacking the ability to tell when he was wanted and when he wasn't, Tommy approached the pack of girls, jester's cap pulled tight over his head. He pretended to trip, falling into a somersault that left him sprawled on his back at their feet.

With thin-lipped smiles and a smirk or two, the four girls stepped over him. Cassidy's face flushed as she watched them take in the picnic table. The balloons drifting from the handle of each cup. The old hats and chipped china. For a moment the glamour of her imagination shifted and she saw it all through their eyes. Mortification seared hot against the inside of her ribs.

A handful of other neighborhood kids arrived soon after, some accompanied by their parents, who all gathered on the porch, where a different sort of tea party had been set up for adults. It took a while, but slowly Cassidy's bruised imagination limped back.

But it did not make a full recovery. Because while the group of girls from up the street were excruciatingly polite, they made no effort to play along. They accepted their mugs when offered and took a small sip of iced tea before leaving the chipped porcelain cups to sweat on the table. They guessed only halfheartedly at the riddles Cassidy had so painstakingly concocted.

The four girls were a weight at the end of the table, a constant drag on the spirit of things. It seemed to leave the few other kids confused, not knowing whether to play along with Cassidy or scorn her efforts. And so the party became like a balloon slowly, agonizingly losing air.

Until finally an acceptable amount of time had passed for the event to be over. The group of girls from down from the street left the way they came: all in a pack, heads tilted to one another in hushed whispers. One of their comments escaped their little bubble to float across the yard: "I mean, a tea party? Really? So dumb."

The other three girls nodded. A hot wash of tears flooded Cassidy's eyes, and she turned quickly away. Which is how she ended up facing the forest.

Even through the blur of tears, she recognized the curve of the March Hare's ears, the white of them set off against the dappled shadows thrown by the canopy of trees. She dropped her chin, a new sort of embarrassment running hot through her—the kind she felt the first time her mom understood how unpopular Cassidy was when she overheard the girls down the street taunting her.

She felt that she had somehow let the March Hare down. That the glamour she'd spun of herself for him had been pulled from his eyes and he was seeing the truth of her for the first time.

As the last guest left, Cassidy concentrated on clearing the table and not looking back at the forest.

The next day Cassidy returned her copy of *Alice in Wonderland* to the library and deleted the movie from the DVR. She balled up her costume, shoving it deep into her closet, and returned the tablecloth to the bottom of the drawer in the corner cupboard. She no longer ventured into the forest.

She was done with tea parties and she was done with her imagination.

Or so she thought. But one afternoon, as fall bit at the edges of weary leaves, she saw a piece of paper caught on a branch just past the end of her yard. When she plucked it free, she realized that it was not, as she'd assumed, a scrap of stray garbage but was instead an invitation. *Her* invitation.

Except that the information she'd painstakingly written had been crossed out. In its place was a new date and time. She searched the forest for a flash of white, but there was nothing more than the expected riot of fall.

Seventeen Years Old

Jack never did say much about what happened to him. He'd been drunk, he explained, and most of the night was a blur. But he did make one thing clear: "Stay out of the clearing, Tommy," he'd told his brother. "Promise me."

Tommy repeated it all to Cassidy, his eyes full of questions. "I'm not sure I believe him," he confessed. "There's something Jack's not telling me." He waited for Cassidy to fill in the resulting silence with details.

She could have told him. She could have explained that she was pretty sure it had been the March Hare. That he was a master at making one thing look like another and that Jack probably hadn't tripped.

But she didn't.

Instead she made a concerted effort to return to life as normal. Which meant avoiding Tommy, ignoring Jack, and staying out of the woods.

Her eighteenth birthday came and went and she spent most of the night sitting in the dark at her window, watching the edge of the forest for the familiar flash of white that never came.

For a while, she thought that so long as she stayed out of the clearing, so long as she didn't give the March Hare cause, everything would be okay. Everyone around her would stay safe. And as summer tipped into fall, that was true.

But then, one night a familiar wash of chills stole her from sleep. The remnants of a nightmare still wrapped around her like a spiderweb as she strained against the darkness. Her heart thudded, the house silent, as she slipped from the bed and moved to the window.

He stood at the edge of the yard, half hidden by barren branches. At first she thought the splash of dark against his fur was shadow thrown from the moon. But then as he stepped backward into the woods she saw that the shape of the stain didn't change.

She swallowed, the sudden taste of tea, bitter and hot, clogging her throat. Along with it came the bright coppery memory of blood, wetly thick. Her heart tripped faster and faster as the March Hare retreated. The last she saw of him were the ears, no longer white but a dingier, tattered gray, pausing. Waiting. And then disappearing into the forest.

Without a second thought, she started for the stairs, but before she pushed her way outside, she hesitated. She glanced over her shoulder into the kitchen. In two steps she had their largest knife in her hand, and then she was racing across the yard and plunging into the forest.

The brittle fall leaves collapsed under her feet, a loud crunching swish in the night. Even before she reached the clearing she knew it wasn't like ten years ago. She could smell the blood. It coated the inside of her nostrils, infiltrating her lungs.

This was worse than before. This was more. This was a massacre.

Eight Years Old

It wasn't until she'd crossed from her yard into the forest a few days later that Cassidy admitted to herself that she was going to accept the strange invitation. Curiosity demanded it.

The path through the trees felt unfamiliar under her feet, the swath of fallen leaves and hungry brambles creating a new landscape for her to navigate. She was so focused on looking down that it wasn't until she'd crossed into the wide sweep of grass that she glanced up.

She blinked, hard, thinking that surely her eyes betrayed her. But as she stood frozen on the cusp of the clearing, the scene before her remained unchanged. The table was there, as before, along with the half-rotted tablecloth and an assortment of cups and saucers.

Now, however, each stump around the table except for two—one at either end—was occupied. There were four of them, two on each side, and Cassidy recognized them instantly: the group of girls from down the street. The ones who'd laughed at her for her tea-party-themed birthday.

They did not laugh now. Nor did they breathe or their hearts beat. Even at a glance it was obvious that the girls were all dead. Cassidy knew she should be horrified. She should be screaming; already the wail of horror sat trapped in her throat, pulsing and ready to escape.

But she did not let it free. Nor did she allow her feet to turn and carry her home. Instead she approached the table slowly. In the center of it, steam clouded from the spout of a teapot and drifted lazily from the cups set in front of each girl.

This was a true tea party. Nothing about it imaginary.

Cassidy's ribs ached at the force of her pulse, the thunder of it in her ears. It was impossible for her to swallow, and her breath broke through her lips in wheezing pants.

Her knees felt weak and so she allowed herself to sink onto her stump. In front of her, her apron sat folded and ready, the blue ruffle now an echo of the surrounding girls' lips.

"Good day," she whispered. Needing some sort of sound to break the moment open. And break the moment it did, because in response each of the girls nodded at her.

Choking, Cassidy fell backward off her stump, digging her hands and heels into the soft ground as she scrambled across the clearing. The girls replied by lifting their right hands as though in a toast to her. Four chipped cups dangled from four sets of limp fingers, steaming tea sloshing over the rims from the movement.

It was only then that Cassidy noticed the wires. They were thin and clear, like fishing line, and they draped from the branches overhead to wrap around the girls' wrists and temples.

Turning the girls into macabre marionette puppets. A new thought struck in her gut as she traced the path of the wires up into the trees and down again, searching for the source of their movement.

She knew what she would find even before she laid eyes on the white ears. The March Hare watched her, his hands dancing in the shadows, causing the girls to shift and move. Teacups swinging toward their mouths and splashing them with scalding tea.

The sound came from somewhere deep inside her, a dark expanse she hadn't known existed until that moment. It was not a scream or a wail, but laughter. And while it may have been edged by panic, it was filled with something horrid and grotesque.

The right thing to do would be to turn back and run screaming for home. Tell her parents and bring the police dogs to bear against the March Hare.

But Cassidy did none of those things. Instead she pushed herself from the ground and pulled the white apron with blue frills over her head. First, she curtsied toward the March Hare, who dipped his head in response, ears flicking forward and then back up again.

Then she took her seat at the table and slipped her finger through the handle of her teacup. "A very happy unbirthday to me." She lifted a salute to the girls. Each one saluted her in return. "Exactly so," Cassidy murmured in appreciation. The tea was delicious.

Eighteen Years Old

When Cassidy stumbled through the last of the trees, the scene broke open before her. Even worse than she'd expected. The fat moon overhead lit on a half dozen corpses thrown around the table, and whereas a decade before the bodies had been posed to give the impression of life, now death was apparent on every one of them.

Blood dripped from fingers and elbows, seeped through sweatshirts and sweaters. Throats were ripped open with long ragged gashes that practically severed head from torso. Eyes stared at nothing, mouths open and spattered red. Their deaths had been violent and gruesome.

As she took it all in, she couldn't stop the words from whispering through her lips: "Off with their heads." And again, just as she had a decade ago, she felt a dark-edged laughter circling inside her. She choked it back, but still a bit of it escaped as a whimper.

Unable to help herself, she crept closer. She recognized the faces—all of them from her class at school. Perhaps they'd been friends once upon a time, the way neighborhood kids are always forced upon each other for birthdays and holiday picnics, but now she'd call them nothing more than acquaintances.

In front of each sat a cracked teacup filled with beer, traces of foam still clinging to the rims. A keg lay on its side off to the edge of the clearing, its nozzle flipped open, slowly draining into the trampled grass. The scent of it added a sweetness to the air, rounding out the bitterness of blood.

She turned, eyes scanning for a flash of white in the trees. But there was nothing, only the distant crunch of leaves and snapping branches, escalating as someone stormed toward the clearing. Not the March Hare, Cassidy knew. The forest belonged to him, holding tight to every one of his secrets, including the sound of his movements.

Cassidy heard Tommy calling her name just as he came stumbling from the trees, pulling up short at the sight of the bodies. His face blanched, throat convulsing. "Jesus," he breathed, pressing the back of his knuckles against his lips. He took two steps toward her and then hesitated, his panic-rimmed eyes dropping to her waist and going wide.

"Cassidy . . . ?" He swallowed. "Are you . . . ?"

She glanced down to find a wide stain of blackness across the hem of her shirt. It grew steadily outward, the edges a duller shade of gray, the moonlight having robbed it of all color. Confused, she quickly pressed a hand to her abdomen, as though needing to make sure her flesh was still intact. But as her fingers probed, she found no wounds. Only that she'd been leaning against the table, the fabric of her shirt soaking in the blood pooled there.

She lurched back, plucking the warm, sticky wet from her skin. "It's not mine," she quickly reassured him.

Tommy let out a trembling breath, his shoulders sagging with relief.

"And I didn't do this," she felt compelled to add.

His lips twitched in a smile, like even the idea of her involvement was absurd. "Of course you didn't." He said it so without thought that it set Cassidy's teeth on edge.

With arms crossed, he circled the clearing slowly, keeping a steady distance from the table as he took it all in. It was several moments before he was able to control the ragged edge to his breathing, the shuddering of his shoulders. He kicked at the ground, shaking his head sharply. "So stupid. I told them not to do this."

Cassidy blinked. "You knew?"

"I'd heard rumors." He paused before adding, "With tonight being the tenth anniversary since they found the bodies and all."

"Yes, I'm aware of that." She bit the edges of the words, keeping them short and sharp.

Tommy's eyes flicked to the knife still clutched in her hand and then away. He rolled his shoulders, continuing his arc around the clearing. Placing the table between them. "They thought it would be funny to throw a tea party out here. Figured it would be ironic, I guess."

Her stomach turned over and her neck flushed. It was just like with Jack, sitting on the table and toasting her. Mocking her.

This place didn't belong to them, she wanted to shout. It didn't even belong to Cassidy. It had always been the domain of the March Hare, his unending party to do with as he chose. She didn't understand how she could know this so clearly and they could be so dense.

Nothing good ever came out of the forest.

Tommy cleared his throat and frowned. "This isn't like last time." There was hesitation to his voice, a cautiousness that hadn't been there before.

Her back stiffened. "I didn't kill them." She said it again because she needed him to understand.

"I know." His response was just as quick as before, but this time he didn't meet her eyes.

Already Cassidy felt the weight of what would come next. It would start all over: the police, the media, the questions. They would probably bring the dogs again, the forest would grow flush with experts searching for clues.

The March Hare would be driven away once more. Or maybe this time he would be caught. Something seized in her chest. Not just at the thought of the March Hare being captured, but also at what it might mean for her if he was.

She realized, then, that silence had stretched between them and she glanced up to find Tommy considering her. He stood at the head of the table while she remained at the foot. If she sat, it would be like always: her usual spot. The only thing missing was the apron.

Tommy was the one to break the silence. "I used to follow you, you know. When we were kids and you'd go into the woods all the time."

The momentum of Cassidy's heart slowed, almost to a stop. "That must have been terribly boring for you." Her voice was breathier than usual, strained. "All I'd do is sit here and have imaginary tea parties."

There was a shift in his eyes. It made him look unfamiliar somehow. "I saw what he did to you, Cassidy."

She inhaled, sharp. Her back crawled as though spiders skated over her flesh. "Everyone saw what he did—it was on the front page of the newspaper."

He shook his head. "I watched it happen—you being strung up."

For a long moment she simply looked at him. All these years he'd known. And he'd said nothing to her. "But you didn't stop him. You didn't tell anyone."

She didn't have to take her eyes from Tommy to see the shift in the forest behind him. The pale ghost of white separating from the shadows.

"I was six," he protested, throwing his hands into the air. "What could I have done? Who would have believed me if I'd told them there was a monster in the woods?" He moved around the table toward her, as though closing the distance would make her understand.

Behind him, the March Hare echoed his movement, stepping fully into the clearing.

"For years I thought I was crazy—that I'd made it up." He shoved a hand into his hair. "But then Jack." His voice cracked on his brother's name.

Her mouth went dry. "He told you what happened?"

He shook his head. "If it had just been an accident, he wouldn't have been so scared. He's different now, Cassidy. And I finally figured out why."

The March Hare loomed so close behind Tommy now that he filled the periphery of her vision. How Tommy couldn't sense him, how his skin didn't crawl with chillbumps, how the air practically vibrated, she didn't know.

"I'm sorry," he whispered, and to his credit he sounded sincere. "I've kept your secret for this long. But after Jack. After this—" He rested his hands on her shoulders. "We can't let anyone else get hurt. We have to tell them the truth."

The tears blurring her eyes turned the edges of Tommy's outline fuzzy so that in some places it was difficult to determine where one ended and the other began. "Not all monsters are filled with darkness." She wanted him to understand this so badly that her voice trembled.

He didn't even hesitate. "This one is."

CARRIE RYAN

She allowed herself a moment to admire Tommy, the way he stood so resolute, like a knight charging after the monster. He just didn't grasp that this fight wasn't his to wage.

"Exactly so," she finally said.

Of course Tommy would think she was talking to him. He exhaled as though relieved and the start of a smile eased the tension around his lips. By the time he realized that she'd spoken the words to someone over his shoulder, it was already too late.

His eyes went wide. First with confusion, then shock, then pain. The March Hare had moved swiftly. Reaching from behind, he raked his claws across Tommy's chest, flaying it open.

Tommy tried to suck in a gasp, but it gurgled in his lungs and came back out, speckled red. Death rolled over him like a storm building, at first soft and distant, then boiling dark and streaked sharp with lightning until it swallowed him whole.

His legs gave and he slipped to the ground so that there was nothing left between her and the March Hare. The front of the creature was a matted scarlet that looked almost black in the moonlight. The sharp claws on his hands dripped with it.

Cassidy still held the knife in her hand. With one swing she could bury it in the creature's abdomen. But instead she sank to her knees next to Tommy. The way he lay on the ground reminded her of her Alice in Wonderland–themed birthday party. How he'd worn the jester's hat and tumbled into a somersault, landing on his back in front of the girls from down the block.

Maybe if she'd invited him into the forest all those years ago, things would have ended differently. But she doubted it. Darkness grew where it would and took what it wanted. It staked its claim and never let go.

And no one else could pry you free of it.

She pressed a hand against his cheek, the vibrancy of warmth still waging a lost battle. "I'm sorry," she told him. Carefully she slipped the knife into his hand. "I can't go back to who I was yesterday."

With a sigh she closed her eyes and dropped her head. As before, it would be her turn next. She'd known this from the moment she'd stepped into the clearing and seen the bodies.

Eight Years Old

Police swarmed the neighborhood, searching for the four missing girls, but since they'd last been spotted at school, the authorities had yet to turn their attention to the nearby forest.

It was only a matter of time, though. Cassidy understood this. Even so, she returned to the tea party in the clearing each successive afternoon. The girls had begun to decay, taking on a sickly smell that reached deeper and deeper into the forest with the passage of time.

Where in the beginning their skin had been ugly shades of brown and pink splotched with swaths of purple where the blood had initially settled, now their bodies swelled and stretched. There was no give in the fishing line wrapped around their wrists and the skin split beneath it. A glistening liquid oozed out, smearing on the table and dripping into their tea.

Their eyes were little more than slits, and their mouths, once a delicate shade of blue, were now black, stretched into gruesome O's. They still saluted her when she arrived. They still nodded in response to her inquiries to their well-being. They still banged the table in appreciation of her riddles.

They still sat with her, permanent fixtures at a never-ending tea party.

But of course it had to end. It was on the fourth day that she'd heard the authorities planned to shift the search to the forest the next morning. Which made today her final tea party. And what a grand one it had been with singing and laughter and toasts of admiration.

Once the tea was gone and the light turned ashen, however, Cassidy grew anxious. She worried that once the police found the table in the clearing they'd figure out she'd been there and she'd get in trouble. They'd start asking questions and Cassidy wouldn't have the answers. Because who would believe her about a man-sized white rabbit?

She plucked at the ruffle on her apron, the taste of tea turning bitter down the back of her throat. In front of her the girls collapsed against the table, one by one, as though their strings had been cut.

It would be her turn next. Somehow she already understood this.

Heart thudding, she rose to face the March Hare as he stepped into the clearing. There was something important she should say to him, but the words wouldn't come. Instead she curtsied, deeply. He bowed in return and Cassidy knew that if she wanted to end it in that moment, she could. With his head bent before her and his neck exposed, he was vulnerable.

But she did not take advantage of it. She could run. She could fight. But she could never escape the March Hare.

When he straightened she tried to meet his eyes, but even standing this close, they receded into darkness in a way she couldn't understand. As though they simply did not exist.

After a moment, he motioned for her to lift her hands into the air between them. Overhead, two lengths of fishing line drifted from the branches, whispering in the wind like the filament of a spider's web.

The March Hare took one and wrapped it tight around her right wrist, until it bit into her skin. Tears stung her eyes and she winced when he repeated the action with her left.

He seemed careful to avoid touching her in the process, his claw-tipped fingers deftly tying complicated knots. But when he was done, he hesitated. Her hands hung in front of her, as though she were sleepwalking or a zombie. He stepped closer to her, until the tips of her fingers brushed against the fur of his chest.

She was surprised at the warmth of it. He took another step, so that her palm was pressed flat against him. Under the shifting muscle, she felt his heart. That he had a heart at all took Cassidy by surprise, much less the way it pounded ferociously.

"Exactly so," she whispered.

He nodded, his crisply white ears falling forward before snapping back up.

The rest of it came swiftly and unexpectedly violent. His hands closed around her throat, claws biting into skin as he squeezed. As the light danced behind her eyes and her lungs turned inside out, she fought him.

But it was useless. He was larger and when he threw her forward onto her knees, the fishing line cut into her wrists, yanking her hands over her head. She didn't even have enough air left in her lungs to scream or beg.

Panic began to drum a frantic beat inside her. Pain sent bright explosions rocketing through her body. It was hard to breathe, her throat bruised and her lungs spasming with sobs and terror.

Perhaps Cassidy had been wrong about the March Hare. Perhaps he was nothing more than a monster, a killer of girls. A wielder of fury and retribution.

Eighteen Years Old

She was everywhere in the clearing: her footsteps in the grass, her fingerprints in the blood, her hair caught in the branches. As before, the only way to erase her complicity was to involve her beyond any measure of doubt. The March Hare had understood this then, even if Cassidy hadn't.

But she understood now.

The only difference was that this time there would be someone to blame: Tommy, raving about monsters in the woods. And, just as they had a decade ago, no one would ask too many questions because no one ever really wanted the truth.

They wanted the safe answer. The one that allowed them to fall asleep to the promise of dreams. The one that allowed them to forget about the white rabbit the size of a man and his clearing in the forest.

The one that reassured them that all monsters are filled with darkness.

"Make it convincing," Cassidy whispered, standing to face the March Hare. He pressed the tips of his claws against her abdomen. She winced. "But not too much," she amended breathlessly.

He nodded, one dingy ear falling forward and struggling to stand back up.

Eight Years Old, Eighteen Years Old

Cassidy was barely conscious when the March Hare, finally finished, gingerly lifted her onto her stump and gently slid a teacup onto her finger. She strained her senses and thought she heard a long sigh and the creak of old bones as he settled at the other end of the table.

He stayed there with her through the night. Every time she struggled to open her eyes, she'd see him, the ghostly outline of white ears against the threatening shadows.

Perhaps he had killed her after all. Perhaps he hadn't. There was only one thing Cassidy Evans knew for sure: It had been a marvelous tea party.

Inspired by the 1865 novel *Alice's Adventures in Wonderland* by Lewis Carroll and the 1951 animated film *Alice in Wonderland*

EMMELINE

CAT WINTERS

Northern France, 1918

Six feet from where I knitted, my bedroom came to an end and dropped to a cold, stinking pit of ash and bricks and shrapnel that was once our music room. Vacant eyes where windowpanes once hung stared out at the darkened countryside. The walls resembled Roman ruins, and stars peered down through a gaping hole where the roof used to protect my bed. *Mon Dieu*, that poor bed—now just a charred heap of wood buried down in the ground. Even on a clear summer night like this one, when warm breezes swept inside the rest of the house and delivered the *pop-pop-pop* of distant rifle fire, my ghost of a room suffered a bitter chill.

In the farthest corner, beneath the shadows of the ceiling's splintered remnants, I shivered on the floor. I knitted my red scarf. I enjoyed the spectacle of moonlight pushing its way through the wreckage and dreamed of motion pictures such as *Notre-Dame de Paris*. The flirty old moon eased his way across the warped and sooty floorboards and kissed my bare toes, turning my feet as luminous as the skin of the cinema stars.

Ah, I thought with a pleased wiggle of my toes.

From somewhere down below, in the untouched part of the house, male voices and bursts of laughter rose into the night. My mother's voice carried a welcoming calm, and silverware clanked genially on plates. *Our benevolent troops.*

Tipsy singing followed the meal—a war ditty bellowed in English, "Pack Up Your Troubles in Your Old Kit Bag." One of the younger children giggled, and my sister Claudine joined in with her off-key warbling. Poor, tone-deaf Claudine. She never could carry a tune, even when we performed our little pageants for the family, before the war.

My room grew colder. I drew my knees to my chest and pulled my half-finished scarf around my waist. Still my teeth chattered. My bones ached. The moon sidled closer, but its cinematic beams, all glamour and trickery, carried no warmth.

Three more songs into the evening, when moonlight bathed my entire skirt in a brilliant shade of white, footsteps approached the craggy opening where my door once stood. I grabbed a hunk of rubble—brick and a wedge of old plaster that made my hands chalky—and lifted my arm, ready for whichever sibling stalked down the teetering hallway to try to catch sight of me.

Someone taller than my brothers and sisters climbed the toppled black fragments of wood and entered my room. It was a soldier, a young one, with blond hair that was almost brown and eyes that looked to be blue or even gray from where I sat. His uniform was a little baggy in the hips, stern and tight in the tunic, olive green in color. Not a German. *Thank heavens.*

He wore tall leather boots that ended just below his knees. The thick soles made a loud shuffling as he inched and creaked across the floorboards, toward the jagged drop below. He leaned forward with his arms slightly out for balance and surveyed the annihilation—what was once a beautiful buttercup-yellow room full of Mama's piano and Grandfather's violin and music, music, music. The soldier's lips formed a small O, followed by a low whistle.

In the shadows, I tilted my head, considering. This stranger in my broken bedroom, with his ethereal skin and striking eyes, cut a handsome figure in the moonlight. Handsome enough for motion pictures. His nose and jaw looked strong and well-proportioned. His body was lean yet muscular. And warm. I sensed the heat of him from across the room.

I slid my feet farther into the light and cleared my throat.

The boy gave a start. "Who's there?"

He squinted into my dark corner, craned his head, took a single step toward me.

"Hello?" he asked in English, and after another step, he straightened his neck and grinned in a dopey sort of way, just then discovering he was alone with a seventeen-year-old girl.

I shifted my gaze downward, a small smile on my lips, and set the chunk of brick and plaster aside.

"Do you speak English?" he asked.

"*Oui.*"

"You do? Wait"—another step—"did you say yes in French because you understood me?"

"*Oui.*"

"Or do you answer *oui* to any question you don't understand?"

I shot him a glare. "I would say no if a foreigner came up here and asked me a question I did not understand. Or *nein* if you were one of our damned Boche occupiers."

"I didn't . . ." He put up his hands. "I'm not a German."

"My grandmother was from England"—I returned to my silver needles and yarn—"but you sound nothing like her. I bet you're a Yank."

"That's right."

"Ah. Our noble American saviors."

He shifted his eyes back to the pit. "Did the Krauts fire this shell through the roof?"

I shrugged. "Does it matter who dropped it there?"

"I . . . Well, I guess not. Unless it makes you feel better to blame someone. I bet anything it was the Krauts."

I shrugged a second time. I didn't know which troops shot the shell into our house, and I didn't want to know. I blamed everyone for it.

The soldier peeked at me again. "What's your name?"

"I'm not going to tell you."

"Why not?"

"Because—" I bit down on my lip.

"Because what?" he asked.

"Well . . . sometimes a girl should keep a trace of mystery about her, no?" I glanced up at him from beneath my lashes. "It's part of the games men and women play."

His big American boots clomped to the sturdier side of the room, where he leaned his hand against the blackened wall. "I don't have much time for games right now."

"Hmm." I fussed with a long piece of scarlet fuzz. "What is *your* name?"

"Well, that's not fair. Why should I tell you mine if you won't tell me yours?"

"Because you're an intruder in my bedroom."

"Christ! This was your bedroom?"

I nodded with my lips pursed tight. "It was. It still is, as long as I watch out for the fall to the first floor and don't mind the soot. The bed's long gone, although I swear I can see my headboard under all the bricks if I look down in the right light. My favorite pair of shoes too. Black ones, with two little straps and fancy buttons."

The soldier plopped his back against the wall and fished for something in one of the deep pockets on his chest. "All right, I'll give you a hint."

"A hint?"

"About my name," he said. "I'm named after an author."

"Hmm. What nationality?"

"American."

"Of course." I wound the yarn with nimble fingers and rummaged in my brain for Yank writers. "Poe?"

"No."

"Twain?"

"No."

"Ah"—I cast a glance at his brooding posture—"you could easily be a Lord Byron. Moody and passionate."

"Byron's British." He shoved a cigarette between his lips and ignited a flame with the flick of a dull brass lighter.

"Hey!" I sat up straight. "What are you doing?"

"Having a smoke. What does it look like?" He tilted his head toward the wavering wisp of orange and blue, and all I could see was my room engulfed in a crackling inferno.

"Don't!" I sprang from my corner and blew out the light with a force that shook through his hair and lashes. He froze and stared at me with wide smoky-gray eyes, his pupils swelling, his eyebrows arched. The unlit cigarette teetered on his lips.

I slunk back two feet, closer to the shadows. "Why would you light a match in a burned-up room that stinks of fire?"

"I just . . ." The cigarette fell out of his mouth and plunked to the floor without a sound. "I just wanted a smoke."

I wrapped my arms around myself. "Why are you staring at me like that?"

"I'm wondering . . ." He closed his mouth and swallowed.

"Wondering what?"

"Why a girl—a beautiful girl—would spend her time in a room that stinks of fire." He swallowed again. "What are you doing up here?"

I relaxed my shoulders. "You think I am beautiful?"

He released a shaky breath and ran his fingers through the blond hair at his forehead, exposing a grisly collection of long red scabs that crisscrossed his hand.

"Oh . . . your poor skin," I said, and stepped forward into the light. "What cut you? Not bayonets, I hope?"

"No." He lowered his fingers and looked at them. "Barbed wire. We run large sheets of metal fencing across no-man's-land to separate our trenches from the Krauts', and all sorts of macabre things get stuck in it."

"Including your hands?"

"Yeah, my hands, and my pants, and my . . ." He kneeled down and patted the floor until he found that horrible old cigarette. "My friends . . . my enemies." He stood back up. "They get snared, and there's nothing we can do besides pull the things out when bullets aren't whizzing past our skulls." He crammed the cigarette between his lips without lighting it and slumped against the wall's black filth. His eyes traveled toward the pit. Air fluttered through his nostrils in an unsteady patter. His mind went somewhere else. Every limb, every muscle and contour of his face took on that same war-weary rigidness I'd seen before. I half believed that if I leaned my ear next to his, I would hear the sound of artillery fire.

"I've always liked spending time with soldiers," I said, and I rubbed my finger through the soot on the wall, pleased with the mark I'd made. "At least the kind ones. The handsome, boyish ones. They make me feel I'm more than just a starving girl in a battle region."

He turned his head toward me, and his eyes warmed and softened. He liked what he saw—I could tell by the way he held his mouth on the cigarette, rolling the wrinkled white cylinder back and forth with his lips, the way I used to play with sticks of candy.

"Do you want to be my sweetheart?" I asked with a boldness I'd learned from all the young soldiers—both the French and the German—who had taught me the ways of seduction.

The right side of his mouth edged into a grin. "Your sweetheart?"

"*Oui.*"

"You won't even tell me your name."

"It's Emmeline."

"Emmeline? Hmm, that's pretty." He cocked his head, and his eyes brightened. His skin pinked up. "Say, you look just like Lillian Gish, now that I take a good look at you in the moonlight."

"The American film actress?"

"Yeah, you've got those same big, dark eyes. The same long, curly hair."

"Oh, I love the cinema." Using my finger as a paintbrush and the muck on the wall as my paint, I drew a crude sketch of a movie projector with giant reels and a boxy body. "I haven't seen a motion picture since before the war. My favorite was *Notre-Dame de Paris*, about the hunchback, with Stacia Napierkowska as the tragic Gypsy Esméralda."

"You like monster films?"

"Just the beautiful ones."

"Beautiful monsters?"

"*Oui.*"

"Huh. I'd like to see that." He smirked and shifted his weight. "Do you get Lillian Gish pictures over here in France?"

"No"—I shook my head—"not up here in the north. The Boche only allowed German films when they occupied our village. I've seen her photograph, though, in a magazine my sister once stole from a burn pile for me."

"Well, she's a real looker."

"Does that mean you like how I look?"

He smiled and breathed a whisper of a laugh that confirmed that he did.

"Come here." I stepped backward and beckoned with my finger toward my shadowed corner.

"Where?"

"Come with me, Yank soldier. I want to take good care of you."

He drew the cigarette out of his mouth and knitted his brows. "What are you, a vampire?"

"That's not a nice question to ask a girl." I settled back down on the floor and picked up my yarn. "Why would you say such a thing?"

"You're the only girl I know who wants to 'take care' of a fellow in the bombed ruins of a bedroom in the dark of night. I think I might have to call you Carmilla instead of Emmeline."

"Who is Carmilla?"

"A bewitching female vampire from an old novella."

"Oh." I resumed my knitting. "Well . . . I am not a vampire."

"You don't bite?" he asked with a grin that showed off a dimple in his right cheek.

"Tell me your name, Mr. Poe"—I smiled as well—"and I'll let you come close enough to find out."

He tucked the cigarette into his pocket and wandered toward me, and my swaying needles, and the thin blue rug that concealed some of the ugliness in the room. Three yards away, his boots triggered a groan in the floor that seemed to be a protest against his weight. He stopped and sidled over to the safety of the wall.

"My mother was a teacher," he said. "She named me Emerson— after good old Ralph Waldo."

I shrugged. "I've never heard of him."

"He was an essayist and a poet we Americans have to learn about in school. Friends back home called me by my initials, or sometimes they used Sonny, which I hate more than anything. Or else they'd just call me by my last name, Jones."

"Emmeline and Emerson." I snickered and coaxed the yarn around the needles. "That almost sounds too silly to be the names of a leading man and his lady."

"I beg your pardon?"

I met his eyes. "Come lie down next to me, Emerson Jones. Escape the bloody war with me."

He grinned with a sheepish hunch of his shoulders and peeked back at the space where the door should have stood. "Your family might come up. Or one of the fellas will decide to go nosing around like I did."

"You and your Yank troops are occupying our house?"

"No, your mother is just letting us stay in the barn for the night. She's cooking us a meal in exchange for food and supplies. I just . . ." He rubbed the back of his neck and seemed a little off-balance. "I got curious about this part of the house when she ordered us—no, *barked* at us—not to come up here."

"Ah, a mischief-seeker." I patted the floor beside me. "Come lie down, lovely Emerson. I swear I am not a vampire. I will not bite."

He sauntered over the precise way I expected a Yank to walk, with a cowboy sort of swagger to his hips. Less graceful than a Frenchman, not as stiff as the German boy who once spent time with me up here, after the shell blasted through the roof.

My American soldier stood over me with his hands at his sides. "Is this something you've done before? 'Escaped' with soldiers?"

I tutted at him. "You sound like my mother."

"I'm just curious what type of girl you are."

"Are you sure you truly want to know?"

He crossed his arms over his chest. "Yes."

I ran my fingers over the completed five feet of my darling scarlet scarf. "Well . . . I am an imaginative girl. A romantic one. One who tells ghost stories to test the bravery of boys who are being a little bit rude."

"Really?" He grinned. "Well, go on, then. Test me."

"Are you certain?"

"Tell me a ghost story that'll make me tremble in these big old boots of mine."

"All right. I only know one such story, and it goes like this . . ." I took a deep breath. "One afternoon when I was knitting in my bed"—I nodded toward the missing half of the room—"that stray shell that's buried down there in the ground plummeted through the roof"—I licked my parched lips—"and killed me."

He turned his head toward the void where my bed should have been.

"Now . . . it seems," I continued, with chills running across my arms, "I'm stuck up here . . . all alone. *Maman* yells at the other children if they sneak down the hallway to hunt for me. She uses the word *morte*—or dead—to keep them away, which hurts worse than the pain of the shell itself. At least that was a swift and instant pain." I sighed.

My beautiful American lowered himself down to his knees in front of me, and his eyes were gentle.

"Well?" I toyed with the soft red yarn. "Did that frighten you?"

"I'm like that too," he said.

I snorted a laugh. "What? Dead?"

"No." He cracked a small smile. "'I have been half in love with easeful Death,' like Keats said in 'Ode to a Nightingale.' I'm obsessed with the idea of dying. I write poems about it. I imagine the same type of things you're imagining. 'Now more than ever seems it rich to die, / To cease upon the midnight with no pain.'"

My mouth fell open. "You're in love . . . with death?"

His smile widened. He remained crouched in front of me. "I don't usually stumble across a girl who's drawn to my dark view of the world, but I have to say"—he rubbed his chin and looked me over—"I find it awfully attractive."

My eager fingers trembled on the scarf. "Is that why you joined the war? To die?"

"God, no." He settled back on his heels. "My father badgered me into enlisting. He's always trying to do his best to make a man out of me."

"Why would he need to do that? You seem manly enough."

"Why, thank you." His cheeks reddened, and he beamed with a bit of the devil in his eyes. "But I grew up in a house crammed full of sisters, and I was Pop's only chance for some extra masculinity in the place. Two years ago he even pushed me to join the football team, but instead"—he chuckled from deep in the crook of his throat—"I published a satirical poem about high school pigskins in the school's literary journal. Even received an award for it."

"What are 'high school pigskins'?"

"It's what we call our great American football."

"Oh." I nodded. "Well, no wonder your *maman* named you after an author. You should be creating your beautiful poetry instead of hunting down the Boche."

"Yeah, well, that's not what my father thought." Again, he pulled out his cigarette and stuck it in his mouth, but he didn't dare light it. *Good boy.*

"Earlier this year," he continued with the stick wedged between his teeth, "my older sister decided to volunteer as a Red Cross nurse in the war. She's always been the charitable type, so it wasn't all that surprising. Pop then sat me down and said, 'By God, boy, if our sweet Amy—a five-foot-tall girl, no less—is risking her neck over in France, then you sure as hell better make a goddamned soldier out of yourself.'"

Emerson stayed stone-still for a moment and seemed to hear the echo of his father's words in the room with us, so much so that I peeked behind me just to make sure his "pop" wasn't there. The unlit cigarette quaked in his mouth. Another rousing American war song echoed down below. Then he shrugged. "So . . . here I am."

"I'm sorry." I gulped. "Do you like being a soldier?"

"Do you like living in the charred ruins of a house that reeks of hell?"

"Of course not."

"Well, the trenches are worse, I can tell you that. Blood and bullets and bodies from all sides, and there's no escape. No relief. I'm sick to my stomach all the time out there."

"I thought you said you were drawn to darkness."

"Not that type." His teeth clamped down on the cigarette. "Less gore and shrieking would be preferable. 'Easeful Death.'"

I set the yarn and the needles aside and lured the cigarette out of his mouth with my thumb and middle finger. The heat of his breath warmed the back of my hand.

"Let's forget the gore for a while." I flicked the cigarette across the floor. "How does that sound, *mon beau soldat?*"

He took another peek over his shoulder. "This burned old ghost of a room doesn't seem all that private."

"No one ever comes up here. Even if they did, we'd hear their footsteps creaking down the hallway long before they reached us."

"Are you sure you want me to be with you like this?"

I nodded and touched his knee. "I'm not a wild girl, Emerson. Just a terribly, terribly lonely one who feels better around boys who help me forget all my troubles."

"All right." He nodded. "I can certainly try to help you forget."

I smiled. "Lie down."

With a low moan in the boards, Emerson shifted and stretched out on his back beside me in the barren corner. He lowered his blond head to the faded blue rug and wove his fingers through mine. "Jesus!" His hand flew away. "You're frosty cold. Don't you ever go downstairs, Carmilla?"

"Don't call me that name. Just kiss me." I leaned over and kissed his soft lips in the shadows of the ruins, tasting sweet outside air and sunshine. "Please . . . say my real name."

"Emmeline," he whispered, and he shivered beneath me. "It's really freezing in here for the summer."

"Forget the chill. Just forget everything terrible and painful and pretend we're a handsome couple in a motion picture." I kissed him again, and although he still shuddered, he let me unbutton his army tunic all the way down to the bottom. My fingers slid beneath his cotton undershirt and found skin smooth and warm as a fever.

His eyelids fluttered. He relaxed beneath my touch. It must not have felt so cold anymore.

"See"—I kissed the salty curve of his neck—"we're like two lovers, caught in the flickering shadow and light of a beautiful film on a screen."

He gave a small nod and a murmur.

I let my hand wander down to his belt and the flat metal buttons of his olive-green trousers. His clothing carried the smells of the trenches, dirt and grime and worse, but the scents of war didn't matter one bit to a girl who dwelled in a house of ash. He was solid and handsome and compassionate, and he thawed my room's unfathomable chill.

I lifted up my skirts, wiggled my drawers down to the floor, and, with a graceful sweep of my right leg, I climbed on top of him. One never saw such a sight on the screen—a girl, adjusting her underclothing, straddling a boy—but I knew that's what happened whenever scenes of romance faded to blackness.

He tensed. "Are you sure about this? Your mother . . ."

"She never comes up here—I swear. No one likes to be here. We're all alone."

He closed his eyes and tipped back his head, and the strain of the war lifted from his face as steam rises from water. Sighs escaped his half-opened lips, and my old friend the moon stole closer. Light glinted off the tips of my silver needles and brightened the fingers clasping hold of my legs.

See, this is lovely, I told myself. *So lovely. You don't need anything more than this.*

I kept him close for as long as I could—two silhouettes intertwined in the dark, rocking together, without any thought to bombs or bayonets or the *rat-a-tat-tat* of rifle fire across the open fields. That's why I always adored such paramours. They were paintbrushes dipped in white that smeared away all the ugly colors.

Afterward, he lowered his shoulders back down to the floor and let his head drift to his left. His body relaxed, as if trading the battlefield for paradise.

I pulled the red scarf off the floor and gathered it into a ball in my hand.

"Get comfortable, my Emerson." I climbed off him, and he rolled onto his side, facing away from the corner, where I stowed the needles and yarn. He fastened some of his clothing back over himself, and I nestled beside him and curled my whole self around his back with my arm strapped over his chest.

"Your mother could still come up," he said in a voice gone drowsy and low.

"I keep telling you, she doesn't like to be in here."

"Your brothers and sisters . . ."

"Claudine hates me these days. She calls me horrific names. They all do. Not like you." I pressed my chest against his back and drew the heat from his body. "You stayed with me, even when I told you my ghost story."

"But I'm just . . ."

"Just what?"

"Just . . . another soldier . . . taking advantage of a French girl."

"No."

"Yes. I even have a girl back home."

"A sweetheart?"

He nodded against my cheek. "I don't think I'll want anything to do with her when I'm back, though. She wouldn't understand a single part of this. She was just a pretty neighborhood girl who tolerated my strange ways."

"No, she wouldn't understand at all. Stay with me. Close your eyes and stay."

"Hmm, I'd like to . . ."

I held myself against him and shared his beating heart, his flushed skin, the lulling rhythm of his chest rising and falling beneath my outstretched hand. He fell asleep. The moon slipped away. The red yarn beckoned.

The last time I hosted a boy in my ruined room, trouble followed. But that was simply a matter of being too hasty. All that urgent stabbing, the swift flow of blood, the howls—that wasn't how it was supposed to be. The Germans had to carry the other boy away, half-dead and whimpering, yet alive enough to keep from staying with me. They blamed my father for the violence and shot him dead in our front garden.

This time would be different.

Go on, I told myself with a desperate taste, sharp as metal, burning stronger and stronger inside my mouth. After all that I suffered from the war and my family, I deserved something more.

My American soldier slept with his whole body gone slack and his breathing soft and steady. He stayed on his side with his head tilted just enough to leave an opening between his neck and the floor. He hadn't yet refastened the top buttons of his tunic, so the smooth skin below the edge of his hair remained exposed and vulnerable. I kissed him there once, right above his top vertebra, drawing goose-flesh without waking him.

My fingers reached into the dark corner for my red scarf—the scarf I never seemed able to complete. I'd been knitting until my fingers ached and chafed, just so some anonymous French soldier could wear it without knowing its creator's tiniest likes and dislikes. He wouldn't know I resembled Lillian Gish, or adored Stacia Napier-kowska, or hated to be alone in my apocalypse room. How much better a use for the scarf—tightly knitted with care and love—than to wrap it around the neck of sleeping, lovely Emerson.

I wound it around his throat once, twice, three times without him stirring. I closed my eyes and imagined a delicate tug. A gentle urg-ing. Nothing sharp or jolting, like a needle through the flesh or a missile plunged through one's roof. It would be more like a siren call to a sailor. Pure and poetic. Absent of agony.

Now more than ever seems it rich to die,
To cease upon the midnight with no pain.

Wasn't that what he had said?

My fists clasped the loose ends of the scarf behind his neck. I counted to three and then . . . I pulled.

Emerson awoke with a start and a gasp and grabbed for the noose around his windpipe. His boots banged against the floor—*thump, thump, thump, thump, thump.*

"No! It's all right. Don't make a sound." I yanked the scarf with all my strength, but he kicked and struggled with a racket that would surely draw attention.

"No, Emerson! Stop fighting and come with me. Come with me!"

The needles swung in the air, still attached to my unfinished creation, and his boots knocked the ground in a cloud of ash. *Thump! Thump! Thump! Thump! Thump!*

"No! Stop or I'll have to stab you instead—I swear I will."

His hands were in my hair, my face, pushing me away. His boots kept pounding. The rest of him writhed and grunted and struggled.

"Come with me. Hold still. Hold still! *Merde!*"

Footsteps hurtled toward us from the hall.

"No!"

I gave a good tug then, one that stopped him from gasping and thrashing. He arched his back and was almost there—I felt him rushing toward me. The room warmed and brightened. I was Stacia Napierkowska in brilliant black-and-white, and he was my leading man, come to share my broken bedroom while the moon transformed us both into ravishing silver creatures.

Five young men in uniforms like his pounded into the room with footsteps that hurt my ears. The floor swayed. They called his name, furrowed their brows, forced off the scarf, wrenched him away from me. With one final burst of energy, I slashed the tip of a silver needle across the back of his neck and painted a streak of red on one of the last parts of his body untouched by battle, the same place I'd kissed mere moments before.

The soldiers surrounded him, but I saw his boots moving about, caught a glimpse of his blond hair and bruised throat. He panted and choked, and his friends spoke all at once:

"What happened?"

"What's wrong with you?"

"You could have fallen into that god-awful pit!"

"Was that a seizure?"

"What the hell happened?"

I crouched on all fours to see past his protectors' arms and legs. From within the wall of olive-green bodies, my soldier's gray eyes locked upon me. He jumped to his feet.

"There she is! The g-girl. The girl's still here."

A dark-haired soldier with scabs on his forehead turned my way, and soon the whole crowd was gawking at my corner, including Claudine, who had stumbled in behind them.

"Why'd you do that, Emmeline?" Emerson pushed toward me, but his comrades pulled him back. "I was gentle with you."

"Emerson?" asked a fellow soldier.

"I was nothing but gentle. Why'd you attack me like—like some animal?"

"Emerson—"

"She tried to kill me." He struggled to get at me, his teeth gritted, his knuckles blanching. "She tried to—"

"Jones!" shouted the dark-haired one with a tug that knocked him off his feet. "There's no one there."

My American soldier's eyes changed at those words. *Mon Dieu,* how they changed. He gaped at me with the uncomprehending stare of a person whose mind told him one thing while his eyes insisted on another. In another moment, he'd refuse to even look at me. I knew I'd soon become something he'd fight to forget for the rest of his living days.

"She's . . . but . . ." He grabbed hold of his throat and struggled to swallow.

"Please stay," I said. "Make my life as romantic as it should have been. You said you were 'half in love with easeful Death,' and I could help you. I could bleed your troubles away."

The troops didn't have to carry this one out like my pale German soldier, whose groans still haunted me. My American boy got up like the man his father wanted him to be and shoved his comrades aside, turning his back on death like a fool. The last part of him I glimpsed before he climbed out of my room was the red slash I'd made on his neck—the same shock of scarlet as my unfinished scarf, now curled in a pile on the floor.

One day soon, I assured myself as his footsteps grew fainter, *that wound will harden into a scar, and every time his hand brushes it, he'll be forced to think of me. He'll be sorry if the Germans shoot off his arm or the side of his face, and he'll realize I could have kept him in one piece. We could have been rapturous and beautiful together. He will be sorry no one will ever truly understand him.*

The gaggle of Yanks followed him out, until only Claudine lingered in my shell of a doorway.

"You need to go, Emmeline," she said in French, and she screwed up her mouth and wrinkled her forehead. She looked so much harsher and uglier than a fifteen-year-old girl who used to share beds and rag dolls and secrets with me. Her brown hair hung to her waist in a ratty mess, and her threadbare dress drooped over the protruding bones of her malnourished body. "It was horrifying enough you attacked that German boy and got Papa killed, but the Yanks are supposed to be helping us. Get out." She grabbed hold of a piece of the plaster wall. It crumbled to dust in her hands. "Get out for good. Stay away. You don't belong here anymore."

I called her name, but she clambered over the rubble and escaped down the corridor on whining broken floorboards. I swore I heard her cough up tears, as if she missed me after all.

It was just I alone in the room again. Only the weakest rays of moonlight loitered with me, and the darkness forced itself upon my shoulders.

Across the floor near my empty corner, a metal object caught my eye. I raised my chin and crawled through the ashes to a small brass cylinder.

Emerson's lighter.

"Ahhh," I said in a whispered sigh. He carried my mark on the back of his neck. Now I possessed something of him.

I tucked the lighter beneath the blue rug that concealed my other soldier's bloodstains. I nestled this new trinket next to a button from a German army uniform. Treasures from those who slipped away.

Boys were curious creatures by nature. Soon there would be another young man who would steal into the wreckage to see the forbidden part of our poor old house. One day I would get things right, and someone would choose me over the war. Someone would treat me as if I were Stacia Napierkowska, and I would take good care of him, and he would stay with me.

I snuggled my shoulder blades back against the wall and returned to my knitting, with the lump of Emerson's lighter rising beneath the rug. The next night my old friend the moon would return, casting his silvery spell, and I would wait. I was always a patient girl.

I could wait.

Inspired by the 1930 film *All Quiet on the Western Front*, Daphne du Maurier's 1952 short story "Kiss Me Again, Stranger," and the 1922 film *Nosferatu*

VERSE CHORUS VERSE

LEIGH BARDUGO

Kara Adams clutched her daughter in a tight hug, turning Jaycee slightly in her arms to make sure the cameras got the best angle. Kara wasn't proud of it, but she did it, and Jaycee would thank her later when she saw the footage on TMZ.

Babygirl had put on a lot of weight at Wellways, but it would come off when she started rehearsing for the tour—Kara would make sure of that. They'd have a new chef on the bus, raw foods, lots of kale. Jaycee had gotten stuck with Kara's rotten metabolism, and that meant she put the flab on fast and took it off slow. She had dropped the weight before, though never without a little help. Besides, Kara still had a prescription for Adderall and she could always have her doctor up the dose. That wasn't quite playing by the rules that the staff at Wellways had laid out, but they didn't have to shake their asses in front of a stadium full of twenty thousand people. Besides, it was alcohol that had gotten Jaycee into trouble, not a little pick-me-up. Wasn't any different than a stiff cup of coffee.

Cameras flashed. It was blinding, like watching a whole sky full of constellations go off. Jaycee did look better. She was smiling and waving, a little pale maybe, but that was nothing a little bronzer wouldn't fix. Her hair had grown out since she'd given it that buzz cut that had landed her on the cover of *Star* and *OK!* and every other supermarket rag. A few more weeks and it would be long enough for a cute bob. Kara would get someone they could trust to handle the story with an upbeat spin, something like *Jaycee Adams: New Life, New 'Do!*

"How are you feeling, Jaycee?" one of the reporters shouted.

"Good!" said Jaycee, grinning broadly. "Happy, healthy, very blessed."

"You gonna visit Carlos Ravelo?"

That was the kid Jaycee had hit with her SUV on the way home from the Attic, a club on Sunset. It didn't matter that she wasn't old enough to drink. Jaycee Adams did not get carded, especially not when she was ordering up bottles in the VIP section of a new club desperate to get a mention on a decent gossip blog. Jaycee's lawyers had claimed she'd been on prescription painkillers for a knee injury she'd gotten during choreography, but the blood and urine tests had told a different story: weed and tequila, Jaycee's favorite way to relax. Luckily the Ravelo kid had been fine, a little banged up, but a fat check had put him back in the pink fast enough.

"Carlos is the sweetest," Jaycee said. "We've been e-mailing. He's even doing some songwriting. He's good!"

She drew out that *gooood,* really letting her drawl come through. It wasn't even deliberate. Jaycee was just a natural, always had been, funny and sweet and charming. Kara had known it from the first time Jaycee had put on her tap shoes, from the first pageant, from the first warbled note of "Can You Feel the Love Tonight." That was her showstopper, the song that first got her noticed. Because Jaycee actually had talent, not like these other girls coming up.

"Meet anyone fun in rehab, Jaycee? How's Marcus?"

Kara stiffened, but Jaycee only wagged her finger. "You know it wasn't rehab. Just needed a little rest to get my head together. I had the time to do some soul-searching and now I can't wait to get into the studio to record."

A natural. A real pro. Every producer Jaycee had worked with said the same thing. She'd managed to dodge the Marcus Price question entirely. That little bastard. Just the sound of his name made Kara's blood boil. She knew he'd been the one to leak those topless photos of Jaycee. Of course, Jaycee had been dumb enough to send them.

"Isn't Wellways a rehab?" shouted another reporter. Couldn't let it go, could they?

"It's a place to get better," Jaycee replied. "And that's what I needed to do."

"Okay everybody," said Kara. "Time to get my baby home. Cornbread won't keep."

They all laughed at that, good-natured, happy to have gotten their shots and a few quick quotes. You had to give the beasts a little meat. Otherwise they could turn on you.

Jaycee was quiet on the ride home from the airport. Kara had wanted to pick her up at Wellways, get a shot of Jaycee with some of the more normal-looking kids, laughing and sitting in the sun, make it look more like a summer camp and less like Jaycee was some kind of criminal. *A place to get better.* Exactly. But the head nurse had insisted that wouldn't be possible.

"We value quiet here," Louise had said over the phone. "We're not going to disrupt the other clients'"—they always called them clients, not patients—"treatment so that you can hold a press conference. Why don't you just take Jaycee straight home and let her have a few days without that dog and pony show?"

Kara had heard the judgment in Louise's voice. She hadn't met her, but she didn't need to. Kara could picture the woman perfectly: wide Midwestern hips and a no-nonsense haircut to prove she meant business. And Kara knew what Louise thought; she got the message loud and clear: Kara was the bad mother, the stage mom, offering her poor daughter up to the paparazzi for a cheap buck.

But what Louise didn't understand, what these women never understood, was that if Jaycee didn't get in front of this story, then the press would just make something up and it wouldn't be pretty. Kara had seen it happen with that girl who broke down all over Twitter and the other one, the cute one with the freckles who ended up making a movie with that porn star. This had to be Jaycee's triumphant return, not the first hint of a downward spiral. You had to come out proud and unashamed, show them you were ready to move on, give them a little piece so they didn't take a bigger one, get them on your side. That was how the game was played. Jaycee had worked hard for what she had, and Kara wasn't going to let anyone take it.

So they'd booked the flight and Kara had tipped off one of the friendlier paps, and when Jaycee had arrived at LAX, the mob had been waiting at the luggage claim. Jaycee had been ready—hair clean, looking adorable in pink sweats and a matching hoodie. It was too bad about the weight gain, but they might be able to spin that too, a role model piece for one of the teen magazines: *Healthy and Happy at Last. Jaycee Adams Loves Her New Curves!*

"You okay, baby?" Kara asked as they sped down the freeway. "You want a soda?" The car service had sent a big black Suburban and it was stocked with all of Jaycee's favorites.

Jaycee shook her head. Now that they were away from the cameras, her face had a funny slack quality, as if it had taken all of her energy to put on a smile for the reporters.

"Was that true?" Kara asked. "What you said about Carlos?"

"He sent me some songs. Louise cleared them and printed them out for me. They're really not bad." *Louise cleared them.* Wellways only allowed supervised Internet access and Kara had gotten just that one phone call from Jaycee the whole time she'd been away.

Kara shifted on the leather seat and fiddled with the knob that controlled the air-conditioning. She didn't like to think of that call. Her daughter had a beautiful voice—even just talking—sweet and husky, a star's voice. But that night it had been panicked, trembling, barely a rasp.

"Mama," she'd whispered. "Mama, please get me out of here. I want to come home."

"Jaycee—"

"Please. You don't understand. There's something here."

Lying on her bed that night, Kara had looked out at the moonlight shining off the Pacific and rolled her eyes. Babygirl must still be coming down from whatever was in her system. "Jaycee, you know what the judge said. You just need to stay focused and—"

"Mama, please come get me. *Please.* Oh god—" The phone had clattered as if Jaycee had put it down in a rush. But the handset must not have settled in the cradle, because Kara could still hear Jaycee and now her daughter was sobbing.

"Please," Jaycee begged, but she wasn't talking to her mother anymore, Kara felt sure of it. Then Kara heard the whir of some kind of machine starting up. It sounded almost like a power tool, maybe a saw. Something about that metallic whine had raised the hairs on her arms.

She'd sat up on the bed. "Jaycee?"

The whine rose to a grinding shriek as if it were being held right up to the phone, then there was a click and after a long moment, a dial tone. Kara had tried to call back but she'd just gotten the Wellways switchboard. "You have reached Wellways, where healing begins. Our business hours are . . ."

Before she'd known what she was doing, Kara had been in the hallway, toeing on her shoes, reaching for her purse, car keys in hand. She could get to the airport in under an hour. There were commuter flights still leaving up until midnight.

Then she'd stopped, hand on the doorknob. If Jaycee came out early, she'd be violating the conditions of her sentencing. She might have to go to jail. She'd lose endorsements for sure. Kara was being silly. Wellways had a great reputation and her daughter had a flair for the dramatic.

Kara had put her purse down, then her keys. She'd turned on the television in the living room and made a bed for herself on the couch. She'd had this feeling that if she went back to her bedroom, when she rested her head on her pillow, she would hear that high metallic whine, right up against her ear.

She'd called the next morning, demanded to speak to her daughter and to know just what kind of program they were running up there. But when she finally got Jaycee on the line after hassling with the receptionist and then that nurse, she'd just said, "I'm fine, Mama."

"What was that last night? You about scared me to death."

"You're making me late for yoga." Jaycee's voice was sandpaper rough, strained and whispery, the way it got when she had too many shows back to back. Or when she'd been crying.

"Baby—"

Louise came back on the line. "Jaycee had a tough night but she's settling in now. You can call again tomorrow." And then she'd hung up.

When Jaycee's court-mandated stay was over, Wellways had wanted to keep her there another six weeks to "successfully embed recovery behaviors." Just another bunch of leeches looking to bleed them for another chunk of change. And who disappears for *twelve* weeks? You might as well be dead.

Now Kara looked at her daughter, head leaning against the car window. She wondered if she should ask Jaycee about the night of the call. No, she decided, it would keep. Trouble always did.

Jaycee had taken a town car all the way up the coast from Los Angeles to Wellways, her new headphones clapped over her ears, watching the coast roll by on her left, listening to the new tracks her producer had sent along. She'd been sure Mama would insist on going with her, but Kara had booked a spot on one of the big morning talk shows to discuss Jaycee's road to recovery. "Damage control, baby-girl." Jaycee had been relieved at first, glad she wouldn't have to sit through two hours of her mother talking strategy. Now she felt annoyed. *Poor little girl all on her own.* That's the way it would look. Jaycee was tempted to check her phone to see if clips of her mother's appearance were already circulating online. She turned up the volume on her headphones instead.

Mama had insisted driving was the best strategy for avoiding the paparazzi, but they were waiting at the Wellways entrance just the same. They descended on the town car, pressing themselves against the windows, jostling one another and shouting her name. The windows were so darkly tinted that Jaycee wasn't sure why they bothered. They weren't going to get a shot. Some part of her wanted to roll the window down and do something outrageous. Flash her tits, show them the mess of her chopped-up hair, her new tongue piercing, let them know exactly what she thought of them.

But before she could work up the courage, the wrought iron gates opened and the car was gliding through. If she'd been high, she would have done it in a second.

The gates closed and the paps were left behind. No trespassing on private property. Jaycee knew that wouldn't keep them out for long. A breaking and entering charge and even a night in jail would be worth it for a picture of Jaycee Adams in hospital scrubs or whatever shitty outfit they put her in. The tabloid bosses would bail their photographers out—just part of the price of doing business.

The car followed a winding gravel drive past green lawns and dense woods until at last the Wellways building came into view. The place looked like a resort—red tile roofs and two white wings stretching out from a central bell tower, all fronted by an arched colonnade. It reminded her of Marcus's mansion in Malibu, same Spanish style. But she didn't want to think about Marcus. They'd toured together last fall. He was a little older, and so funny, smart about the industry. He could make her laugh just by pulling a face. They'd played their guitars, talked about recording a duet. But that had all changed when his new album dropped. It just hadn't gotten heat the way hers had, and that was a shame because it was good, really good. She'd told him so and she'd meant it, but that had only seemed to make him madder. And then those pictures had surfaced. He claimed his ex-assistant had done it, that she was sore over being fired, but Jaycee didn't quite believe him. As the car rounded a bend, the shadows shifted. The building's arches seemed to yawn like a row of dark mouths. Jaycee rubbed her arms.

When the town car rolled to a stop, the driver came around to open her door. Jaycee stepped out and stretched, sliding off her headphones. They were on a high wooded hill that overlooked the highway and the blue sea beyond. She couldn't see the gates they'd come through, but she guessed most of the paparazzi were dispersing, making plans to return after dark, or maybe getting into their SUVs to head back to LA in search of some other story. Jaycee was surprised at the twinge she felt, like watching Mama drive away on the first day of school. The driver took her bag out of the trunk, then slammed it closed and stood waiting for instruction. Jaycee realized she could actually hear the break of the waves in the distance. Maybe her room would have a view.

No one had come out to greet her. They were probably making a show of the fact that she'd be treated the same as anyone else here. Jaycee blew out an annoyed breath. They could pretend all they wanted. She *wasn't* like everyone else, and she sure as heck wasn't some high school junkie popping Oxy or cutting herself for thrills.

"Guess you can go," she said.

The driver nodded, then mumbled, "Have a . . . good stay."

"Thanks," she replied sourly, but she still wanted to chase after him, hop back in the car, and beg him to take her home.

Jaycee straightened her shoulders, fluffed her hair, and headed up the stairs. The doors slid open with a whoosh, and she walked into a plush, high-ceilinged lobby. It was carpeted in soft beige, the dark wood furniture upholstered in earth tones, the walls decorated with vague watercolors of the coastline. Some kind of music was playing, one of those meandering melodies played on a flute with no real structure.

The woman behind the big, round welcome desk was young and pretty. She smiled at Jaycee and Jaycee smiled back, full wattage. "Jaycee Adams," she said, leaning her elbows on the counter.

"Of course," the receptionist said warmly. "Welcome to Wellways. I'm going to need you to fill out some forms and someone will come get you in just a few minutes."

She handed Jaycee a pen and a clipboard full of paperwork. Jaycee hesitated. Mama had always filled out these forms when she was younger, even when Jaycee had gone on the pill. She'd been thirteen, but Mama and her manager had insisted on it. She needed to be on a cycle where she didn't have to worry about getting her period more than once or twice a year. No cramps, no bloating, nothing to worry about when she was touring or before an awards show.

She sat down in one of the overstuffed chairs and slowly started filling out the forms. It felt strange, like she was making a confession: birth date, weight, height, allergies to medications, surgeries in the last year. Then she got to smoking, alcohol consumption, and drug use, and it was hard not to smirk. Why did they even bother asking? She went down the column checking the *never* boxes. All she needed was for a form like this to leak online.

An older woman appeared through the pair of swinging doors behind the welcome desk. She looked like she was in her fifties and wore scrubs with little Winnie-the-Poohs on them and a pair of those ugly rubber Crocs in purple.

"Hey, Hollywood," she said to Jaycee with a big grin. "You hungover?"

"What?" Jaycee sputtered.

The nurse held up her hands in a placating gesture. "Lots of people like a last hoorah the night before they go dry."

"No," Jaycee said icily. "I'm fine." She'd had a little weed before she'd gotten in the car, but just for motion sickness.

"Good, then let's lose the sunglasses and get you squared away."

Jaycee wanted to throw her Ray-Bans in the old bag's face, but she took them off and tucked them in her bag. "Sorry, ma'am," she said in her sweetest drawl, the good Southern girl who didn't mean no harm.

"Much better," the nurse said with a wink. She tucked the clipboard with Jaycee's paperwork on it under her arm and gave the woman at the desk a pat on the shoulder. "You can take your break in fifteen, Angie."

Angie smiled, but as Jaycee hitched her bag over her shoulder she saw the receptionist had her hands balled into fists, pressing them hard against her thighs.

She hurried to follow the nurse through the swinging doors. As they swished closed, she felt that same little-girl twinge, like she was Alice shrinking down to a smaller version of herself.

"I'm Nurse Allen, but everyone calls me Louise. Or Lou if you like."

"Thanks," Jaycee said, and flashed another high-wattage smile. "Do you have kids, Lou?"

"Did have. Lost him in Afghanistan."

"I'm sorry," Jaycee said, internally kicking herself. She'd hoped Lou might have grandkids who wanted a signed poster or tickets to a show. She could work with that.

"Me too, kiddo."

She led Jaycee down a long hall carpeted in the same beige as the lobby, past some kind of rec room where people were playing cards or watching a TV in the corner. Everyone turned to stare at Jaycee as she passed. She saw the looks of surprise and recognition. One guy sat up and smacked his friend on the arm. She saw his mouth form the words *no way*.

They passed through another set of doors and Lou used her keys to open up an examination room. The floor was speckled tile here, and there was a black-and-white photograph of a grove of oak trees on the wall. Through the narrow window, Jaycee could see a glimpse of green lawn, a sprinkler turning in a slow circle, leaving an arc of water that shimmered briefly with rainbows.

"Hop up," Louise instructed, patting the paper cover on the table.

Jaycee hoisted herself up and Louise said, "Okay, kiddo, here's what's gonna happen. I'm going to get you checked out, take down all your stats, and help you settle in. Then you can have a shower or a nap before you meet the group."

Jaycee rolled her eyes.

"Yes, that's right, you've gotta go to group just like everyone else, Hollywood."

Jaycee felt a stab of resentment. "I'm not an addict, okay? I'm like any other kid who drinks a little too much at a party, only I've got the world watching."

"You hit another kid with your car, and alcohol wasn't all that was in your system, was it?"

Jaycee shrugged.

"Jaycee, we're the only addiction program for teens on the West Coast. We've got all kinds here and they're not all lowlifes and burn-outs." Her eyes crinkled and she gave a little chuckle. "Might be good for you to meet some kids who don't have agents or entourages."

Jaycee pressed her lips together. Was she really supposed to open up in a room full of strangers when anything she said could end up on the cover of *Us*? Jaycee Adams's daddy issues. Jaycee Adams molested by photographer. Jaycee Adams crying over spilled milk.

Louise looked down at the clipboard.

"I see you marked *never* for drug use. Jaycee, I've seen the police report."

Jaycee shrugged again.

"What about cigarettes?"

"Once in a while," Jaycee admitted. That wasn't illegal. "At parties."

Louise glanced at the clipboard. "No to alcohol?" She sighed and pulled up a chair. "Listen up, kiddo. Whether or not you think you need it, you're here for the duration, until we clear you or the court says different. And whether or not you want it, I'm going to do my best to help you while you're here. Think of it as a vacation. No one's going to look at you or take your picture. Cell phones aren't allowed here. Not even on the staff."

"You think your gates are going to stop the paparazzi?"

"Oh, sweetie," the nurse said, laying a hand on her thigh. "It's electrified. No one gets over that fence."

No one gets over that fence. It should have been reassuring, but it gave Jaycee a cold feeling in her stomach. She realized there was dirt under Louise's fingernails. Maybe she'd been working outside.

"You're safe here," said Louise, "and I want to help you, but I need you to be honest with me. Think about it: If we started leaking private patient information, would anyone ever come here again?"

She had a point. "Okay."

Louise smiled. She had yellowing teeth, smoker's teeth. *Hypocrite,* thought Jaycee, but she smiled back.

"Now let's try this again. Alcohol?"

"Yes."

"How many drinks per day?"

"Sometimes none."

"Other times?"

"If I'm partying I don't really keep track."

"Drugs?"

"Um, marijuana sometimes."

"That it? What about prescription medication?"

Jaycee paused. "Ambien, Adderall, Xanax, Vicodin, Oxy once in a while."

"You have scripts for all those?"

LEIGH BARDUGO

Jaycee shook her head.

"Your mom does?"

She heard the disapproval in Louise's voice. "Yeah."

"Sexually active?"

Jaycee blushed and hated herself for it. "Not exactly."

"Don't know how it's done?"

Jaycee laughed nervously. "I'm just not with anyone right now."

"But you've had intercourse."

"No."

"Not even with Marcus Price?"

Jaycee shifted uncomfortably. "No," she said, surprised at the question.

"But you did other things, didn't you?"

"What?"

"Any history of depression in your family?"

Jaycee blinked. "I—no."

"Violent behavior?"

"My granddaddy had a temper."

"Addiction?"

She didn't want to talk about her dad. Besides, he was an alcoholic, not an addict. "No."

"That wasn't so tough, was it?" Louise said, and gave Jaycee another quick pat on the leg. "Now I just need some blood and we'll be all set. You okay with needles?"

Jaycee nodded and held out her arm. Louise took a slim band of rubber from a drawer and tied it tightly in place above her elbow. Jaycee's hand started to throb. She couldn't stop looking at the thin line of grime embedded beneath each of Louise's nails. She hadn't spent much time in hospitals or doctors' offices, but she'd never seen a nurse with dirty hands.

Louise took an empty syringe from the drawer. "Make a fist."

"Uh . . . no gloves?"

Louise released a laugh that sounded almost like a grunt. "Don't tell me my job, Jaycee, and I won't tell you yours." She grinned again. Up close, her teeth looked more brown than yellow. They were oddly thick, with dirty little ridges. *Not like teeth,* Jaycee thought. *Like tusks.*

Louise took hold of Jaycee's arm and Jaycee saw that the nurse had coarse, dark hairs on the backs of her wrists.

"So you didn't put out for that boy?" Louise asked, and jabbed the needle into Jaycee's arm.

"What?" Jaycee squeaked.

Louise leaned in closer. The smell coming off of her was sweat and the ashy vegetable stink of dumpsters in a hotel alley. Why hadn't Jaycee noticed it before? She tried to breathe through her mouth.

"You said no intercourse."

"Hey—" Jaycee said, trying to pull back.

"Careful," Louise said pleasantly, giving the needle a shove. Jaycee hissed in a breath. It stung. "He religious?"

"What? No." Jaycee watched the test tube fill with blood. Louise popped it out, then clicked another into place. "He didn't pressure me. We wanted to wait."

Louise chuckled. Moments ago her laugh had seemed warm and friendly; now it had an ugly, knowing sound to it. Jaycee focused on her blood pooling in the plastic tube, so red, it was almost black. She was starting to feel dizzy.

"You eat today?" Louise asked.

She'd had a smoothie for breakfast, but that had been hours ago. Jaycee shook her head and the world started to spin.

Louise popped the second tube out and locked a third into place.

How much blood does she need? "I don't think—" Jaycee tried to say, but the words felt funny and shapeless in her mouth.

"Maybe he didn't want to be in you. You ever think that might be the problem, kiddo?"

"I think I need to lie down."

"Maybe he knows what you are." The nurse's eyes looked bloodshot, her nostrils curiously wide and dark. Flecks of foam had formed in the corners of her mouth.

Jaycee tried to stand, but her knees buckled. Dimly she was aware that there was still a needle in her arm. The room tipped and she hit the white floor with a loud crack. She saw the soles of Louise's purple Crocs. They were caked with something black and foul. *I'm going to die here,* she thought, and then the world went dark.

By the time they got home from the airport, it was late and they'd missed the sunset. Kara walked through the house, turning on lights.

"No cornbread?" Jaycee asked, eyes roaming over the immaculate kitchen. Like the rest of the house, it was all clean, modern surfaces, bright white, glass and chrome.

"I've got fruit and quinoa," Kara said cheerily. "Vacation's over. Time to get you fighting trim. You can have my chili and cornbread when you lose that little pooch."

She expected sass back or maybe an embarrassed laugh, but her daughter just stared at her with that same slack expression, as if Kara were speaking some foreign language. "Oh, don't look at me like that," Kara said, surprised by the nervousness in her own voice. "I'm just trying to take care of you."

"Where's Inger?"

"She has the night off," said Kara. "House is tidy enough and I figured we could do for ourselves like old times." Except old times would have been canned soup in a studio apartment in Huntsville.

They had a light dinner, took a call from Jaycee's film agent, then Kara got Jaycee settled in her room. "Big day tomorrow," she said. "Can't wait to hear what you've been cooking up." She planted a kiss on her daughter's head. Jaycee's blond hair was soft as corn silk, just like when she was little. Made it almost impossible to curl. "So glad you're home, baby."

"Me too," Jaycee said, but her face hadn't changed.

Kara put the dishes in the sink, then took a little sliver of Ambien and washed it down with some white wine. On her way back down the hall, she peeked in on Jaycee. She was sitting cross-legged on her bed, and had her old acoustic guitar out, the one that had belonged to her daddy. She wasn't playing, just tuning it, humming a little to herself, a single low, flat note. Still, it was good she had a guitar in her hands. Jaycee was mostly known for ballads and upbeat dance songs, but Kara felt sure they were going to get an anthem out of all this—Jaycee as a fighter, the phoenix rising from the flames.

As she turned from the doorway, she heard Jaycee settle on a chord, then another, pulling out a melody. It sounded familiar, but it was only when Kara was in her bathroom, putting on her face cream, that she remembered the song:

They say you're crazy, I'm crazy too
Made crooked just like you
Lost my mind, lost my way
Found my crooked path to you

A silly song, but it had been a big hit in the nineties. It brought back memories of that last summer before things had gone really bad, driving around town in Trent's new Sebring. Who had recorded it? Some one-hit wonder, but she couldn't remember the name.

She wiped the lotion off her hands and sat down at her laptop to look up the lyrics. It was an easy find: "Malia Mayes Will Have Her Way." Words by Rafe Beckman. Music by Rafe Beckman and Subterfuge. Now Kara remembered—Subterfuge. She hadn't heard that name in forever. But that's what the music business was like.

She glanced through the search results and clicked on *Rafe Beckman: The Invisible Man,* skimming the first paragraph. In 1998, Rafe had split from Subterfuge and gone into the studio to record his first solo album. But he'd packed up less than a month later when the body of a young girl was found dead on the premises. He hadn't released a single song since and had refused to join in the Subterfuge reunion tour. He'd been holed up in his Hollywood Hills house ever since. Kara clicked her tongue. Nasty stuff, but not really surprising, given all the drugs floating around. And these were hard drugs, cocaine and heroin, not the stuff Jaycee and her friends messed around with.

Kara prepared to close the window and check her e-mail when two words jumped out at her: *Las Brisas.* She frowned. That was the town where Wellways was located, a sunny haven for surfers and retirees, all pristine California coastline and forested headlands.

She clicked through and felt a chill settle in her belly. The website didn't look like it had been updated in ages, but it bore a muddy image of an old photo. The caption read: *1998—Rafe enters the studio to record his still unreleased solo album.* Rafe Beckman stood glaring at the camera in long hair and torn jeans. The building behind him looked like a Spanish mission, big and white with an arched colonnade. Kara recognized it from the Wellways brochure.

Below that was a harmless-looking picture of trees that bore the caption: *Starlet Malia Mayes hanged herself from this oak in the arboretum in 1952. In June of 1998, Rafe Beckman split from Subterfuge and rented the abandoned Central Coast Hospital and Center for Mental Hygiene, a former mental institution and site of the infamous Malia Mayes suicide that inspired Subterfuge's hit "Malia Mayes Will Have Her Way."*

Kara read on, frowning. Wellways actually *had* been a mission, then a girls' school, a rest home for recovering tuberculosis patients, and finally a state mental hospital until it was closed down in the wake of the Mayes suicide.

Rafe bought the notorious building and converted it into a recording studio, but left less than a month later when the body of a seventeen-year-old fan was found floating in one of the old therapy pools.

Seventeen. Just a year older than Jaycee. Kara scanned down, the skin on her arms prickling cold. The next photo was of a body bag being wheeled out on a coroner's cart. The death had been ruled accidental overdose, but an employee from the coroner's office had leaked photographs that didn't bear that out. There was a link that read: *Photos after the jump. GRAPHIC MATERIAL.* Kara hesitated, her cursor hovering over those capital letters. She could hear Jaycee singing down the hall, *They say you're crazy, I'm crazy too.* She clicked through.

Jaycee had been at Wellways nearly a week, but it felt like a year. No phone, no Internet, and only one hour of TV in the afternoons. They almost always ended up watching an *NCIS* rerun. She told herself to enjoy "disconnecting," but she didn't feel peaceful or free, only restless.

Nights were the worst. It was after curfew now, and that meant that if you weren't in your room, you had better be in the bathroom. No excuses. There was nothing to do but lie in bed and think or read something from the Wellways library. She'd grabbed a biography of the Dalai Lama, but she hadn't gotten past the first page.

That morning, they'd had to go around the circle in group and talk about their "real addictions."

The other kids had been there long enough that their group leader, Dr. Michaels, had them perfectly trained. One by one they'd spoken up like little barking seals:

"My dad's approval."

"Adrenaline."

"Attention from guys."

Then they'd gotten to Harper, one of those sad, soft, goth girls. Apparently the Wellways staff hadn't let her keep her jewelry, because her ears and nose and lip were riddled with holes where her piercings should have been. Her black hair had grown out so that it was mostly a kind of sad gray-brown. Pathetic. She'd looked directly at Jaycee and said, "Shitty music. Can't get enough of it."

Jaycee had smiled sweetly and given her the finger. But she'd felt vindicated. This was the proof that there was no point to her being in group.

Dr. Michaels had shaken his head. "Harper, we've talked about this before. When you act out that way, you disrespect the group and you disrespect yourself. Come on." He'd stood and beckoned to her.

Harper had rolled her eyes. "It was a joke," she said sullenly, shuffling after him. Then all of a sudden it was as if a current had passed through the little ring of chairs. The fat kid biting his thumbnail, the redheaded girl with the long hair, the boy with the out-of-control unibrow who hadn't stopped staring at Jaycee's chest for more than a heartbeat—they all sat up straighter. A stiffness came into them, like they knew they were on camera but were trying to act natural.

Jaycee turned and saw Louise headed across the room. Today she had on scrubs with clusters of pink hearts and those same purple Crocs. Her reading glasses hung from a chain that bumped against her solid bosom. Jaycee hadn't seen much of Louise since the nurse had checked her in that first day. The blunt she'd smoked before the drive and low blood sugar had made her all kinds of woozy and left her with a weird blur of memories. She'd shrugged them off, wondering if maybe it *was* a good thing that she had to detox a little. Louise was a bit of a hard-ass, but she was nice enough. As Dr. Michaels approached her with Harper in tow, the nurse's face showed only resignation and concern.

"Harper needs a time-out and a chore assignment, Lou," said Dr. Michaels.

Louise gave a small sigh. "We'll get it sorted. What's the infraction?"

"Disrespecting her peers and violating the safe space of group."

"Gotta watch that tongue, kiddo," Louise said. "Come on."

Harper glanced back once at the group. Jaycee was tempted to flash her another "fuck you," but the panicked look in Harper's eyes had been enough to wipe the idea from her mind. Jaycee knew that expression from the days when her daddy used to hunt—white-eyed and panicked, the look of an animal caught in a trap. That was when she'd realized the way the other kids were sitting—not like they were on camera. They were keeping still like small creatures when a predator was near.

Jaycee hadn't seen Harper again until right before sunset when she'd gone out for a run. It was the last thing she wanted to do, but if she got too lazy while she was away, she'd never hear the end of it from Mama.

The kids from group had been clustered under the arches near the front steps, so she'd had to go around them: the fat kid, Unibrow, that vague redhead—Althea maybe? And Harper, red-eyed and chewing on a pen cap. Had she been crying? Big baby. Louise had probably just given her kitchen duty or something.

They went silent as Jaycee passed and Unibrow moved his knees so she could get by. She could practically feel his eyes on her ass as she descended the steps. When she reached the gravel path, she was surprised to hear him say, "Steer clear of the oaks."

Jaycee turned, and bent her knee to stretch her quads. "Why?" Unibrow's throat worked slightly, Adam's apple bobbing up and down. Jaycee rolled her eyes. "Why is everyone here so fucking weird?"

"It's where Malia Mayes . . . you know," he managed.

"No, I don't know."

He swallowed, a flush climbing up his cheeks. "Hung herself."

"Hanged," said the fat kid.

Jaycee switched legs, hooked her hand around her other ankle. "You're messing with me."

"After they gave her the spike," said Fatty with a snicker. "Icepick right through the eye."

"This place just keeps getting better."

Harper leaned back on her elbows, ankles crossed. "Lobotomies were all the rage back then," she said around her mangled pen cap. "They did lots of them here. That's what they used to do to bad girls in the forties and fifties."

"Not just girls," said Unibrow.

Althea reached out and brushed her fingers along Jaycee's hand. Jaycee flinched back, then blushed, embarrassed. "They fed it," Althea said. "They shouldn't have done that." Her freckles stood out on her pale skin like punctuation. She was pretty, Jaycee realized, model pretty with those giant eyes and her cloud of red hair. "It learned appetite."

Jaycee's brows shot up. "Wow. Someone's fuses are blown."

Harper shrugged. "Whole lotta lobotomies," she said, lingering over the syllables and earning another laugh from the fat kid. "All that rage and aggression had to go somewhere. Maybe this place just sopped it up."

It learned appetite. Jaycee suppressed a shudder.

"Straight shot to the frontal lobe," said Harper, pantomiming a jab with her pen cap. "Sure cure for misbehaving celebrities."

Malia Mayes. The name came back to Jaycee now. She'd been some kind of actress, really young when she hit it big. So they *were* messing with her. "Hilarious."

"I'm not kidding," said Harper. She was smiling a little, as if she was enjoying herself, but her voice sounded tense, like a string tuned too tight, like she was daring herself to keep talking. "You know what the friars called this place back when it was a mission? Casa de Sangre. They abandoned it. Said there was something living in the walls."

"Oh my god, spare me your creepy goth crap."

Harper lifted a shoulder. "It's getting dark. Sure you want to go for a run?"

"Am I supposed to be scared? I have a tour coming up—" Fatty and Unibrow exchanged a glance. "What?" Jaycee said, hands on hips. "It's my job."

Althea shook her head. "You leave when it lets you go."

Jaycee started to laugh. "What have you been smoking?"

No one else was smiling. Harper uncrossed her ankles and Jaycee glimpsed some kind of tattoo. "None of us were supposed to be here this long," she said. "Those gates shut, people forget about you."

Jaycee snorted. "They're not going to forget about *me*." But was that really true? Mama wouldn't. Everyone else? If she just disappeared? Stopped making music? Stopped doing shows? *Whatever happened to Jaycee Adams?* She overdosed, joined a cult, strung herself up on an old oak tree. Jaycee glanced toward the oak grove at the southern end of the lawn—stout limbs, leafy branches casting shadows on the sun-dappled grass. California-postcard pretty. But there was something off about those shadows. She blinked. There was no breeze, but they were moving, swaying slightly. Jaycee shook her head, annoyed. "What is wrong with you guys? And what's the deal with Louise? You all looked like you were going to piss yourselves today."

Nobody said anything. Fatty stared at his feet. Althea's gaze was soft and unfocused. Unibrow's eyes darted from Jaycee's boobs, to her shoulder, to the lawn, and back to her boobs.

Harper fiddled with the pen cap. All the daring seemed to have drained out of her. Her voice was barely a whisper when she said, "She's just one of its faces."

"You can make a trade," said Althea. "If you want to go home. Sometimes."

Unbelievable. Had all these kids been crazy before they got here, or had this place made them nuts?

"Yeah. Okay," she said, and took off at a jog. But she'd headed north, away from the oaks, and she'd made sure to be inside before dark.

Now she gathered her hair into a bun and grabbed her little plastic basket of toiletries, the only things she'd been allowed to bring—her special facial cleanser, toothbrush and toothpaste, sweet-smelling shampoo, and her favorite conditioner.

She headed down the hall to the girls' bathroom wearing a soft gray Wellways T-shirt and sweats. They'd given her three sets when she arrived. It was like living in pajamas.

The corridor was dark and cold. The dorms were in the older parts of the building and they felt more like a hospital than a spa. Jaycee's flip-flops made loud smacking sounds on the linoleum. Somewhere she could hear a low chuffing, like someone trying to stifle sobs. She thought of Althea's fractured stare, of Harper's red eyes, the bravado in her voice as she'd talked about Malia Mayes and the old mission. *Something living inside the walls.* Whatever. It wasn't a warning; it was a joke. Besides, Harper was a bitch.

Jaycee pushed open the door and set her basket down on the row of metal sinks. The mirrors were spotless, reflecting the empty, white tile room, silent except for the clank of pipes and the drip of water. She brushed her teeth, plucked a few stray hairs from her eyebrows. Her cheeks were already filling out. The other kids complained about the food, but Jaycee couldn't get enough of it—soft white rolls and vats of instant macaroni and cheese. Mama was going to kill her.

She lathered her face and when she bent to rinse away the soap, she heard a faint high whine, then a little pop. She stood up straight, water dripping down her neck into the collar of her T-shirt. She looked to her right, to the swinging door that led to the showers. The high whine came again, then a pop and a bright flash of light through the circular window in the door. Was someone taking pictures?

She turned off the faucet.

Pop. Pop. Pop. Jaycee looked around the white tile bathroom. If Harper was pulling some kind of stupid prank—

Pop. She could hear a voice now, a man's voice talking. *Good, good. Arch your back a little. Better. Keep your eyes on me.*

Jaycee pushed the door open. The light was bright enough to make her squint. But even as her eyes adjusted, she couldn't make sense of what she was seeing. She'd been in the shower room before—a big space with stalls along the walls and benches in the middle where you could set down your belongings. But now the benches were gone and there was just an old-fashioned claw-footed bathtub full of bubbles sitting in the middle of the white tile floor. The room was flooded with light—not the steady gray buzz of the fluorescents overhead, but the hot, intense glare of stage lights.

"Come on in, kiddo," Louise said from behind her.

Jaycee startled and stepped forward, the door swinging shut behind her as she did. Louise was there in those scrubs with the pink hearts, her reading glasses hanging from a purple chain.

"Go on, kiddo," she said. "Water's getting cold."

Jaycee's mouth felt dry. She'd begun to sweat. "I already showered."

"I don't have all night." The echo deepened Louise's voice and the words chimed an ugly chord inside Jaycee. She remembered the feel of her legs slick with soap. *I don't have all day.*

"I—"

"You've done it before, Jaycee. Get in the tub."

Jaycee looked back at the bathtub, the bubbles piled high around the rim. Louise was right. She had been it in before, or in a tub just like it. It was the tub that had made her famous. She'd been fourteen when they did the photo shoot, her new album about to drop. No one had expected much. She had done okay with her first single, and landed a minor role as a minor character in a minor kids' television show. Her publicist had pulled in a ton of favors to get her into the *Slide* summer music issue. It was supposed to be a kind of girly, retro look with her sitting on the edge of the tub in a fluffy pink towel, talking on a pink cell, and they'd even landed Gary Todd as the photographer.

From moment one, he'd made it clear that the job was beneath him. He'd complained that she was stiff, that she looked nervous, that there was *nothing new here*. She'd known she was failing, but the angrier he got, the more awkward she became. She could feel herself flushing, her chest going blotchy. It had been hard not to cry.

What's next? he'd snarled. *Engagement portraits? Kids' birthday parties?* Then he'd kicked over a chair and shouted, "Clear the room." Jaycee hadn't wanted her mother to leave, but Kara had reminded her that Gary's assistant would be there the whole time, a slender girl wearing a long black sweater with sleeves so long, it looked as if she had no hands.

"I don't have all day," Todd had grumbled, and Jaycee's mother had grabbed her chin. "Shape up, Jaycee. You can do this, babygirl."

After the others had left, he'd taken a few more shots, scowling and swearing. Then finally he'd said it: "Let's try it with you in the tub." The funny thing was that Jaycee had almost felt relieved.

He swore that the shots would only be her in the water, that the bubbles would hide everything, but the lights kept going pop pop pop as she removed her panties and the bra she'd kept on beneath the towel. He wasn't shouting anymore. Now he was just crooning, *Good, good, beautiful, beautiful.*

She'd gotten in the tub. The water was cold and felt strangely slippery. They'd used dishwashing liquid to get the foam to pile high.

Good, he'd said. *Lean back, open your mouth, look at me like you want me.* Her heart had been hammering, but she'd done it anyway. *Lift your leg up on the edge. That's it, point your toe. Beautiful. Beautiful. We're going to get the cover, gorgeous. You want that, right?* And when he'd rolled up his sleeve, and put his hand in the water, when he'd pushed her thighs apart, she'd let him as the assistant looked on and the camera went pop pop pop. *Shape up, Jaycee.*

They'd gotten the cover, and that single shot had set her career on fire. It showed Jaycee in the tub, one bare leg propped on the lip, mouth open, expectant, the bubbles barely covering her body, the reflection of the photographer in the water. It was lewd, tawdry, and it sold more issues of *Slide* than any cover that year. Jaycee's album had exploded and the rest was history.

Jaycee remembered that Mama had taken her to McDonald's that night. She hadn't blinked twice when Jaycee ordered a shake and fries and two cheeseburgers. Now that famous photo was framed in their living room and every time she walked past it, Jaycee could hear Gary Todd's voice. *You want the cover, don't you? Then tell me. Say yes.*

"Go on, babygirl," said Louise.

Jaycee walked across the bathroom floor. When she looked down at the tub, the bubbles were gone. The tub was full of murky brown water, a dry, milky sheen to its surface, peppered with little starbursts of white mold.

"It's dirty," Jaycee whispered.

Louise chuckled softly. "So are you, kiddo. So are you. It's why that boy didn't want you." Something moved beneath the surface of the water. "He knows what you are. That's why he put those pictures out there, so everyone else would know too. Now get in the tub."

Jaycee was cold when she pulled off the sweats and the gray T-shirt, when she stepped into the filth of the water, the film of the surface parting in oily ripples beneath her toes. She lowered herself down as the flashbulbs popped, as the high whine of them filled her ears. It didn't sound like cameras now, more like a machine, a drill or a saw, like metal against bone.

She was shaking, the lights growing brighter and brighter as the thing in the water curled around her ankle. She wasn't sure if it was her mother's voice or Louise's that said gently, "Go on, babygirl. It has to be fed."

Kara slammed the laptop shut, but the image of the dead groupie was burned into her mind: a young girl with chestnut hair, half of her face *eaten* away by someone or something, the remaining skin studded with uneven rings of bite marks like bloody, haphazard embroidery.

She could still hear Jaycee singing that god-awful song in the other room, but now it didn't sound like grinding, crunchy guitar pop. It sounded like a lament.

Made crooked just like you.

Kara thought of that day they'd been driving to the Wind Creek casino. She'd been nineteen, barely older than Jaycee was now; Trent had been at the wheel, Jaycee in her car seat in the back. When that song had come on the radio, they'd all sung along.

They say you're crazy, I'm crazy too.

It had started off as a good day, one of the best days, but it hadn't ended that way. It had ended with them arguing in the parking lot of the casino, Trent yelling, his shirt stuck to his body from the heat, that weavy awful sound he got in his voice when he'd had one too many. He'd been drinking the whole time, sipping on that Big Gulp from the 7-Eleven, a Coke slushie that he'd doused with rum. She'd been able to smell it, but she'd pretended to herself that it was just the sweet chemical scent of the air freshener and the gasoline. That's why he'd been in such a good mood.

And then his mood had soured, like the wrong switch got flipped. The worst part was the way he cycled high and then low. One minute he'd be calling her a whore, demanding to know who she was spreading her legs for while he was at work, threatening to call their friends, her mother, the people at the salon where she worked. She'd be yelling right back, giving as good as she got, then suddenly, he'd be on his knees, crying. *You're going to leave me, aren't you? You can see I'm shit and you're going to leave me. Don't leave me, baby. Please don't leave me.* Clutching at her hips, crying into the folds of her skirt. Then as if someone had picked up the remote and skipped back to the last channel—*You're going to leave me, aren't you? Well FUCK YOU.*

He was up and on his feet, screaming in the parking lot, Jaycee crying in the backseat, her little face red and crumpled, a crowd gathering to watch the show. Concerned, sure. But smug too. These morons in their stonewashed jeans with their sunburned shoulders and beat-up cars, getting their chance to laugh at someone else for a change. She could feel their eyes. They were judging Trent, but judging her worst of all: *Why doesn't she just walk away? Doesn't she have any self-respect? What kind of mother lets her kid see something like that?*

Trent had always been that way. And the worst part, the part that Kara could never talk about, never admit to anyone but herself, was that there was a time when she'd liked it. No, she'd loved it. She'd loved his jealousy, his intensity, the way that broken little boy in him came squalling to the surface, how he'd get so wound up that he'd put a fist through a wall, then take her in his arms moaning *Love me, love me, love me.* She'd been drunk on his wildness and the fact that she'd been the one to tame him, crazy Trent Connors, beautiful and dangerous and tripwire lean.

She wasn't sure when she realized that when Trent called her worthless, he meant it. But she remembered standing in the parking lot that day, seeing the scorn in all those people's eyes, and wondering if he might be right. There'd been a guy wearing a Pearl Jam T-shirt. He'd had little bits of boiled egg in his beard and one of those big jutting bellies that looked hard as a melon, Eddie Vedder's face stretched over it so it looked like he was screaming instead of singing. When the cruiser pulled up, its red and blue lights flashing, its siren making that bright, humiliating chirp, that loser with *food* in his beard, with a belly so big, he probably hadn't seen his own dick since 1980, had shaken his head and smiled. *Here we go,* that smile said. *What did you expect from trash?*

Kara hadn't pressed charges, but Trent had a record and Jaycee was crying. CPS got involved and there had been house visits and a report filed. That was the report that the tabloids dragged out when Jaycee got arrested. It had been online and on TV. It had been everywhere. For Kara, it was like standing in that parking lot all over again, her makeup smeared, her face sunburned. But instead of ten or fifteen people, it was thousands and thousands of people laughing, leaving comments, calling her a bad mother. *What do you expect from trash?*

They'd put up one of Trent's old mug shots with a headline: *Like Father, Like Daughter. But Where's Mom?* and in that minute, Kara had hated Jaycee. She'd understood that she would always be standing in that parking lot. No matter how many tickets Jaycee sold, or how many charities they gave to, they'd always be trash.

So maybe Kara had wanted to punish Jaycee a little. She'd been a nightmare since she'd turned thirteen, challenging Kara on every decision, breaking house rules, sneering that she was the one who paid the mortgage and if she wanted to go out, she'd damn well go out. Maybe Kara hadn't looked closely enough at Wellways because she'd just wanted Jaycee to be someone else's problem for a while. The night that Jaycee had called from Wellways, Kara had heard how scared she was, but as she'd hesitated by the door, the waves had whispered back to her with every beat on the shore:

LEIGH BARDUGO

trash, trash, trash, a refrain that had drowned out Jaycee's terrified voice, and that high metallic whine. She'd known that if she went to get Jaycee, the headlines would start all over again. Everyone would be watching.

But she could apologize now, walk down the hall and say, "I'm sorry, baby. Tell me what happened there." Because it couldn't be all that bad, and once it was out in the open, they'd both feel better. She'd apologize and then she'd get Jaycee to sing something else.

Kara pulled on her robe. The hall was very dark and the ceiling seemed strangely far away. The only illumination came from the bright square of light cast from Jaycee's doorway. It was like being in a chapel, Jaycee's voice flying warm and resonant through the eaves. *They say you're crazy. I'm crazy too.*

Kara was halfway down the hall when she heard another voice join Jaycee's in high, sweet harmony.

Lost my mind, lost my way
Found my crooked path to you
We will be home soon

Kara stumbled, putting her hand to the wall for balance. It felt damp beneath her fingers, as if moisture was seeping through from somewhere. Her chest was tight, the breath caught there, captive against her ribs. Something was in that room with her daughter. *Someone,* she corrected, regretting the wine and especially that little bit of Ambien. Someone was in that room and Jaycee was not allowed guests. She was going to get a talking-to no matter how rough she'd had it at Wellways.

She forced herself to walk down the hall, disturbed to find her legs were shaking. Jaycee was sitting on the bed with her back to the door, her blond hair shining in the lamplight, her guitar in her lap. There was no one else there. Kara could still hear two voices singing;

the harmony went on, pure and perfect. *It's an MP3,* Kara told herself, *some kind of recording.*

"Jaycee?" she whispered. "Baby?"

Jaycee didn't turn. Kara could see her face reflected in the big windows, half in shadow, as if something had taken a bite from it. Jaycee's fingers moved over the neck of the guitar. Her hand looked like a fat spider stretching long white legs, twitching in slow spasms as the chords formed—G, A, A, D minor, G—the spider flexed.

"*Jaycee,*" she said more firmly. "I'm talking to you."

The spider stopped. The girl on the bed turned and Kara's stomach dropped. Jaycee's face was whole, but it wasn't her face at all. Her forehead was broader, her nose a little flatter, a pretty face, and even without the bite marks on her cheek, it was easy enough to recognize the girl from the coroner's photo.

"What is it, Mama?" Her features shifted; the eyes became luminous and damp, the mouth puckering red, a silver-screen starlet's face.

Kara blinked and the girl was gone. It was just Jaycee sitting on the edge of the bed with that beat-up old guitar.

"I thought . . . I thought I heard someone singing with you."

Jaycee looked at her blankly. Then her lips stretched over her teeth. It wasn't quite a smile. "I sang a lot while I was away."

"That's good, baby."

"I sang until I screamed."

"What?"

"It liked that sound best."

Kara swallowed. *You have to say the words. You have to say it and then she'll stop.* "I'm sorry, baby."

Jaycee set down the guitar. She rose from the bed. She seemed taller, longer. Her face was pale and strange and when she opened her mouth, the black space between her lips was too deep. It seemed to grow and elongate like a cavern.

"No, Mama," she said, and she spoke again with two voices. "You're not." Three voices. "Not yet." Ten voices. A choir now.

Kara heard a little whimper and realized it had come from her. She gripped the door frame as the thing that was not her daughter crossed the room, her too-long limbs moving in silence, the white nightgown obscenely short, a little girl's nightgown.

"I am, baby. I am," Kara said, her voice thready and weak.

The thing put its hand on Kara's shoulder. Kara wanted to scream but she was afraid to, afraid that if she opened her mouth near it, something might climb in. Gently, it turned her.

"Shape up, Mama. You've gotta give a little to get a little." Down the hall, Kara could see a light beneath her bathroom door. Had she left it that way? She could hear the sound of running water, and below it a shrill whine. The whine grew higher, the piercing wail of some hungry machine, the sound of appetite. The thing that was not Jaycee, that was a thousand Jaycees, led her down the hall. "You'll learn to be sorry, Mama. But first you have to get in the tub."

Inspired by Nirvana's "Frances Farmer Will Have Her Revenge on Seattle"

Hide-and-Seek

Megan Shepherd

> *Beware a man who comes in a black coat with a bird on his shoulder. If you see him, it means you are already dead. He is Crow Cullom, death's harbinger, and the only way to win back your life is to challenge death to a game. But be warned, death has never lost . . .*

—Excerpt taken from *A Patchwork Death*,
a book of Appalachian folktales

PART I: SUNSET

Annie stepped onto the front porch. The screen door thwacked behind her, echoing through the narrow valley loud enough to scare a flock of crows into flight. They disappeared over the ridge into the fading summer sun. She pressed a hand to her rib cage and slowly sank into one of the rusty metal chairs, watching for the crows to come back. She hoped they would. She was already feeling sleepy. It was a heavy sort of feeling, but not unpleasant—like being wrapped in a winter blanket. She let her arm fall away from her ribs, releasing a gush of blood that soaked her new sundress, rolled down her bare leg, pooled thickly on the uneven boards.

Dying wasn't so bad, not really.

Not when you could go out like this, on a summer's evening with the fireflies winking in the trees. She always thought dying would be a scream into a void, a thrashing, a searing. Not this slow and sleepy drip.

Behind her, inside the house, heavy footsteps moved fast. A man's voice making a telephone call. *An accident,* he said, his voice slurred with gin. While Annie was sitting here dying among the fireflies, he was probably cleaning his fingerprints off the knife and rehearsing the drunken lies he'd tell the police.

A crow landed on the porch railing. It was one of the ones that had flown away. Or was it? It seemed bigger than most, and blacker, like its feathers had lost all sheen, but Annie thought that might just be blood loss blurring her vision. The bird cocked its head.

"Annie Noland."

A man had spoken, not the crow, and it came from the side of the porch. She wanted to turn toward it, but her movements were sluggish. She tried to stand, but her legs didn't work. She collapsed to the hard porch floor with a crash. Painless. She barely felt anything at all.

Footsteps came up the stairs—slow, calm, not like her stepdad's panicked ones inside the house. A man's black boots, polished, but with an unreflective sheen like the bird's feathers. Then the hem of a black coat, stained with salt rings. The man crouched down so that his face was in her line of sight, and she *knew*. That sea-tangled black hair, the rough face that seemed ageless.

Beware a man who comes in a black coat with a bird on his shoulder, her grandmother had read from the old book of Appalachian folk tales when Annie was a little girl. *If you see him, it means you are already dead.*

The crow landed on the man's shoulder and cawed.

"You're Crow Cullom." Annie's voice was barely audible, but he seemed to hear her just fine. "I thought you were only a story."

The crow cocked its head.

"I'm much more than a story, *chère*," Crow Cullom said. "And it's a pleasure not to have to introduce myself. So few people know me." He smiled. "The residents of this valley have always been an exception."

His boots scuffed as he stood to help her up. She felt nothing as he slid his hands under her arms. He had no temperature to him, no pressure, no smell other than the faintest odor of the sea. But then that started to change. She detected a flicker of warmth. Her legs moved a little more easily. By the time she slumped into the chair, the sluggishness was gone. Her entire body hummed with life.

"Did you heal me?" she asked, touching her blood-soaked dress.

He gave a brittle laugh. "No, *chère*. I took away the last traces of your life. You're in the in-between now. You needn't worry about feeling pain anymore."

Annie looked through the gash in her red-wet dress. The wound was still there, a gruesome slice through layers of skin and fat and flesh, but it had stopped bleeding. Not worsening, but not healed either. She smoothed the fabric back.

Crow Cullom extended a pale hand. "I have come to take your soul to death's realm. There are no worries there." There was a scar across his palm, just as there had been in the inky black drawing in her grandmother's book of legends. Annie used to trace that draw-

MEGAN SHEPHERD

ing of his scar as a little girl. Her grandmother had said it was from where he'd taken his own life many, many, many years ago.

A door slammed from inside the house, and Crow Cullom's head turned. His eyes narrowed as a figure slunk out the back door, moving with a drunk's uneasy lurch. A car roared to life, just as sirens started from somewhere deep in the valley. His eyes shifted to Annie's slashed dress.

She grabbed his wrist, staining him with a bloody handprint.

"I don't want to go. Not yet."

"Death waits for no one, Annie. Didn't your grandmother teach you that?"

She gripped the chair arms with her newfound strength, pushing herself up, and then took a step down the stairs. "She taught me that I have the right to challenge it. To challenge death." Night was falling on the valley, and the light was growing faint, but she could still make out the flicker of surprise on his face. "A game," she added. "Of my choosing, for my right to return to the realm of the living. Isn't that how it goes?"

"A game?" His lips curled in a smile. "You *do* know the legends. Very well, you pick the game, but I, as death's representative, set the terms. And I should warn you, *chère*. Death has never lost."

Annie forced herself to stand straighter. The sirens were getting closer now.

"What will it be, then?" Crow Cullom asked, seemingly unconcerned. "Not chess. I grow so weary of chess. I played Go Fish with a Russian dissident once, on death's behalf—it was delightful. None of these modern video games with the flashing lights, I hope. They're so dull. Push a button and just—"

"Hide-and-seek."

When she was a little girl, she'd played hide-and-seek in the valley every summer with Suze at the Dixon Farm down the road—the only daughter in a family with four sons. Annie knew every inch of the valley, down into town, to her high school and the train tracks beyond. *It has to be a game you're good at,* her grandmother had said, *if you have any chance of winning.*

Crow Cullom raised an eyebrow. "Very well—but it won't be *me* searching for you, but death itself. Death is a force of nature, like luck and fear and fate; think of me as a referee of sorts. An impartial party. A riveted spectator. You'll never know what form death might take. A tree branch falling. A hunter's stray bullet. You'll have to be very alert. If at the end of twenty-four hours you have successfully hidden from death, you shall win back your life. Any collateral damage between now and then shall be undone." He produced a silver ring from his pocket. "But if you die before sunset tomorrow, the damage remains, and this ring will claim its wearer's soul." He held out his scarred palm.

She hesitated.

"I need your hand, Annie. This is a pact, and all pacts must be sealed."

She slowly gave him her left hand, sticky with her own blood. He slid the cool metal around her fourth finger. His smile indicated that she would lose.

"When does the game begin?" she asked.

"Now."

The crow took wing, soaring off into the sky as the sun dipped below the ridge. Crow Cullom followed it down the dusty road toward town, disappearing among the fireflies until he was as dark as the rest of the world.

PART 2: EVENING

Annie tested the ring, trying to twist if off her ring finger, but it didn't budge, as if she was married to the game. The sound of sirens grew louder and red and blue lights flashed on the road up the valley, and suddenly it all came crashing back to her. The kitchen knife slicing under her ribs. Her warm blood splashing on the porch floor. Her own *murder*. She spun toward the garage, but her stepdad's truck, of course, was gone.

The police were almost there.

They couldn't find her.

She crashed into the woods, pulse racing. The world spun. Overhead, storm clouds were rolling in. The air seemed soaked in feverish sweat. Suddenly she wanted the sluggishness of death again, or the euphoria of the in-between, now that life meant, any second, something would be hunting her down.

It was darker in the woods. The full moon came only in cracks from the leaves and the massing clouds overhead. But she knew these woods. It was why she had chosen this game. Her sandals found the paths she knew by heart, and she dashed along a dry creek bed that flanked the road. She'd go to the Dixons' farm on the other side of the valley—she knew all the good hiding spots there, from the horse stalls to their abandoned chicken coop. The creek split around a flat riverbank shaded by an enormous oak where she and Suze used to hold make-believe tea parties. She dropped to her knees. Ferns had overgrown the area, but she ran her hands through them until she brushed something hard and metal. An old fork. The marker for their treasure box. She tore at the dirt beneath the fork until she found the bucket they'd buried all those years ago. Tea party supplies: nuts for squirrels, old broken china, and a knife to cut cake. Her hand curled around the knife. It was old and rusted, the blade long since dulled. She paused for a second, considered climbing the tree and hiding in its branches, but one wrong move and she could come crashing down.

She wouldn't make it *that* easy for death.

She veered up the bank instead, pushing through a tunnel of rhododendron that spit her out on the road a quarter mile from the Dixon farm.

Sudden lights blinded her. She hissed against the glare, covering her eyes.

"Don't move," a voice blared through an intercom.

She squinted into the light, heart racing, and made out the side of a police car. The lights were headlights. A car door slammed, and she flinched. The officer coming around in front of the car had a gun strapped to his hip, a baton on the other side. She spotted a police rifle between the driver and passenger seat. Even the car, engine running and just ten feet away, could plow her down.

"Don't move, Annie." She recognized the voice. Officer Burton— he worked at their school during the year. There had been rumors of him hooking up with students, and she didn't like the way he had a half dozen pit bulls tied up with stakes behind his house, but he'd always looked the other way when she'd cut class, and once he'd even driven her home when her stepdad had forgotten to pick her up.

His hand dropped to the gun. "We got a call from your dad. Said you'd gone wild, tried to hurt him. Then we found his car in a ditch with blood on the seats. You want to tell me why you're covered in blood?"

She'd tried to hurt *him*? That bastard. Her eyes darted between the farm and the woods. "Everything's fine, Burton."

"You don't look fine. Your dad said you might have been on drugs. Said you'd been unpredictable recently." His hand clicked open his holster. "And now he's gone missing, and that's a mighty big knife in your hands. We have to take you in for some questions. That's all."

She couldn't let them take her in. The whole point of the game was to hide, and in a jail cell she'd be trapped. Death could seek her there so easily: Faulty wiring. A roof collapse. Another inmate, drunk and angry.

So she ran.

Burton cursed and pulled the gun on her, fumbling with the safety just as she dove into the woods. She braced herself for the sound of the gunshot, death's first attempt, but nothing came. Her sandal caught on a root and she went smashing to the ground, stopping herself a second before her head connected with a broken, sharp branch.

"Get back here, Annie!"

Panic blinded her. Another inch and the branch would have impaled her. This was how death was going to play it, then. It was going to throw surprises at her. Show her a loaded gun and then try to kill her with a sharpened branch.

Officer Burton called for her again, and another car door slammed, and she shoved herself up and started running. The torn sandal dragged behind her. She kicked it off, then raced through the woods until they opened on the edge of the Dixon farm, where she skidded to a halt before she crashed into their electric horse fence.

NO VOLTAGE, the sign said.

"Nice try," she muttered. The Dixons always left the fence electrified, and the rains had been heavy recently—the far end of the pasture was probably flooded, which meant the wire could be live enough to sizzle a person alive.

The clouds were rolling in fast now. She dropped to her stomach to shimmy under the bottom wire, like she'd done a thousand times playing hide-and-seek with Suze. She pushed free of the fence and raced across the field, dodging the horses. She needed to get rid of her bloody dress, and she needed better shoes.

Annie collapsed against the side of the Dixons' double-wide trailer, breathing hard. In the last twenty minutes, a gun had been aimed at her, she'd nearly been impaled, and she'd ducked an electric fence—all after she'd *already* died. This was going to be the longest twenty-four hours of her life.

The Dixon trucks were gone; Suze's parents and brothers usually went to Chapel Hill on the weekends for the big game, but Suze didn't love basketball. There was no sign of her, though. Probably gone into town to meet up with kids from school. Annie figured she could break in a window, borrow some baggy clothes—Suze was pushing six feet—maybe some food and a better knife. Hide out in the barn, where she'd watch any seekers coming from the hayloft, just as she used to as a little girl.

A shadow circled in the darkness.

It landed six feet away.

A crow with dull feathers.

It cocked its head at her. Watching, no matter where she hid.

PART 3: NIGHTTIME

Annie used her rusty tea party knife to pry open the Dixons' bathroom window. She shimmied into it, climbing down carefully onto

　　　　MEGAN SHEPHERD

the toilet, listening hard. The last thing she needed was Mr. Dixon coming to relieve himself after dinner and finding a blood-soaked girl with a rusty knife crouched on his toilet.

She pushed open the bathroom door an inch, peeking through the crack. The kitchen light glared, buzzing faintly, but they usually left that on when they went to town. Otherwise the house was silent. She tiptoed down their carpeted hallway, the knife tight in her hand, alert. She made it to Suze's room—more of a closet, really, since her brothers were all crammed in the two extra bedrooms. It was filled with messy stacks of library books and beat-up soccer gear. She started pulling open drawers until she found a pair of running shorts and a tank top, then peeled herself out of the bloody dress. Toweled off with Suze's soccer jersey. Left everything balled in the corner of the room. It was such a mess anyway, Suze wouldn't find Annie's clothes for days.

She tugged on a pair of Suze's sneakers—a few sizes too big, but she laced them up tight—grabbed a backpack, then tiptoed to the bathroom and started shoving in medical supplies and any prescription bottles she could find. Who knew what tricks death had planned for her—swarming bees? Escaped fugitives? She paused, remembering that Mr. Dixon kept a gun. She had found it once while playing hide-and-seek with Suze. She'd crawled under their kitchen sink, ducking amid Mr. Dixon's empty beer bottles and Mrs. Dixon's cleaning supplies, and there it had been, strapped to the bottom of the sink.

She'd never asked Suze about it. She'd been too scared.

Now she headed for the kitchen. The old light buzzed, high-pitched and whining. Annie had overheard Mrs. Dixon tell Suze to change the bulb last week, but in typical Suze fashion, it was untouched. A bowl of popcorn sat on the counter, still warm. She opened the sink cabinet and shoved Mr. Dixon's beer bottles to the floor—some things never changed—and felt along the top of the sink. Her fingers grazed a nylon holster with Velcro holding it in place. Something trilled, like an insect. Annie froze.

"Uh, Annie, if I were you, I would crawl backward very slowly."

Suze. But she sounded terrified, and there wasn't much that frightened Suze Dixon. The trilling sound grew stronger. Annie jerked, her head slamming against the bottom of the sink.

"Suze, just—"

"Seriously, Annie. Don't move. There's a rattlesnake coiled up in there. I found it a minute ago while taking out the trash. I was just getting a shovel from the barn to take care of it."

The same trilling came again, and Annie's stomach shrank. *Not an insect.* She couldn't see much, but her eyes landed on something coiled and glistening behind the cleaning supplies. The rattle came again.

"Just back out, really slowly, and I'll kill it," Suze said.

"No," Annie tried to whisper. "You just get out of here. Get away from me. I'm not safe."

"Yeah, no shit. You're cozied up to a six-foot rattlesnake."

"No, I mean *me*. I'm not—"

The rattlesnake lunged, and Annie jerked out, scattering beer cans. It sank its teeth into a Miller Lite she thrust at it as she scrambled out. The snake came right after her, nearly on her. It reared back—

Suze slammed down the shovel.

The rattle stopped.

Annie balled herself up on the floor, checking for bites, watching the snake twitch and rattle in death throes, unwilling to feel any relief. Twenty-one hours were left and anything could happen. Death must have put the snake there knowing about Mr. Dixon's gun—it was anticipating her hiding spots.

"Jesus." Suze picked up the dead rattler by the tail, kicking it slightly. She let it fall back down at Annie's feet. "You know, you could have just called if you wanted to come over."

Annie finally relaxed her hold on the rusty knife. She pushed to her feet, leaning over to catch her breath, feeling like she might throw up in the sink. "I thought you'd gone to town."

Suze kicked the snake again, then grabbed a handful of popcorn from the bowl on the counter. "So you always break in when the house is empty? That's not very comforting."

"I needed your dad's gun."

"That's *really* not comforting." Suze frowned. "Are you wearing my clothes? This isn't about those sirens all over your side of the valley, is it? Wait—is that *blood* on your arm?"

Suze moved closer, but Annie jerked away. She grabbed the kitchen towel and wiped the last of the blood off. "I can't explain. You'd never believe me anyway. I just need to borrow that gun for a while. And I need to hide out in your barn."

Annie crouched to unstrap the gun from beneath the sink, but Suze got to it first. She held it high above Annie's head.

"Hang on. You're not getting this until you explain what the hell's going on."

Sirens wailed from outside. At the same time, rain kicked up, pelting the windows. Lightning crashed, and Annie flinched. From somewhere outside, a horse let out a high-pitched squeal.

"It's a long story. You wouldn't believe me. It's a game—a twisted one. And I have less than twenty-one hours left to win."

Annie stood on tiptoe to reach for the gun, but Suze didn't lower it until her eyes caught on Annie's hand. She tucked the gun in her waistband and grabbed Annie's fingers, splaying them. In the flickering kitchen light, Crow Cullom's ring gleamed with unnatural brightness.

Suze gasped. "I know this ring." She dropped Annie's hand and ran into her bedroom. There was the sound of shuffling books and papers. She came back, out of breath, an old leather book clutched in her hands. The same book Annie had tucked away in the back of her closet ever since her grandmother died. *A Patchwork Death*. Suze flipped through the pages until she found a drawing of the ring and shoved it in Annie's face. "The game . . . that's part of it. If you die, you can challenge death for a chance to return to life. There's a man in black with birds who governs the game. Crow Cullom. Is that what happened. Are you *dead?*"

Annie let her hair hang in her face as she leaned over the counter. Her fingers wrinkled over her borrowed tank top, where the gash still throbbed beneath. She took a deep breath and lifted the shirt, revealing the gruesome slash—deep and wet and raw.

Suze made a face. "Holy shit. What happened?"

Annie covered the wound. "My stepdad happened. And a knife. And a bottle of gin. And a grudge he couldn't let sit."

"That bastard! I could kill him—"

"It doesn't matter. I should be dead, but I'm in the in-between, just alive until sunset tomorrow unless I win this game. Hide-and-seek. Against death." She toed the dead snake. "Hence this." Lightning crashed outside, close enough, it felt like it hit the house. "And that. That's why I said stay away, Suze. I don't want you caught up in this." She held out her hand for the gun, but Suze clutched it to her chest.

"No way *death* is after you and I'm letting you do this alone. Hide-and-seek? Please. Nothing's a match for the two of us at hide-and-seek, especially not with this." She waved the gun. "Remember

MEGAN SHEPHERD

why we even started playing that game? It was second grade. I'd just moved here. My brothers were all such assholes, shoving me around, picking on me because they could. You found me hiding in that clearing in the creek, where we had the tea parties. You turned it into a game. Taught me all the places around here I could hide from them until I got tall enough to kick *their* asses. You helped me then, Annie. Let me help you now."

Lightning crashed again, this time even closer, and they both shrieked as sparks flew out of the kitchen light. Darkness absorbed the room. For a second there was a tense silence. Then Annie sniffed the air.

"That's smoke. The lightning must have struck the house."

They ran for the door, but flames erupted in the living room. The house caught quick, everything cheap and flammable, pushing them back toward the rear bedrooms. Suze aimed the gun at the flames like they'd come to life, clutching *A Patchwork Death*. Annie ran to the bathroom. She shoved at the window, but it had jammed when she'd come in, and now it wouldn't budge. The flames were spreading up the carpet, racing toward them.

Annie hurled herself at a bedroom window, smashing the tea party knife hilt against the glass. Through the darkness and pelting rain, she could make out a dull-winged crow on the other side, flapping its wings against the glass, taunting her. She slammed the knife at the glass again and it smashed open. She hurled the knife at the crow, who took off into the darkness.

"This way!" she yelled. Suze hurried to the bedroom and slammed the door just as flames reached the other side. Smoke poured through the door cracks as Annie used her elbow to break out the shards of glass. She shimmied through, dropping to the muddy ground below, and helped Suze climb out.

"Couldn't have just picked charades, could you?" Suze yelled.

Annie searched the ground for her knife, but it was gone. The roof splintered behind them, and they ran from the house just as something exploded. Suze skidded to a stop and threw a look over her shoulder. Flames reflected in her watery eyes. The smoldering house. All her belongings—gone.

Annie blinked as she looked between Suze and the wreckage. It wasn't fair. The Dixons were innocent.

She glanced at the book clutched in Suze's arms, and her grandmother's voice returned to her. *Don't expect death to play by the rules,* she had read. *Death is not a person. Death cannot be reasoned with. In death, as in life, nothing is fair.*

Thunder cracked the night, and Annie jumped. "We can't stay out here!"

"Head to the barn," Suze yelled above the wind, and then, "Shit, I left the door open—the horses got out!"

The horses were stampeding in the field, set on edge from the storm. Annie and Suze ran from the raging house through the torrential rain to the Dixons' old barn, dodging holes in the pawed-up pasture. They'd played hide-and-seek in this barn for years when they'd been younger, burying themselves in the hay bales, crouching in the horse stalls, hiding behind the feed bins. Now the hay could so easily catch on fire. The feed could smother them if the bins broke. But Annie didn't know where else to go.

Suze threw open the barn door at the same time a gunshot rang out from the slurry darkness.

Annie screamed and ducked as a bullet shattered into the siding just above her head. She whirled to find Officer Burton by the road, car lights flashing, gun aimed at them. He was yelling something she couldn't hear over the storm.

MEGAN SHEPHERD

Annie's pulse raced. His car door was open, the keys in the ignition, and he was a good thirty feet away. If she could beat him to it, she could drive deeper into the woods and hide out in the mountains, away from Suze and anyone else who might get caught up in the game.

"I owe you for that snake," Annie called over her shoulder to Suze, and took off toward the car. Officer Burton must have guessed her plan, because he ran toward it too, and then suddenly Annie was facedown in the mud, tackled, a second before she reached the car.

"Stay down! He's going for his gun!" She smelled popcorn—it was Suze, pinning her down just as Officer Burton got to the car and pulled out his rifle. The wind howled, pushing at the trees, and there was a giant *snap*. The old oak tree they'd used to climb pitched toward the ground.

"Suze—run!" Annie scrambled up, digging her fingers into her friend's shoulders, trying to pull Suze out of the way as the whole trembling tree crashed toward the ground. She screamed and braced herself around Suze.

The ripping trunk fractured the night.

The tree crashed to earth, shaking the ground. Annie and Suze were both screaming, until after a breath, and then two, Annie realized they were untouched. She shoved to her feet, blinking through the rain.

The tree had fallen in the opposite direction, leveling everything—including the police car and Officer Burton. Suze pushed to her feet beside her, watching in horror. A puddle of blood was already forming in the dirt. One fleshy white arm stuck out from under the tree.

"Oh god." Annie pressed a hand over her mouth. Officer Burton maybe wasn't the most upstanding citizen, but he didn't deserve to die. She started for the body, but Suze grabbed her and dragged her toward the barn.

"It's too late for him. It's another trap. We have to *hide,* that's the entire point!" Suze threw the door open. They crowded inside, where it smelled warm and thick with animals. It was an old barn—water drizzled in from the leaky roof—but it felt safe. Familiar.

Annie collapsed against the closed door.

In front of her, in the center of the barn, a crow flapped its wings.

Anger unfurled in her like an animal ready to strike. She launched herself at the bird.

"That was supposed to be me!" she yelled, seeing again Officer Burton's blood in the dirt, and she collapsed into sobs, Suze holding on to her fiercely.

The crow cocked its head, and flew outside.

PART 4: MORNING

When the sun rose the next morning, the storm was all but gone. They had huddled in the hayloft the rest of the night, Suze with her gun aimed toward the door, Annie flipping through *A Patchwork Death* for more clues, hugging her knees in close, every nerve alert, waiting for death's next attempt. Crow Cullom had said, once this terrible twenty-four hours was over, that the world would reset itself if she won. Her stepdad would have never gone to the police. The Dixons' house would never have burned. Officer Burton would be alive again.

But if she didn't win, all this destruction would remain.

She spun the ring on her fourth finger, uselessly tugging at it.

Suze eyed her closely. "Can't you take it off?"

"Not unless I win. And if I don't, I'm dead for good."

Suze scratched her chin with the grip of the gun. "Shittiest engagement ring ever."

Hours passed with nothing but the dying storm outside. Suze eventually even fell asleep in the hay, gun hugged tight. Annie would have thought death had taken pity on her if she didn't know better. This temporary reprieve only made her more on edge, more careless—more likely to fail when the next attempt did come.

She unwound her tight limbs and crawled to the hayloft window with the book clutched in one arm. By the early morning light, she flipped to the page with Crow Cullom walking along a dusty road, a crow circling above him.

There is only one rule in Crow Cullom's games, the caption said. *Only the dead can play.*

Annie slammed the book closed, looking out from the hayloft at the wreckage of the Dixon house and the oak tree smashed over the police car. Why hadn't more police come yet? Either Burton hadn't radioed in his last location, or Crow Cullom was working his tricks to keep them away. She could barely make out the lumps of Burton's body beneath the tree. It didn't seem fair. If only the dead could play, then Officer Burton should be alive right now, hungover with a pit bull drooling on his face while the TV flickered infomercials.

A crow circled lazily in the sky against a backdrop of summer-morning blue, and landed on the highest branch of the oak tree, right above the puddle of Officer Burton's blood.

Rage gripped Annie. She slammed the book closed, pausing only to pry the gun from Suze's fingers gently enough not to wake her, and started down the ladder. She slipped out of the barn door and jogged across the grass to where the crow calmly watched her.

It dropped down and started picking the flesh off Officer Burton's arm.

Annie raised the gun, so angry it shook, and let off a shot at the bird. The bullet tore through the quiet morning and shattered a branch just above the bird. The bird took flight, cawing, and then swooped down behind her. She spun around, the pistol still aimed, but froze.

Crow Cullom stood behind her, his sea-tangled hair unkempt, fresh salt rings on his coat. The bird settled on his shoulder.

She didn't lower the gun.

"It isn't fair," she seethed, and jerked her chin toward Officer Burton's body. "He wasn't part of the game. No one else was supposed to die. Only the dead can play—those are the rules."

"The trap was set for you, Annie. He just got in the way."

"Well, you're about to get in the way of this bullet." She squeezed the trigger. A bullet ripped into his chest, tearing a hole in his black shirt, but he didn't flinch. Another crow landed on the ground beside him.

"You can't kill what's already dead, *chère*."

She gritted her teeth and lowered the gun. The rush of everything caught up with her and her body started shaking, and she spun on the tree and kicked it hard.

"Well?" she spat at him. "You've found me—aren't you going to kill me?"

"It isn't me seeking you. I'm just death's harbinger, not death itself. I've just come to tell you that you're doing remarkably well. It's been twelve hours and you're still alive. I particularly enjoyed the snake. Clever, don't you think? Death always finds a way."

She pointed the gun at Officer Burton's foot. "Clever? An innocent man is dead." She tucked the gun in the back of her pants and folded her arms across her chest.

The playful smile faded from Crow Cullom's face. The bird took off from his shoulder, circling higher and higher, like smoke disappearing into air. His face was bleak and worn as the cliffs at sea now. "Don't mourn him, *chère*. As for the rules, you're right. Only the dead are supposed to play, but I'll admit that, as death's referee, I blur the rules on occasion. For Burton, I made an exception. Cheating has its place, you see—the man was a monster. He tortured dogs. Raised them to fight against one another." Crow Cullom looked with disdain as one of his birds landed on the officer's hand again and started picking off the flesh. "I was happy to bend the rules of death, if it meant ridding the world of one more miscreant."

Annie stared at the crow picking at Officer Burton's pinkie finger. She didn't want to believe Crow Cullom, but something itched in the back of her head. All those times she'd driven by Officer Burton's house and seen the kennels out back, the pit bulls tied to stakes.

"What about my stepdad, then? Why don't you kill him? He's a monster."

Crow Cullom sighed. "The universe is not a fair place."

"You don't say." But the truth was, she didn't know exactly what to think. This man, with his crows, was a legend come to life. A folktale that had walked off the pages to claim her soul—but standing in his salt-stained clothes, rubbing the scar on his palm, he seemed like so much more than a story.

She twisted the ring around her finger.

He pointed behind her. "I have been a spectator until now. And I have enjoyed watching you play. I suggest, if you wish to keep playing, that you hide *now*."

She whirled around. The Dixon horses, still jumpy and panicked from last night's storm, were stampeding toward her, tearing at the ground. She could just make out Suze in the hayloft window waving frantically and screaming.

She didn't give Crow Cullom a second look as she raced across the farm.

PART 5: AFTERNOON

Annie threw herself into the streambed, splashing in Suze's oversized old sneakers. She'd lost the gun in her dash. It must have fallen in the field, but she didn't dare go back for it. One of the horses—the big one Suze could never catch—had stampeded for her, nearly catching her under its iron-clad hooves before she'd rolled away at the last second. She'd fled into the forest, where the thick rhododendron on either side of the bank would protect her from sight. Her pulse pounding in her ears, she made her way along the slick rocks, straining to listen for any approaching danger.

How did someone hide from death? It could come from any direction. A moss-slick rock to trip on. A satellite falling from the sky. A tiny insect carrying a deadly disease.

She reached a split in the stream and stopped. She could follow the larger stream down the valley, but that led to town, where she didn't dare go. The police would still be looking for her, especially if they'd found Officer Burton's body. Not to mention all the cars that might swerve off the streets and hit her, or the streetlights that might short out and electrocute her, or someone's air-conditioning unit falling from an upper story.

No, town was too dangerous.

She had no choice but to continue upstream, back toward her stepdad's house. Ever since her real dad had left one night and never come back, and then cancer got her mom, and her grandmother not long after, it had just been Annie and her stepdad and his bottles of gin. He'd threatened to beat some sense into her so many times, just like he had her mom. But he never had. Not until last night, when he'd been deep into the bottle and they'd argued over her college applications and she'd said the one thing she knew she never, ever should.

I'm glad the cancer killed Mom—before you did.

It had all been a blur after that. He'd raised his fist. She'd grabbed for a knife, but he'd beaten her to it. Then there'd been warm blood pooling on the porch floor, and a man in a salt-stained coat walking up the dusty porch steps.

Her foot sank into a deep puddle, and she froze. Voices. Filtering through the leaves. She crouched down and climbed through the rhododendron until she could see the road, maybe a half mile off from her house. Three police officers, heavily armed, scanned the trees.

She ducked, silencing her breath, but her foot slipped and splashed back into the creek.

One of them spun and raised his pistol. "There—in the trees."

"Annie Noland!" another officer said. "Show yourself with your hands up!"

Annie cursed. They wouldn't be armed unless they thought she was a real threat. They must have found Officer Burton's body.

Did they think *she'd* killed him?

"She's wearing a white tank top," one said. "Annie, come out!"

She gritted her teeth, weighing the chances they'd actually shoot. On any other day, no. But today death was out to get her. Someone could misfire, or get spooked and fire too soon. She couldn't risk it.

She tore up the stream instead, knowing she could run faster through the woods than they could. A shot rang off behind her. She gasped and ran faster. Leaves blurred by as she plunged through an opening in the trees and ran up the bank, sliding and slipping. Another gun fired. She felt a sting in her arm and cried out, touching her arm, coming away with blood. But it was only a flesh wound, a nick—death had missed her by a few inches.

Through the trees she heard the sound of the police calling, and someone radioing for backup. *Shit.* Sunset—the end of the game—was still an hour off. Plenty of time for the town's entire police force to comb the woods, seeking her like death itself.

She clamped a hand over her arm and stumbled through the woods toward her house. She could at least bandage it so she wouldn't bleed to death—that would be a sneaky way for death to win—and change clothes into something darker, less visible.

She looked off at the ridge, where a crow circled lazily. Her hand tightened over her bleeding arm.

Just one more hour.

She pushed through the leaves until she could make out the shape of her house in the late-afternoon light. She crouched behind the tool shed, looking for signs of movement, but from the tire marks in the mud and grass, it looked like the police had already been there and left. She took a deep breath, ready to dart into the house.

A low growl came from behind her.

She turned slowly. Wolf, her neighbor's German shepherd, stood on the other side of the tool shed, teeth white and gleaming. Her neighbor had trained him as a guard dog, but with Annie he'd always been ridiculously sweet; a big puppy. Now he had a crazed look in his eye, like he didn't recognize her. Slobber hung off his mouth in thick lines. He sniffed the air and growled again. He must have smelled the blood dripping from her shoulder.

She regretted losing the gun—not that she could bring herself to shoot Wolf anyway, especially when death had to be behind this terrible, snarling version of him. As quietly as she could, she opened the shed latch. There would be hammers inside, and axes. She didn't want to kill Wolf, but she wasn't above knocking him out cold.

On the horizon, the sun sank lower.

Wolf lunged for her. She twisted the latch, throwing open the shed door. Wolf smashed into it, just barely missing her leg. She reached for a hammer but froze—everything inside was gone. Every tool, even down to the nails. Her stepdad must have cleared it out, or the police had.

Wolf lunged for her again, and she threw herself into the shed and pulled the door shut behind her, holding it closed as Wolf tore at the other side. Her mind raced. Death must be as desperate as she was now; time was winding down and only one of them could win. Outside, Wolf ripped at the wooden door, scratching at the cracks.

He'd get in eventually, but could the door hold until sunset? Could she wait it out until the game was over and Wolf—and the world—would be reset?

Through the cracks, she saw that Wolf was trying to dig underneath the shed. He'd unearthed some old metal pipes. She crouched in the far corner, hands over her head, until she remembered what those pipes were.

The gas main.

They went from the house to the barn, right under the tool shed.

Her stepdad had never replaced them. They were always leaky and rusted—that's why he'd built the shed here, to hide them from the inspectors.

Wolf dug frantically, nails tearing through the red soil, scratching on the pipes.

Annie's lips parted. All it would take was one scratch, at just the right pressure, to cause a spark. The entire shed could explode.

She pushed up from the floor. In the distance, she could make out the sound of sirens on the road. *Dammit.* The police probably had the entire valley surrounded by now.

The sun was sinking lower and lower. Blood gushing from her arm, dog tearing at the door, police surrounding her, a gas main ready to blow—there was only one place she could hide now: her own house. She'd make a stand.

She took a deep breath, ripped off a strip of her blood-soaked tank top, and twisted it in a ball. She pushed a hand through the crack in the door, Wolf tearing and snarling, and held up the piece of shirt.

"Go get it!" she cried, and threw it as far as she could down the yard. The dog took off after it. She shoved the door open, running for the house, but her shoelace caught. She was pulled to the ground just as she turned to see the metal door scrape against the exposed gas main pipe.

Shit.

Wolf was already coming back, lunging toward her, nearly on her, when the explosion came. It blasted the tool shed apart. Splintering wood crashed over her. She covered her head, braced to be impaled, but she'd avoided the worst of the blast, lying flat on the ground. Wolf lay nearby, dazed and panting heavily.

Annie's ears rang. She could see the lights of the police cars clos-

MEGAN SHEPHERD

ing in. She stumbled to her feet, away from the blazing tool shed, and climbed the porch steps in a daze. Her blood from last night was still there, dried in the cracks. She opened the door and locked it behind her.

She was streaked with soot and dirt and blood. The police would be there any second. But the sun was just a sliver above the ridge now. Just minutes until sunset.

She might win this thing yet.

She stumbled down the hall to her room, then stopped. Her stepdad's door was open. She saw his boot first, then his leg, and her pulse raced faster. He was asleep in bed, passed out with a fresh bottle.

She could only stare. She'd thought he'd be in town, or halfway to Kentucky. Was this what death had planned for her—some twisted end where the past repeated itself, where she'd have to face her stepdad once more?

Annie looked closer at him. He must really be drunk if the shed explosion and all the sirens didn't wake him. Maybe it wasn't death's plan after all. Maybe Crow Cullom had stepped in again—not so impartial of an observer anymore—and taken pity on her. Did death's harbinger have a heart that still felt something?

The sirens were louder now. The sun still hung in the sky, stubborn to disappear. She grabbed her stepdad's camo hunting jacket and pulled it on. If she could get back in the woods, hide out for just a few more minutes, she'd be camouflaged in the shadows and the police might not see her. She pushed open his bedroom window and climbed out. A crow landed in front of her, but she shooed it away. Another one sat on the porch railing, and two more by the ruined tool shed. Dozens of them perched on the porch, huddled in the grass. Annie's breath grew shallow.

The sun was so very nearly gone.

What was death planning now? Was Crow Cullom here, watching, waiting to call the game?

She turned at the side of the house, ready to run for the woods, but a crack ripped the air. She froze. A gunshot? Who had—

An impact like a fist slammed into her. She blinked. Her vision blurred. When she touched her stinging chest, she came away with blood.

The sleepiness of death started to overtake her again.

She turned, the shock of it all numbing her, and found Suze standing in her front yard, Mr. Dixon's gun in hand, eyes wide with horror. She must have seen where the gun had fallen and picked it up.

"Annie! I thought you were him! Your stepdad. Your coat . . ." Suze dropped the gun.

That bastard, Suze had said. *I could kill him for this.*

Annie sank to her knees, surrounded by crows as her blood drained into the red dirt. On the horizon, the last sliver of sun disappeared.

It was sunset.

She had lost the game.

PART 6: SUNSET

Annie collapsed to hands and knees. Crows swarmed the earth, but Suze didn't seem to see them as she ran up. "I didn't know it was you!" Suze cried.

"Just get out of here," Annie choked. "The police are coming. They can't catch you."

"You'll die."

"I'm dead anyway."

Suze looked ready to protest, but Annie shook her head, waving her away until at last Suze turned and ran. She listened to Suze's feet pounding on the dirt road until she couldn't hear them anymore. It was just her and the crows in the twilight. She closed her eyes. Another set of footsteps came, slow and deliberate. When she looked over her shoulder, a man with sea-tangled hair was slowly walking up the dirt road.

Annie clenched her jaw. She'd lost the game. She'd lost her last chance at life. The ring on her finger started to warm. How much longer did she have before it claimed her?

With her last bit of strength she pushed herself up, stumbling through the grass and up the porch steps, back into their house. She found the knife in the kitchen—the one her stepdad had slid against her ribs the night before. Perfectly clean now. When the police came, they'd never know. Her stepdad would get away with it, just like he'd gotten away with beating her mother, when cancer had been the excuse for the bruises.

She stumbled down the hallway as crows cawed outside, louder and louder, and Crow Cullom's boots sounded on the porch steps. She pushed open her stepdad's bedroom door. He was still passed out on the bed. She sank down next to him. Her reflection flashed in the knife blade, streaks of blood and soot on her face.

"If death can cheat, then I can too."

She splayed out her hand on the bedside table and brought the knife down on her own fourth finger. The pain was blistering. It seared all the way to her toes, throbbing and pulsing and she nearly dropped the knife. But she gritted her teeth, and clutched the knife harder until she cut her finger clean off. She let the knife fall to the floor, crying out at the pain. Her finger sat on the bedside table, just sat there. She picked it up with shaking hands and pulled the silver ring off of it. She held it up to the light, thinking back on her grandmother reading her stories in this very house. *Don't expect death to play by the rules,* her grandmother had said.

Annie slipped the ring onto her stepdad's pinkie finger.

Crow Cullom had said if she lost the game, the ring would claim its wearer's soul. He had neglected to specify *whose* soul.

Her stepdad stirred, just slightly. A few mumbled words. One bloodshot eye oozed open, and for a second, their eyes locked. His mouth frowned.

"Annie." His voice was slurred. He tried to sit up, but he groaned like the room was spinning, and lay back down. "You're dead."

"No," she said, and stood up. "You are."

Her stepdad blinked at the strange ring on his finger, tugging it uselessly. Annie turned away; she pressed her good hand to the wound in her chest and made her way back down the hallway, out onto the porch. Crow Cullom was waiting for her, leaning on the railing, a crow perched on his shoulder, looking as ageless as the first time she'd seen him.

She sank into the porch chair, wincing. His eyes went from her missing fourth finger to the window of her stepdad's room.

"You know that's cheating, don't you, *chère*? It's supposed to be *your* soul the ring claims."

"Sometimes there's a place for cheating. Someone told me that once."

For a few seconds, as twilight changed into night, and the crows watched patiently from the porch railings, neither of them spoke. Annie knew that even as death's harbinger, he had a soul. He had compassion. He had interceded in death's game to kill Officer Burton not as a lark, but to rid the world of a monster. Well, her stepdad was a monster too.

Crow Cullom smiled. Annie felt that sleepy blanket of death lift, and her body started to pulse again, and feel warm, and *hurt*.

"It's been thrilling watching you play, *chère*. As for the police searching for you, and your stepdad's body, you needn't worry. It all ends with the game. Your friend's house will return to normal. The dog will too. Any damage shall be corrected—except perhaps Office Burton, and your stepdad. Let's leave them to rot where they lie, what do you say? Alcohol poisoning seems a likely enough excuse for your father, and as for Burton, it was stupid to stand beneath a falling tree." He paused, eyes falling to her hand. "But your finger. That you shall forever lose—a toll for cheating." The corner of his mouth twitched in a smile. "I look forward to the next time we meet. Hopefully not for many more years, but one never knows."

Crow Cullom left her on the porch, walking down the dirt road just like the drawing in her grandmother's book. His crows went with him, except for one. The inky one with the dull feathers. It cocked its head at her and cawed.

Annie leaned back in the chair, hesitantly lifting her shirt. The wound was nothing but a scratch now, and healing rapidly. As she watched, the last of the redness faded until her stomach was smooth again. When she glanced toward the side of the house, the tool shed was standing, and Wolf was nosing around it as calmly as always. Warmth spread out to her limbs. The sirens had vanished. When she went back inside, she knew her stepdad would be dead, the ring gone. Taken to death's realm in her place. She'd never have to see him again.

She looked down at her left hand, with the missing finger.

She might have lost at hide-and-seek, but she had won at a much bigger game.

She watched Crow Cullom disappear among the fireflies, and wondered, when he came for her next, hopefully when she was old and gray-haired, what game they would play—and if she could cheat him once more.

Inspired by the 2000 film *Final Destination*, the 1994 film *The Crow*, and the 1991 film *Bill & Ted's Bogus Journey*

THE DARK, SCARY PARTS AND ALL
DANIELLE PAIGE

"I wanted to hear more of what the monster had to say," I said as my class broke out in giggles behind me. I was used to their laughter, and a lot worse. What I wasn't used to was Damien Thorne staring at me. But Honors English was my favorite, and today we were discussing *Frankenstein*—Mary Shelley's—which I loved a lot more than I hated them. Or at least most of them.

"Go on, Marnie," Ms. Demetrios said.

I cleared my throat. And blinked to my left. I was imagining it. I had to be. Sure, it looked like those deep, blue-gray eyes were stuck on me. But Damien Thorne was not supposed to be looking at me. He was supposed to be looking at someone with longer limbs, a face with more angles than circles, and a dress that was bought this decade.

I kept talking.

"We hear the whole story from the perspective of the ship captain and Victor himself . . . the guy who created him. Not from the monster." I could hear the giggles get louder. I raised my volume. "But the monster is the most interesting thing in the story, and he barely gets a voice. Imagine being cobbled together. Imagine discovering *what* you are and knowing that no one will ever love you, not even your maker. He does some awful, awful things. But all he wants is someone to love him. Which is, in a way, the most human, the most un-monstrous thing of all."

Ms. Demetrios smiled. Most everyone else either snickered or rolled their eyes. Everyone but Damien Thorne. All I got from him was a continued stare. Was he making fun of me? Probably. But just before I turned away—did he nod?

"Well, that is a smart, if expected, interpretation of Frankenstein's creature," Ms. Demetrios said.

I gulped. I wanted to be more than "expected." Ms. Demetrios picked up a paper from the pile on her desk. I could tell from the loopy handwriting it was mine.

"But what wowed me in your essay was the comparison you drew to the modern context. 'We live in a world where transplanting a hand or even a face is now possible. Perhaps in the modern world Frankenstein's creature would be lauded as a scientific breakthrough, greeted as a marvel instead of a monster.'"

I felt a surge of pride despite the looks on my classmates' faces. I didn't turn to see Damien again. Being the smartest girl in class was what I had over everyone in here. One of the few things. Another giggle erupted behind me—this time I knew who it belonged to without turning. I had spoken too long, too passionately, the teacher had singled me out, and there would be a punishment for that. Everly York only cared about the stories she starred in. And her attention span wasn't much longer than her tweets.

I waited for it.

"Maybe someday someone will make a monster mate for you, Marnie Monster," she hissed. It was an old grade-school name that just never went away. Everly made sure of that. She always started it. In fact, she started it all.

DANIELLE PAIGE

My first day of school in Harlow was on Halloween in fifth grade. My father didn't know or care enough to dress me up. I broke out in a rash. I was nervous—about the new school and the new people— and it manifested as disgusting, itchy, red bumps all over every inch of me, including my face. Just in time for Halloween. Just in time for Everly. When I showed up at school in a sea of pretty princesses, I was dressed as myself. Everly took one look at me and said, "Ew! What *are* you?" in front of the whole class at recess.

"Nothing," I said, scratching the red welts on my arms.

She corrected me: "You don't even need a costume, *Marnie* . . . *Marnie Monster.*"

She turned around, plastic, translucent wings bobbing. My eyes stung, tears on the verge, and it made me even madder. My hands hurt as I reached for the wings and yanked them as hard as I could. Everly fell backward and landed on her green tulle skirt. Or at least I think she did; I didn't stick around to see her fall, I only heard it as I ran. Back into the school and into the bathroom. I stayed in a stall until Mrs. Austin found me and gave me a lecture about "sticks and stones and names that can never hurt you."

Mrs. Austin was wrong. It was stupid, and the name should have gone away like the rash did a few days later. But it didn't. Marnie Monster was forever. Everly had written my story and I kept playing my part. I let her use me to remind everyone how popular she was by contrast. It was almost boring, and yet . . .

When I glanced back, Everly literally puckered up and blew me a kiss.

"*Marnie, Monster, Monster, Monster . . .*" The chant began quietly.

It still got to me.

Ms. Demetrios searched the class for the culprits, lowering her wire rims on her nose.

"Monster, Monster, Monster, Monster . . ."

"Enough," Ms. Demetrios ordered. But the voices continued.

My face warmed. I stayed quiet. Speaking up wouldn't help.

"I second what Marnie said," came a voice to my left.

Damien Thorne.

"I'm Team Monster," he added. He lifted a shoulder in a shrug.

And the chanting stopped.

"Hey." He said it simply, like he was picking up a conversation we'd started long ago.

It was after class now. He'd walked up to my desk and I'd wanted to blurt "Thank you"—but knew his act of chivalry would only make Everly worse. A couple girls huddled in the doorway, looking at us and whispering. All it took was one glance from Damien to send them scurrying off to their next class.

Damien Thorne had an origin story. The beyond-tragic kind that could either have landed him in rehab or made him a superhero. Despite the fact that—or maybe *because*—both his parents were taken from him at a young age, he was on top in our school. Straight A's, captain of the lacrosse team, resident of an estate—an actual *estate*—at the edge of town, and possessor of the most intense, most magnetic stare I'd ever encountered.

He was handsome, but not like the jock good-looks of Shawn Coleman or the model-y thing that James had going. Damien looked like something out of a book—a Heathcliff, someone dark and brooding but with just the tiniest hint—was it his mouth? his eyes?—of humor.

"Sorry about those guys," he said, messing up his black hair and then shoving his hand into a pocket.

"Why should you be sorry? You didn't make them idiots."

He laughed. His nose scrunched up a little when he did, and I realized he was even cuter up close.

"Marnie Campbell, defender of the literary underdog," he said.

"Is that supposed to be a compliment?" I asked, genuinely bewildered.

"Yes, it is. I like a good subplot," he said, looking down at my paper and touching the *A+* inked there.

I grabbed it up and shoved it in my bag.

"Sounds like you practically wrote some monster fan fic. Does your love of the antihero extend to other classics?" I glanced up. He was smiling, joking—but not meanly.

I managed a shrug. "Some."

"What are you doing tonight?" he asked unblinkingly.

"Homework," I said, not sure where this was going.

"No, you're not."

"I'm not?"

"No, you're going out with me."

"Why?" I almost whispered.

"Because I don't think anyone here is nearly as interesting as you."

Was he serious? Damien had said maybe five words to me in the seven years I'd known him. It didn't make any sense. But my heart began double-timing in my chest. Damien Thorne was asking me out.

The warning bell rang. I knew a girl like me should not take an offer from a boy like him.

Stories like this did not end well.

Not for girls who got called Monster. But the way Damien was looking at me . . .

I wasn't the prettiest girl in school. But neither was Everly. Somehow she had everyone convinced that we lay on opposite ends of the spectrum. But pretty wasn't always symmetry and flawless skin. Pretty was sometimes a verb. And Everly prettied better than anyone. She tossed her hair and batted her lashes and owned every room. I slouched and hid and tried to take up as little space as possible.

I returned Damien's stare, thinking suddenly about all the things I'd never allowed myself to think about. Holding hands in the hallways. Going to prom. Kissing outside my front door.

There was more to Damien than just his good looks—it was something behind his eyes, or about his mouth. An intelligence.

A curiosity.

A mischief.

A promise.

I thought about saying yes.

But then he took a sudden step back.

"Don't answer yet," he said, taking another backward stride toward the door. "I like a little suspense."

I was the girl who lived in *that house*. You know it. The one that's been worn down to the point of no return, where you wonder what's buried in the backyard.

When I got home it was empty except for the flea-market furniture and broken TV. The fridge was empty too. I grabbed a handful of stale cereal from the cabinet and made my way to my room, past the peeling paint and up the termite-infested staircase. The house said everything about Dad. He didn't care what it looked like. He didn't care how embarrassing it was. It was a roof and walls and it was the bare minimum of what he needed for himself and for me.

Dad had his music—though he hadn't quote-unquote *made it*.

Some part of me was irked that he hadn't, that he wasn't a better musician, more successful. After all, he'd traded me for his music a long time ago. But the music Dad loved wasn't rock and roll, it was jazz. And he wasn't a star, he was a good bass man. He'd played on some pretty big records and for pretty big jazz stars, if you liked that sort of thing.

Dad and Mom had been those kids who got pregnant in high school. Mom wanted to give me up for adoption, but Grams took me in and raised me. Dad visited his mom and me for holidays and weekends. But my mother never did. Instead she committed suicide when I was three. Hanged herself. I used to wonder why she didn't do something easier, like take pills. Now I think Mom didn't want easy, she wanted certain. Hanging takes commitment. Hanging means no second chances. I used to have nightmares of her eyes bulging, her neck breaking as she hung suspended from the beams of her bedroom ceiling. Grams never really talked about it, and my dad pretended like Mom never existed.

And this week he pretended harder. Mom's suicide-iversary was three days away and every hour of it, every minute, Dad would fill with more gigs, more girls, and more booze than ever. And that was saying a lot. I didn't blame him for this week. It couldn't be easy to lose Mom the way that he did. But I did blame him for the rest of the time. Because when he wasn't forgetting about her, he was forgetting about me.

When I was ten, Dad came back for good and moved the two of us into this hellhole we live in because it was what he could afford. He got a gig playing jazz at a local club—and when he wasn't playing, he was drinking away the money he made playing. We've been stuck here ever since. For a long time, I think I was waiting for Dad to start hating me for taking him away from the road. But he never did. Then at some point, I realized what I was really waiting for. Him to start loving me. But that never seemed to happen either.

I curled up with our next book for class, *Dracula*. And I closed it when Dracula meets Mina for the first time. I felt a wave of sadness for the original vampire. He, like Frankenstein's monster, wants to love and be loved, and that so wasn't going to happen. I drifted off into sleep, a dream, where I'm back at some kind of gothic version of school, in the auditorium. Damien is there, sitting on a throne—for real, a throne—and looking down at me.

He stands and reaches out his hand to me. A super-waify girl I've never seen puts a crown of thorns on each of our heads. Damien's crown has small horns protruding from both sides. And music swells—some kind of cross between opera and electropop. We start to dance. Everyone's there from school. But instead of making fun of me, they're looking at us in a kind of awe. Except for Everly. She looks around, big eyes all disbelieving, and tries to cut in on our dance. I excuse myself and do something that surprises me and her at once. I punch her in the face. She stumbles, straightens, and pulls back her hand to fight, but her eye begins to bleed where I punched her. The blood gushes and she puts up a hand to stop it. But it isn't just her eye that's bleeding. Her whole face begins to welt and blood comes streaming out of every pore. She opens her mouth to scream.

When I woke it was me who was screaming. The sheets were wet with sweat, and I thought I could smell smoke.

What the hell was that? I threw back the covers and noticed the window was open. I could hear dogs outside barking.

I hated Everly. Still, my subconscious had taken it to a whole new level.

When I looked outside, the only thing staring up at me were the naked patches of dirt in our backyard. I slammed the window down and closed the curtains tight.

I made it through half the next day without seeing Damien or Everly. By the time I got to the cafeteria I was half convinced that none of yesterday had really happened. Maybe him asking me out was just another dream, equally vivid. I still sat at the table closest to the kitchen, which was the equivalent of high school no-man's-land. There were three of us. Me, Jenny Dash, and Silent Jason sat there every day and never became friends. Jenny was super-smart and too busy with maintaining her GPA to maintain basic social interactions. Silent Jason didn't speak. Ever. He only communicated through really cool, sometimes scary drawings.

After yesterday and the nightmare, I welcomed the silence, the total lack of attention. So it took me a few seconds to realize Jason was speaking to me

"Just because you're chosen, doesn't mean you don't have a choice."

I'd never even heard Silent Jason's voice.

"What?"

"You heard me," he spat.

I'd never seen him angry either. He was leaning too far forward, into my space, so close, I could smell the sloppy joe on his breath. Normally he was hunched over his tray or his sketchbook. I always assumed *he* of all people was on my side. Maybe it was yesterday's brush with Everly, or last night's lack of sleep, but out of nowhere, my words rose up to meet his. "If you have something to say to me, Jason, say it. Or shut the fuck up."

I stared at him, daring him.

I thought about Marnie Monster.

About Everly. About Dad.

My hands had balled into fists and my nails dug into my skin. I was madder than I'd realized. Maybe I was always mad.

If I heard one more unkind thing . . . from Jason, from anyone . . .

Jason opened his mouth to speak. But something was wrong. He didn't put his hands on his throat like they do in the movies, but I knew he was choking.

I jumped to my feet.

Jenny called for help.

Shawn Coleman stepped in and pounded him hard on the back. When that didn't work, he wrapped his arms around Jason and squeezed beneath his rib cage.

Across the cafeteria I saw Damien staring at the commotion. Everyone was staring, silent.

Then Jason coughed and choked up something that projectiled out of his mouth and onto the floor. It was black and wet and round. It looked like coal. Jason was weird, but what in the world? I remembered that Portia in *Julius Caesar* committed suicide by eating coals. But Silent Jason wasn't exactly a Shakespeare nerd. Maybe it was some kind of drug?

Mr. Harrison, the lunch monitor, was at Jason's side now. Escorting him out. Another teacher picked up the small, black thing with a napkin and followed.

"God, Marnie Monster." I hadn't even seen Everly standing by the next table over. She was wearing a short sequined dress and sunglasses in the middle of the cafeteria in the middle of the day as if she were avoiding the paparazzi. "Must you really try to kill the first guy that gives you the time of day?"

The cafeteria, silent during the Jason commotion, now filled with sound. Laughter. Everly was a bitch, and I wasn't going to sit around and watch this escalate into a chant. I started to pull my stuff together—I was going to the library—but noticed that Jason had left his sketchbook; it was on the floor. I grabbed it. Once outside the cafeteria, I flipped it open, telling myself that I just wanted to see what goth comic book heroine he had created today. But really, I wanted answers. What was wrong with him? What was wrong with me? My reaction was outsized—the weird shit Jason was saying had nothing to do with me and everything to do with him being crazy enough to suck down a coal briquette.

I glanced around. No one was paying attention to me. Then I looked down at the open notebook. And I laughed. There on the first page was an illustration of *me,* wearing some kind of superhero costume, with crazy-big boobs and a butt that even a Kardashian couldn't compete with. I turned the page: me standing in front of my house. This time I looked normal, but my house looked haunted or something. Me in class. Me walking home. Drawing after drawing of me. A little creepy. But a little flattering. I kept flipping. The last drawing made me stop in the middle of the hallway.

It was Damien and me, holding hands. I was wearing a white gown, and we were both wearing crowns. Like prom queen and king, only the crowns were made of thorns. And Damien's crown had horns on it.

Wait a minute . . .

I felt someone fall in step beside me. Damien.

I slammed the book shut.

"I was just— This isn't mine. Silent Jason—I mean, Jason dropped it."

"Jason's quite the artist," Damien said.

"I was just returning it."

Damien nodded. "Can I see it?"

I stammered a little, and quickly flipped through the images. "It's really nothing. Just a lot of drawings of people." When I got to the end, I was ready to slam it shut again, but I didn't this time. Because the last page was different. Instead of me and Damien, it was some other couple. And there were no thorned crowns. Just a superhero couple watching a sunset.

"What the . . ." I started flipping through again, but none of the illustrations were the same. Instead there were all different kinds of people—at home, in class, walking along the street . . .

"Are you okay?" Damien touched my shoulder.

"I—think so" was all I could get out.

A school counselor told me once that Mom's death was probably related to some kind of depression. But what if Mom was crazy? What if I was too? She wasn't that much older than I am now when she hanged herself. I always thought of my mother as something separate from me. But what if in addition to leaving me, she'd also left me with something else—some kind of madness?

"Are you sure?" Damien looked genuinely concerned now. He put his hand on my arm.

I felt a warmth spread from under his fingers and throughout the rest of me. It wasn't just that no one ever touched me. It was that he was the one who just had. My insides strained for more. *Do it again.* Damien, unaware of the effect he was having on me, was still waiting for a response. What did he see when he looked at me? Did he see what the rest of them saw? A know-it-all? A mess of brown hair and brown eyes and sharp features that I was waiting to grow into? Not pretty, but not a monster either? Or did he see something else? Something that even I couldn't see yet?

DANIELLE PAIGE

"Marnie?"

The bell rang. The hallway began to fill.

"I'm fine." I shook him off and opened my bag to shove the sketch-book inside. When I looked up, I noticed Everly walking by with her minions. She stopped talking and started staring. But not at me this time. At Damien.

I didn't know why I didn't see it before.

Everly didn't go after me yesterday for the sake of going after me. She was defending her territory.

"She likes you," I blurted.

"And?" he asked, frowning.

"And she thinks you like me. Which is ridiculous. But she thinks it. So just stop and she'll stop."

He shook his head. "It's not ridiculous. And I can't stop."

"Can you just go?" I said, even though my heart was suddenly speeding up and I could hear it in my ears.

His face fell. He stepped out of my way, and I walked right by him. By the time I got to the staircase, Damien was already gone, swallowed into the stream of people.

I wanted to follow him into the crowd suddenly, but Jason's words, the ones he choked on, came back to me. *Just because you're chosen, doesn't mean you don't have a choice.*

Later, when I got to English, Everly was waiting, sitting pretty in her sunglasses.

"Everly, please remove those. You are not famous here," Ms. Demetrios said.

I stifled a laugh.

She kind of was.

"Everly, do you want to remove them here or in the principal's office?"

Everly shoved the glasses down. A blue-and-black bruise had bloomed around her eye.

Everly had a black eye.

The same eye I punched in my dream.

"Who did this to you?" Ms. Demetrios shifted into first aid mode. "We have a zero-tolerance policy at Harlow High for violence."

Everly turned to stare at me.

"Marnie?" Ms. Demetrios looked stunned.

"I didn't do that. I didn't touch her." I did. But it was a dream. It was only a dream.

I looked around for Damien. I'd told him I didn't want his help. And what was he going to do? Flirt with her into making her change her story?

Damien was flipping through his copy of *Dracula*, not even remotely interested in what was unfolding. Had I really hurt him that badly?

"Marnie, I am shocked . . ." Ms. Demetrios started.

"I didn't do it!" I insisted.

Damien sighed loudly from down the row.

Everly sighed too. "She's right, she didn't touch me—just looking at her made me want to punch my own eye out."

Ms. Demetrios looked visibly relieved for a moment, before going into full-on angry-teacher mode. "Everly, go to the principal's office."

When Everly reached the door, she cut a look to Damien and then back to me, as if I were indeed responsible. Her look said what I already knew. She was just getting started.

× × ×

DANIELLE PAIGE

That night I lay awake in bed. The events of the past two days were just too weird. Everly had a black eye, and it was after I dreamed about punching her right in that spot. And Jason choked on god knows what after I snapped at him. But none of this had anything to do with me. It couldn't.

I heard my father stumble in around three a.m. This was the way he celebrated the anniversary of Mom's death. She was his wife. But she was my mother. Why didn't he get that? He didn't make it to the stairs—I heard him crash onto the couch in the living room. He mumbled to himself, and then one shoe after the other hit the hardwood floor.

I wanted to wake him up. I wanted to ask him about Mom. It was suddenly important to know the details of her crazy, and not just because tomorrow was the anniversary of her suicide. Was she like me? Was what was happening to me—had it happened to her? I'd always figured that Mom was depressed. But now my mind spun a new scenario. Mom had become a danger to herself and others. What if I was the danger now?

When I got to my locker in the morning, I was still trying to shake it all off. I was not my mother. There were logical reasons for everything that had happened. I could think my way out of this, I could think my way out of anything. I took a deep breath, feeling calmer, more anchored, and then I opened my locker and stifled a scream.

A doll hung, bloody, suspended by a tiny noose. The doll looked like a Barbie, only its hair had been bleached and teased on top of its head, standing straight up. The Bride of Frankenstein.

Behind me, there was a cackle of laughter—led by Everly—and the flash of cell phones.

I didn't turn around at first. I didn't want them to see me. I didn't want them to capture the redness in my cheeks or the tears in my eyes so they could Snapchat it to everyone in school who didn't get to witness it for themselves. I stood there, face burning, throat aching, and a hand reached past me, into the locker, and yanked the doll down.

Damien didn't say anything. He just grabbed the doll and my chemistry book and slammed the locker shut. He steered me past Everly and her laughing minions. And they parted for him.

I let myself be steered. Then he dropped me at my chemistry classroom without a word before walking away.

There was another "bride" doll on my seat in AP French.

"*Qu'est-ce que c'est, Mademoiselle* Marnie?" Mrs. LaCroix frowned at me. *What is that?*

I bit back my answer, saying only, "*Je ne sais pas.*" I don't know.

The nightmare continued in AP calc, where Brian Marks proceeded to pick up the doll and put it down his pants before putting it back on my desk. And in AP history, I managed to get to class in time to hide the next doll in my backpack. At least they weren't hanging by the neck. But by the time I marched to the cafeteria and found a doll in my seat at the loser table, I felt the anger grip me so hard, I saw white. I grabbed the doll and shoved it headfirst into my mashed potatoes. *Stupid doll, stupid life, fucking Everly.*

But before I could leave, Damien sat down at my table.

I shook my head at him. "Thanks for earlier, but I thought we agreed that you would stay away."

He ignored that, saying instead, "Do you want me to make her stop? I can. Just say the word."

I searched his face. *How* could he stop her? Everly was Everly. I took the seat beside him. "Don't do that. Don't come to my rescue. Don't sit with me. Don't talk to me."

I stared him down. He didn't move.

"I can handle myself." It was a lie. I was doing a terrible job so far.

"I know. There are a lot of things you can do. But your approach is all wrong."

"I'm not approaching, I'm avoiding. And if you would just—"

"Everly is a lot of things, Marnie . . . but she is never, ever ignored."

I shrugged.

Damien kept talking. "You think it's like a storm. Like you're driving through it, and all you have to do is pull over and wait for it to pass. But it's not like that. It's like being in the woods with a bear and you can't remember if you're supposed to make yourself big or small or run. What if doing nothing means you get eaten alive?"

I stared at him. Who did Damien think he was? It was easy for him to say. He was a rich kid with perfect grades and a perfect life. I breathed heavily through my nose and clenched and unclenched my fists. I needed to keep my shit together.

"Trust me, Marnie. It's time to stand up for yourself." He sounded like one of those assemblies about bullying that everyone nodded along to at the time but ultimately ignored.

I felt my eyes prickle and my fists ball tighter. What did he know? He'd lost people he'd loved, but they hadn't *taken* themselves away. And everyone left . . . they adored him.

The glass bottle of apple juice on the table in front of us suddenly shattered.

I jumped.

"What the hell?" Jenny Dash leaped up from the table.

Damien's mouth dropped open for a second. Then he just shrugged. "That wasn't you?" he asked as if he was kidding, but his look was as serious as a grave.

When I walked into English, I got that sinking feeling of dread again. Maybe it was the singing.

"*Here comes the bride. Here comes the bride. Here comes the bride,*" Everly sang. The others joined in.

On my seat was another Frankenstein Bride Barbie.

"Everly, you have been warned," said an exasperated Ms. Demetrios.

What was wrong with her?

I bit my lip, but what Damien said bubbled up in me. Riding it out wasn't working. I couldn't tell if I was going crazy or what, but I felt myself facing a rising ocean of anger. I didn't just want it to stop. *I* wanted to be the one who stopped it. I looked at Damien—who smiled up at me. Like he understood what I was thinking. Like he was encouraging me. I turned back to Everly.

"Aren't you a little old to be playing with dolls?"

She blinked, surprise spilling over her features. And then she laughed.

Damien was smiling broader now. He was proud of me.

But what good had saying something done? I didn't feel better. I felt angrier than I had before. I wanted *her* to know what it felt like. I wanted *her* to hurt like she had hurt me.

"All right, let's take out our books," Ms. Demetrios said.

The yellow paperback of *Dracula* sat on my desk dumbly next to the doll. This should have been when I reeled it in. Took deep breaths. Found my calm, focused on saying something smarter and better than Everly, than anyone.

But my breath got more ragged. My hands flipped through the book, my eyes searching for the sections I'd highlighted. But the words blurred with the threat of angry tears, and I felt an overwhelming desire to turn and face her instead of hiding in the pages of the book or staring at Ms. Demetrios's oversized cursive on the chalkboard.

"You know what's really sad?" Everly mock-whispered. "That you were right all those years ago."

I glanced at her from the corner of my eye. She caught it and continued.

"When we first met. You said you were *nothing*." She smiled, showing me her bright, white teeth. "And you were exactly right. You. Are. Nothing."

I turned back to face her again, my jaw clenched, and caught sight of Damien. His eyes were narrowed on her too. It wasn't protective this time—it was as if we shared my anger. As if we were hating her on the same frequency. As if I wasn't alone in this. It made me feel stronger, braver, when I said, "Fuck you, Everly."

The wall of windows that looked out on the parking lot shook at my words. "Excuse me?" Everly snapped.

Ms. Demetrios was looking at us now, but I didn't care.

"You heard me," I said louder. "After high school, girls like you become nothing—not girls like me. Enjoy it while it lasts, Everly. Because you've fucking peaked."

Everly snarled—actually *snarled*—and reached across her desk to grab my hair, but something inside me snapped and I blocked her arm and I moved to push her back. But I didn't touch her. My hands froze just before I reached her. They were shaking. *I* was shaking. As if the anger I felt had frozen them in place. My arms jerked up toward the wall of windows. My limbs weren't my own. They belonged to my anger.

Everly tried to swipe at me again. A smile forming on her lips. She thought she had won.

There was a sudden scratching sound and a crash.

A giant branch from the oak tree outside smashed through the window, its twisted, heavy bark swinging through the air, inches from Everly. She leaped from her seat.

If she hadn't had the reflexes of a cheerleader, she would have been crushed at her desk.

There was screaming. Stacey Blonder had a cut on her face from the falling glass, and Faith Sarah was torn between helping her and backing away. Ms. Demetrios was ushering people out of their seats to the classroom door. "Stay away from the glass and line up!"

Everly didn't move. She inspected herself for cuts before glaring at me. Her look was questioning, as if she was trying to figure out what had happened—as if I'd somehow had something to do with it.

I was frozen in my seat, even though my head screamed at me to run. Damien got up, barely looking back at Everly, and made his way to me.

The wind picked up and blew in through the broken window. Beyond it, tree branches danced as if they weren't done with us, as if they wanted inside too.

"Everyone out!" Ms. Demetrios put an arm around Stacey, who had her scarf pressed to her cheek, and began to lead her to the door.

Damien took a deep breath, looking infinitely calmer than everyone else. He took my hand and yanked me to my feet, putting me back in motion. As we reached the door, the wall of windows crashed at our backs. Glass chased us as we rushed to clear the door.

It was the wind. Of course it was.

"You okay?" he asked.

Amazingly, no one looked further hurt.

He grabbed my hand and pulled me deeper into the hallway.

"What was that?" I didn't just mean the glass. There was the dream. And the drawings. All of it.

"Nature," he said, still holding my hand.

But since when did nature have such good timing? It didn't feel like nature. It felt like the books we read in class—how the settings of stories reflected what was happening with the characters. If they were feeling dark and stormy, cue the storm clouds. But this was real life. And if I didn't know better, I'd think that somehow I had made that branch reach out and almost smash Everly to pieces.

I looked down at Damien's hand, still holding mine.

Did I make this happen too? Damien Thorne didn't even know I'd existed until a few days ago. And now Mom's suicide-iversary was here. Had I subconsciously chosen this day to become her crazy mirror image? I looked at our hands again. His fingers, long and strong and sure, wrapped around mine. I couldn't conjure this. I couldn't conjure him, could I?

"You sure you're okay?" Damien asked again. I nodded. He let go, his face resigned, and turned to walk away. But suddenly, I didn't want to run. I wanted company. And if whatever I was doing had brought him to me, how bad could it be? And why couldn't I keep him?

"Wait," I said.

He was a gentleman, if those still existed. He was a door-holding throwback to some other time or place. I was surprised, but pleased.

We sat together in the dark at the local college theater. *Annie Hall*, my favorite. And we laughed at almost the exact same times and stole glances at each other's profile. We walked out of the theater somehow closer. And he took me to the Diner on 5th, where the cool kids hung out on Friday nights. He wanted to be seen with me.

"You don't scare me, Marnie," he said after opening the door to his ridiculously compact, ridiculously expensive silver sports car.

I got out, trying to keep my knees together in my only nice dress, a vintage blue number that I had buttoned and unbuttoned a few times while debating my level of first-date modesty. I'd settled on three buttons unbuttoned.

"Excuse me?"

"You wanted to bite my head off in the cafeteria the other day. But I am not going anywhere."

Mercifully nothing about what happened in Ms. Demetrios's class. Nothing about the Barbie Brides or the broken windows.

"You want a gold star for that?" I squinted up at him as we approached the diner's glass doors.

"Nah." He laughed, nose scrunching. Then his face went serious. "I just want to know what I did wrong so I don't do it again."

I didn't say anything. I felt myself recoiling. I didn't want him to ruin it. The night was supposed to be so perfect.

I stopped in front of the doors, knowing I was probably blowing it—but somehow I couldn't help myself.

"You didn't do anything. I was the one who was wrong. I was—I guess I was comparing how you lost your parents to how I lost mine. Which is pretty awful. Your two accidents versus my one suicide. Which is worse? And I know better, I know that all that matters is *gone*. Not how." My voice sounded harsher than I wanted it to. Why couldn't I just keep my mouth shut?

He didn't blink. "A misery competition," he said with a sad smile. "I think it all matters. *How* always matters."

I shook my head. "But to compare us—"

"It's no worse than using a dead-parents sob story to get a pretty girl to think I'm more than some spoiled rich kid."

He laughed, letting me off the hook. My heart unclenched. My date had surprised me. He was nicer than me. And it was the weirdest thing—there wasn't an ounce of pity in his niceness. Just curiosity.

When he pushed open the door and I stepped inside, no one was there. It was completely empty except for the waitress.

"Weird, huh?" I said.

But he owned it. Like he'd planned it.

"It's more romantic this way. We have it all to ourselves. Only the best for Marnie Campbell."

He picked out my favorite song on the jukebox, "Wonderwall," by Oasis. It was like magic. How did he know that song was mine? How did he know about the movie? The questions floated up, but I didn't think too hard about their answers. I was always too cautious, too careful. Tonight I didn't want to think about my mother's death. I wanted this distraction.

The waitress delivered our milkshakes. Chocolate for me. Strawberry for Damien. I never ordered. Again, he just knew.

"How did you know?"

"Magic," he said with a wink. Boys my age didn't wink. But somehow he pulled it off. He was somehow immune to awkwardness.

"Lucky girl," the waitress whispered to me when she gave us the check. Even she knew he was out of my league.

I checked my watch.

"Don't worry, I'll get you home by a respectable hour."

I wasn't checking for that. I still couldn't figure out how not one person had come into the diner in the hour we'd been here.

"My dad doesn't care. And my mom is long gone." It was the first time I'd said that out loud to anyone—it didn't feel good to say it. But saying it reminded me that I was free to stay and talk and drink my milkshake. I was free to enjoy this little bit of magic. Even if it was just coincidence. Even if it was just tonight. After today, I'd no longer think of this day as the anniversary of my mother's suicide. After today, it would be the anniversary of my first-ever date.

"Sometimes not caring is kinder than caring," he said.

For a second, I didn't realize he was referring to what I'd said about my dad. I looked down at my shake.

"My parents weren't my parents," he said. He was twisting a straw wrapper around his finger. "I was adopted and raised by the Thornes. My birth father has been in touch, but he always wants something from me," he added, his voice suddenly distant. That intense stare he normally wore softened focus, as if he was thinking about the adoptive parents he lost. Or the birth father he'd found.

"I—I'm sorry, Damien. I didn't realize. What does . . . what does he want from you?"

"My dad? He wants more. World domination," he deadpanned.

I laughed. "Oh, so politics, then?"

He shrugged. "Something like that."

"And what do *you* want?"

"Sometimes I think I just want what Frankenstein's monster wanted," he said. Then he leaned in and kissed me. Or maybe I kissed him. I wondered if he knew it was my first. I wondered if I should have warned him. But then I wasn't wondering or thinking at all because I was all body, all lips, like I'd been somehow outside of myself all this time, and only now could I feel my heart beating in my chest, my ears, my throat. My skin alive, every nerve pulsing, every pore opening, so that when his lips left mine, my breathing was ragged. I wasn't ready for it to end. I didn't want him to stop.

He exhaled and smiled at me. I blinked, gathering myself, finding my voice. His hands had made their way around my waist, and he did not remove them now.

I swallowed. "The way I see it, you don't owe him anything. The only person you owe anything to is you."

He nodded as if he appreciated my words but knew they didn't change anything.

"Hey, I should get you home," he said, his arms, to my disappointment, loosening around me.

"What about you?" he asked, back in the car. "How's your big brain going to conquer the world?"

I shrugged. "Lawyer maybe."

I could see my breath. Damien reached down and turned up the heat. The weather in Harlow always seemed about ten degrees colder than the city.

"Don't you want to be a writer?"

I was going to pick something practical—something that made the most money, something that ensured I would never be like my father. Doctor. Lawyer. Wall Street. But Damien was right. I did always like stories. Writing them and reading them. *Frankenstein*, *Dracula*, *The Metamorphosis*—maybe I'd read one too many.

"How do you know that?"

He studied me for a beat, then said, "Been going to school with you for, like, seven years, Marnie. No one loves words like you do. I've seen it in class. You name-drop authors like other girls drop boy bands."

I felt myself smiling from the inside out. He noticed things about me. How had I gone this long without anyone noticing anything good?

He turned to me when we got to Chambers, the street that led to my side of town.

"Do you mind if we make a quick pit stop by my place?"

We pulled into the drive of his house. It was massive. It was the size of one of those English castles, only totally modern. Skinny windows lined the facade. And manicured shrubbery bookended the house. His nanny had become his guardian after his parents died. I saw a light on in one of the upstairs rooms and wondered if it was her.

He led me inside through the opulent foyer. There was a family portrait of a baby Damien and a happy-looking couple. I felt my chest clench for his parents and a twinge of guilt shuddered through me for ever doubting the magnitude of his loss. His might have been bigger after all.

And then I heard the barking.

Two impossibly lean, impossibly large dogs were racing toward us. Rottweilers, but enormous. I wondered if they had been bred that way on purpose.

Damien broke into a smile. They leaped on him simultaneously and he rubbed their faces until they settled down. They turned their massive heads to me. A low growl coming from both of them at once. I took a step back.

Damien gently chastised them. "We like her."

The growling stopped. One of them licked my hand.

"A lot," he added. "Dogs, meet Marnie. Marnie meet Dogs."

"Don't they have names?"

"I call these two Cerberus and Erebus. But there are more. Security." He looked toward the floor-to-ceiling windows, and I thought I saw dog-shaped shadows prowling the manicured, tastefully lit grounds in the distance.

Damien grabbed my hand and pulled me down the hall. More photos lined the walls—pictures of his parents in happier times.

When we got to the great room, I gasped. Not just because it was grander than any room I'd ever been in, but because of who was standing in it.

"What is she doing here?" I said. Everly was wearing a flimsy nightgown down to the floor. And she was standing in the center of what looked like a star with a circle around it that had been scarred deep into the elaborately inlaid wood floor. A pentagram.

There was no furniture. Only a massive black marble fireplace and dozens of lit candles. *What the hell?* I looked at Everly, lit by the flickering light. I could see she was wearing nothing underneath the gown. A pentagram equaled witchcraft or devil-worship or something, but what was it doing in Damien's living room? And Everly equaled trouble, but what kind?

"What is this?" I was breathing heavy now.

Was she Damien's girlfriend? Was he hoping for some kind of creepy fantasy come true?

"You know what? Never mind, I don't need to know." I took a deep breath and prepared to storm past the killer guard dogs. Facing them seemed less scary than whatever was going on in here.

"I got her for you," Damien said, and I stopped. "What happens here," he continued, "is entirely up to you."

I turned. "I don't want *anything* to happen here. Not with her. I hate her."

"Exactly," Damien said simply.

Everly picked up a knife from the nearby table and held it to her neck.

"What? Wait—Everly, don't!" I took a step toward her. What *was* this? Some kind of bizarre proposition? But the pentagram. And the knife . . . Was she depressed? Crazy? Was I?

I looked from the shiny blade to her eyes and I got my answer. My stomach twisted.

Her gaze was utterly vacant.

Which could mean only one thing.

I was doing this to her. It was true. It was me.

"I am sorry for calling you those names," Everly said, sounding sincere.

I always knew it would take nothing short of a knife to her throat to get Everly to apologize to me, but I didn't think she would be the one holding it. I didn't know I'd be the one . . . what? *Compelling* her?

"What names?" Damien asked.

A tear fell from Everly's mascara-smeared eyes.

"Monster, Monster, Monster . . ."

The word stung, even still. But I ordered myself to be calm, to stop this.

"It's okay, Everly. Listen. Don't do this. I'm not mad at you anymore." And I realized I meant it.

"Monster, Monster, Monster . . . I—I don't even know how you can show your face in public, and those *clothes.*" Her mouth was moving, but her eyes were pleading. Part of me wanted to hate her. Part of me wanted to remember how nasty she was. And I did remember, my anger was there just beneath the surface as always—as predictable as a reflex. But . . .

My knees felt weak and I righted myself. I tried to concentrate on pushing it back down. I didn't understand what was happening. Damien had brought her here. He'd put me and her and my anger all here in the same room. But why? Because he'd figured out my—my power or whatever it was, and wanted to see it in full bloody array? Because he liked me and wanted to support me in getting a little revenge?

"I don't want her to die, I want her to suffer," I said to him quickly, trying to find a way out, a way that didn't involve blood.

"You do the very same thing in class. You hit a wall and it doesn't stop you. You just keep looking for another solution . . . You should see your face . . . it's so pretty when you're thinking so hard," he said, sizing me up, oblivious to how weird his flattery was next to the girl with a knife.

Why was it still at Everly's neck? I did not want this. No part of me wanted her to die. I didn't feel anger anymore. I felt fear. Was I still doing this? I wasn't. I couldn't be. I turned to Damien.

"Who are you?"

He broke out into another smile. A smile that belonged in the hall-ways of our school, in the dark of the movie theater, or in the bright of the diner, but not here. "I thought you would never ask."

"Make her put the knife down," I said.

The knife fell to the floor.

"Just because you asked me to."

"Who are you, Damien?"

"Dear old Dad probably wouldn't do the same. Or maybe he would. There's a misconception about him—about both of us. Just because he is who he is doesn't mean he doesn't love. And I love too, Marnie—"

"Dear old Dad?"

He looked down pointedly. I inhaled. My brain circling his mean-ing but refusing to land.

"I bet you've heard the story. My favorite one about him. He falls in love with a girl and takes her home. Only her family doesn't ap-prove. Literally no one approves, and she's persuaded to leave him. Only, she can't resist and she comes back to him. Again and again and again. In fact, every year she ends up spending half her year with him and half with her family."

Was he talking about . . . Wait. Was he talking about Persephone and Hades? Aka the devil kidnapping his bride and forcing her to spend half the year in the Underworld? But the way he was talking . . . like it was some kind of beautiful love story, and more importantly, like the devil was his . . . *father?*

I wanted to laugh. A joke. An elaborate, insane joke. The cool kids playing a joke on the monster girl who lived in the ghost house. Everly was in on it. And Damien too. And I'd known—I'd known not to get involved. My lungs contracted painfully. But there was relief mixed in with the hurt. I wasn't Carrie at the prom. I had no supernatural abilities. No way to wipe out my enemies. I was just a girl getting my heart broken into a million pieces.

Then I did laugh. The anger filling me up. And I let it, wishing for a second that I actually *did* have the power to take Damien out with a sigh.

"You totally got me. And wow, you really committed, Damien. Bravo. You win. You're a first-class asshole. Just like her."

"You don't believe me," he said, shaking his head.

He nodded at Everly then, and she picked up the knife. In one swift move she sliced one of her wrists. She cocked her head as if genuinely surprised by the sight of her own blood. "What the hell?" I shrieked, running over and grabbing the knife from her, tossing it to the floor. She went down all at once—deadweight. I tore off my sweater, crouched, wrapped it around her wrist. A red stain bloomed on the fabric. *"What did you do? Did you give her something?"* It had to be drugs. No one cut their wrists because the cutest guy in school ordered them to. I looked up at him. "Call 911!"

He took a step back; he looked disappointed in me. This wasn't an act or a trick. He believed it. And somehow he'd pulled Everly into his delusion.

DANIELLE PAIGE

"You think you're the devil," I said. The dad stuff. The dogs.

"His son, actually."

Oh my god, he was mentally ill. I finally liked someone, and he thought he was the Antichrist.

I grabbed my phone and dialed, but it flew out of my hand and hit the wall across the room, shattering into pieces.

I stared at Damien.

It was never me.

He was doing this. He was doing all of this. But how?

"Everly—we have to go. Let's go!" I pulled her closer to me. I could feel her trembling, half-conscious.

"It's only a flesh wound." Damien sighed. "She'll be fine. If that's what you really want."

"Do you hear yourself? I thought she was one of your friends!"

He laughed. "I don't have friends. Only subjects." He smiled at me. "What you said in class, Marnie . . . about wanting to know the monster?"

"It wasn't an invitation. I wanted to get an A. Ms. Demetrios likes someone to play . . . devil's advocate. I didn't mean it literally."

Damien laughed at "devil's advocate." But then his face fell. He looked struck for the briefest of moments, like he'd made a miscalculation. Then just as quickly, his pretty features rearranged themselves back into calm resolution.

"What you said, you meant. I know it. I felt it."

"Maybe your evil Spidey senses are off. You don't know me."

"Maybe you don't know yourself, Marnie."

I dragged Everly and looked back at the door, where Cerberus and Erebus appeared to have several more heads than before. I tripped. But held tight to Everly. If she weren't bleeding, I'd be running. I could be running now, getting away from here, from all this. What had she ever done for me? I pushed down the thought. I couldn't leave her. I wouldn't. I wasn't that person.

"I lied before when I said I thought you were less boring than everyone else. I will never lie to you again. I knew already. Just today in class you wished you had the power to get rid of her. I know what you think. I know every dirty thought and every sweet one. I know what movies you like and how much you hate your dad and that you sometimes wish your mother had just taken you with her."

My stomach twisted. "What I think and what I actually do are two different things. That's what makes us good or evil. I am not like you."

"I didn't have a choice in that," he said. "I never had a choice. I killed my own mother before I went to kindergarten. Not because I wanted to, because I was a kid who was jealous and angry and didn't know what he was capable of. My dad was different. It was harder. *He* tried to kill *me*. It was self-defense. I didn't want to. I didn't."

"You have a choice now." I was inching us closer to the door as I spoke, Everly still shaking, eyes closed.

"I choose you."

I stopped. These words—I'd wanted to hear them for so long. And here they were. And they were awful. "Will you let her live if I let you have me?" My voice was hoarse.

He shook his head. "Free will. You have to come to me because you want to."

"Why, though? Why me? What is wrong with me that you'd pick me?"

"I have seen inside you, Marnie. We're more alike than you think. You have darkness and light. Bitterness and compassion. And I can give you power."

"And what—I sign over my soul?"

"I want to share what I have with someone. With you." Damien looked at me. "Even a monster wants to be loved."

"You have your fans. You have Everly. She's literally willing to kill herself for you—you don't need me—"

"You should hear their thoughts." He shook his head dismissively.

There was silence, and I realized, ashamed, that I was waiting to hear how I was different.

"But you, Marnie. You were the first broken thing I ever met who didn't want to be someone else. Who didn't want to be fixed. You wanted out of that house. But you never wanted to be Everly. You never wanted to be anyone else. Even Everly wants to be someone else. Probably a Kardashian, but still . . . Even I, when I started to realize what I was. I wanted to change. I wanted to heal instead of hurt. I would kill things, small things, and try to bring them back to life. My power didn't work that way. *I* didn't work that way. And eventually, I had to accept that."

A vision of Damien and a roomful of dead crows flashed across my mind. I shuddered. Damien was lost. He was a broken thing too. But he also broke others.

"And my soul?" I asked again. I let Everly go, easing her to the floor and stepping closer to Damien.

"Is yours. I only want your heart."

"You promise not to kill anyone," I said, moving still closer to him. Close enough to kiss, though my mind screamed to run. But I felt the pull again. The power. I had slipped the knife in my pocket when I'd wrapped Everly's wrist with my sweater. I slipped it out again now. I kissed him, deeply, revulsion warring with wanting.

The knife went in easier than I thought it would. Blood gushed from his neck. A look of surprise crossed his pretty face. And a hint of a smile.

I pulled Everly from the floor, dragging her. *"Run!"*

The dogs came straight at us, teeth bared, glinting in the candle-light. I braced myself. But it was the barest brush—they'd raced past us to their owner, sniffing and whining.

A hoarse laugh rose in my throat.

Damien didn't need me.

He had his dogs.

We made it to the neighbors' house. They promised to call the police. They were an elderly couple, gray-haired and slow-moving.

We sat in their opulent drawing room. Me cradling Everly, who looked at me in weary surprise as the old couple went searching for bandages and blankets.

"Why did you help me?" she asked, her eyes watery, exhausted.

I shrugged. "I couldn't let that happen to you. You didn't deserve that."

"I mean, why did you disobey the master? You are so lucky, you have been chosen." Her eyes glazed over, lids lowering.

I heard the door open, but realized too late that I hadn't heard sirens. When I looked up, he was there.

The neighbors belonged to him. Of course. Everly too.

His neck was healed. He was wearing a fresh blue shirt. You hear that phrase—"devastatingly handsome." This is what it looked like.

"Let's get you home." He gently pulled me up from the couch. I didn't even notice Everly had crawled away. "I don't want you to miss curfew."

He put a hand on my back—was he going to kill me or kiss me?

"What happens now?" I asked. Or maybe I screamed.

"I take you home. I try again tomorrow."

"I will never love you," I said. Or maybe I was still screaming.

"You do already. You just need time to admit it."

I shook my head. "You're crazy," I said. Or maybe I was crying.

"This morning, you thought that you couldn't kill someone. Tonight you didn't hesitate."

I said something, or maybe nothing.

"Lucky girl, so ungrateful," the old woman said, cutting a glance at me as she bent over Everly's wound in the front hall.

Lucky girl? It was the third time I'd heard it today. Everly, the waitress, and now this old woman.

World domination, Damien had said, and I'd laughed.

He'd started with his neighbors. I recalled the way the classroom full of kids stopped chanting when he talked, the deferential looks even Ms. Demetrios gave him. How many people in town already worshiped him? How would I ever get away?

He took my hand and led me to the car.

What would happen if I ran? Would his love for me stop him from coming after me? I would find my moment. Bide my time.

A thought—not mine—pushed into my head.

I like hide-and-seek.

Damien winked at me. Then he held open the door, like nothing had happened, like we had eaten our burgers and drunk our shakes and held hands, and he would drive me home and kiss me outside my front door.

I slipped inside the car.

"I had to wait until you were ready. It was so hard, Marnie. Watching you all those years. But I knew the day would come when we could be together. When we didn't have to be alone anymore."

We pulled into my overgrown driveway. The lights in my house were all off.

Damien glanced at me, something like hope on his face. He was planning for us. A future.

I put my fingers around the door handle. I'd begun the night wanting to erase the stain of what my mom did. I'd wanted to erase the last few days of wild thoughts and anger and everything that had been building in me for years and years. Only Damien didn't. He wanted me to embrace them—the anger, the spite, the malice. To embrace him. He wanted me to embrace myself. The dark, scary parts and all.

I looked at my bleak little house, where no one cared a thing about me. I looked at Damien, who would put the world at my feet if I wanted him to.

A thought, errant and wrong crept in and took root.

What if I didn't run?

Then:

Monster Marnie . . . Monster Marnie . . .

The words pushed into my head, but they weren't coming from Damien or Everly or anyone else . . . and they didn't sound so bad.

Inspired by the 1976 film *The Omen* and Mary Shelley's *Frankenstein*

The Flicker, the Fingers, the Beat, the Sigh

April Geneviève Tucholke

She was looking at me when the car hit her, straight at me, eyes round and wide behind the square, black, nerd-cool frames. Her body hit the windshield, thud, brakes, screaming, yellow hair fanning out like the sinking summer sun.

"Is the flask empty?"

Grace leaned up from the backseat and hit me on the arm, palm slapping the meat of my shoulder. "Yo, brother, is the flask empty?"

"Long gone, sis." The pink thermos was rolling around on the floor by my feet, nothing left but a watery slush of melted ice, coffee, and vodka.

She sighed, and slunk back.

"You've drunk enough, Grace." Scout's voice was snappy, like her eyes.

I looked over at my girlfriend, slim hands on the wheel, pointed chin, flattish nose, narrow shoulders, long black hair. Pale blue moonshine was pouring through the windshield and coating her in its eerie glow. Damn, she was beautiful.

"Stop staring at me." Scout laughed her low, bubbly laugh.

"I can't."

"Moonlight always makes you dreamy and sentimental, T."

"I'm an artist. We're all dreamy and sentimental."

Scout had lean limbs and chubby toes. She read Tolstoy and did yoga and made curry chicken and grape salad sandwiches on buttery croissants. She was going to Harvard. Her parents had a hole-in-the-wall diner and that was all they had. But she was going to Harvard.

Finals were over, graduation a few days away, and this was the first night in months Scout hadn't worked or studied past midnight.

"Answer my damn question, Theodore."

I looked back at Asher. He had his hands all over my sister and a huge grin on his face. Asher had been my best friend since the sixth grade. He was the high school quarterback, beefy and alpha, such a cliché. But he was always up for anything and always in a good mood. He was dating my sister and I was cool with it. Grace had a dark side, and he evened her out. They looked good together. Both had brown curly hair and big blue eyes. Grace's friends gave them the couple name *Gasher,* and said their babies were going to be *sooooooocuuuuute.*

"Don't call me Theodore. And stop groping each other, Gasher. My eyes are bleeding."

Grace groaned. "We are *Grace* and *Asher*. Don't combine our names. It makes me hate the world." My sister pushed Asher away and leaned against the door. "I'm glad the flask is empty. I feel sick. Mixing locally distilled vodka and locally roasted espresso. What were we thinking?"

"We were thinking PORTLAND." Asher kissed my sister's neck

and then hit me in the side with his fist. "Theodore, answer the question. This is important. We've done best seventies horror flick, best eighties horror flick . . . what's the best nineties? Because I say *Army of Darkness* and I know best. Hail to the king, baby."

Asher pawed at my sister and she laughed and slapped his hands away.

"Everyone knows the best nineties horror film is *Silence of the Lambs*." Scout glanced back over her shoulder, and her long hair swished against my arm.

"You *would* say that."

She looked at me, and raised her black eyebrows.

I lowered my voice, so Gasher wouldn't hear me in the backseat. "You and Clarice. You have certain things in common."

"Don't analyze me, T," she said, snappy, snappy. But then she put her fingers on the collar of my shirt, knuckles rubbing softly against my skin. "We're supposed to be celebrating, not going full *Spellbound* on each other. For tonight I'm dumb as a post and ambitious as a pothead in Eugene. All right?"

Scout had worked her ass off senior year. But we'd all needed this. Road trip to the city. Late-night eats at the food carts, crazy PDX food like avocado milkshakes and fried plantain crepes. Getting lost in the biggest indie bookstore in the world, a whole block long. Running through Nob Hill, the twinkling lights a yellow-white blur. Getting olive oil ice cream at the Salt & Straw. Asher whooping and laughing for no reason, picking up the girls and throwing them over his shoulder like they weighed nothing. Everyone but me sipping iced Stumptown espresso and Crater Lake vodka from a pink Hydro Flask in Scout's purse.

I'd let Scout drive even though she'd been drinking and I hadn't. No one told Scout no.

I loved how my girlfriend drove. Aggressive. Confident. In control. Elbows perfectly bent at ninety-degree angles. Queen of the damn road in her sensible blue Toyota Corolla.

"*The Sixth Sense. Scream.*" Grace, answering Asher's question. "Best nineties horror movies, hands down."

I spun around. "No way. *The Blair Witch Project.* People thought it was real. Three kids in the woods, lost, hearing creepy noises . . . it *felt* real. That movie scared the hell out of me."

Asher put his hands up in the air. "That was a one-concept indie with a jerky camera that gave people motion sickness. Let's agree to disagree. Moving on . . . what's the scariest urban legend?"

"Oh, I've got this one." Scout looked sideways at me and shivered, her torso and shoulders wriggling sexily. "You're driving alone at night on a deserted back road, but someone is hiding in the backseat of your car. Your eyes meet his in the rearview mirror as moonlight gleams off the butcher knife he holds in his hand . . ."

Grace screamed, a shrill, fake scream. Asher put his hands over his ears. "*Stop with the shrieking,* Grace. Seriously."

"Not a chance. And the scariest urban legend is the Bloody Mary one. Chanting her name three times into a mirror in a dark room, trying to conjure her blood-covered ghost . . . I still can't look in mirrors when the lights are off. That story singlehandedly destroyed my childhood innocence."

"I thought I did that." Asher.

I turned around again. "Thanks for that, Asher. Now I have to beat the hell out of you."

"I'd like to see you try, painter-boy." Laugh, laugh, laugh. "Both of you girls are wrong. The scariest urban legend is that one with the unpopular girl who goes to the prom with the hottest guy in school but a serial killer murders the dude after the first dance, guts him, and then dumps a bucket of his blood all over the girl while she stands onstage, calling his name. Brilliant stuff."

Scout reached back and hit Asher on the knee. "That's not an urban legend, you idiot. It's a book by Stephen King. And it was a bucket of pig's blood. And they poured it on the unpopular girl because she was meek and naïve and pathetic."

Scout looked at me, quick. Her eyes went big, and she made a fake-scared face. "What about the one where the girl thinks her dog is under the bed, licking her hand, and she hears this dripping noise, *drip, drip, drip,* but she can't figure out where it's coming from. The next morning she finds her dog in the bathroom, hanging from the shower head, his neck cut . . . and then she realizes it was the *killer,* under her bed, licking her hand . . ."

"Oh, fuck *that.* You win, Scout." Asher reached up and high-fived my girlfriend.

I looked out the window. The dark highway curved against the crashing Pacific, Portland back to Wolf Cove, the notorious 101.

"Wait a sec, Gasher." I grinned at them over my shoulder. "What about *The Drowned Girl?* You know, the one set right here on the Oregon coast—the shy girl that gets led on by a guy as a joke and when he dumps her in front of all his friends she throws herself off the cliffs. And then she comes back from the dead to haunt him. He keeps thinking he sees her in the water, and he can't go swimming anymore, or even take a shower, and he goes stark raving mad, convinced she's still alive, swimming with the fish down at the bottom of the sea, and someday she'll turn up naked on the beach with her hair as long as seaweed and her eyes black and glassy like a seal's, and she'll drag him into the water, to swim with her in the darkness for all time . . ."

Grace stuck her head up between the seats and scowled at me.

"That story didn't happen here. It was in the Caribbean. And her boyfriend lured her into the water knowing she couldn't swim because he was *eeeeeeevil*."

Scout laughed, short and deep. "What kind of dick would lead a girl on as a joke? He deserved what he got." And then she winked at me, right eyelid, long lashes, slow.

Asher hit me in the side. Again. "No way, Theo. An urban legend needs blood, and a batshit-mad serial killer, and screaming chicks. Lots of hot, screaming chicks." Asher leaned back in his seat and put his arms behind his head. "I'm calling this one, and I say the scariest urban legend is the one with the clown and the babysitter. *The kids are in bed, and she's watching TV, but she keeps thinking the clown statue in the corner of the room is staring at her, and she finally calls the parents to ask about it, and they say, WHAT CLOWN STATUE?* Because, *snap,* it's not a statue, it's a killer dwarf dressed as a clown."

"Oh my god. I hate clowns. I *hate* them." Grace shrieked right in my ear, just one long *IHATECLOWNS* wail.

Asher rolled down his window and stuck his head out, hair whipping in the wind. "FUUUUUUUCK CLOWNS . . ."

Scout had driven this road a hundred times, a thousand times, and she was laughing and I was laughing and my girlfriend was smart and going to Harvard and I'd gotten into an art school in Italy and everything was fucking awesome . . .

And then I saw the girl out of the corner of my eyes—headlights sparking off her thick glasses, moon sparking off her blond hair as it whisked across the windshield.

Canary London had a weird name and she seemed to embrace it, wearing tweedish wool skirts with pulled-up socks, and big glasses on a small nose, and letting her hair frizz in the ocean humidity until it looked like a blond cotton ball. She never talked in class but seemed to know all the answers when called on. I'd been going to school with her since kindergarten, but she was still a mystery to me, as foreign and unfathomable as the sea creatures that lurked in the ocean deep.

Grace told me once that Canary lived alone with her grandfather in one of the decrepit old sea captain houses on Widow Lane, the ones that flooded every time it stormed. The ones that smelled like salt and seawater on cool summer mornings, and rotting fish on hot summer afternoons. The ones with cockroaches and cat-sized rats . . . or so went the rumors.

Canary and I were assigned an English project together when we were juniors—*Jane Austen vs. Dorothy Parker: A Battle of Wit*. Canary met me after class and told me to follow her. I did. I thought she was taking me to the study hall, but nope. I followed her into an empty room in a dark hallway between the stage and the teachers' lounge. The door was hidden in shadows and painted the color of the walls. Nearly impossible to see unless you knew it was there.

"It used to house theater props, but the teachers have forgotten it's here." Canary had a breathy, husky voice that surprised me every time I heard it. I expected a girl who rarely talked and lived alone with her grandfather in a rotting rat hole on Widow Lane to have a shy, high voice, I guess.

I glanced around. Cardboard trees, a rack of dusty Renaissance costumes, Venetian masks, a stuffed raven, an old vintage sofa.

"I found this nook last year. I was . . . sad, and needed a place to hide for a while. You're the first person I've shown it to." Canary looked up at me, and her hazel eyes were clear and pretty behind the chunky glasses. "I've added some of my own things," she said, and waved a hand over an old star-patterned quilt on the floor, and a black lamp, and a pile of tattered paperbacks in the corner—*Jamaica Inn, Rebecca, The Shadow over Innsmouth and Other Lovecraftian Sea Stories, The Folk Keeper, Bloody Jack* . . . all books I'd read before. And liked.

She sat down on the quilt, and I sat down next to her. I gave her a look like *Thanks for showing me this place.* She smiled, and I saw she had two cutely crooked front teeth. She pushed her glasses back up her nose with small fingers and my heart beat faster, watching her do it. I don't know why.

We lay on our stomachs, English literature books between our elbows, and studied in the soft light from Canary's lamp. Theater kids walked by outside, talking, making noise, acting out scenes, oblivious to the door, and the nook, and us.

I kissed her.

She kissed me back.

Her glasses pressed into my cheekbone.

Her lips were soft.

Canary London.

The next day Scout asked me out after art class. She marched up, threw her black hair behind her shoulder, and said I drew better nudes than any kid born in Wolf Cove had a right to.

Me and her, after that. Me and her. Canary and the nook and the kissing, forgotten.

"What do I do? What the hell should I do? Do I just keep driving? I'm just going to keep driving, oh, god, WHAT THE HELL DO I DO?"

Scout was screaming and screaming and Asher was shouting *eff eff eff eff eff* and Grace was saying my name over and over and gripping my arm, *squeezing* it, and I . . . I just stared straight ahead.

"*I'm so fucked, I'm so fucked, so help me god, I'm so fucked . . .*"

I put my hand on Scout's leg. Pinched her knee between my thumb and pinkie the way she liked. "It's going to be all right, Scout," I said. Slow. Calm. "One step at a time. We need to see if she's dead—she might just be stunned. Come on, keep it together. Think of Clarice."

Scout shut her mouth.

Asher shut his mouth.

We all got out of the car.

Canary was a pile of clothes next to the yellow line, fifty yards ahead, right in the beam of the headlights, one leg splayed out, scuffed white oxford, striped sock slipping down her calf.

My heart stopped.

Started back up again.

"Grace, check her pulse." My sister was going into pre-med, and volunteered at the clinic on weekends.

She shook her head. "No, Theo, no, I can't, *I can't* . . ."

"Do it. *Now.*"

Grace kneeled down on the road. She closed her eyes, reached into the mess of hair and clothes, pulled out a limp wrist, and wrapped her fingers around it.

A pause.

An endless pause.

The waves beat against the rocks, a hundred feet below.

Crash, crash, crash.

Asher paced up and down the highway, ten feet up, turn, ten feet back.

Scout slumped to the ground, hands to her heart.

I stood still, still as the body on the road.

WOODSON

The waves crashed.

Crash, crash, crash.

I took a step forward, toward Scout . . .

My foot went *crunch*.

I bent down and picked up a pair of glasses. The right lens was smashed. I held the black frames in my hand, cradled in my palm.

It started to rain. I looked at Scout. Drops slid down the side of her face, drip, drip. I realized then that I'd never seen her cry. All those nights of studying, slaving away in the diner to make tuition, and the AP classes, and the volunteering at a million non-profits to help her get that scholarship. She hadn't cried. Not once.

"She's dead." Grace's voice cut through the waves and the rain. She stood. Turned toward Scout. "She's dead. *She's dead, and you killed her.*"

Scout jumped up and *ran* at my sister. Ran right at her. Hands to shoulders, push, Grace stumbled backward, hit the car. She started crying and Scout started screaming again and the whole damn world was ending . . .

"Stop it," I shouted. *"Stop it stop it stop it stop it."*

But Scout screamed right over me. "How can you say that, Grace? You saw. You *all* saw. She came out of nowhere. You were distracting me. You and Asher, screaming *fuck clowns*. It's your fault if it's anyone's. I'm not even drunk anymore. You and Asher are wasted and you weren't wearing your seat belts. I was wearing my seat belt. I *always* wear my seat belt. It's not my fault. *It's not my fault. IT'S NOT MY FAULT.*"

Asher stopped pacing. "We've got to call the cops."

Grace went to his side, leaned against him, and nodded.

Asher reached in his coat and pulled out his phone—

Scout, wiry arm white-blue in the moonlight. She smacked the

APRIL GENEVIEVE TUCHOLKE

phone out of his hand. It skidded down the road, and stopped an inch from the dip of Canary's dead knee.

"*Fuck* that. *I'm not going to jail.*" Scout stared at Asher, and she was bigger than him, she really was right then, with her five feet two facing his six feet three. "I've worked too damn hard. My parents have worked too damn hard. I'm not going to jail. I'm *not*. Where am I going, Asher?"

Silence.

"*Where am I going, Asher?*"

"Harvard," Asher said.

"That's right. And you don't want to lose your football scholarship to Austin, do you?"

He shook his head.

She whipped around and stared at my sister. "You're not going to get into a good med school with this on your record, Grace. You know you won't."

My turn. "They won't let you leave the country to attend that exclusive Italian art school, Theo."

We all just stood there, saying nothing.

And the waves went *crash, crash, crash*.

Scout screamed. One long, gut-wrenching scream. And then she slumped down to the road again.

The rain made her hair stick to her face, and it creased her cheeks with black scars.

Asher looked down and saw the crushed eyeglasses in my hand. "So who was it?" he asked, long, long after the fact. "Who did we kill, anyway?"

"Canary. Canary London." Raindrops down my face, across my neck, behind my ears.

Scout. Knees still on the road. She looked up. Straight at me.

"Canary lived near here," I said. "Widow Lane is the next turn to the left, half a mile ahead."

"Shut up, Theo." Grace hit me with one hand and pointed with the other. "Headlights. Someone's coming. *Someone's coming.*"

Senior year. Prom. Note in my locker.

Meet me in the nook.

I went.

She kissed me for an hour, not on the lips, everywhere else. Down my cheeks, across my neck, behind my ears, up my spine. She pulled on the loops of my jeans and kissed the skin she found underneath.

I fiddled with the tiny buttons on her white shirt, which she called a *blouse*. "Put your hand in my blouse, Theo," she said.

I did.

"Theo?" she said later, husky voice in my ear. "Do you remember that time in sixth grade, when Scout and her friends were making fun of my name and my thick glasses at recess?" She paused. "You ripped off your coat like a rock star and said you'd beat up the next person who made fun of me, girl or guy."

I nodded. I remembered. "I just did what needed to be done."

"I've always liked that about you."

And then she asked. I don't know why. She knew I was with Scout. Everyone knew I was with Scout. Scout liked to run her hands over me in between classes, staring down the born-again prudes with fight-me eyes. She'd kiss me against my locker while I quizzed her on upcoming tests, and slap me when she got a question wrong. Scout was noticeable. We were noticeable.

Still, Canary asked me to prom.

APRIL GENEVIEVE TUCHOLKE

And I wanted to go with her, I really did, so I just said yes, fuck the consequences.

Scout, up again, on her feet, screaming. "We have to get rid of the body, we can't put her in the car, we'll get DNA all over it, is she bleeding, did anyone check? *We can't get her blood all over my seats, my parents, we can't, I'm so fucked, I'm so fucked . . .*"

I'd never seen Scout lose it like this. Not the day she took the SATs, not when she opened her acceptance letter from Harvard, not the autumn night we carved pumpkins and both lost our virginity with the sweet smell of spiced cider in the air. Not ever.

I brushed the raindrops off my forehead, quick slap, and then pointed at the rock wall on the other side of the road. "Asher, Scout, drag Canary back into the shadows on the other side of the car and stay there. Now, *right now.*"

The headlights got closer.

Asher and Scout grabbed her arms, one each. Pulled. Back she went, out of the headlights, into the dark.

I took my sister by the shoulders. "Grace, listen. *Listen.* If they stop, we're going to tell them that we're geocaching, all right? You have to act bored. You have to act like nothing's wrong."

Grace nodded, fast.

The headlights got closer.

Closer.

Slowed . . .

Stopped.

My heartbeat. Loud and big as the surf.

Red truck. Window rolling down.

"Anything wrong?"

It was Mr. Dunn, our math teacher.

"Hey, Mr. Dunn," I said. Like it was nothing. "We're geocaching. Asher and Scout are determined to find this ammo box."

"Damn rain. My hair is totally ruined." Grace, right on cue, making me proud. She pushed wet brown strands behind her ear and scowled. "They're both so stubborn. Had to get this cache, *tonight*. You know how Scout is. She has to get an A in everything, even geocaching."

Mr. Dunn stared at us. His eyes narrowed. He was one of the smartest teachers at our school. Grace had a crush on him, and so did Scout.

"Geocaching," he repeated. Slowly. He stared over my shoulder toward the car. I fought the urge to flinch. I knew he couldn't see anything. It was all rain and shadows. "Well, get off the road, Theo. One of you could get hit."

I nodded.

The window rolled up.

The red truck drove off.

A pause.

Crash.

Crash.

I went to the prom with Canary. Scout said it would be good for her. That she deserved it, for asking me to go when she knew I had a girlfriend.

I did nothing to stop it.

Scout was waiting. She was ready.

Half an hour in, and I was slow-dancing with Canary. We were out of the nook, out in the wide open, our classmates all around us,

APRIL GENEVIEVE TUCHOLKE

her gangly arms around my neck, my hands on her waist, fingertips along her spine, her cheek on my shoulder, her back bare to the waist, the edge of her old-fashioned dress swooping across the floor . . .

I leaned down and kissed the tip of her nose. She smiled up at me, two slightly crooked front teeth. Her eyes behind the thick glasses were soft. Blissful.

I felt someone watching me. I looked over Canary's canary-yellow hair. There she was, standing at the edge of the gym. Black pants, black sweater, black boots, black hair tucked into a black cap, the brim pulled down low.

She nodded at me.

I dropped my hands from Canary's waist and stepped back.

Scout ran toward us, pail in hand. I smelled it, I gagged on it, the sea stench, clouds of it, everywhere, everywhere . . .

Salt, rotting fish, sand, ocean.

Scout threw the bucket of seawater. It arced up, came back down, *splash*. Canary's green silk dress turned black.

Scout threw the pail again. She got every putrid, stinking drop out, down to the rotting fish at the very bottom. It bounced off Canary's small chest and landed at her toes.

She just stood there, and took it.

People screamed.

People laughed.

Scout left the pail on the gym floor and disappeared into the crowd, sliding into the shadows before anyone thought to stop her.

Canary was all alone in the middle of the streamer-strewn dance floor, dead fish at her feet, hair and dress soaked with the reeking sea.

I didn't go to her.

I walked away.

I don't even remember doing it . . . I just melted into the crowd and the next thing I knew I was sitting in my car by myself, listening to Philip Glass and feeling nothing but relief.

That was all I cared about, right then.

The next day I got another note in my locker.

Nook. Now.

She was waiting for me, sitting on the old sofa, light green blouse, plaid wool skirt, gray socks pulled up to her lower thighs, frizzy hair sticking out six inches from her cheekbones.

"I want to show you something," she said.

Nothing about the dance, nothing about what happened, nothing, just nothing. She knew it was Scout who threw the pail. It was all over school. They were whispering it in the halls. She must have heard.

And me. I didn't defend her when it happened. I didn't tell Scout to stop. I didn't do anything.

But she'd forgiven me anyway.

Scout thought Canary was weak and pathetic, and she hated her for it. Scout didn't forgive people. She was proud, and aggressive, and stubborn. And she liked being that way.

But Canary had strength too. It took strength to be quiet. It took strength to be kind. It took strength to let other people's cruelty bounce right off of you.

I dropped down to my knees beside her. I kissed the skin of her right leg where it met the gray sock. I stroked her calf with my palm. I pulled off her shoe and ran my thumb underneath her toes.

She reached into her backpack and pulled out a little homemade book. Thirty pages, stapled together. It was filled with drawings—*her* drawings—all dark, thick lines, spooky and haunting.

"It's the story of a sad girl and a sad boy who accidentally stumble through a magical door into a wonderful parallel world. They fall in love. But when one of them goes too far, and tries to take their love back into the real world . . . it dies."

I looked through the illustrations.

Two figures, one tall with a dimple and wavy hair, one a gangly blond with glasses, both kissing in front of a crashing sea.

Two figures reading a book in a one-sail boat, a group of seagulls leaning in, listening to the story.

Two figures on the sand, sharing a night picnic under a starry sky.

Two figures swimming underwater, holding hands, schools of tiny fish surrounding them like stars around the moon.

"I've got it." Scout pointed at a sign by the side of the road. "We'll put her in the churn."

We all turned and looked.

DEVIL'S CHURN TRAIL

Carved into a rectangular sign, illuminated in the headlights.

Mr. Dunn's truck was barely out of sight, just going around the next curve . . . going . . . gone.

"We have a witness." Scout stared down the empty road. "We can't just leave her here and we can't put her in my car. I'll say we hit a deer. It will explain the dent, but it won't explain blood on my seats or a corpse in the trunk. Look, she's already dead. What does it matter now? *We have to put her in the churn.*"

The screaming, wailing Scout on her knees in the road was gone. Just like that. The Straight-A Scout was back.

Devil's Churn was a rock-lined inlet that used to be a sea cave, until the roof collapsed. And now it was a tourist attraction. The waves hit it so hard the spray touched the stars.

"Someone else could come along any minute . . ." Grace looked from the Devil's Churn sign, to the empty highway, to Canary. Her face was wet. From rain, from tears.

"There's no time, *there's no time.*" Scout was the one pacing now. Back and forth between the sign and Canary. "She'll be banged up beyond recognition. *If* they even find her body. People fall into the churn every year, they're eaten up by the waves and never seen again. Asher, pick her up. We'll carry her there. *PICK HER UP.*"

Asher shook his head, fast and hard. "No. I'm not doing it, Scout."

Scout screamed. But it was different this time. Head back. No panic, no fear. Just frustration.

I saw them. Headlights gleaming down the curve behind us, only a half mile away, no time, *no time* . . .

I shoved Canary's smashed glasses in my pocket, leaned down, slid my hands underneath her, lifted, lifted . . .

And then she was in my arms.

Head hanging back, frizzy yellow hair swinging. Her face looked naked without the nerd frames.

Her eyes were closed. I didn't know if they would be.

There was no blood. Not on the car. Not on her. Not anywhere.

"For fuck's sake let's just get this done," I said.

And they followed me, across the road, to the trail. It was narrow, paved, covered with overgrown ferns and wild azaleas and rhododendrons and completely hidden from the highway.

Down.

Down.

The ocean got louder.

Louder.

I heard a car go by on the road. Then another.

I wasn't big and meaty like Asher, but Canary weighed nothing in my arms.

APRIL GENEVIEVE TUCHOLKE

Her neck still felt warm on my skin. Her knees were tucked into the crook of my right elbow. They fit perfectly. Her skirt had ridden up, and I could see the pale skin of her thighs.

I heard it. The waves of the churn.

Crash.

Crash.

We went around a corner, hugged a rusty railing. And there it was. The waves were white in the moonlight, and spitting mad.

Note in my locker this morning.

Meet me at Devil's Churn after sunset. I'll wait for you by the side of the road.

I'd planned to go. I'd *wanted* to go. And I wasn't going to tell Scout this time, so she could laugh and laugh afterward, hanging on every detail. No. Just me and Canary. Out of the nook. Out in the real world. The two of us. No one else knowing.

And then Scout said we were going to Portland to party . . .

. . . and I forgot. I forgot about the churn. And Canary.

She'd waited for me for hours. For *hours.*

"Do it, Theo." Scout looked at me. Her eyes were inky black. Sad. Unflinching. *"Just do it,"* she shouted, ribs stretching beneath her brown T-shirt, lungs straining against the howling of the sea. "Don't think about it. *Just put her in."*

"Don't do it, Theo, don't do it. Please don't do it." Grace was crying again. Asher put his arms around her and she huddled into him and kept crying. *"Don't do it, you'll regret it, you'll regret it . . ."*

I went up the rim. Toes on the rock edge. I looked down, over Canary's body. Thirty feet to the water. The waves were cruel. Brutal. The spray hit my face and it was sharper than the rain. Little wet knives.

Did I imagine it?

Did I imagine the flicker?

It could have been shadows, playing across her eyelids.

Did I imagine the feel of her fingers, gripping my shirt?

It could have been the wind.

Did I imagine the sudden *beat beat* in her neck, cradled in the bend of my arm? Did I imagine the sigh? The breath that fogged up into the cold sea air?

I threw her in.

I put Canary in the churn.

I put her in, and watched her fall, all the way down. I watched until she disappeared into the white fluff.

I reached into my pocket, got out the black, chunky glasses, and threw them in after her.

Scout and I split up, after the churn. She never went to Harvard. She was driving back from Portland a few weeks later and her car spun out of control on the same stretch of road where we hit Canary. She went over the edge, sensible blue Toyota Corolla, rocks, waves, gone.

Asher snapped a vertebra his first game at Austin. He's in a wheelchair now.

Grace dropped her class ring down the garbage disposal while doing dishes. She reached in with her fingers to fetch it out, stretching . . . stretching . . . almost there . . .

Her hand was a useless, mangled mess. She'd never be a surgeon.

I didn't go to Italy.

I moved to Portland, and took art classes at a community college. I didn't make any friends. People avoided me. I had nightmares. I kept dreaming of Canary, kept lifting her up and throwing her in Devil's Churn, over and over again. I screamed in my sleep and my roommate complained and moved out.

I quit college after the first year. I live in a rat-infested cottage on Widow Lane now. It's small. You could almost call it a nook. I don't make much money, doing janitorial work at the Wolf Cove Aquarium. I can't afford any of the nicer apartments closer to town. And besides, I need to walk the beach. I need to watch the waves.

They never found her body.

Sometimes . . . sometimes I get this idea that she's still going to wash ashore. She'll look the same, exactly the same, just like the day I threw her in, the cold ocean preserving her like fish packed in ice. She'll float right in, right here at the foot of Widow Lane, where she used to live.

Sometimes I walk through the waves, knee deep, and I can't tell if it's the seaweed tickling my calves or her blond, blond hair.

Her grandfather died soon after she went missing. She was all he had.

I paint. Sea things. Waves and caps and crests and breakers and tides.

And I paint the beach. Over and over. Stormy sky, long stretch of sand, empty except for a naked girl with black, glassy eyes and yellow hair, long as seaweed, down to her toes.

Sometimes I wake up in the middle of the night and I think she's lying next to me, her hair spread out on my chest, her soft breaths going in and out like waves hitting rocks, *shush, shush*. I talk to her and she talks back, but her voice is different now, not breathy like it used to be, but deep, and distant, like the sea is pressing on it.

I've stopped eating fish. I see them at the seafood market in Wolf Cove. The salmon and the bass and the tuna. I look into their slippery, beady eyes . . . and I wonder if they saw her, swimming, down there in the dark. I wonder if she ran her small fingers down their scales as they swam by.

I wonder if she's going to come back. I wonder if she's going to come get me and drag me into the water with her.

Sometimes . . . sometimes I think I want her to.

Did I imagine it?

The flicker?

The fingers?

The beat?

The sigh?

Did I?

FAT GIRL WITH A KNIFE

Jonathan Maberry

-1-

She had a pretty name but she knew she wasn't pretty.

Kind of a thing with the girls in her family. None of the Allgood girls were making magazine covers.

Her oldest sister, Rose, was one of those college teacher types. Tall, thin, meatless, kind of gray-looking, with too much nose, no chin at all, and eyes that looked perpetually disappointed. She taught art history, so there was that. No one she taught would ever get a job in that field. There probably weren't jobs in that field. When was there ever a want-ad for art historian?

The sister between Rose and her was named Violet. She was the family rebel. Skinny because that's what drugs do; but not skinny in any way that made her look good. Best thing you could say about how she looked was that she looked dangerous. Skinny like a knife blade. Cold as one too. And her moods and actions tended to leave blood on the walls. Her track record with "choices" left her parents bleeding year after year. Violet was in Detroit now. Out of rehab again. No one expected it to stick.

Then there was the little one, Jasmine. She kept trying to get people to call her Jazz, but no one did. Jasmine was a red-haired bowling ball with crazy teeth. It would be cute except that Jasmine wasn't nice. She wasn't charming. She was a little monster and she *liked* being a little monster. People didn't let her be around their pets.

That left Dahlia.

Her.

Pretty name. She liked her name. She liked being herself. She liked who she was. She had a good mind. She had good thoughts. She understood the books she read and had insight into the music she downloaded. She didn't have many friends, but the ones she had knew they could trust her. And she wasn't mean-spirited, though there were people who could make a compelling counterargument. A lot of her problems, Dahlia knew, were the end results of the universe being a total bitch.

Dahlia always thought that she deserved the whole package. A great name. A nice face. At least a decent body. A name like Dahlia should be carried around on good legs or have some good boobs as conversation pieces. That would be fair. That would be nice.

Failing that, good skin would be cool.

Or great hair. You can get a lot of mileage out of great hair.

Anything would have been acceptable. Dahlia figured she didn't actually need much. The weight was bad enough; the complexion was insult to injury. But an eating disorder? Seriously? Why go there? Why make it *that* much harder to get through life? Just a little freaking courtesy from the powers that be. Let the gods of social interaction cut her *some* kind of break.

But . . . no.

Dahlia Allgood was, as so many kids had gone to great lengths to point out to her over the years, all bad. At least from the outside.

No amount of time in the gym—at school or the one her parents set up in the garage—seemed able to shake the extra weight from her body. She was fat. She wasn't big-boned. She wasn't a "solidly built girl," as her aunt Flora often said. It wasn't baby fat, and she knew she probably wouldn't grow out of it. She'd have to be fifteen feet tall to smooth it all out. She wasn't. Though at five-eight, she was a good height for punching loud-mouth jerks of both sexes. She'd always been fat and kids have always been kids. Faces had been punched. Faces would be punched. That's how it was.

But, yeah, she was fat and she knew it.

She hated it. She cried oceans about it. She yelled at God about it.

But she accepted it.

Dahlia also knew that there was precedent in her family for this being a lifelong thing. She had three aunts who collectively looked like the defensive line of the Green Bay Packers. Aunt Ivy was the biggest. Six feet tall, three hundred pounds. Dahlia suspected Ivy had thrown some punches of her own in her day. Ivy wasn't one to take anything from anyone.

Mom was no Sally Stick Figure either. She was always on one of those celebrity diets. Last year it was the Celery and Carrot Diet, and all she did was fart and turn orange. Before that it was a Cottage Cheese Diet that packed on twenty extra pounds. Apparently the "eat all you want" part of the pitch wasn't exactly true. This year it was the Salmon Diet. Dahlia figured that it was only a matter of time before Mom grew gills and began swimming upstream to spawn.

Well, maybe that would have happened if the world hadn't ended.

-2-

It did. The world ended.

On a Friday.

Somehow it didn't surprise Dahlia Allgood that the world would end on a Friday. What better way to screw up the weekend?

-3-

Like most important things in the world, Dahlia wasn't paying that much attention to it. To the world. To current events.

She was planning revenge.

Again.

It wasn't an obsession with her, but she had some frequent flier miles. If people didn't push her, she wouldn't even think about pushing back.

She was fat and unattractive. That wasn't up for debate, and she couldn't change a few thousand years of developing standards for beauty. On the other hand, neither of those facts made it okay for anyone to mess with her.

That's what people didn't seem to get.

Maybe someone sent a mass text that it was okay to say things about her weight. Or stick pictures of pork products on her locker. Or make *oink-oink* noises when she was puffing her way around the track in gym. If so, she didn't get that text and she did not approve of the message.

Screw that.

It's not that she was one of the mean girls. Dahlia suspected the mean girls were the ones who hated themselves the most. And Dahlia didn't even hate herself. She liked herself. She liked her mind. She liked her taste in music and books and boys and things that mattered. She didn't laugh when people tripped. She didn't take it as a personal win when someone else—someone thinner or prettier—hit an emotional wall. Dahlia knew she had her faults, but being a heartless or vindictive jerk wasn't part of that.

Revenge was a different thing. That wasn't being vindictive. It was—as she once read in an old novel—a thirst for justice. Dahlia wanted to be either a lawyer or a cop, so that whole justice thing was cool with her.

Justice—or, let's call it by the right name, revenge—had to be managed, though. You had to understand your own limits, and be real with your own level of cool. Dahlia spent enough time in her head to know who she was. And wasn't. So, when someone did something to her, she didn't try to swap cool insults, or posture with attitude, or any of that. Instead she got even.

When Marcy Van Der Meer—and, side note, Dahlia didn't think anyone in an urban high school should have a last name with three separate words—sent her those pictures last month? Yeah, she took action. The pictures had apparently been taken in the hall that time Dahlia dropped her books. The worst of them was taken from directly behind her as she bent over to pick them up. Can we say *butt crack*?

The picture went out to a whole lot of kids. To pretty much everyone who thought they mattered. Or everyone Marcy though mattered. Everyone who would laugh.

Dahlia had spent half an hour crying in the bathroom. Big, noisy, blubbering sobs. Nose-runny sobs, the kind that blow snot bubbles. The kind that hurt your chest. The kind that she knew, with absolute clarity, were going to leave a mark on her forever. Even if she never saw Marcy again after school, even if Dahlia somehow became thin and gorgeous, she was never going to lose the memory of how it felt to cry like that. Knowing that while she cried made it all a lot worse.

Then she washed her face and brushed her mouse-colored hair and plotted her revenge.

Dahlia swiped Marcy's car keys during second period. She slipped them back into her bag before last bell. Marcy could never prove that it was Dahlia who smeared dog poop all over her leather seats and packed it like cement into the air-conditioning vents. Who could prove that the bundle of it she left duct-taped to the engine had been her doing? No one could be put under oath to say they saw Dahlia anywhere near the car. And besides, the keys were in Marcy's purse when she went to look for them, right?

Okay, sure, it was petty. And childish. And maybe criminal. All of that.

Did it feel good afterward?

Dahlia wasn't sure how she felt about it. She thought it was just; but she didn't spend a lot of time actually gloating. Except maybe a couple of days later when somebody wrote "Marcy Van Der Poop" on her locker with a Sharpie. That hadn't been Dahlia, and she had no idea who'd done it. That? Yeah, she spent a lot of happy hours chuckling over that. It didn't take away the memory of that time crying in the bathroom, but it made it easier to carry it around.

It was that kind of war.

Like when Chuck Bellamy talked his brain-deprived minion, Dault, into running up behind her and pulling down the top of her sundress. Or, tried to, anyway. Dahlia was a big girl, but she had small boobs. She could risk wearing a sundress on a hot day with no bra. Chuck and Dault saw that as a challenge. They thought she was an easy target.

They underestimated Dahlia.

Dahlia heard Dault's big feet slapping on the ground and turned just as he reached for the top hem of her dress.

Funny thing about those jujitsu lessons. She'd only taken them for one summer, but there was some useful stuff. And fingers are like breadsticks if you twist them the right way.

Dault had to go to the nurse and then the hospital for splints, and he dimed Chuck pretty thoroughly. Both of them got suspended. There was some talk about filing sexual harassment charges, but Dahlia said she'd pass if it was only this one time. She was making eye contact with Chuck when she said that. Although Chuck was a mouth-breathing Neanderthal, he understood the implications of being on a sexual predator watch list.

Dahlia never wore a sundress to school again. It was a defeat even though she'd won the round. The thought of how it would feel to be exposed like that . . . Everyone had a cell phone, every cell phone had a camera. One photo would kill her, and she knew it. So she took her small victory and let them win that war.

So, it was like that.

But over time, had anyone actually been paying attention and keeping score, they'd have realized that there were very few repeat offenders.

Sadly, a lot of kids seem to have "insult the fat girl" on their bucket list. It's right there, just above "insult the ugly girl." So they kept at it.

And she kept getting her revenge.

Today it was going to be Tucker Anderson's car. Dahlia had filched one of her dad's knives. Dad had a lot of knives. It probably wasn't because he was surrounded by so many large, fierce women, but Dahlia couldn't rule it out. Dad liked to hunt. Every once in a while he'd take off so he could kill something. Over the last five years he'd killed five deer, all of them females. Dahlia tried not to read anything into that.

She did wish her dad would have tried to be a little cooler about it. When they watched *The Walking Dead* together, Dahlia asked him if he ever considered using a crossbow, like that cute redneck, Daryl. Dad said no. He'd never even touched a crossbow. He said guns were easier. Ah well.

The knife she took was a Buck hunting knife with a bone handle and a four-inch blade. The kind of knife that would get her expelled and maybe arrested if anyone found it. She kept it hidden, and in a few minutes she planned to slip out to the parking lot and slash all four of Tucker's tires. Why? He'd Photoshopped her face onto a bunch of downloaded porn of really fat women having ugly kinds of sex. Bizarre stuff that Dahlia, who considered herself open-minded and worldly, couldn't quite grasp, and then glued them to the outside of the first-floor girls' bathroom.

Tucker didn't get caught because guys like Tucker don't get caught. Word got around, though. Tucker was tight with Chuck, Dault, and Marcy. This was the latest battle in the war. Her enemies were persistent and effortlessly cruel. Dahlia was clever and careful.

Then, as we know, the world ended.

-4-

Here's how it happened as far as Dahlia was concerned.

She didn't watch the news that morning, hadn't read the papers—because who reads newspapers?—and hadn't cruised the top stories on Twitter. The first she knew about anything going wrong was when good old Marcy Van Der Poop came screaming into the girls' room.

Dahlia was in a stall and she tensed. Not because Marcy was

screaming—girls scream all the time; they have the lungs for it, so why not?—but because it was an inconvenient time. Dahlia hated using the bathroom for anything more elaborate than taking a pee. Last night's Taco Thursday at the Allgood house was messing with that agenda in some pretty horrific ways. Dahlia had waited until the middle of a class period to slip out and visit the most remote girls' room in the entire school for just this purpose.

But in came Marcy, screaming her head off.

Dahlia jammed her hand against the stall door to make sure it would stay shut.

She waited for the scream to turn into a laugh. Or to break off and be part of some phone call. Or for it to be anything except what it was.

Marcy kept screaming, though.

Until she stopped.

Suddenly.

With a big in-gulp of air.

Dahlia leaned forward to listen. There was only a crack between the door and frame and she could see a sliver of Marcy as she leaned over the sink.

Was she throwing up?

Washing her face?

What the hell was she doing?

Then she saw Marcy's shoulders rise and fall. Very fast. The way someone will when . . .

That's when she heard the sobs.

Long. Deep. Badly broken sobs.

The kind of sobs Dahlia was way too familiar with.

Out there, on the other side of that sliver, Marcy Van Der Meer's knees buckled and she slid down to the floor. To the floor of the girls' bathroom. A public bathroom.

Marcy curled herself into a hitching, twitching, spasming ball.

She pulled herself all the way under the bank of dirty sinks.

Sobbing.

Crying like some broken thing.

Dahlia, despite everything, felt something in her own eyes. On her cheeks.

She tried to be shocked at the presence of tears.

Marcy was the hateful witch. If she wasn't messing with Dahlia directly, then she was getting her friends and minions to do it. She was the subject of a thousand of Dahlia's fantasies about vehicular manslaughter, about STDs that transformed her into a mottled crone, about being eaten by rats.

Marcy the hag.

Huddled on the filthy floor, her head buried down, arms wrapped around her body, knees drawn up. Her pretty red blouse streaked with dirt. Crying so deeply that it made almost no sound. Crying the way people do when the sobs hurt like punches.

Dahlia sat there. Frozen. Kind of stunned, really. Marcy?

Marcy was way too self-conscious to be like that.

Ever.

Unless . . . What could have happened to her to put Marcy here, on that floor, in that condition? Until now Dahlia wouldn't have bet Marcy had enough of a genuine human soul to be this hurt.

The bathroom was filled with the girl's pain.

Dahlia knew that what she had to do was nothing. She needed to sit there and finish her business and pretend that she wasn't here at all. She needed to keep that stall door locked. She needed to not even breathe very loud. That's what she needed to do.

Absolutely.

-5-

It's not what she did, though. Because, when it was all said and done, she was Dahlia Allgood.

And Dahlia Allgood wasn't a monster.

-6-

She finished in the toilet. Got dressed. Stood up. Leaned her forehead against the cold metal of the stall door for a long ten seconds. Reached back and flushed. Then she opened the door.

Turning that lock took more courage than anything she'd ever done. She wasn't at all sure why she did it. She pulled the door in, stepped out. Stood there. The sound of the flushing toilet was loud and she waited through the cycle until there was silence.

Marcy Van Der Meer lay in the same position. Her body trembled with those deep sobs. If she heard the flush, or cared about it, she gave no sign at all.

Dahlia went over to the left-hand bank of sinks, the ones farther from Marcy. The ones closer to the door. She washed her hands, cutting looks in the mirror at the girl. Waiting for her to look up. To say something. To go back to being Marcy. It was so much easier to despise someone if they stayed shallow and hateful.

But . . .

"Hey," said Dahlia. Her throat was phlegmy and her voice broke on the word. She coughed to clear it, then tried again. "Hey. Um . . . hey, are you . . . y' know . . . okay?"

Marcy did not move, did not react. She didn't even seem to have heard.

"Marcy—?"

Nothing. Dahlia stood there, feeling the weight of indecision. The exit door was right there. Marcy hadn't looked up, she had no idea who was in the bathroom. She'd never know if Dahlia left. That was the easy decision. Just go. Step out of whatever drama Marcy was wrapped up in. Let the little snot sort it out for herself. Dahlia didn't have to do anything or say anything. This wasn't hers to handle. Marcy hadn't even asked for help.

Just go.

On the other hand . . .

Dahlia chewed her lip. Marcy looked bad. Soaked and dirty now, small and helpless.

She wanted to walk away. She wanted to sneer at her. Maybe give her a nice solid kick in her skinny little ass. She wanted to use this moment of alone time to lay into her and tell her what a total piece of crap she was.

That's what Dahlia truly wanted to do.

She stood there. The overhead lights threw her shadows across the floor. A big pear shape. Too small up top, too big everywhere else. Weird hair. Thick arms, thicker legs. A shadow of a girl who would never—ever—get looked at the way this weeping girl would. And it occurred to Dahlia that if the circumstances were reversed, Marcy would see it as an open door and a formal invite to unload her cruelty guns. No . . . she'd have reacted to this opportunity as if it were a moral imperative. There wouldn't be any internal debate over what to do. That path would be swept clear and lighted with torches.

Sure. That was true.

But part of what made Dahlia *not* one of *them*—the overgrown single-cell organisms pretending to be the cute kids at school—was the fact that she wasn't wired the same way. Not outside, God knows, but not inside either. Dahlia was Dahlia. Different species altogether.

She took a step. Away from the door.

"Marcy . . ." she said, softening her voice. "Are you okay? What happened?"

The girl stopped trembling.

Just like that. She froze.

Yeah, thought Dahlia, *you heard me that time.*

She wanted to roll her eyes at the coming drama, but there was no one around who mattered to see it.

Dahlia tried to imagine what the agenda would be. First Marcy would be vulnerable because of whatever brought her in here. Breakup with Mason, her studly boyfriend du jour. Something like that. There would be some pseudo in-the-moment girl talk about how rotten boys are, blah-blah-blah. As if they both knew, as if they both had the same kinds of problems. Dahlia would help her up and there would be shared tissues, or handfuls of toilet paper. Anything to wipe Marcy's nose and blot her eyes. That would transition onto her clothes, which were wet and stained. Somehow Dahlia—the rescuer—would have to make useful suggestions for how to clean the clothes, or maybe volunteer to go to Marcy's car or locker for a clean sweater. Then, as soon as Marcy felt solid ground under her feet again, she would clamp her popular girl cool in place and, by doing that, distance herself from Dahlia. After it was all over, Marcy would either play the role of the queen who occasionally gave a secret nod of marginal acceptance to the peasant who helped her. Or the whole thing would spin around and Marcy would be ten times more vicious just to prove to Dahlia that she had never—*ever*—been vulnerable. It was some version of that kind of script.

Marcy still, at this point, had not turned. Dahlia could still get the heck out of there.

But . . . she *had* reacted. She'd stopped sobbing. She was listening.

Ah, crap, thought Dahlia, knowing she was trapped inside the drama now. Moving forward was inevitable. It was like being on a conveyor belt heading to the checkout scanner.

"Marcy?" she said again. "Are you hurt? Can I . . . like . . . help in some way?"

An awkward line, awkwardly delivered.

Marcy did not move. Her body remained absolutely still. At first that was normal. People freeze when they realize someone else is there, or when they need to decide how to react. But that lasts a second or two.

This was lasting too long. It wasn't normal anymore. Getting less normal with each second that peeled itself off the clock and dropped onto that dirty bathroom floor.

Dahlia took another step closer. And another. That was when she began to notice that there were other things that weren't normal.

The dirt on Marcy's red blouse was wrong somehow.

The blouse wasn't just stained. It was torn. Ripped. Ragged in places.

And the red color was wrong. It was darker in some places. One shade of dark red where it had soaked up water from the floor. A different and much darker shade of red around the right shoulder and sleeve.

Much, much darker.

A thick, glistening dark red that looked like . . .

"Marcy—?"

Marcy Van Der Meer's body suddenly began to tremble again. To shudder. To convulse.

That's when Dahlia knew that something was a lot more wrong than boyfriend problems.

Marcy's arms and legs abruptly began thrashing and whipping around, striking the row of sinks, hammering on the floor, banging off the pipes. Marcy's head snapped from side to side and she uttered a long, low, juddery, inarticulate moan of mingled pain and—

And what?

Dahlia almost ran away.

Almost.

Instead she grabbed Marcy's shoulders and pulled her away from the sinks, dragged her to the middle of the floor. Marcy was a tiny thing, a hundred pounds. Dahlia was strong. Size gives you some advantages. Dahlia turned Marcy over onto her back, terrified that this was an epileptic seizure. She had nothing to put between the girl's teeth to keep her from biting her tongue. Instead she dug into the purse she wore slung over her shoulder. Found Dad's knife, removed the blade and shoved it back into the bag, took the heavy leather sheath and pried Marcy's clenched teeth apart. Marcy snapped and seemed to be trying to bite her, but it was the seizure. Dahlia forced the sheath between Marcy's teeth and those perfect pearly whites bit deep into the hand-tooled leather.

The seizure went on and on. It locked Marcy's muscles and at the same time made her thrash. It had to be pulling muscles, maybe tearing some. Marcy's skirt rode high on her thighs, exposing pink underwear. Embarrassed for them both, Dahlia tugged the skirt down, smoothed it. Then she gathered Marcy to her, wrapped her arms around Marcy's, pulled the soaked and convulsing enemy to her, and held her there. Protected. As safe as the moment allowed, waiting for the storm to pass.

All the while she looked at the dark stains on Marcy's shoulder. At the ragged red of her shirt. At the skin that was exposed by the torn material.

There was a cut there and she bent closer to look.

No. Not a cut.

A *bite*.

She looked down at Marcy. Her eyes had rolled up high and white and there was no expression at all on her rigid face. Those teeth kept biting into the leather. What *was* this? Was it epilepsy at all? Or was it something else? There were no rattlesnakes or poisonous anythings around as far as Dahlia knew. What else could give a bite that might make someone sick? A rabid dog? She racked her brain for what she knew of rabies. Was that something that happened fast? She didn't think so. Maybe this was unrelated to the bite. An allergic reaction. Something.

The spasms stopped suddenly. Bang, just like that.

Marcy Van Der Meer went totally limp in Dahlia's arms, her arms and legs sprawled out. Like she suddenly passed out. Like she was . . .

"Marcy?" asked Dahlia.

She craned her neck to look at Marcy's face.

The eyes were still rolled back, the facial muscles slack now, mouth hanging open. The leather sheath slid out from between her teeth, dark with spit.

Except that it wasn't spit.

Not really.

The pale deerskin leather of the knife sheath was stained with something that glistened almost purple in the glare of the bathroom fluorescents.

"Marcy?" Dahlia repeated, shaking her a little. "Come on now, this isn't funny."

It wasn't. Nor was Marcy making a joke. Dahlia knew it.

It took a whole lot of courage for Dahlia to press her fingers into the side of Marcy's throat. Probably the toughest thing she'd ever had to do. They taught how to do it in health class. How to take a pulse.

She checked. She tried to listen with her fingers.

Nothing.

She moved her fingers, pressed deeper.

Nothing.

Then.

Something.

A pulse.

Maybe a pulse.

Something.

There it was again.

Not a pulse.

A twitch.

"Thank God," said Dahlia, and she realized with absolute clarity that she *was* relieved that Marcy wasn't dead. Dahlia fished around for the actual pulse. That would have been better, more reassuring.

Felt another twitch. Not in the throat this time. Marcy's right hand jumped. Right hand. Then, a moment later, her left leg kicked out.

"No," said Dahlia, fearing a fresh wave of convulsions.

The twitches kept up. Left hand. Left arm. Hip buck. Both feet. Random, though. Not intense. Not with the kind of raw power that had racked Marcy a few minutes ago.

It was then that Dahlia realized that this whole time she could have been calling for help. *Should* have been calling. She shifted to lay Marcy on the floor, then dug into her purse to find her cell. It was there, right under the knife. Directly under it. The knife Dahlia forgot she'd put unsheathed into the bag.

"Ow!" she cried, and whipped her hand out, trailing drops of blood. Dahlia gaped at the two-inch slice along the side of her hand.

Not deep, but bloody. And it hurt like hell. Blood welled from it and ran down her wrist, dropped to the floor, spattered on Marcy's already bloodstained blouse.

She opened the bag, removed the knife, set it on the floor next to her, found some tissues, found the phone, she punched 911 and tucked the phone between cheek and shoulder, pressing the tissues to the cut.

The phone rang.

And rang. And, strangely, kept ringing. Dahlia frowned. Shouldn't the police answer 911 calls pretty quickly? Six rings? Seven? Eight?

"Come on!" she growled.

The phone kept ringing.

No one ever answered.

Dahlia finally lowered her phone, punched the button to end the call. Chewed her lip for a moment, trying to decide who to call next.

She called her mom.

The phone rang.

And rang. And went to voicemail.

She tried her aunt Ivy. Same thing. She tried her dad. His line rang twice and the call was answered.

Or—the call went through. But no one actually said anything. Not Dad, not anyone. After two rings Dahlia heard an open line and some noise. Sounds that she couldn't quite make sense of.

"Dad?" she asked, then repeated it with more urgency. "Dad? *Dad?*"

The sounds on the other end of the call were weird. Messy-sounding. Like a dog burying its muzzle in a big bowl of Alpo.

But Dad never answered that call.

That's when Dahlia started to really get scared.

That was the point—after all those failed calls, after that bizarre, noisy, not-a-real-answer call—that she realized that something was wrong. A lot more wrong than Marcy Van Der Poop having a bad day.

She turned to look at Marcy.

Marcy, as it happened, had just turned to look at her.

Marcy's eyes were no longer rolled up in their sockets. She looked right at Dahlia. And then Marcy smiled.

Though, even in the moment, even shocked and scared, Dahlia knew that this wasn't a smile. The lips pulled back, there was a lot of teeth, but there was no happiness in that smile. There wasn't even the usual mean spite. There was nothing.

Just like in the eyes.

There . . .

. . . was . . .

. . . nothing.

That's when Dahlia really got scared.

That's when Marcy suddenly sat up, reached for her with hands that no longer twitched, and tried to bite Dahlia's face off.

-7-

Marcy let out a scream like a panther. High and shrill and ear-shattering.

She flung herself at Dahlia and suddenly the little princess was all fingernails and snapping teeth and surprising strength. The two girls fell back onto the wet floor. Dahlia screamed too. Really loud. A big, long wail of total surprise and horror.

Teeth snapped together with a porcelain *clack* an inch from her throat. Marcy bore her down and began climbing on top of her, moving weirdly, moving more like an animal than a girl. She was far stronger than Dahlia would have imagined, but it wasn't some kind of superpower. No, Marcy was simply going totally nuts on her, throwing everything she had into attacking. Being insane.

Being . . .

Dahlia had no word for it. All she could do or think about was not dying.

The teeth snapped again and Dahlia twisted away, but it was so close that for a moment she and the crazy girl were cheek to cheek.

"Stop it!" screamed Dahlia, shoving at Marcy with all her strength.

Marcy flipped up and over and thudded hard onto the concrete floor. She lay there, stunned for a moment.

Dahlia was stunned too. She'd never really used her full strength before either. Never had to. Not even in jujitsu or field hockey or any of the other things she'd tried as part of a failed fitness and weight loss program. She'd never tried to really push it to the limit before. Why would she?

But now.

Marcy had gone flying like she was made of crepe paper.

Dahlia stared for a second. She said, "Hunh."

Marcy stared back. She hissed.

And flung herself at Dahlia as if falling hard on the ground didn't matter.

Dahlia punched her.

In the face.

In that prom-girl face.

Hard.

Really damn hard.

Dahlia wasn't sure what was going to happen. She didn't think it through. She was way too scared for anything as orderly as that. She just hauled off and hit.

Knuckles met expensive nose job.

Nose collapsed.

Marcy's head rocked back on her neck.

She went flying backward. Landed hard. Again.

Dahlia scrambled to her feet and in doing so kicked something that went skittering across the floor.

The knife.

She looked at it. Marcy, with her smashed nose and vacant eyes, looked at it.

With another mountain lion scream, Marcy scrambled onto hands and feet and launched herself at Dahlia. For a long half second Dahlia contemplated grabbing that knife; it was right there. But this was Marcy. Crazy, sure, maybe on something, and certainly no kind of friend. Still Marcy, though. Dahlia had known her since second grade. Hated her since then, but that didn't make this a grab-a-knife-and-stab-her moment.

Did it?

Marcy slammed into her, but Dahlia was ready for it. She stepped into the rush and hip-checked the little blonde.

Marcy hit Dahlia. And Marcy rebounded. As if she'd hit a wall.

Any time before that moment, such a clash, such a demonstration of body weight and mass, would have crushed Dahlia. It would have meant a whole night of crying in her room and eating ice cream and writing hate letters to herself in her diary.

That was a moment ago. That was maybe yesterday. This morning. Now, though, things were different.

Marcy hit the edge of a sink and fell. But it didn't stop her. She got back to her feet as if pain didn't matter. She rushed forward again.

So, Dahlia punched her again.

This time she put her whole heart and soul into it. Along with her entire body.

The impact was huge.

Marcy's head stopped right at the end of that punch. Her body kept going, though, and it looked like someone had pulled a rug out from under her feet. They flew into the air and Marcy flipped backward and down.

Which is when a bad, bad moment got worse.

Marcy landed on the back of her head.

The sound was awful. A big, dropped-cantaloupe splat of a sound. The kind of sound that can never ever be something good.

Red splashed outward from the back of Marcy's head. Her body flopped onto the ground, arms and legs wide, clothes going the wrong way, eyes wide.

And Marcy Van Der Meer did not move again.

Not then. And, Dahlia knew with sudden and total horror, not ever again.

She stood there, wide-legged, panting like she'd run up three flights of stairs, eyes bugging out, mouth agape, fist still clenched. Right there on the floor, still close enough to bend down and touch, was a dead person. A *murdered* person.

Right there was her victim.

Her lips mouthed a few words. Maybe curses, maybe prayers. Maybe nonsense. Didn't matter. Nothing she could say was going to hit the reset button. Marcy was dead. Her brains were leaking out of her skull. Her blood was mixing with the dirty water on the bathroom floor.

Dahlia was frozen into the moment, as if she and Marcy were figures in a digital photo. In a strange way she could actually see this image. It was framed and hung on the wall of her mind.

This is when my life ended, she thought. Not just Marcy's. Hers too.

She was thinking that, and the words kept replaying in her head, when she heard the screams from outside.

-8-

For a wild, irrational moment Dahlia thought someone had seen her kill Marcy and that's what they were screaming about.

The moment passed.

The screams were too loud. And there were too many of them.

Plus, it wasn't just girl screams. There were guys screaming too.

Dahlia tore herself out of the framed image of that moment and stepped back into the real world. There were no windows in the girls' room, so she tottered over to the door, her feet unsteady beneath her. The ground seemed to tilt and rock.

At the door she paused, listened. Definitely screams.

In the hallway.

She took a breath and opened the door.

The bathroom was on the basement level. This part of the school was usually empty during class. Just the bathroom, the janitor's office, the boiler room, and the gym.

She only opened the door a crack, just enough to peer out.

Dault was out there, and she froze.

Dault was running, and he was screaming.

There were three other kids chasing him. Freshmen, Dahlia thought, but she didn't know their names. They howled as they chased Dault. Howled like wildcats. Howled like Marcy had done.

Dault's screams were different. Normal human screams, but completely filled with panic. He ran past the bathroom door with the three freshmen right behind him. The group of them passed another group. Two kids—Joe Something and Tammy Something. Tenth graders. They were on their hands and knees on either side of one of Marcy's friends. Kim.

Kim lay sprawled like Marcy was sprawled. All wide-open and still.

While Joe and Tammy bent over her and . . .

Dahlia's mind absolutely refused to finish the thought.

What Joe and Tammy were doing was obvious. All that blood, the torn skin and clothes. But it was impossible. This wasn't TV. This wasn't a monster movie.

This was real life and it was right now and this could not be happening.

Tammy was burying her face in Kim's stomach and shook her head the way a dog will. When tearing at . . .

No, no, no, no . . .

"No!" Dahlia's thoughts bubbled out as words. "No!"

She kept saying it.

Quiet at first.

Then loud.

Then way too loud.

Joe and Tammy stopped doing what they were doing and they both looked across the hall at the girls' bathroom door. At her. They bared their bloody teeth and snarled. Their eyes were empty, but there was hate and hunger in those snarls.

Suddenly Joe and Tammy were not kneeling. They leaped to their feet and came howling across the hall toward the bathroom door. Dahlia screamed and threw her weight against it, slamming it shut. There were two solid thuds from outside and the hardwood shook with what had to have been a bone-breaking impact. No cries of pain, though.

Then the pounding of fists. Hammering, hammering. And those snarls.

Far down the hall, Dault was yelling for help, begging for someone to help him. No one seemed to.

Dahlia kept herself pressed against the door. There were no locks on the bathroom doors. There were no other exits. Behind her on the floor were three things. A dead girl who had been every bit as fierce as the two attacking the door. A cell phone that had seemed to try to tell her that something was wrong with the world.

And the knife.

Dad's knife.

Just lying there.

Almost within reach.

She looked at it as the door shuddered and shuddered. She thought about what was happening. People acting crazy. People—go on, she told herself, say it—eating people. Marcy had been bitten. Marcy had gone into some kind of shock and seemed to stop breathing. No. She had stopped breathing. Then Marcy had opened her eyes and gone all bitey.

As much as Dahlia knew that this was insane and impossible, she knew there was a name for what was happening. Not a name that belonged to TV and movies and games anymore. A name that was right here. Close enough to bite her.

She looked down at Marcy as if the corpse could confirm it. And . . . maybe it did. Nothing Dahlia had done to the girl had worked. Not until she made her fall down and smash her skull. Not until Marcy's brain had been damaged.

All of those facts tumbled together like puzzle pieces that were trying to force themselves into a picture. A picture that had that name.

Began with a z.

"Aim for the head," whispered Dahlia, and her voice was thick with tears. "Oh God, oh God, oh God."

Tammy and Joe kept slamming into the door. The knife was still there. Very good blade. And Dahlia was very strong. She knew how to put her weight into a punch. Or a stab.

"...*God*..."

When she realized that she had to let go of the door to grab the knife, it changed something inside of her. She waited until the next bang on the door, waited for them to pull back to hit it again, then she let go and dove for the knife, scooped it up as the door slammed inward, spun, met their charge.

Tammy, smaller and faster, came first.

Dahlia kicked her in the stomach. Not a good kick, but solid. Tammy jerked to a stop and bent forward. Dahlia swung the knife as hard as she could and buried the point in the top of the girl's skull. In that spot where babies' skulls are soft. The blade went in with a wet crunch. Tammy dropped as quickly and suddenly as if Dahlia had thrown a switch. One minute zombie, next minute dead.

That left Joe.

A sophmore boy. Average for his age. As tall as Dahlia.

Not quite in her weight class.

She tore the knife free, grabbed him by the shirt with her other hand, swung him around into the sinks, forced him down and . . . *stab*. She put some real mass into it.

Joe died.

Dahlia staggered back and let him slide to the floor.

Outside she heard Dault screaming as he ran in and out of rooms, through openings in the accordion walls, trying to shake the pack of pursuers.

Dahlia caught a glimpse of her own face in the row of mirrors.

Fat girl with crazy hair and bloodstains on her clothes. Fat girl with wild eyes.

Fat girl with a knife.

Despite everything—despite the insanity of it, the horror of it, the knowledge that things were all going to slide down the toilet in her world—Dahlia Allgood smiled at herself.

Then she lumbered over to the door, tore it open, and yelled to Dault.

"Over here!"

He saw her and almost stopped. She was bloody, she had that knife. "W-what—?"

"Get in here," said Dahlia raising the blade. "I'll protect you."

Yeah.

She was smiling as she said that.

Inspired by the 2009 film *Zombieland* and the 1968 film *Night of the Living Dead*

SLEEPLESS

JAY KRISTOFF

She takes her time.

I'm used to it by now. It's always the same. She'll be late to her own funeral, this girl. But she's worth waiting for. When I think about her, I still get that unbearable lightness in my stomach. You know the kind—halfway between giddy and puking your lungs up. I can't remember a girl making me feel this way before. Or at least, I don't want to.

Funny thing is, I don't even know her real name.

The house creaks around me, arthritis swelling old timber bones. The dark outside my bedroom window is full of crickets and the pulse of the distant freeway. If I listen hard enough, I can hear the rumble of farm machinery and soft voices. I wonder what the hell anyone out here has to talk about, but I can't make out the words.

I was half-asleep. Dreaming of long blond hair and pretty blue eyes. The selfie she sent is stuck to the old laptop on the bed beside me. When the speakers ping to let me know she's finally arrived, me and the butterflies in my stomach all wake up at once. When I see her avi on the screen, their fizzy wings start beating at my insides.

I think she might be the one.

2muchcOff33_grrl: hey wolfie

My fingers don't shake much as I type my reply.

wolfboy_97: hey cOff33

2muchcOff33_grrl: wut u doin

wolfboy_97: waitin on u like alwayz ☺

2muchcOff33_grrl: ya soz, my mom being a cow

wolfboy_97: lol mine 2

2muchcOff33_grrl: wut she on ur case about now?

wolfboy_97: got a C in history and she flipped

2muchcOff33_grrl: flip over a C lol

wolfboy_97: ikr

2muchcOff33_grrl: i could help.

2muchcOff33_grrl: I'm real gud @ history

wolfboy_97: didn't know that

2muchcOff33_grrl: o ya

2muchcOff33_grrl: can learn a lot

2muchcOff33_grrl: mistakes of the past & all

wolfboy_97: ooh deep

2muchcOff33_grrl: not like ur other girls huh

wolfboy_97: ur not like anyone i know

2muchcOff33_grrl: ☺

wolfboy_97: so wut u doin?

2muchcOff33_grrl: homework

wolfboy_97: *yawn*

2muchcOff33_grrl: maybe u should try it sometime, C boy

wolfboy_97: so mean ☹

2muchcOff33_grrl: u luv it

wolfboy_97: maybe. u luv me?

2muchcOff33_grrl: mmmmaybe

wolfboy_97: only maybe?

2muchcOff33_grrl: how can I say I luv u if I've nvr met u?

wolfboy_97: lol u've met me every nite for 6 months

2muchcOff33_grrl: chat not the same as IRL

2muchcOff33_grrl: i thought u'd *wanna* meet me

2muchcOff33_grrl: thought u boys were only after 1 thing :P

wolfboy_97: i not like dat

2muchcOff33_grrl: pity ;)

wolfboy_97: 0_0

2muchcOff33_grrl: u goin 2 school 2morrow?

wolfboy_97: ya why?

2muchcOff33_grrl: i dun wanna sleep

wolfboy_97: bad dreams again?

2muchcOff33_grrl: always

wolfboy_97: ☹

wolfboy_97: wut r ur dreams about?

2muchcOff33_grrl: voices

wolfboy_97: wut they say?

2muchcOff33_grrl: sad stuff

2muchcOff33_grrl: makes me cry

2muchcOff33_grrl: makes me mad

2muchcOff33_grrl: sometimes when I open my eyes i think i can still hear them

wolfboy_97: D:

2muchcOff33_grrl: need sumthing to keep me awake tonite

2muchcOff33_grrl: coffee not working

2muchcOff33_grrl: figured I'd use u ;)

wolfboy_97: orly

2muchcOff33_grrl: ya rly

2muchcOff33_grrl: wut u wearing?

wolfboy_97: just sum shorts.

wolfboy_97: y

wolfboy_97: wut U wearing?

2muchcOff33_grrl: i show u

2muchcOff33_grrl: rdy?

wolfboy_97: k

2muchcOff33_grrl: imgfile:thong_1.jpg

wolfboy_97: @_@

"Justin!"

The shout jars me out of the moment. Chokes the blood flow south. I slap the laptop closed and roll out of bed, shrug on a band T-shirt old enough to be in the vintage stores. Her voice trails down the hallway again.

"Justin!"

"Coming, Momma!"

The scent of roses and vanilla wraps me tight as I step out of my room. Cloying. Choking. I hurry down the creaking floorboards toward her door. A crucifix of plain, dark wood nailed into its center. A ribbon of light spilling beneath. The walls are lined with dusty family pictures. Soldiers and nurses. Black-and-white. Watching as I walk past.

I knock gently, step inside. And there she is. Wrapped in a fluffy pink robe embroidered with tiny red flowers. Surrounded by plump white pillows and a thin gauze of mosquito netting. Scented candles burn on the nightstand, vanilla and roses thick in the air. Her hair is the color of old straw. Crow's-feet eyes of milky blue. Staring right at me.

Through me.

"What were you doing?" she demands.

"Nothing, Momma."

"You were talking to her again, weren't you?"

"No, I wasn't."

"Don't you lie to me, boy, God and almighty Jesus help me, don't you lie."

I'm not looking at her face, but I can feel her eyes on me. Sometimes I swear I can feel them when I leave the house. When I sleep or eat or shower. She never blinks.

"I'm not lying, Momma."

"She's just like the others, you know. They're all the same. They only want one thing. You hear me?"

"I hear you, Momma."

Bible on the nightstand beside her scented candles, open to her favorite book.

The last book.

"They don't love you, Justin," she says. "Nobody loves you like I do. A boy's best friend is always his momma. You know that, don't you?"

"Yes, Momma."

"You're a good boy. My special boy."

I know what comes next.

The butterflies in my stomach are all dead.

"Come give your momma a kiss."

The three feet to her side feel like miles. I paw my way through the mosquito netting and sit beside her on the creaking mattress. The bed that's been her prison since the accident. This close, I can see how thin she's gotten. Skin stretched on her bones. She used to sing to me when I was little. Songs of praise and glory to His name. She stopped the day Dad left us, though.

My stepmom is two years older than I am.

I guess I wouldn't feel like singing either . . .

I take her hand. Stick-thin fingers. Cracker-brittle bones.

"I love you, Justin."

"I love you too, Momma."

"Don't you ever leave me."

"I won't. I promise."

Where would I go?

As I lean in close, I smell what's coming for her, dark and sickly sweet under the candle smoke. I kiss her cheek. Sandpaper skin against my lips. Her eyes still locked on mine.

"My special boy."

2muchcOff33_grrl: where'd u go last nite

I'm in the living room, sprawled on the couch. The TV is on; coupon sales and silicon lips and the milk-carton faces of missing people on the news. A Mexican guy a little younger than me with greasy hair and pock-marked skin. Yearbook photos of a girl with an orthodontist smile and long blond pigtails. Some old kiddyqueer the cops probably won't look too hard for, all comb-over and empty eyes.

Black-and-white photographs on the walls and dirty dishes on the coffee table and slowly dying pot plants. I try to keep the place clean, but it's hard to find the time. I suggested to Momma we get a maid once. She got so angry, she didn't talk to me for a week.

I didn't mind much.

wolfboy_97: internet went down, sorry

2muchcOff33_grrl: u missed out, had 2 keep myself awake

wolfboy_97: ☹

2muchcOff33_grrl: beginning 2 think u dun like me anymore

wolfboy_97: u kidding i'm crazy 4 u

2muchcOff33_grrl: y u bail every time i get sexty then

wolfboy_97: told u my net went down.

2muchcOff33_grrl: :P

2muchcOff33_grrl: so

wolfboy_97: so?

2muchcOff33_grrl: so when can we meet irl?

wolfboy_97: not yet

2muchcOff33_grrl: y not? i want to see u so bad

2muchcOff33_grrl: u only 1 town over

wolfboy_97: soon ok?

wolfboy_97: i want it 2 b rite

wolfboy_97: 2 b perfect

2muchcOff33_grrl: sigh

2muchcOff33_grrl: well in other news

2muchcOff33_grrl: my mom being a total psycho again

wolfboy_97: wuts up

2muchcOff33_grrl: i swear she wants to put me in a freakin
convent

wolfboy_97: noooooo

2muchcOff33_grrl: lol

wolfboy_97: you haven't told her about us have u

2muchcOff33_grrl: god no, she'd explode

2muchcOff33_grrl: she just doesn't shut up, you know? she has no
idea wut it's like. She's always on my back. sometimes i just wanna
pack up everything and spilt.

wolfboy_97: i know exactly what u mean

wolfboy_97: sometimes I wish I'd have gone with my dad when he
took off. he was kinda awesome

wolfboy_97: but ur stronger than them. ur the most amazing
person i know

2muchcOff33_grrl: u always know how to cheer me up ☺

wolfboy_97: i really like u

2muchcOff33_grrl: I like u 2 <3

wolfboy_97: i think about u all the time

2muchcOff33_grrl: what u think about

I look at her picture taped to my laptop screen. Her skin is like milk. Her hair is liquid summer. Her photo wears a sly, knowing smile that makes me smile back every time I look at it. Her eyes take me away. Someplace quiet no one else can see.

wolfboy_97: i think about being with u

2muchcOff33_grrl: like dinner at mcdonalds and 2 for 1 movie

"being with me"?

wolfboy_97: no

2muchcOff33_grrl: what then?

wolfboy_97: being alone with u

2muchcOff33_grrl: and what will u do when ur alone with me ☺

wolfboy_97: stuff ;D

2muchcOff33_grrl: lol, do tell

wolfboy_97: i been looking at the pic u sent me last nite

2muchcOff33_grrl: excite u?

wolfboy_97: yeah

2muchcOff33_grrl: u want me?

wolfboy_97: y—

"Justin!"

I close my eyes and try not to sigh. Try not to think bad thoughts. To wish she'd just go away like Dad did. How much easier it would be. How much quieter in my head. I know it's wrong, but sometimes I think it'd be better if I was just on my own. I pray to God and almighty Jesus for strength, but they don't listen. They never listen.

Honor thy father and thy mother.

"Yeah, Momma?"

"What are you doing?"

"Talking to a friend on the computer."

Her voice rises an octave. "Is it that tramp again?"

I sigh, push the laptop aside. Stalk through the house, toward the back door. Pizza boxes and dirty dishes and dust bunnies in the corners. She wanted to sit on the porch tonight. Listen to the crickets sing. Insisted I drag her from the bed, wheel her out to watch the sunset. It can't be good for her skin, but I didn't have the strength to argue.

I push open the back door, stare down at her in her wheelchair. All the crickets in the yard fall silent. Like they're waiting. She looks so small. So thin. I know it must be hard for her. She just never thinks how hard it must be for me.

"Momma, please don't talk that way."

Her eyes are on the horizon. Dying sunlight reflected in that milky blue.

"I don't like it here anymore. Take me back. Take me back, Justin."

She does this sometimes. Tells me to take her back to the place the county put her after the accident. They said I couldn't look after her, that they'd take care of her. She says it was nice, to get on my nerves, but we both know it was horrible. Gray stone and cheap pine and padded walls. Crowds of gawping visitors on a Sunday, milling about like pigs at a trough.

"I'm not taking you back," I say. "This is your home. No good son would leave his momma in a place like that."

"And you're a good son, are you?"

"I try to be."

"You keep this up, you're going to burn, Justin. You're going to burn in hell."

"Momma—"

"I know what you're thinking. I can see it in you. You're going to leave me, just like *him*. Some teenage piece of tail wags itself at you and that's all it takes. I know it."

"Momma, stop it."

"She's nothing but a tramp, Justin. She's just like all the others. Sending you pictures of herself. It's ungodly."

I glance back into the house. ". . . How did you know that?"

She's refusing to look at me. Thin lips drawn back against her teeth.

"They're all alike," she spits. "Wicked. No good. Dirty girls."

The words I bite back taste like sour milk in my mouth.

"Momma, stop it. She's really nice. She's sweet and funny and—"

"And the woman was arrayed in purple and scarlet color," she hisses, "and decked with gold and precious stones and pearls, having a golden cup in her hand full of abominations and filthiness of her fornicati—"

I'm tired of this. Of scripture and revelation, of those eyes that never blink, of her always being inside my head. I grab her wheelchair handles, drag her in through the back door. She shrieks protest, but I don't listen. Trundling her through the sprawling rooms, past those staring photos and Bible pages in dusty frames. Every word is a nail driven into my head. I pick her up, and she weighs almost nothing in my arms. And careful as I can, I put her back into her bed, back into the cloying stink of those scented candles and musty pages. Screaming all the while.

Tramps. Harlots. Floozies. Trollops. Jezebels.

Shut up, shut up, shut up.

I slam the door, muffling her venom. Snatch up my computer. Fling open the stairwell door and stomp down into the cellar. It's always quiet down here. Thick concrete walls and rich, dark earth.

Sheets of old plastic. My dad's tools hanging on the walls. The only things he left behind. The only place I can really go to escape her voice.

I'll wait down here awhile. She'll be calm in an hour or two. Everything will be normal.

Normal.

wolfboy_97: sorry, back

2muchc0ff33_grrl: missed u

wolfboy_97: ☺

wolfboy_97: we shud do it u know

2muchc0ff33_grrl: um slow down stud

2muchc0ff33_grrl: u run a mile when I send you a pic of my undies

wolfboy_97: lol no

wolfboy_97: i mean run away together

2muchc0ff33_grrl: lol, ur crazy

wolfboy_97: only about u

2muchc0ff33_grrl: u don't know me.

wolfboy_97: I know ur amazing

2muchc0ff33_grrl: might not think that the 1st night i wake up screaming next 2 u

wolfboy_97: i wouldn't care. Coz u'd be waking up next 2 me

2muchc0ff33_grrl: I'm a total headache, wolfie

wolfboy_97: u can't be as bad as my other gf's lol

2muchc0ff33_grrl: o so I'm ur gf now?

wolfboy_97: . . . aren't u?

2muchc0ff33_grrl: tell me bout them

wolfboy_97: who

2muchc0ff33_grrl: ur old gfs

wolfboy_97: y?

2muchcOff33_grrl: told you. I'm good @ history. Mistakes of the past and all

wolfboy_97: this is like a golden rule or sumthng. Never talk about exes

2muchcOff33_grrl: if ur as hawt as ur pics, they must have been too

2muchcOff33_grrl: so

2muchcOff33_grrl: were they?

wolfboy_97: lol i'm not talking about this

2muchcOff33_grrl: WERE THEY

wolfboy_97: . . .

wolfboy_97: they were pretty, yeah

2muchcOff33_grrl: prettier than me?

2muchcOff33_grrl: think carefully b4 u answer, wolfboy

wolfboy_97: ur way prettier

2muchcOff33_grrl: huzzah u have passed the test!

2muchcOff33_grrl: how many gfs u had?

wolfboy_97: I plead the 5th

2muchcOff33_grrl: afraid u'll incriminate urself?

wolfboy_97: u make me smile

2muchcOff33_grrl: lol i make u squirm

2muchcOff33_grrl: crazy headcase psycho girl I told u

wolfboy_97: i like that ur psycho

wolfboy_97: i'm psycho too ☺

wolfboy_97: hello?

wolfboy_97: u there?

2muchcOff33_grrl: *sighs* gotta jet, wolfie. mom screaming again

2muchcOff33_grrl: back around 10

wolfboy_97: k

2muchcOff33_grrl: xxx

I stare at her kisses for I don't know how long. The sound of the world down here is muted. Soft and dark but for the house breathing. I can't hear Momma yelling anymore.

My mind drifts, wandering in the unwelcome direction of former girlfriends. Why'd she ask about them? Why take me there? Now I'm remembering and it makes me sad. I don't like thinking about how it never works out.

Shy Alice with her freckles and her glasses who never really kissed me back.

Lucy with her tattooed arms and pierced tongue.

Sally, who never really talked much, but still liked to scream my name.

A parade of imperfections and unhappy endings. Failed experiments. Sometimes I wonder if the right girl is out there. Sometimes I wonder if Momma isn't right about all of them.

No.

C0ff33's different. She's special. She's the one.

Just like me. Lost. Lonely. Looking for someone.

Someone special.

That special boy.

I met her on Reddit. Some true-crime author AMA. I visit lots of chat rooms. Books and hobbies and music and movements. Just watching. People would say I lurk, but I hate that word. Sounds like I'm some kind of creeper, and I'm totally not. I just don't talk unless I've got something to say. Mark Twain said it's better to remain silent and be thought of as a fool than to run your mouth and remove all doubt.

Anyway, after the AMA was done, she got into a flame war with some nub who insisted Pedro Lopez was the worst serial killer in history. I watched her take him apart, smart and funny all at once. Explaining Lopez was second-string, that Luis Garavito had over four hundred possible vics. The nub disappeared with his tail between his legs.

I sat staring at her name. 2muchcOff33_grrl.

I don't drink coffee. Gives me headaches.

Took me ten minutes to muster the courage and PM her.

wolfboy_97: ur wrong btw

2muchcOff33_grrl: wut

wolfboy_97: about Garavito

2muchcOff33_grrl: omg another Lopez fanboy? Learn 2 google, kid

wolfboy_97: not Lopez. Harold Shipman

2muchcOff33_grrl: lol he bushleague. 250ish

wolfboy_97: your wikifu sucks, they solved over 400 murders off Shipman.

wolfboy_97: but they think it could've maybe been 1000

wolfboy_97: and Lopez maybe beats Garavito. No way for them rly know who the #1 is

2muchcOff33_grrl: who the hell r u, guinness?

wolfboy_97: just another freak

wolfboy_97: like u

2muchcOff33_grrl: well thank u very much

wolfboy_97: freaks beat normal any day

2muchcOff33_grrl: I'm not a freak, I'm special

wolfboy_97: ha that's just wut my mom says

2muchcOff33_grrl: *crickets*

wolfboy_97: where u from

2muchcOff33_grrl: winterset

wolfboy_97: iowa?

2muchc0ff33_grrl: check out the big brain on brettttt

wolfboy_97: lol i go to high school like 1 town over from you

2muchc0ff33_grrl: omg its fate

wolfboy_97: obvs ☺

wolfboy_97: how old r u

2muchc0ff33_grrl: 16

2muchc0ff33_grrl: u?

wolfboy_97: 17

wolfboy_97: u like true crime, huh

2muchc0ff33_grrl: meh. maybe. thinking about doing forensics in college

wolfboy_97: CSI winterset!

2muchc0ff33_grrl: lol

2muchc0ff33_grrl: sumthin like that

2muchc0ff33_grrl: what about u

wolfboy_97: wut about me

2muchc0ff33_grrl: what you wanna do when u grow up

wolfboy_97: my dad says growing up is overrated

And that's how it started. Simple as that. She joked about it, but maybe it *was* fate. I'd just finished with Sally maybe two weeks before. The breakup hadn't gone well—I didn't take it too good. But when I was with c0ff33, it didn't seem to hurt so much.

I sent her my pic, she sent me hers. The online courting waltz, pieces of us shared in the cricket-song dark. It's funny how I've never asked her real name, but she knows me better than anyone. Sometimes I'm afraid of what'll happen when we meet. Afraid it'll turn out like everything else. We're perfect while we hide behind our little screens. We can be whoever we want in the dark. But there's no delete key IRL. No way to undo the mistakes we make.

Maybe it's better this way.

I plod up the stairs. Up to my room. Find the shoebox under my bed. Ticket stubs from ball games my dad took me to when I was a kid. Shells I collected from some summer at the beach. A piece of polished bone. Tongue stud (Lucy's idea, and a bad one—they totally ruin your teeth). An old orthodontic retainer. Rubbers. And right at the bottom, I find it. A gold ring, set with tiny diamond flecks. A single word engraved on the inner band.

I remember the day I found it on the bedroom floor. Momma's fingers had gotten too thin for it to stay on anymore. I remember the way it looked on Alice's hand. How Lucy freaked when I gave it to her. The empty band of skin around Sally's finger where it used to be, thirty seconds after she broke my heart.

There's no delete key IRL.

No way to take back "I love you."

It's 11:45 PM, and she was supposed to meet me at 10:00.

She always takes her time.

2muchc0ff33_grrl: u hear about this SK on the news

My stomach drops into my toes as she appears on-screen. Full of new butterflies. A pesticide breeze blows in through the open window. The crickets are singing, all in time.

wolfboy_97: hello 2 u 2

2muchc0ff33_grrl: u hear about it?

wolfboy_97: i don't watch the news

2muchc0ff33_grrl: cops found belongings at his house from five different girls

wolfboy_97: jesus

2muchc0ff33_grrl: he kept their jewelry, how stupid is that

wolfboy_97: lotta serial killers keep trophies

2muchc0ff33_grrl: i know that. It's just real dumb. if u wanna get away with it, i mean

wolfboy_97: maybe he didn't wanna get away with it?

2muchc0ff33_grrl: well, he didn't. been missing for twelve days now. sum1 got him

wolfboy_97: good

2muchc0ff33_grrl: who you figure did him?

wolfboy_97: dunno

2muchc0ff33_grrl: come on, u read about this stuff all the time

wolfboy_97: maybe it was just bad luck.

wolfboy_97: walked out in front of a bus when texting ruh rohhhhh

2muchc0ff33_grrl: lol

2muchc0ff33_grrl: vigilante maybe?

wolfboy_97: not likely. he's prolly just holed up sumwhere.

2muchc0ff33_grrl: wouldn't that be cool, tho. Sum1 out there hunting these freaks down and giving them what they deserve

wolfboy_97: i guess. Cops sure can't do it. Only time they catch an SK, it's usually an accident or the guy being stupid

2muchc0ff33_grrl: not accident. karma

2muchc0ff33_grrl: u believe in karma, wolfie? Universe bringing us wut we deserve?

wolfboy_97: nah

2muchc0ff33_grrl: y not?

wolfboy_97: coz I got u. and no way I deserve u

2muchc0ff33_grrl: oooooooh, SMOOTH talker

wolfboy_97: :D

2muchc0ff33_grrl: u don't deserve me, huh

wolfboy_97: nope

2muchc0ff33_grrl: so have u been a bad boy, wolfie?

wolfboy_97: lol I'm very well behaved I'll have u know :D

2muchcOff33_grrl: mmm

2muchcOff33_grrl: u want me 2 be a bad girl 4 u.

My hand slips down toward my boxers. My mouth is dry as dust.

wolfboy_97: i don't know

2muchcOff33_grrl: tell me wut u'll do when u meet me

2muchcOff33_grrl: will u be bad 4 me baby

wolfboy_97: u torturing me

2muchcOff33_grrl: lol, not yet

2muchcOff33_grrl: but when i do

2muchcOff33_grrl: it's gonna be soooooo good

"Justin!"

Her voice is like a bucket of cold water thrown in my face. It wakes me up. Drags me back. And just for a moment, I hate it. Hate this. Hate her.

"Justin!"

I glance at the flashing cursor on the screen. Search for the girl beyond it. Wondering if she really is the one to get me away from this place. Away from her. Away from me. Is she real? Can I make her real?

"Justin, I'm cold! Come close the window!"

I wonder if there *is* such a thing as karma. Or God. Or whatever.

2muchcOff33_grrl: u there?

I wonder what I did to deserve a life like this.

But I know what I have to do to change it.

wolfboy_97: I got u something

2muchcOff33_grrl: got me what?

wolfboy_97: present

2muchcOff33_grrl: omg what?

wolfboy_97: I show u

wolfboy_97: rdy?

2muchcOff33_grrl: yesssssss

wolfboy_97: imgfile:ring_1.jpg

2muchcOff33_grrl: *squeeeeeeees*

wolfboy_97: u like?

2muchcOff33_grrl: OMFG ITS BEAUTIFUL

2muchcOff33_grrl: WUT'S THE ENGRAVING SAY I CAN'T READ IT

wolfboy_97: "forever"

wolfboy_97: gonna give it to you when we meet

2muchcOff33_grrl: WHEN

2muchcOff33_grrl: WHEN

wolfboy_97: u luv me?

2muchcOff33_grrl: I luv u

2muchcOff33_grrl: OMG IT'S BEAUTIFUL I LUV U

2muchcOff33_grrl: *dies*

wolfboy_97: lol, don't do that

"Justin!"

wolfboy_97: i gtg

2muchcOff33_grrl: ok

2muchcOff33_grrl: I luv u

2muchcOff33_grrl: I LUV U

I drag myself out of bed, trudge past those black-and-white faces toward her door.

"Coming, Momma."

2muchcOff33_grrl: omg

2muchcOff33_grrl: omfg

I open my eyes. It's nearly midnight. The house is so quiet, I can hear it breathing. The pinging on my laptop is loud enough to wake the dead. I look to Momma's room, slap at the volume control as my chat window fills with her name.

2muchcOff33_grrl: wolfie

2muchcOff33_grrl: u there

2muchcOff33_grrl: pls

wolfboy_97: wuts up?

2muchcOff33_grrl: omfg, my mom

wolfboy_97: wut about her

2muchcOff33_grrl: she went through my computer

2muchcOff33_grrl: she read my logs

2muchcOff33_grrl: saw the pics I sent u

Cold fingertips brush my spine. I can't seem to breathe right.

wolfboy_97: 0_o

wolfboy_97: what did she say

2muchcOff33_grrl: SHE FREAKED WTF U THINK

wolfboy_97: ok ok calm down

2muchcOff33_grrl: she said she gonna cut off my net

2muchcOff33_grrl: that I'm not allowed to c u anymore

2muchcOff33_grrl: i told u she's a PSYCHO

wolfboy_97: where r u now?

2muchcOff33_grrl: bus station

wolfboy_97: wtf

2muchcOff33_grrl: did u mean what u said

wolfboy_97: what did I say?

2muchcOff33_grrl: that u wanted to run away with me

. . .

. . .

wolfboy_97: yes

2muchcOff33_grrl: then come get me

2muchcOff33_grrl: let's just go

2muchcOff33_grrl: u and me

2muchcOff33_grrl: now

wolfboy_97: does ur mom know ur gone

2muchcOff33_grrl: no, I waited til she went to sleep

wolfboy_97: did u tell anyone else about us?

2muchcOff33_grrl: who the hell am I gonna tell?

2muchcOff33_grrl: COME GET ME

It wasn't meant to be like this. This was supposed to happen when we both wanted it. I'm not ready for it yet. I haven't even started to—

2muchcOff33_grrl: wolfie pls

2muchcOff33_grrl: wolfie I luv u

I should let her go. If she's run away, the cops will be looking for her. I could get into so much trouble. My mind is running through the maybes. This is stupid. This is crazy.

But what if she's the one?

wolfboy_97: ok

wolfboy_97: ok I'll come

2muchcOff33_grrl: omg thank u baby

wolfboy_97: its gonna be ok, i promise

2muchcOff33_grrl: ok ok

2muchcOff33_grrl: i'm ok

wolfboy_97: it's gonna take too long 4 me to get to winterset tho

wolfboy_97: i can't drive

wolfboy_97: my dad can, tho. he just outside of ur town. i'll get him to come get u.

2muchcOff33_grrl: ur dad? Won't he tell the cops?

wolfboy_97: no, he's cool. trust me

wolfboy_97: he's a real cool guy

wolfboy_97: he'll take u to his place, I'll come pick u up in the morning, ok?

2muchcOff33_grrl: ok

wolfboy_97: don't wait at the bus station tho

wolfboy_97: too many ppl

wolfboy_97: wait two blocks south, he'll come get u there

2muchcOff33_grrl: wolfie I'm freaked out

wolfboy_97: its gonna be ok, i promise

2muchcOff33_grrl: ok

wolfboy_97: we'll be together soon

2muchcOff33_grrl: forever?

wolfboy_97: and ever

Amen.

A storm is coming in from the north. Rain like knives.

My hands are shaking the whole drive there. Windshield wipers squeaking in time with my pulse. I'm not sure what I'll say. She thinks I'm perfect behind my little screen. I can be whoever she wants in the dark. But there's no delete key IRL.

What if she can't love who I am out here?

The brakes on my dad's truck squeal as it pulls up to the curb. Gravel crunches under the tires as the headlights die. I look at the streets around me. Empty asphalt and dark windows. Lifeless neon and howling wind and rain, rain, rain.

Nobody for miles.

My breath fogs up the glass and the storm comes down in floods. But finally I see her skulking down the street, and I know it's an awful cliché, but I swear my heart skips a beat. Even in the gloom I recognize her, the half-moon crescent of her cheek picked out in the streetlamp's light. Raindrops glittering as they fall around her, like her own personal fireworks show. Long blond hair flowing from beneath her hoodie, leather jacket, and tight, tight jeans. Gliding slow through the dark. She looks up, sees the truck, but even then, her pace doesn't quicken. Ever and always, she takes her time.

I roll down the window so she can see me. Distrust in her eyes. I give her my most disarming smile.

"Hey there, coffee girl," I say. "You look soaked."

"Who're you?" she asks.

"I'm Justin." I smile. "I'm Wolfie's dad."

She stares out the window the whole way back. Doesn't look at me at all. That's okay, though, I expected it at first. Her lips are slightly blue, and she's shivering. It'll be better once we get home. Get her out of those wet clothes.

"Are you cold?" I ask.

"I'm always cold."

I turn on the heater, and the dashboard rattles and shakes.

"I'll take you back to my place. You can have a shower, get warmed up."

"Is Wolfie there?"

"He'll be there in the morning."

She nods, chews at her lip. I watch out of the corner of my eye, and my mouth goes dry.

"Bad scene at home, huh?" I ask.

"Yeah."

"I know what that's like."

"Runs in the family?"

"What do you mean?"

"Wolfie doesn't get on with his mom either. Says she's a real psycho."

I bristle a little. "I'm sure he never said that. They might butt heads sometimes, but—"

"He hates her. I can tell. The way he talks about her."

My knuckles are white on the steering wheel. "I'm sure that's not true."

"She sounds like a real freak." A sideways glance. "No offense. I mean, he told me you split when he was young. I don't blame you. You must know what she's like."

No, no, this isn't working at all.

"It's kinda funny," I say. "You guys meeting online and living so close to each other."

She shrugs. Damp blond hair plastered to her throat. Her skin is moonlight pale.

"Wolfie and me are fate."

"You really think that? Some people are just meant to be together?"

"I think everything happens for a reason."

"Well, Wolfie's very lucky, then. You seem like a wonderful girl." I steal another glance. "Beautiful too."

"It's real cool of you, you know." She shifts a little in her seat. "Helping us out like this."

"Well, I'm a nice guy."

She looks at me and smiles, and it seems the sun has come out from behind the clouds.

"Yeah. Wolfie always said."

The windshield wipers are too slow to keep up with my heartbeat now. The road hisses under our tires as we drive through the thundering night. I see her stifle a yawn against her sleeve. I notice dark circles under her eyes.

"What's your real name, anyway?"

"Cassie."

The word echoes in my head like a prayer.

"You look tired, Cassie."

"Yeah, I don't sleep much."

"Is that why you call yourself coffee girl?"

"Coffee's my best friend. I have bad dreams."

I put one hand on her lap. Just the briefest touch. Light as feathers.

"Everyone has bad dreams."

She stares out the window. Blue eyes fixed beyond the foggy glass.

"Not like mine."

The brakes squeal as we pull into the driveway. I have an umbrella, run around to her side of the truck. As we dash toward the porch, I put my arm around her waist to keep her close. She's so cold. I can feel the chill coming off her skin.

It makes me shiver.

Inside, the rain beats down on the roof like a million tin drums. Thunder rattles the windows in their frames. I shake the wet out of my hair, watch as she shrugs off her backpack, offer to take her jacket. As I hang it on the coatrack, I can smell her perfume on the leather. Feel a faint breeze somewhere on the back of my neck that sets goose bumps loose all over my skin.

Her eyes are so blue.

"The bathroom is up the hall. You can have a shower, get out of those clothes. I'll get a fire going. Did you bring pajamas?"

"Yeah." She shivers. "Couldn't fit my robe, though."

She must feel it too. This is perfect. Just too perfect.

"I have one I can loan you," I say. "I'll leave it outside the bathroom door."

"Okay. Thanks."

"Down the hall." I smile. "Second on the right."

She tosses her hair over her shoulder. Turns and walks away. I watch her hips sway. Think about the shape of her lips. Raindrops beading on her skin.

She must feel it too.

She said it was fate.

This time it's going to be all right.

This time it's going to be perfect.

Not like the other times.

Alice was my first and I made a mess of it—first times are usually that way, they say. I gave her too much Flunitrazepam and she just never woke up. She was too thin. Too shy. That was her problem. Momma told me I needed a girl with a backbone, so I kept a piece of it. A little polished piece of bone in a shoebox. All that remains of shy little Alice.

Lucy was my second and she was much better. She had a bad mouth, though. The things she called me when she woke up—I couldn't keep her after that. Momma wouldn't have stood for someone like Lucy living under her roof. I tried to keep her tongue, but it just turned to rot after a while. A silver barbell's all that's left.

Sally woke up too early. I'm still learning how much I should use in their drinks. I get the tablets online, keep them above the kitchen sink—the shiny white kind that dissolve easy, not the blue ones that stain the liquid. But it's hard to guess the dose. She screamed when her eyes fluttered open. Screamed my name and kicked and flailed. Bit me with those perfect teeth her orthodontist must have made a fortune on. I still have the scar. Still have her retainer too. The ground got the rest.

They didn't understand. They weren't the one. But Cassie's different. She said bad things about Momma and I'd never think those things, but the start is always hard, isn't it? Before people really get to know each other? It'll be okay this time. She loves me. She'll understand the person behind the screen is the same person in front of her now. Of course she will.

She has to.

I don't know what I'll do if she doesn't.

I feel sandpaper skin against my lips. Smell vanilla and roses over my shoulder.

Yes, you do.

I'm pretending to read when she steps out of the bathroom in a swirl of warm steam. Damp blond hair framing an angel's face. She's wearing black bunny slippers with X's for eyes. Her pajamas are black too, patterned with skeleton teddy bears. I don't like them. At all.

But the robe is perfect. Fluffy and pink. Embroidered with dozens of tiny red flowers. She looks beautiful. She looks—

"I look ridiculous in this thing," she says.

"No, you look great."

"I look like someone's mother. Someone's tragic, saggy, seven-million-year-old mother." She plops down on the couch opposite me, plucking at the hem. "I look like I murdered Martha Stewart and stole her skin."

My butterflies are all dead.

"I don't have anything else," I manage to say. "I'm sorry."

"It's only for tonight, right?" She gives me a thin smile that doesn't reach her eyes.

This isn't going well at all. She moves differently than I thought she would. Slumps in the chair with her legs slightly spread instead of crossing them like a lady. Picking at the browning leaves of the potted plant beside her. And her voice is wrong. Her accent is hard. And she chews her fingernails. I don't like that.

"When's Wolfie coming?"

"He'll be here in the morning, like I said."

Silence stretches for miles between us, broken only by the rolling thunder. Her gaze roams the room—she's obviously looking for something to say. It's so easy for us, usually. We talk for hours. Words flowing like water. Surely she can still sense that? Surely she can find something worthwhile talking ab—

"How long you lived out here?" she asks.

The question's so banal, it makes my teeth ache.

"A long time."

"God, I'd go crazy out here all by myself. Don't you miss the city?"

"I like the quiet."

"I think I'd kill myself out of boredom."

No, no, no.

"Wolfie lives in a place like this, right?" she continues. "Some old crappy farm thing? God, no wonder he wants to split. Psycho mom aside, I mean."

My hands curl into fists on my armrests.

She seems to remember herself. Something like apology creeps into her voice, matched by that eyeless smile. "I mean, I'm sure it's okay for a guy like you."

". . . A guy like me?"

"Yeah. Old. I mean, older. You know."

It feels like I've been stabbed in the stomach and all the air is leaking out of me. Flames are crackling in the fireplace. The wind outside sounds like howling wolves.

Someone's tragic, saggy, seven-million-year-old mother . . .

I look into her eyes and I suddenly realize they aren't blue at all.

A guy like you. Old. Older. You know.

They're gray.

She's just like the others, you know. They're all the same . . .

Shiny white pills in the cupboard above the sink.

"Would you like something to drink?" I hear myself say.

"Yeah, coffee would be awesome."

She's still speaking as I walk toward the kitchen, but I can't hear what she says. I want to ask her to keep her voice down in case she wakes up Momma, but suddenly I can't stand the thought of looking at her. It's not the same. It's *never* the same. It's so easy when it's all happening behind a screen. So clean. You never have to notice that their eyes have dark shadows under them, or they fidget when they talk, or their fingernails are chewed down to the quick. I should never have brought her here.

There's no delete key in real life.

I bring back the coffees (I know the way she likes it, I know everything about her), watch her nurse it in her lap, waiting for it to cool. She's still talking and I want her to shut up in case Momma hears, but I don't want to be rude.

Drink it, drink it.

"Are you okay?" she asks.

The apologetic smile on my face feels made out of plastic.

"Just tired."

"I'm cold."

Wood snaps in the fireplace, sparks spilling up the chimney like fireflies. I get up and throw another log into the burning mouth, let the flames tumble and catch. I'm not sure how long I stand there, watching the heat lick and the bark blacken, trying not to hear her talk about her bad dreams and the voices she hears when she closes her eyes and everything about her I once wanted, and now want to rip bleeding out of her chest. But I'm still. So still and quiet.

Like a good little boy.

When I turn back around, the butterflies in my stomach wake up as I see her draining the last of her coffee, thumping the mug onto the table.

She doesn't use the coaster.

"Urg, what flavor was that? Sweaty underwear?"

"Just instant."

"Tasted like something died in it."

"Justin!"

My stomach lurches. Cassie's eyelids are fluttering, the corners of her mouth starting to sag. She runs her hand across her eyes, blinking hard.

"Justin!"

"Excuse me for a moment." I smile. "I'll be right back."

Down the hallway on shaking legs, past the black-and-white stares toward the crucifix door. I knew she'd wake her, I *knew* it. She's spoiling everything, God why can't it ever be—

"Justin!"

"I'm here, Momma," I say, pushing the bedroom door open. It smells damp in here. Wrong. I think the rain is creeping in some-where, rotting the wood.

Momma is staring at me. Through me. "Who are you talking to? I heard voices."

"Nobody."

"Don't you lie to me, boy, God and almighty Jesus help me, don't you lie."

"It's just the television, Momma."

"You think I don't see, don't you? You think I don't know what you get up to?"

"Momma, go back to sleep."

"Don't you take that tone with me!"

"I'm not taking a tone!"

"You're just like him, Justin. Just like your daddy."

"I'm *not* like him!" I shout. "I'm still here. I'm a good son! A good boy! Who got you back from that awful place they put you in after the accident? Who looked after you?"

"It's not an accident when it's on purpose, Justin."

My butterflies are all dead again.

"I said I was sorry!"

"I was happy where I was. It was quiet there. I could sleep."

"No." I shake my head. "No. You belong here, this is your home."

"I belong in the ground, Justin," she sighs. "Put me back."

"Who'rrre you talk . . . talking to?"

I whirl and see Cassie standing behind me with those wide eyes that are gray, not blue.

"Is she . . . ?"

And she's looking past me to the thing in the bed—that thing of dry skin and cracker-brittle bones I dug up out of that awful place they put her. I said I was sorry. It was an accident. Oh God, I didn't mean to hurt you, Momma. And Cassie's hand creeps up to her mouth as she realizes her hair is the same color and the robe I gave her is identical and all the rain and the candles in the world still can't quite cover the smell.

"Is she . . . dead?"

Pale blue eyes that never blink.

Her voice always inside my head.

Only inside my head?

"Don't you talk that way about my momma."

"Oh, Jesus," Cassie whispers. "Oh, my God . . ."

She turns to run, but the pills have got her now. Her hands on the walls as she tries to keep her balance, stumbling and knocking one of the photos loose. It's an old one—soldiers and nurses—my mom and dad during the war. It shatters on the ground, glass shards spinning slow in the air until they fall, down, down, just like Cassie, down to her knees and then to the boards, hair the color of damp straw splayed about her head in a ragged halo.

I stoop and heft her over my shoulder, boots crunching in broken glass.

"I'm going down to the cellar for a while, Momma."

I close the bedroom door behind me.

Momma doesn't say a word.

I lay Cassie down on the workbench, plastic sheet beneath her. I've slipped Momma's ring onto her finger and she looks so perfect. So pretty. So peaceful now. With all those bad dreams, I bet she hasn't slept this good in years. I almost want to leave her a little longer to enjoy it. But I suppose she can sleep forever now.

A breeze is tickling the back of my neck as I look through my dad's tools, taking the ones I want to start with. Wood saw. Pliers. Claw hammer. I plonk them onto the table beside Cassie, watch her chest rise and fall. There are goose bumps on my skin. It's really cold in here.

I don't want to strap her down yet. I'm not sure what part I want to keep. I want to wait until I can't wait anymore. Until the need makes me shake. And so I rip open her backpack, upend it on another workbench. Sifting through the socks and tees and underwear, pulling apart her toiletries bag—paint for those blue lips and polish for those too-chewed fingernails. I'm beginning to think there's nothing worth keeping until I search the side pocket, find it sitting in there like it was just waiting for me.

Her diary.

I glance at her on the table, smile sneaking and creeping to the corners of my mouth. Opening up these pages will be like opening up her head. I have to keep it. It's too perfect.

I flip through with trembling hands, eyes scanning the text.

. . . Mom on my case again about staying out so late. She just doesn't . . .

. . . no sleep again, yay for double-caff . . .

. . . sometimes wonder why they picked me . . .

. . . bad dreams . . .

. . . the worst. She swears like a goddamn sailor. I try to . . .

There's nothing in here, I realize. My frown deepens and I keep flipping, page after page.

There's no reference to Wolfie at all.

But she said she loved me . . .

. . . followed him home from work last night. Some crappy dishpig job . . .

. . . think I found another one . . .

. . . nightmares again. Latino kids with their eyes missing. They showed me his face. Long greasy hair and acne scars. I know where he put . . .

What the hell is this?

And from inside the pages, something tumbles. A photograph, fluttering down to the concrete at my boots. As I stoop to pick it up, I see there's a red X marked across it. The face still looks familiar, though. Hollow eyes. Terrible comb-over. I've seen it somewhere before . . .

Television, I realize.

That missing kiddyqueer they were talking about on the news . . .

wolfboy_97: wut r ur dreams about?

2muchc0ff33_grrl: voices

wolfboy_97: wut they say?

2muchc0ff33_grrl: sad stuff

2muchc0ff33_grrl: makes me cry

2muchc0ff33_grrl: makes me mad

2muchc0ff33_grrl: sometimes when I open my eyes i think i can still hear them

No.

. . . followed him home from work last night . . .

. . . sometimes wonder why they picked me . . .

. . . They showed me his face . . .

2muchc0ff33_grrl: wouldn't that be cool, tho. Sum1 out there hunting these freaks down and giving them what they deserve

I turn and she's sitting up on the workbench. Head slightly tilted, staring at me with those bruised gray eyes. Skeleton teddy bears on her pajamas. Claw hammer in her hand.

She swings it faster than I can move. It catches me on the jaw and I feel the bone shatter, taste bright copper in my mouth. I stumble, legs going out from under me. Knees cracking on the concrete, sharp pain lancing through the bloody haze over my eyes. And as she brings the hammer down again, her words cut like razors in the dark.

"Sorry, Wolfie."

I wake up and all I taste is blood, metallic in my mouth. The light-globe above me is etched in triplicate—three burning suns to blind me. My head doesn't feel right. I try to speak, remembering too late my jaw is broken. Bone grinding bone. Whatever I was going to say turns into a bubbling whimper.

I'm still in the cellar, I realize. Strapped to the table. The suns over-head are eclipsed as she leans slowly over me, looking down. Gray eyes and blue lips.

It's freezing, I realize. Her breath hangs in the air between us as she speaks.

"You cold, Wolfie?"

I can't speak. Nod instead.

"Can't say I'm real sorry about your comfort level. But it gets cold when they get angry. And they're real angry at you, Wolfie."

They?

I glance around the room, seeing nothing but blank concrete and my father's tools on the walls. Some are missing, I realize. Not in their places.

"Don't bother looking for them." She wiggles her fingers in front of my eyes. "You gotta have the touch. The curse. The crazy. What-ever you wanna call it. Alice doesn't look too bad, but it's not like you'd want to see Sally and Lucy, anyway. They mostly keep the shape they died in, see. And you didn't let them die easy, did you?"

I try to speak, but it's just a gargle of pain and bone splinters.

"Shhhh," she whispers, putting her finger to her lips. "You don't have to explain. They told me all about it. Chatroom creeper. IM flatterer. Solid pro at spotting the easy pickings in the crowd, right? Lonely girls. Sad girls. Lost girls. Big bad wolf, huh?"

She picks up the wood saw. Holds it in front of my eyes.

"This is what you used on Lucy, right?" Her gaze flickers along the saw-tooth blade. "They told me what you did to them. What you did it with. So I didn't drink your coffee, Wolfie. Your plant looked thirsty. Mistakes of the past, remember? I'm real good at history."

I flail at the straps holding me down. But she's bound me tight. My muscles cord and tendons stretch, but it's no good. No good.

"Wuh . . ." I wince, agony nearly drowning me. "Wuh . . ."

"What do I want?"

I nod. Tears running down my cheeks.

"I want to sleep, Wolfie." She sighs the words, and I see the red veins scrawled across those big gray eyes. "Just a single night without one of them finding me. Pleading. Waking me in the dark. They just wander, see. The Sleepless. Looking for someone who can hear them. And eventually they find me. They won't leave me alone." She rubs at her temples, frozen white spilling from her lips. "The only way to shut them up is to give them justice. Vengeance. Whatever you call it. Then they can sleep."

Another sigh.

"Then maybe I can too."

I jerk against the straps again, leather and buckles cutting into my skin. She pats my shoulder, somewhat apologetically.

Lifts the wood saw.

"So, this is really going to hurt. And from what I understand, the place you go after this hurts a lot worse. But don't hate the player, hate the game, right?"

I feel metal teeth replace her hand on my shoulder.

The first tiny sting.

"Noohh . . ." I try to say. "Muh . . ."

"Mother?"

A weak nod.

"The thing in that bed stopped being your mother a long time ago, Wolfie. But she'll be cremated. Along with this house. Along with you."

No.

She leans in close. Whispers in my ear.

"This is for Alice. And Lucy. And Sally. And all the others you would've done for if someone like me didn't stop you." She shrugs, and her smile doesn't reach her eyes. "At least someone's going to sleep easy tonight."

Metal teeth gleam in the dirty light.

I pray to God and almighty Jesus she makes it quick.

They don't listen, though.

They never listened.

And she takes her time.

Inspired by the 1960 film *Psycho* and Mudvayne's "Nothing to Gein"

M

STEFAN BACHMANN

She could hear them below in the garden, the hiss of their feet in the cool grass, voices soft as moth wings as they whispered to one another. A childish screech floated up toward her window. Then they were singing again, the sound of it eerily high-pitched and wavering:

A *is for Anna, who licks all the forks*
B *is for Bobby, who's thin as a stork*
C *is for Camden, who ought to be kicked . . .*

She smiled at that: Camden did need be kicked. Lady Gortley had said so the other day at luncheon, whispering it to her husband while young cousin Camden had a screaming tantrum on the floor. Everyone at the table had heard the remark. And somehow the children had heard it too, though they ate in the nursery, in another part of the house entirely.

She moved closer to the window. A breeze was drifting through the open panes. She felt it on her face, felt it stirring the lace at her sleeves, a slow current, heavy with sunlight and the thick scent of apple blossoms. She extended one hand until her fingertips brushed the warmth of the light. Then she stopped, still in the shadows. If the children looked up now, they would not see her. They mustn't.

She heard one of them call out, a girl's voice, sharp and prickly as a briar branch. Then the pack moved around the corner of the house. There were more children today, now that the hunting party was here, and all the guests. The song went on, cold and distant now, as if sung in the shadows of a courtyard:

J is for Jamie, alone in the park
K is for Kerstin, who's good for a lark
L is for Louis, who douses the spark
M is for Misha, who sits in the dark . . .

She stiffened at the sound of her name, then turned her back on the window and felt her way to the other side of her chamber. Her hands brushed the sunlight-warmed smoothness of a tassel, the rich fur of velvet, sleek porcelain, brass, dark wood, growing colder as she sank farther into the room. She sat down in her chair. It creaked inelegantly under her.

It had taken them eight months, then, to realize the cousin in the attic, whom no one spoke of, and whom no one wanted to speak to, was worthy of inclusion in their songs. The children seemed to know everything that went on at Hatfield—they were like a dwarfish, all-knowing jury—but they had never sung of her before. Not until today.

Whenever she went downstairs to join the Gortleys for their family tea (which she did as seldom as possible, because going downstairs felt, to her, akin to drowning), she never once heard the children speak. She could imagine them sitting in their starched collars, eyes grave and full of secrets, but she never heard them whisper or laugh,

STEFAN BACHMANN

and there was certainly none of the running and shrill singing she heard now. Sometimes she wondered if the children were not ghosts, conjured up by her own mind, and that if she stumbled into the garden and felt about with her hands she would find no one there, because what child would sing such songs as these?

But they sounded real enough now.

O *is for Oscar, who might be a pig,*
P *is Patrick, who definitely is.*

Misha sorted through the names in her head, trying to pin them to the sachets of sounds and smells with which she recognized people. *J* for Jamie and *L* for Louis were no doubt two of the guests who had come up for the foxhunts that weekend. She was related to a Jamie, and a Louis, too, but of course, these might be different ones. Kerstin was a housemaid, a loud, jolly girl, from what little Misha knew of her. She liked to sing "I'm the Queen of London-Town" while bustling laundry across the green toward the stone wash-house. Oscar was a stable boy, Patrick a duke. And then there was *M. M* for Misha, *who sits in the dark.* They were right about that, the children. She did sit in the dark. She did other things too, but no one knew.

Misha sat very still, her thumb rubbing over a ridge in the armrest. K *is for Kerstin, who's good for a lark.*

Misha often wondered whether she would have been like Kerstin if she had been born to a charwoman instead of a lord. Would she have grown up jolly and loud? Would she have been able to see? But what was the use of thinking about it. Misha *had* been born to a lord, and the lord had died, and then had begun the endless passing about among relatives, from house to house, from London to Oxford to Wiltshire to here, like some sort of odd and awkward present, a lead goose thrust among the china and delicate figurines on a mantel. No one had wanted the great, ungainly girl for long, because she couldn't sew, that Misha, and she couldn't sing, and she couldn't speak interestingly, and she couldn't see.

She had seen, once. She remembered being small, dancing in a garden much like the children outside were doing now. She remembered white smocks and scratchy stockings, laughing and jeering, and the brilliant green of the grass, so brilliant, it made her eyes sting and water to think of it. And then she remembered cramped rooms and medicine bottles and sickness. They had pressed a poultice over her eyes, soaked in strong herbs to help her sleep. It had burned them. The last thing she recalled seeing was a shape in the cloth, a long, thin tear in the upper right corner through which the light came. And then the light was gone, and there was only pain and darkness . . .

W's for William, who's such a great boor
X is for Xavier, who happens to snore
Y is for Ylenia, who snaps like a stick
Z is for Zelda, who drinks like a tick

Misha's fingers were running over the armrest frantically now. The dinner gong would be ringing soon. That meant going downstairs, drowning, resurfacing stiff and silent in the dining room while the chorus of dinner conversation drew around her like a net, while she listened to the bitter grievances and false friendlinesses whispered across her lap, as if she were deaf as well as blind. She heard every word, of course. She often thought of witty things to say in response, and she waited for other people to say them, but no one did. She could imagine the rows of faces if she tried to, the stunned silence, then the sneers and pitying smirks. It was like a cage almost, the image they had of her, and she could not break out of it for fear of hurting herself. And so she would sit, stiff and hollow, like a doll, but inside, there were colors swirling, and faces like flowers, opening and smiling, and wind and words—

Someone was at the door. Misha's heart gave a terrible squirm; she struggled up out of her thoughts. She sat very still, listening. She heard a woman's voice, high and giggly, and the light tap of a slipper. Then the heavy tread and deep voice of a man. A hand was placed on the doorknob.

"It—it is *occupied*," she coughed, but the words came out in barely a whisper.

The knob turned. Misha half rose, then scrabbled toward the door, hoping she could lock it in time, or that they would hear her and leave. The latch clicked open. She froze, hunched over, halfway to the door.

She tried to straighten herself, look composed, but it was too late for that. She could feel the two figures in the doorway, watching her.

"Oh!" said a woman's voice. "Good gracious, we didn't realize—"

Go away, go away. Misha wanted to sink into the floor, into the dust and beetles between the beams. She heard a nervous titter, heard the woman's hand on her companion's arm. "Come along, darling, we'll find somewhere else . . ."

But they didn't move, and if Misha's instincts were not mistaken, the man continued to stare at her, his presence hanging in the doorway, filling it.

"Come on, will you?" the woman said, testily now. *Lady Willoughby. That's who it was. Ginty Willoughby, second cousin once removed.*

Silence. Misha felt ill. She heard a sound like a throat clearing, and teeth coming together inside a mouth. Then the door closed abruptly, and the footsteps moved away.

Misha felt her way backward toward her chair and collapsed into it. The visitors had left behind an odious smell, like lavender and tobacco, far too strong. The children outside were not singing anymore. No doubt they had been called in for dinner. It wouldn't be five minutes before the gong for the grown-ups rang.

She got up and went to the washbasin. Her fingers shook against the porcelain, rattling like bones. She felt drained and tired, as if the mere seconds of facing the strangers had taken the last of her energy.

Stop it, Misha. Stop being so frightened of everything.

But she couldn't stop. She carried fear with her like a little animal, curled in the nook behind her heart, and it whispered to her: *You are weak, you are frightened, and you will never dare do anything at all.*

She felt about on the floor for her shoes, which she had kicked off. She went and closed the windows. Far down in the house, the dinner gong sounded. She spent a great deal of time clasping a necklace. Then she clenched her hands at her side, opened the door, and poked her head out, breathing heavily.

The hallway was curiously quiet, as if it were holding its breath. Three stories down, in the entrance hall with its great stone staircase and tapestries, she heard guests arriving, the distant rumble of their voices, but up here there was nothing. Less than nothing: an odd, aching void, as if something *had* been here, and had been ripped from the air so suddenly it had left a hole.

A floorboard creaked softly somewhere farther on. Misha listened, her heart beating hard and quick, like a stone mallet.

Oh, stop! She set off purposefully up the hall in the direction of the stairs. *Seven, eight, nine,* she counted, and her hand caught the newel post at the top of the banister. She started down. A sound reached her ears: a soft knocking and the scuff of shoes. Someone else was on the stairs.

She paused, suddenly afraid it was the man and woman again, hanging about for a joke. She took another step down. Her face brushed against something. There was an odd smell in the air, like unwashed skin, and she could sense something in front of her. She was fairly sure it wasn't a person. It was *almost* the feeling she got when she was near another human being, but this was more like a weight, something solid, displacing the air. She swept her hand out in an arc. She felt cloth again. And all at once something hot dripped onto her face, and she stumbled forward, and suddenly the cloth was everywhere, tangling with her. Her head knocked into something. She felt skin, strangely heavy and clammy, and a face, upside down. Her fingers wriggled across a mouth, hair hanging down, and Misha's feet were slapping about as if— No. *No, not blood, she was dreaming, there was no one there, there was no sleeping woman hanging before her, and no blood, NO BLOOD.*

Something rushed past her. And then she felt a mouth press close to her ear and a thick arm snake around her neck and clamp tight like a noose. A man. He was breathing heavily, gasping, as if he had run a great distance, and his arm went tighter and tighter, and he gasped and breathed, and at last, when Misha thought she was to die too, he said in a rough, country voice that sounded of earth and gravel: "Not a word, old girl, or it'll be you hanging from the lights, and your guts a-slipperin' and a-slidin' on the stairs."

He let go of her neck. And then she was alone, standing in silence next to the dead woman. It was a full two minutes before she began to scream.

× × ×

Dinner was called off, but the murder had done little to dampen anyone's appetite, and so all the food was laid out on a buffet in the front hall, and everyone ate there, standing and speaking to one another frantically. Misha was brought into the drawing room, where a police inspector tried to pry words from her head like teeth. She barely spoke. She heard him. She heard all his questions, and she heard the vexation begin to rise in his voice, and she heard Lady Gortley take him to the other end of the room and whisper: "Do be patient, Mr. Bilgeberry. I'm afraid she's a bit simple, and now with this beastly murder business and her finding poor Lady Willoughby like that . . . Oh, I can't imagine. Hanging upside down, and the blood just dripping. Thank heavens she's blind."

Misha stared out in front of her, into nothing. She held her hands clasped tightly in her lap. It was all she could do not to rub them raw. They said the murderer had being trying to haul Lady Willoughby's body up into the attic, through the trapdoor above the landing. He had let her fall when Misha had interrupted him, and the body had tangled with the antlers in the chandelier. One of the prongs had driven clean through her leg. A servant had washed the gore off Misha—she had felt the warm water and the rub of the cloth—but somehow it was as if the blood were still there, drying stickily between her fingers.

"Miss Markham?" The inspector was leaning over her again. She could smell his breath, rot and meat and the sherry Lady Gortley had been so liberally offering him, and which he had been accepting gratefully. "We will try again: You were the only one in that level of the house. Your rooms are only a few steps from the stairwell where the woman was savagely attacked with a knife. Surely you must have heard *something*!"

Misha turned her head. She imagined how the inspector must

STEFAN BACHMANN

look with that voice and that meaty, rotten breath. No doubt he was a constable, hurried away from his dinner in the village, not a real inspector at all. She imagined spectacles and a brown tartan waistcoat and a great walrus mustache, someone with a family and a cottage, someone who would find this all rather thrilling and flattering, and who really had no idea what he was doing.

"I heard nothing," she said, and the smell of the blood and the lavender and the tobacco flooded over her so that she thought she might be sick in the middle of the drawing room. *Not a word, old girl, or it'll be you hanging from the lights.* "I left my room to go to dinner. And then I was on the stairs, and . . ."

"And what?"

"And there was the body." Her fingers tightened in her lap. She felt like running. If she could get away from that house in its little bowl of gardens and walls, away from the narrow corridors and the guests, all the *J*'s and the *L*'s, the grand and prideful people, maybe she could be happy. Maybe she could burst her cage and brush the splinters from her hair, and never be afraid again.

She sensed the inspector leaning back. "Very well," he said, frostily now, and perhaps a little bit petulantly. She was ruining this for him. "We will speak again in the morning. Miss Markham, if any new scrap of information should surface in your mind, we would be very thankful if you would share it with us." His tone shifted abruptly, all posturing and humble subservience now. "Lady Gortley, if it isn't too much trouble, we will question the others now. And you'll make sure, won't you, that all the servants are accounted for, and that no one should leave the house or grounds, at all? Yes. Not under any circumstances."

× × ×

After the interview, Lady Gortley positioned Misha in a chair in the hallway and left her to speak with Mr. Hudson, the butler. It was then that they descended on Misha. They were not cautious or polite. They buzzed toward her like a cloud of mosquitoes, and they wanted to know everything, gory details, things not even the inspector had asked.

"Were you quite covered in blood? Head to toe?" *Minerva Boulstridge. Great-aunt.*

"Was Lady Willoughby, well—I heard she was wearing all her jewels, every last ring and bauble, and you know that means she was planning to elope." *Emily Howsham. No relation. Guest.*

"What if the blind one did it herself?" *Jamie Thorpe. Cousin. Up from London.*

She recognized many of the peripheral voices too, all of them elegant, shiny like boot-black, and smooth as cream: Lady Dartmouth, whispering behind her fan; Lord Bellham, Duke of Westerdown, also known as Patrick, Definitely a Pig. She could feel their eyes boring into her, pinning her to the chair. Some hung back, what they thought was a safe distance, but she heard them too:

"To think, it was someone in the house. Perhaps one of us. And she can't even tell us who!"

"Horace, look at her nose."

"I see it, I see. She's like an ogress."

"There are convents for girls like her."

"And prisons." Somone laughed.

Misha let their words flow over her, and she retreated from them, surrounding herself in kinder thoughts, pictures of things half remembered from childhood, teapots and clocks, and her characters and friends that she kept in her head, beautiful, kind people with golden hair and rosy cheeks. And all at once, someone snatched her

STEFAN BACHMANN

firmly by the arm and dragged her up. She struggled at first, shocked. She heard a rough voice nearby, and was sure it was the murderer come to finish her off. But then she heard the heavy shoes, and a brisk girl's voice saying: "Sorry, ma'ams, sirs, I was told to take her up, she's quite disturbed, mistress's orders, come along now, Miss Misha."

With that, Misha was dragged from the crowd of spectators and bundled quickly toward the baize servants' door, and Kerstin was muttering, "Wicked folk. Wicked, wicked people."

Fear made Misha raw and empty, scratched her insides to ribbons, as Kerstin helped her up the stairs to the fourth floor. They were going up by the back way, as the front stairs were still occupied by the murder scene. No doubt the landing was strewn with white sheets and shattered flashbulbs, and crawling with policemen like bluebottle flies.

The murderer knew who she was, and yet Misha knew nothing. Nothing except that he smelled of lavender and tobacco and spoke in a strange country voice, and those were things easily falsified. If he decided to kill her, no one could stop him. And if he decided to kill someone else—

"Miss?" Kerstin said, and Misha flinched. Kerstin had never spoken to her directly before, not even when bringing up the breakfast tray, or passing her in the hall. "Miss," Kerstin said again, and she sounded a little breathless, as if she had gathered up all her courage and now she was a steam engine, barreling unstoppably forward. "I'm sorry for all them down there. I just want you to know that I saw someone murdered once, and it weren't a pretty sight, nor sound, and I know— Well, I just know."

Misha's face felt like a mask, cotton skin on porcelain bones, but underneath she had begun to spin. It was strange, what words could do. No one had spoken to her like that since she was a child, like she was a real person, a real girl, and not just a walking list of ailments and deficits.

She didn't answer at first. Kerstin fell silent, as if worried she had spoken out of turn.

"You saw a murder?" Misha said softly, at last. "In the village?"

"No. In Leeds, where I grew up." Kerstin's voice turned eager, and a shade dramatic. "It was a dreadful thing. Guts everywhere, like all that skin a person has is just wrapping, and when it pops you splatter everywhere. And I suppose it wouldn't have mattered if I hadn't seen it. You know, it's not really the sight that sticks with me. It's the feeling. I got there right after it happened, and the *feeling* in the air, like something unnatural horrid had been done that couldn't ever be taken back, like something had left and when it went, it tore a hole right through everything." Kerstin's voice softened suddenly, the bravado gone. "It was dreadful."

Misha wasn't sure what to do. She wanted to say: "That is what I thought. That is what I felt," but she didn't. She climbed the stairs next to the servant girl in silence, feeling strangely light.

"You know, they don't talk about you much, the Gortleys," Kerstin said, at the third-story landing. "Or the servants. You're like a character in a novel. Rather like a secret."

That sounded nice. Being a secret. "It's not like that at all," Misha said. "It's miserable here."

"Isn't it everywhere," Kerstin said matter-of-factly.

"*You're* not miserable. I hear you singing. When you're taking out the washing. *I'm the Queen of London-Town.* You don't sound miserable at all."

"Don't I? Oh. Well, better singing than crying. Anyway, I don't want to be a servant forever. One day I'll get away from here. I'll be an actress or a circus performer. I'll shoot pistols and whisper to snakes."

Kerstin sounded dreamy, and Misha fell into the dream, thinking of bright lights strung across a tent, sawdust kicked into clouds, jangling music drifting from an organ grinder's box. She wanted to pursue the subject, but they were walking down the corridor now, and Kerstin was speaking of murder again. "Tomorrow it'll be a bit fresher, I think. Clearer in your head, and less like an awful nightmare. It was with me. D'you have any idea who might have done it?"

"No. There are thirty guests in the house at least, and just as many visiting servants."

"But did you notice anything? Perhaps a—?"

A floorboard creaked, footsteps approached, and suddenly Misha was surrounded by the smell of tobacco and lavender. Someone passed behind them in the corridor.

Misha stopped, rooted to the floor. Kerstin tried to keep going, but Misha's muscles were locked, her shoulders stiff and high.

"Miss?" Kerstin's fingers squeezed Misha's arm encouragingly. "Miss, go on?"

Misha turned, looking back down the corridor. Someone was standing there. She could feel him. She could feel eyes on her, watching, and through the fog of her vision, she could see a shape, tall and dark, facing her through the swirling gray. She wanted to scream, but the only sound that came from her was a hissing, high-pitched whine. Her hands went tight around Kerstin's arm. She wanted to ask who it was, who was standing there at the end of the passage. Then Kerstin opened the door to Misha's room and pulled her in, hurrying to fold down the bedspread and plump up the pillows.

"Kerstin?" Misha whispered. But by then Kerstin was gone, and the fear returned, creeping around the edges of the door, red and murky.

Misha slept fitfully that night, her sheets twisted around her legs. She had wedged the door shut with a chair and closed all the windows, but it was summer and the night was hot. The temperature seemed to have seeped into the velvet drapes and the wood and the bric-a-brac, and was now releasing itself in puffs of steam, slicking her forehead and dampening her pillow. She could not close her eyes. She felt she could still smell the thick cologne, feel the woman's skirts hanging down from the ceiling, the blood dripping, and the cold arm . . . Every shifting in the house, every scuttle of a rat under the floorboards, sent her skin rising into gooseflesh.

There in the dark, she wondered why the man had not killed her when she had stumbled across Lady Willoughby's body on the stairs. She had practically walked into the murder as it was being committed, and she had witnessed his presence, and surely it would not have been such a great risk to add a blind girl to the scene. But Misha knew why, even if she wished she didn't: He had not killed her because he thought she was not a threat. He thought he could whisper a few horrid words into her ear and it would be enough to frighten her into silence. It had been enough, almost. She *was* frightened, a part of her, but another part was forming too, deep in her chest, and shaping into an angry, spiky little burr, and that part wanted to catch him, wanted to grab him by the hair of his wicked head and drag him to justice. He was still in the house, one of the guests, or more likely one of the guests' servants, judging by his rough voice. And either she caught him, or she waited in fear and silence while he did whatever he pleased and perhaps got away with it.

No, she could not allow that. She was done sitting quietly in her attic room. He would come to regret having spared her.

When morning came, it was a sick sort of relief. Misha stumbled from her bed and shuffled about for her clothing. Kerstin came up several minutes later with the breakfast tray. No sooner was she in than Misha snatched her arm and pulled her into the middle of the room.

"Kerstin, you've got to listen. Is the door closed? Was anyone in the hall?"

"Miss, please, I've got a load of work to do—" Kerstin started, but Misha shook her. She listened for a second, and when she heard no sound, either from the garden or the house, she went on:

"I know who did it. I know who killed Lady Willoughby. At least, I know a little. I know he smells like lavender and tobacco, and I can see him somewhat, like a dark shape in my eye. I know that sounds mad, but it's more than anyone else knows, and we've got to do something or he might kill me. He might kill *you*, Kerstin. Did you see the man that passed us in the hall last night?"

"Do you mean, when you had that little fit and fairly well clawed my arm off? No. I was distracted."

"Oh. Well, that was him. That was the murderer, and you've got to help me catch him. He sounded like a country man, a Yorkshire man perhaps, though come to think of it, he may have put that accent on. He didn't *smell* like a country man. He smelled like lavender and tobacco. Do any of the servants smell like lavender and tobacco? And if they don't, I need you to go through all the men's guest rooms and find a cologne that does. Tobacco and lavender, all right? Can you do that?"

Misha had barely breathed at all during the rush of words, and now that she did, she realized that Kerstin was probably staring at her as if she were the maddest creature alive. "*Can* you do that?" she said again, somewhat suspiciously this time.

Kerstin did not answer at once. Then, quietly, and a little awed, she said: "We passed him? We passed by the very murderer?"

"Yes. And he came into my room right before he did it. He was right there in the doorway with Lady Willoughby."

Suddenly Kerstin tore away from Misha, and she heard her go to the window and pause there. "Oy!" she shouted down at someone. "You shouldn't be out there! Back inside, the lot of you!" She slammed the panes closed and came back to Misha. When she spoke again her voice was breathless and a little bit excited. "He was *right there*? Oh, lawks, the murderer, right there with you . . ."

Misha was about to launch into another plea, when Kerstin said: "I'll help you. I don't believe that you can see him, not unless you aren't blind as a bat as we've always supposed, but I know you were there, and so I'll look. You, miss, should go downstairs and be with the Gortleys and not by yourself."

"No, I can't, I—"

"Then come to the kitchens. Wait there. At least there'll be folk around to watch you. I won't be able to tell you right away, but I'll do my best. Now come on, or Cook will have my head for chicken dinner."

Misha was not convinced she wanted to be in kitchens either, not until she was sure the murderer was not one of the staff, but at least she would not be alone there, and so they both ran from the room, down the back stairs and into the servants' wing. Misha hung back while Kerstin whispered to the cook and the other maids that they would have a guest. A hard wooden chair was brought out for Misha, and she sat down. She listened carefully for a rough voice like gravel and earth, for the dark spike in the corner of her eye that would tell her the murderer was here, but he was not. Misha sat very still on her chair and listened to the bustle swilling around her, the snap of aprons, the crackle of the stoves, the clang of pans, the whispers.

The servants tried to be quiet at first. Even the head cook, the queen of the lower levels second only to the butler and the housekeeper, lowered her voice while giving orders. But after a while of Misha sitting like a statue they seemed to forget about her, and the regular noises of the kitchen returned as loud as ever. She heard their gossip like a constant newspaper reading: The servants' quarters had been searched again; Mr. Hudson, the butler, was disgusted, and said that if it was one of his servants who was the murderer, he would break the perpetrator's neck himself and spare the cost of rope; the entire house was being searched; the old governess, Essa Beet, just down the hall from Misha, was missing from her room, and a side table was knocked over as if there had been a struggle, and no one had seen her in hours; guests were wailing desperately about their wish to leave the wretched place; and Lady Gortley did nothing to dissuade them, because if Miss Beet's body was found, Lady Gortley would be ready to go as well.

Kerstin did not come back to the servants' hall for many hours, or if she did, she had no time to speak. Eventually it was teatime and

Misha was sent away by the cook to have tea with her own people. She did not tell Cook that she didn't have people, that the Gortleys were no more her own sort than the servants. She came into the parlor just as Lady Gortley was arriving, conversing loudly with a guest:

". . . and what *is* that lovely scent I'm smelling everywhere?" Lady Gortley was saying. "Such a rich accord. Is it Guerlain?"

"Oh, it's not Guerlain. I don't know where it's from. All the men found a bottle in their rooms, tiny little ampoules with lovely notes. I was sure you had done it as a welcome gift!"

"Darling, no, I couldn't possibly afford it. The taxes, you know. They'll be the death of us. But it is a strong scent, isn't it? Like tobacco and lavender."

Misha's heart sank into her shoes. She walked to one of the sofas, counting the steps, sat down, and waited as others arrived. Someone arranged herself to her left and began eating daintily. A gentleman sat to her right; the Earl of Prylle, judging by the sound of his bronchitis. The room filled quickly, bodies jamming the space. And everywhere, completely drowning the smell of black tea and scones and finger sandwiches, was the scent of the murderer, rolling from every soul, like purple smoke.

There was one more grand dinner before the end of the hunt. None of the guests were allowed to leave, even the important ones, because Lady Willoughby was the daughter of a councilman, and that made her death much more problematic than it might have been otherwise. Most of the guests huddled together in the drawing room or billiard room, nursing cups of strong drink and murmuring to one another. The brave ones helped in the search for Essa Beet and the murderer, and the less brave spoke fervently of planning to do so. No progress was made on either front.

And so the dinner went on as planned. Misha had taken a new room, a small cupboard of a place lower down in the house, and had told Kerstin not to tell anyone, not even the servants. That morning, as she climbed the stairs on her way back from her bath, she passed an open window. She heard the children again, singing:

F *is for Frederick, who laughs like a hog*
G *is for Ginty, who died like a dog*

Misha shivered and hurried on, the bathwater suddenly cold on her skin. She dressed quickly and started down toward the servants' quarters.

"Misha! Oh, there you are." It was Kerstin, stopping her on the stairs. "You heard about the perfume. I don't know, I don't know how, but he *knew* somehow that we knew, and all the ampoules from the silver cabinet had been stolen and an eye-dropper and fourteen pieces of card-paper, and what's the first thing you do when you have a new perfume, you *try it,* of course, and now—"

"Kerstin, it's all right. We'll catch him another way. There's a dinner tonight. He's not one of the servants. He gave himself away with the scent. If he were a servant, he would have given the scent to the servants, but he knows where I'll be and he wants to throw me off. He made a mistake there. He thought I knew more than I did. I'm going to find a way to get near him tonight, and then I'm going to mark him."

"I told you I didn't believe that nonsense about you being able to see him." They began clattering down toward the kitchens. "You can't *know—*"

"I do know. It's like—it's like a sickness in the air whenever he's close. You don't have to believe me, but it's true. Now. I'll need a bit of red paint and a letter stamp, or something similar, and then I'm going to have to distract him at dinner tonight and mark his suit or his hand, and then I'll need you again, Kerstin. I'll need you to tell me who it is. When we have that, I'll go the police, tell them the entire story, have them follow him about incognito until they've got something to arrest him for. It shouldn't take long. D'you have a stamp?"

"Can't you just point him out to me, and I'll tell you who he is?"

"You're a housemaid, Kerstin! Of course I would if you could get into the dining room, but what'll Mrs. Hawksmith say if she hears you were in with the guests during dinner!"

"She'll say, 'You're sacked,' and that'll be that."

"Precisely. So. A stamp. Do you have one?"

It took Kerstin some time to catch up with Misha's thought processes, but when she did, she said: "Of course I don't have a stamp!" She paused and perhaps she winked, but Misha couldn't see it, so at last Kerstin squeezed her fingers and said: "But I can fetch one. I'll have to sneak into Mr. Hudson's pantry. He's busy enough right now. It shouldn't be difficult. I'll meet you down in the scullery and slip it to you. I'm not sure this will work one bit, but . . ."

But she did it anyway. They found each other an hour later and Kerstin passed her a metal-something and a tiny envelope of red stamping ink, slipping it behind her back as they passed each other, right under Mr. Hudson's nose, as sly as two cats. They agreed that Misha would try to mark his shirt, and then they would meet early the next morning at the latest, and search for the marked clothing among the washing. With that they parted ways, and Misha dressed herself for dinner and crept down to the dining room.

You should have killed me when you had the chance, Misha thought, and she smiled bitterly and trudged into the whirl of sound and bodies.

The dinner was eight courses—soup, jellied salads, fish, fowl, red meat, sorbet, cheese, and a sweet, and the chatter was slow and dull and everyone spoke a little softer, displaying the usual symptoms of worry and righteous anger and grief, though none were quite so sincerely expressed as the worry. The inspector had been allowed to eat with them, and sat drinking up the admiration of the highborn guests like a sponge. Misha knew the murderer was at the table too. When she turned her face one-quarter of an inch to the left, she could see him, far down at the other end, his form like a flickering blot of ink, like his very essence was a blight in the room. She took care not to stare in that direction, but even so she felt him, the weight of his eyes on her, like a dead-cold stone. She did not hear his voice. Or perhaps she did, but she could not separate it from all the other shoe-black voices slipping and hissing and sliding into her ears, smooth as eels.

What did the others see, she wondered. No doubt a suave and smiling shell. Perhaps he was speaking to them, condoling with them, expressing little tuts of outrage over the monster who had hung Lady Willoughby by her legs from the chandelier. And they believed him, simply because he was polite and rich, like them. And suddenly Misha wished everyone were blind, every single person at that long table with its clinking silver and hissing lamps. Because what good did seeing things do, really? For all their squinting, peering eyes, they did not know who was good and who was wicked, who was strong and who was cowardly, who was murdering in their house, and who was trying to save their lives. Eyes were tricks in bone boxes, but everyone believed them.

Misha tried to eat, poking her fork idly about her plate. There wouldn't be much time left. The murderer knew of the incriminating perfume. He knew she was following him, and if he knew that, he would not let her go on with it. He would kill her too. Two murders in one house—three, if Miss Beet was not found soon—was a dreadful number, but he felt secure, no doubt, invisible. He thought he was safe.

You aren't safe, Misha thought, crushing her napkin in her lap. *I see you. And you think you see me, but I'm not what you see, and I'm not what you think.*

M is for Misha, who sits in the dark, the children had sung. They could change that now: *M is for Misha, who faced the dark and vanquished it. M is for Misha, who acted, who caught a murderer and rescued a houseful of aristocrats.* They would have to work on the rhyming, but it sounded infinitely better to her already.

After the dinner came the dancing, and that was when Misha saw her chance and took it. The string quartet (farmers from the manor, buttoned tightly into fine livery like sausages in skins, with lace at their throats so that none of the guests would know) began to tune their instruments. The first piece started, a slow, rather blue-sounding waltz.

Misha stood up and tapped her way toward the dancers. She could feel eyes following her, appraising her dress, her walk, her poise or lack thereof. *They don't know. They don't know who you are, and so they don't matter.* She saw the shadow of the murderer out of the corner of her eye, but she did not go to him. She went to the center of the floor, held out her hand, and said, "Who will dance with me?" as clearly and loudly as she could.

She felt sure she heard the first violin slip a note when she spoke, but she did not flinch. She stood and waited, and let the snickering wash over her. And then she felt a wrinkled hand in hers and an elderly gentleman said, "My dear? Will you permit me?"

His voice was kind enough, but she could hear the wink in it, spoken as much to the audience as to her. She took his hand, and they began to dance. Or he did. She walked, clumsily, stepping here and there and swishing her skirt. The tittering became louder. Her ears began to burn. *They're laughing at you,* her mind told her. *They think you're a mad, foolish girl.* And as much as she did not want it to, it stung her. She danced with the elderly gentleman for several minutes, and then, when she felt the attention begin to shift away, she let herself be passed to another fellow, and then a third, moving closer and closer to the shadow man. She swooped past him, so near she could have reached out and touched him. A new song began, a sharp, scratching three-step in minor. And then she was in his arms.

He did not smell like lavender and tobacco anymore. That scent had been scrubbed off him. He smelled of soap now, milky and nondescript. He took her hand, but he did not speak a word, and his darkness was right in front of her, pulsing, swelling like an inky thundercloud. She felt cold suddenly, terrified. They danced up the floor, down. She dropped one arm for a moment, let the red stamp slip down her sleeve and into her hand. She fingered it, felt the squelch of the ink, the prongs of the letter:

M.

M for Misha.

M for murderer.

It would stain. It would blot his collar and then it would drip over his skin, red as the blood on the staircase. She moved closer to him, close against his chest, and his darkness seemed to be flooding over her, suffocating her. He whispered something in her ear. And then she pretended to trip, and caught him around the neck, pressing the stamp hard into the back of his collar. But she was not quick enough. There was too much ink. She felt it dripping, splattering over his neck. He jerked back with an oath. And before she even realized what was happening he lifted his hand and struck her hard across the face.

The orchestra screeched to a halt. The dancers stopped, and a whisper spread through them. Misha stumbled, her eyes wide, her hand to her burning cheek. She did not cry out. She smelled the tobacco and lavender closing over her as arms took her, and his darkness was drawn away. But it was stronger now than ever, that darkness, a black flame, fuming and roiling against the gray plain of her sight.

"Misha?" Kerstin's face was inches from her own, her breath coming in gasps. "Misha, wake up! Wake up, hurry!"

Misha sat up with a start, her head still heavy with sleep. Her face was aching, and she could feel the purple bruise, tender under her eye. "Kerstin? Did you find it? I got red ink all over his jacket and his face, and I stamped his shirt collar, did you see who it was?"

Kerstin pulled her out of the bed and began practically ramming clothes down over her head. "I was in the kitchens until midnight, silly, of course I didn't."

"And no one said anything?" Misha pulled away. She'd had a suspicion of what the reaction might be. The murderer could have said anything he wanted while Misha was out, that she had been play-ing wicked pranks on unsuspecting gentlemen, that she deserved the slap, like an unruly child. The others would nod their heads and agree because she was not quite all there in the head, that Miss Markham, the typhoid you know, it didn't only take her eyes. And maybe it *had* been stupid to stain his clothes. All it proved was that she couldn't be trusted, that she wasn't sane . . .

But Kerstin believed her. She prodded Misha from the room, her voice low and excited. "We've almost got him now. And when the inspectors are awake, I'll back you up. I'll say I smelled the scent too, and that it's mighty suspicious giving everyone the same perfume as you, when that's the only thing the blind girl knew you by. We'll get him."

They ran together down the stairs and through the herb garden, starting across the green. The sun had not yet risen. Misha felt the air, chilly and brisk, and the wet grass soaking her skirt. She heard Kerstin unlock a rough old door. Then they were inside the echoing cool of the wash-house, and Kerstin was hurrying about.

"The valets will have collected all the shirts the gentlemen wore last night. They won't all be laundered yet, but Moll will have got-ten a head start yesterday." Misha heard Kerstin flipping through the racks of hangers, the whisper of fabrics. "But she won't have gotten that stain out, poor girl. We'll have to apologize afterward. *Oh, I'm the queen of London-Town,*" she began to sing softly. "The shirt-tails'll all have tags on them. Room and name, or at least the valet's name. And even if he was clever and switched the tags, the shirt will have a monogram on it. We'll know for sure."

Kerstin's voice was electric. Misha wanted to join in somehow, but there was nothing she could do there, and so she said: "Hurry! I don't know if anyone saw us, but we mustn't be caught, not out here—"

She heard footsteps, little feet hissing through the grass. The titter of voices.

"Kerstin?" she said through her teeth.

"What?" Kerstin practically screeched over her shoulder, and then she came and stood by Misha, and let out a little gasp.

The children were there. Misha couldn't see them, but she felt them, a coiled, watchful presence. They were simply standing, staring.

"What are you all up so early for?" Kerstin said after a moment, her voice snappish. They did not answer. Misha's hand dug into the fabric of her dress. She tried to say something too, tried to tell them that they needed to be inside, and they needed to be careful, when all at once she heard a whistle, and they were rushing away through the grasses, and gone as quickly as they had come.

Kerstin made a grunting noise and turned back into the wash-house. "I'm just about through with those little devils," she muttered. The sliding ring of hangers resumed.

A minute passed with no results. "How much longer?" Misha cried, her eyes straining, watchful for a shadow, a tall, dark shape.

"There are a *lot* of shirts, all right?" Kerstin said. "And quite a handful look like someone took red ink to them. Are you sure you didn't splatter the entire room?"

Misha waved her hand back desperately, silencing Kerstin. Her neck craned. She thought about running, but it was too late now. There, moving along through the whiteness toward her, was the murderer.

"Get . . . back," Misha whispered, without moving her mouth. "Hide!"

She heard footsteps retreating into the wash-house, a quiet exclamation. Misha backed into the room, her hands sliding over the walls, the equipment, searching for something, anything to use as a

STEFAN BACHMANN

weapon. She turned her head, slowly. He was standing in the door-way, a pillar of darkness, darker than the pre-dawn outside, darker than the fog of her vision. He was standing there, watching her. She went so, so still, but the stillness was all he needed and he took a step toward her. She made one last desperate attempt for a weapon, but her fingers closed on air. Her hands were empty.

"Good morning," he said, and it was his real voice now, no more rough country tones, no more gravel and earth. She didn't move. Not a muscle. Not an eyelid. Outside, the children were singing again:

J *is for Jamie, alone in the park*
K *is for Kerstin, who's good for a lark*

"You tried, old girl. You did. But perhaps you should have left well enough alone. Perhaps you should have been grateful for your spared life and run away with it. You'll join the others now. Essa Beet and Ginty Willoughby."

L *is for Louis, who douses the spark*
M *is for Misha, who squirms in the dark*

It was too late now, too late to tell anyone, too late to scream. She knew who it was: Cousin Jamie from London. She remembered him from long ago, a tall pale boy with a sharp face. He had been in the garden, in that childhood memory of the white smocks and the painfully green grass. Ginty Willoughby was there, ten years old, and sallow from influenza, and several other children too. And Essa Beet, wizened as ever, had been meant to watch them, but she had fallen asleep against the roots of an apple tree. Misha remem-bered a prank being played, how Jamie had rallied the children, how he'd had them carry old Essa Beet softly and silently to the old barn as she slept. How Jamie had tied her wrists and held bees to her skin by their wings. Essa Beet woke up when they stung her. She had screamed. Misha had begun to cry. Later, Jamie had been beaten for it. Lady Thorpe had wept and Lord Thorpe had threatened to send him to India, and yet Misha remembered watching Jamie during all this, standing like a pallid spike in his dark suit, tall and nervous and smug. He had not looked sorry. He had simply been interrupted.

His hand was growing tighter and tighter around Misha's own, and she could feel the sweat spring up in his palm like cold needles—

She stood bolt upright. In one swift motion she tore her hands from his and leaped toward the door, or what she thought was the door, but the man caught her hair and jerked her back savagely. She swung about, pummeling his face. He caught her fingers a second time, and they squeezed in his hands like wet twigs until she thought they would break. She tried to scream. His hand clamped over her mouth.

"Now, now," he said, and his voice was maddeningly patient, a gentle scold. "Quietly. We wouldn't want to frighten the children." And then he dragged her to the door and closed it, and the sound of its latch was like an anvil strike.

"How did you know?" she gasped, struggling against his grip. "How did you— ? Kerstin didn't tell you, she never would have!"

"Oh, Kerstin didn't say a word. She is a good and loyal girl. And no one else knew. But the children did. The children know everything."

Misha tried to scream again, but her throat would not allow it, and her voice box let out nothing but a dry crackle. *Get away, Kerstin,* she thought desperately. *Get out, get out, don't let him find you!*

"So," the man went on, and his breathing was coming quick again. He swallowed thickly. "Let's have some fun, shall we?" And here she heard the snick of a blade being drawn from its sheath.

Misha screamed into his palm, flailed wildly, but he only clamped down harder until her jaws ached. She felt cold metal on her neck. Somewhere out in the gardens the children shrieked with laughter.

And then, behind them, there came the rattle of hangers parting and the pounding of shoes, and something struck Jamie with a metallic thunk so heavily, Misha felt it in her own bones.

"Kerstin?" Misha wriggled out from behind the hand. The shuddering thunk came again, again, whizzing through the air, and Misha knew it was Kerstin, wielding a pressing-iron the size of a birdhouse. She smashed it into the shadow's head. Misha heard the knife skittering out of his hand. He collapsed, but in an instant he was up again, and she saw his darkness coming at Kerstin, his shoulders hunched. Misha launched herself from the floor, following the sound of his blade as it slid across the boards. Her hand found it. She flew at the dark shape.

"*Help us!*" Misha screamed. "*Help us, someone, he's killing us!*" But he wasn't. They were killing him, and he was curling on the ground beneath their blows, and Kerstin had the knife now, and Misha's fingers were over the man's mouth, and she felt a liquid sliding between them, hot as the blood pooling on the stairs . . .

When the inspector woke up, he would see the dots—a gentleman, brutally murdered, an orphan recluse, a lowly country maid of questionable reputation. He would not see the lines, though, that connected them, or the spaces between, where the truth lay. Perhaps Misha and Kerstin would be brought to an insane asylum for deranged females. Perhaps they would be hanged. But not then. Not that day. When the deed was done, and Jamie no longer moved, they took each other's hands and ran from the wash-house and the gardens, away into the morning sunlight. Behind them the children began to sing again, a new song, and a dark one:

J is for Jamie, who gave us quince pies
K is for Kerstin, who stabbed out his eyes
L is for laughter that flew through the green
M is for Misha, who stifled his screams . . .

Inspired by the 1931 film *M* and the 1970s television series *Upstairs, Downstairs*

THE GIRL WITHOUT A FACE
MARIE LU

Out of all twelve bedrooms in the new house, Richard's was the only one with a closet locked from the inside.

His parents couldn't figure out how it happened. The closet's doorknob had no keyhole, for one, and the door didn't seem rusted shut; when Richard peered through the side of the door, he could see that the bolt was pulled straight across, as if done purposefully. Odd. It didn't seem like anything was in there. He couldn't see any shelf or chair legs when he looked through the slit under the door.

Dad joked about it for a while, in the lame, awkward way he had of saying exactly the wrong thing at the wrong time. "A trick door!" he said, nudging Richard in the ribs and giving him an exaggerated wink. "I'll bet the last owner accidentally locked himself in there all the time. Couldn't you picture that? Probably got himself stuck in there for days on end, hollering . . ."

Dad's joke trailed off once he saw Richard's face. They ended up staring at the door together in an uncomfortable silence.

Why did it have to be the *closet* door that couldn't open? It was as if the universe wouldn't leave him alone about closets. And in a giant house this expensive, on a street where doctors and politicians lived, you'd think all the doors would be well-crafted, top-of-the-line. Not made like shit.

Still— "It's fine," he said. "I'll use the dresser," he said. Hoping his parents would agree and just forget about it.

They didn't. At first, they tried halfheartedly to open it. Then they tried in earnest. No good. The hinges refused to pivot. They couldn't even get it to budge. The jokes turned into grumbles about needing to break the whole thing open. They ended up moving Richard to a different bedroom, and that worked for a few days, until the second bedroom's closet door started jamming up too.

"Sorry, honey," Richard's mom said to him. "Must be the cold weather. We'll get a contractor to look at these. You could switch again, if you—"

"Forget it," Richard said, waving a hand. He didn't start a brand-new year in a brand-new house just to dwell on old news again. "No big deal."

In the rush of moving in, the closet situation was forgotten. A month passed, and January became February.

After a while, Richard started getting the distinct impression that someone was watching him sleep. There was a strange weight in his room, as if the furniture or the walls weren't aligned quite right, and sometimes he would feel that weight press against his chest like a stone. At first, he would get up in the middle of the night and rearrange his things. Honor roll plaques. Golf trophies. Decathlon ribbons. His Harvard University early action acceptance letter, encased in a thousand-dollar frame. He would move and move until it all seemed right, and then he would go back to bed.

The next night, though, the weight always returned. He tried not to think about it.

Once, in the middle of the night, winter wind slapped tree branches hard enough against his window to wake him up. He scrubbed a hand over his face, then looked around, puzzled. No, there had been some other sound too. A rustling, maybe. He looked around the room. Everything seemed untouched and in place.

Then the rustle came again. It sounded almost like the shuffle of feet.

He tilted his head, listening for the source.

Nothing again.

Finally, he went back to sleep. As he drifted off, he realized that the shuffling sound seemed to come from behind the closet door.

The next night, he had a dream. In the dream, he was walking down an empty street that he didn't recognize. Fog shrouded the road, blurring the streetlamps. His steps echoed. Up ahead, he saw the faint shape of a girl walking slowly ahead of him. She had long, pale hair, and even though a cold wind blew around him, it didn't seem to stir a single one of her strands. He could tell he was walking faster than her, but he could never seem to catch up. She stayed ahead, right at the edge, where the fog started to swallow everything whole. She never turned around.

Richard jerked awake. Outside, a weak rain had started. He let himself lie still for a while, listening to the storm, until the sweat on his body had dried. Then he looked over at his locked closet.

The door was open.

He frowned. Then he propped himself up on his elbows and squinted into the darkness for a better look.

The door was *wide* open, swung all the way out so that the doorknob touched the wall.

Standing in the middle of its entranceway was the girl. She kept her back turned to him, so that all he could see of her was her long hair.

A strange tingle traveled up his neck and over the back of his head. He sat up. Then he swung his feet over the side of the bed, put on his slippers, and got up. Thunder rumbled outside.

"Hello?" he whispered, keeping his eyes on the girl.

She didn't move.

He took a step forward. Then another. The closet drew closer, and his heart started to pound. He stopped a few feet away from her. He reached a hand out to touch her shoulder.

Before he could, she started to move. She walked into the closet, where it was so black that he couldn't see any of its inner walls, and then she turned to the right and disappeared abruptly into the darkness.

Richard bolted upright in bed.

He had never woken up from his first dream. His eyes darted over to the closet—he half expected the door to be wide open again, and the girl to be standing in front of it, her back turned to him. The faint light of dawn had already started filtering in through his window.

The closet door was locked, as it had always been. When he walked over to it and tried again to pull it open, it stayed tightly shut.

Just a dream. Richard stared at the closet door for a moment longer, then shook his head and started getting ready for school. A poor night's sleep meant a long day ahead.

His friends shrugged it off.

"Was she hot, at least?" one of them asked as they ate their lunches on a bench outside school. For a moment, Richard couldn't even tell who said it—they all looked the same under this slant of winter light, identical in their uniform navy sweaters and scarlet ties and khakis, the crest of their academy embroidered on their right sleeves.

He just smiled with them. His friends were trying to steer the conversation away from the eight-hundred-pound elephant in the yard, and he appreciated that. It did sound kind of stupid in bright daylight, even if the bright daylight was the overcast gray of winter. "Nah," he replied. "I couldn't see her face."

"Maybe she had a butter face," another friend said, "and your dream's trying to take pity on you." The others laughed. Richard went along with it, but the more he did, the colder he felt. A crazy worry entered his mind. *What if the girl could hear them?*

After a while, the bell rang. His friends started heading inside. Richard followed behind them, half listening to their conversation. He didn't want to say anything, but the strange weight on his chest had returned, and he felt as if his friends' chatter was coming from somewhere far away, muffled from behind glass. He grimaced and rubbed his neck. *Poor night's sleep,* he thought again. He glanced out across the schoolyard.

Something in the corner of his vision . . . beyond the white fence and across the street. It was the girl. She was just standing there, her back turned to him. Her pale hair untouched by the breeze.

Richard stared. His breath rose in a cloud of condensation. It took him a long moment to glance back at his friends. "Hey," he called to them. "You guys see that?"

They didn't hear him. Richard turned back to where the girl— But she was gone already. He blinked. She'd been there. *Right there.* Yet the sidewalk was empty, swept clean of leaves by the breeze. His eyes scanned the entire street in both directions, following it until it wrapped around the block and disappeared from view. No sign of her.

He swallowed his words. Suddenly he was glad that his friends hadn't heard him. They would have made fun of him all day for being stupid and seeing things.

He stayed in a fog of thought for most of the afternoon. Each class bled right into the next. It took several hours before the pressure on his chest finally began to lighten. Of course he hadn't seen anything. Did he really believe that something he'd seen inside his dreams could creep into reality? He almost chuckled out loud in class. Hallucinations: He could definitely use more sleep.

Still, a *feeling* lingered in the back of his mind. It distracted him enough that he walked home in a daze, crossing streets when he shouldn't and bumping shoulders against passersby. Cars honked at him at the crosswalks.

There were an awful lot of cars on the streets, actually, when he forced himself to pay attention. He stared at the trail of neon red taillights as he went, letting them blur into a line across his vision. It looked like traffic was being diverted away from his street. He frowned, his mind sharpening again, and then quickened his pace. Unease settled into the pit of his stomach, like he had swallowed something heavy and cold.

When he turned onto the street leading home, he saw the police lights.

The sight sent a familiar ripple of panic through him. There were two cars, both parked outside his parents' home, and the officers were talking to his mother. Richard noticed that one of the cars was a police car, while the other was an animal control truck. His mother's shoulders looked hunched as the men asked her questions. She was still in her suit; the cops must've asked her to come straight from work.

"Richard!" His mother finally saw him. She waved him over frantically as he approached.

"What's going on?" he asked. His eyes darted to the police officers. They stared back at him, expressionless. He bristled. Why did cops always look so damn severe? It wasn't like he did anything.

"Are you Richard Dukaine?" they said.

"Yeah."

One officer motioned him over to a blue tarp laid out on the road. He pulled it aside.

Richard fought back the urge to gag.

It was a deer. At least, it used to be. Someone had gauged both eyes out and snapped all of its legs. Bone shards protruded out of the hide, exposing tangles of sinew and muscle. Blood stained the cement under and around it. It was as if a car had hit the deer—except too perfectly.

Wonder where the car went. Richard didn't know why that was his first thought.

The officer pulled the tarp back over the body. Then he turned to Richard. "We've had two witnesses tell us that they saw you doing this."

"What?" Richard almost choked on the word. "I was at school today. All day." At the pause, he looked from the officers back to his stricken mom. "This is sick. I wasn't here. This—somebody's idea of a twisted joke."

The officer looked at his partner and sighed. "Look, kid," he said, his voice weary. "If it were me, I wouldn't blame you. We all know your old man." He nodded respectfully in Mom's direction. "And your mother. We don't want to give you more trouble in your senior year." He shrugged. "Only wanted to hear your side of the story, see if some kid might've been giving you grief, setting you up."

His mother stepped in before Richard could sputter out an answer. "This is ridiculous," she snapped. "I had to leave work early for this? My son's afternoon, disrupted, over *this?* He's had a rough enough time. I want to know the names of those witnesses."

"Now, ma'am, I'm afraid I can't give out those names—"

"*I want them.* Do you hear me? I will escalate this to . . ."

Richard's confidence grew as his mother went on. Of course they had no proof that he did anything—because he didn't. He lifted his head and looked the closer officer in the eyes. "Tell us who the two witnesses were, and my father will talk to them personally."

The officer hesitated. "No need," he finally said, shaking his head as if he wanted to be done with the whole thing. "I don't want to get everyone all riled up over this. It's just a deer."

Richard's mother narrowed her eyes. "And if you'd stop wasting your time harassing my son, you might find whatever sick child in the neighborhood left this."

They talked for a few more minutes. But soon the cops left, the animal control people removed the corpse, and the evening settled into silence. Richard thought, as he and his mom went back into the house, that some of their neighbors were watching them through the slits of their window blinds. It brought out a strange rush of rage in him. *What did they know?*

Before he could step into the house, he saw her again. The girl was walking away on the opposite side of the street, her hands in the pockets of her coat, her back turned, her pale hair limp and dull. He paused on the steps and stared. He didn't dare blink. His eyes started to water. He had a sudden urge to run over there and shake the girl violently.

But he didn't. All he could do was stand there and watch until she disappeared into the evening, amid the dark tree trunks and lampposts. He moved only when his mother called him back into the house.

Nothing would come of it. Nothing ever came of anything. Richard knew he was protected; the son of a congresswoman and a lawyer, valedictorian of his old high school, multi-million-dollar trust fund, legacy admission into Harvard. He was a good kid. *I'm a good kid.*

The police let it go, and they didn't hear anything more.

Two nights later, Richard was fast asleep when the door of his closet suddenly swung open with a loud bang.

He screamed. His parents came rushing in, and he tried lamely to explain it—but his words sounded slow and dumb. This time, it wasn't a dream. The closet door stayed open, revealing an empty space inside. His parents listened to him with confused frowns, but Richard could tell that they thought he'd simply had a nightmare, that he'd opened the door himself. Dad even walked over to test it several times, as if to prove to Richard that there was nothing to fear. Embarrassing. An eighteen-year-old guy screaming at monsters in the closet. His parents calmed him down. His father promised to have the door locked back up, if he preferred. As if he were a child.

Richard waved them off. No big deal. Maybe something had kept the door stuck and now the winter air had simply loosened it. After a while, he went back to bed, but instead of sleeping, he kept his eyes locked on the closed closet door until morning finally came.

"God, you look like shit," his friend whispered to him when he arrived late to class. "What the hell did you drink last night?"

Richard ignored him. He slouched in his chair, tie rumpled and blazer askew, staring blankly at the whiteboard while their teacher droned on. His mind wandered in a murky swamp of thought.

They had moved across town to get away from it all. His parents had gone through great pains to make sure he could still attend a private academy where some of his friends went. It had seemed like a great idea at the time—maybe it was still a great idea, actually. But Richard sat and felt the weight return to his chest, the awful and oppressive heaviness, until it seemed like he could barely breathe. The teacher's voice faded to a hum, and the world gradually started to look like it was underwater, the walls dark and ugly and rusty green-blue, the light through the windows faded and old, the desks peeling. His classmates continued listening to the lecture, the shadows on their faces cut into sharp angles. The sound of pen against paper grated on his nerves.

Richard's head nodded. He jerked himself awake. It wasn't even noon yet—he really had to get more sleep.

The room looked faded now, the sounds and people far away, identical rows of dark uniforms. His eyes went back up to the whiteboard. He just had to get through his senior classes. Then he was free.

The lights flickered overhead. Richard blinked, looked up and then around. No one else even stirred. His friend sitting beside him just kept on writing into his notebook, his eyes obscured by the shadows that fell across his face. Richard turned his attention back to the teacher.

She looked different somehow. Did she always have light hair? Why did Richard remember that she was supposed to be a brunette? He frowned as she continued to write on the whiteboard. She looked shorter now too, her shoulders more delicate, her body nearly lost inside a chunky, bleak-colored sweater. Her hair spilled down to the middle of her back, loose and limp, dull under the green-yellow light. He started to take notes again. He could barely keep up.

Why was she writing so fast?

Slow down, Richard snapped in his mind as he tried to keep up. But the teacher kept scribbling faster and faster, words and sentences that Richard could no longer even understand, lines and lines of jagged symbols from one end of the whiteboard to the other. He paused, bewildered. She was putting all of her weight into it, her shoulders hunched up, her writing arm jerky with motion. The cold, uneasy feeling seeped back into his stomach. He looked around— everyone else still seemed completely unperturbed. Could they even understand what she was writing? Faster and faster she wrote. The room turned darker, until Richard felt like he was the only one still sitting in there. The girl wrote and wrote and wrote, the marker screaming against the board. Richard tried to cover his ears, but it penetrated right through his skin. It was the girl, of course, the girl was his teacher and she couldn't stop scribbling, scribbling so hard into the whiteboard that she was carving deep grooves into the surface. The nails of her writing hand had started to bleed.

Richard couldn't take it anymore. "You have to stop," he called out. No one listened to him. He raised his voice. "Stop. *Stop!*" He stood up. His chair squealed against the floor. "Stop writing so fast!"

The girl didn't listen.

Richard spit out a curse and hurried up the empty aisle. *Who the hell are you? Why are you following me?* He reached her at the whiteboard, grabbed her shoulders, and spun her around.

He couldn't see her face. Where it should have been, he could only see a heavy film, a blur of skin, like he was staring into a thick sheet of opaque glass framed by pale hair. He shook her as hard as he could. "Stop it," he hissed through his teeth. His shaking turned violent. The girl without a face began to shriek.

Then hands were on him, and somehow he was being pulled off, pulled away from the grotesque creature. He had the dull sensation of being thrown back to the ground. Somewhere, someone kept screaming.

"Stop!" They were screaming at *him*. The world suddenly brightened, and when Richard blinked, he was staring up at the ceiling of the room and his classmates were gathered around him in a wary circle. Two of his friends sat next to him, their hands still wrapped tightly around his arms, both breathing heavily. In front of them, a group of students were comforting a shaking girl, who sobbed uncontrollably.

"What the hell is wrong with you?" one of them yelled at him.

Richard stared numbly back at the girl. She sat in front of him in class. Now she trembled and cried in her friends' arms. Even when the teacher rushed back into the room with security officers at her back, he couldn't move.

But he hadn't grabbed his classmate. He had grabbed the girl without a face. He was sure of it.

Another round of police conversations at home, another emergency work-leave for Mom. They all sat together in the living room while the police interrogated Richard, their eyes weary and unfeeling. This time, a psychiatrist sat with them. Richard answered their questions one after the other.

"And you attacked Miss Evans today because you thought she was someone else?" the officer asked.

What in the world was he supposed to say to that? Richard shrugged in frustration. "I don't know," he muttered. "I must have had some sort of nightmare in class. I didn't sleep well last night. I must have fallen asleep."

He hated the psychiatrist's penetrating look. She peered at him over her glasses. "Have you had any dreams lately, then?"

"No, ma'am."

"Do you still find yourself dreaming about Lillian Stephens?"

Richard's mother straightened, her posture tense. "I'd prefer we not discuss that," she said. "We've gone to great lengths to help Richard forget about—"

"Let him answer the question," the psychiatrist replied calmly.

Richard tightened his jaw until he thought it might break. If the police weren't here, he might insult the psychiatrist right to her face—but with the cops sitting next to him, he had to behave himself. "No, ma'am," he said, keeping his demeanor innocent and confused. "I've been doing better since we moved here. We've put the whole thing behind us and tried to move forward."

"He's graduating in a few months and heading off to Harvard," his mother interjected. "Top grades in all his classes. Isn't that right, honey?"

Richard just wanted his mom to be quiet.

The psychiatrist smiled, but somehow, her smile didn't seem to touch her eyes. "How lovely to hear that you're doing so well," she said.

The questions went on for a while longer, until finally the police officer seemed satisfied with his answers. They didn't leave him alone, though, until he agreed to start seeing the psychiatrist once a week, at least until his graduation. Richard had to play along. So he did.

That night, he lay awake in bed, turned in the direction of his closet, and tried to stop thinking about Lillian Stephens. The whole thing had been so stupid, anyway. It bothered him that the psychiatrist felt the need to bring it up. Did she have any idea how hard it'd been for him to push it all behind him? For him to move on?

Richard grunted and flipped around in bed, turning his back to the closet. Just a weird couple of weeks. He was tired, was all. Screw this. Screw everything.

Slowly, his eyelids started to droop.

A strange noise woke him up. It sounded like a girl, someone crying. He blinked, then sat back up in bed. Was this his house? It took him a long moment to realize that he wasn't in his room at all, but a stranger's. No, not a stranger's. The decorations on the wall had changed, his trophies and plaques replaced with paintings and portraits. Now he remembered; this was his friend's house, and the only time he'd been in here was during a party at the end of last year. He hesitated, then got out of the bed and made his way across the room. Red party cups littered the floor. He had to get out of here and back to his own home, he thought groggily, before his parents found him gone.

The hallway was dark. He couldn't seem to turn on the lights. He stumbled down the corridor, kicking red cups out of the way. As he went, he thought he could still hear the sounds of the party going on around him. People dancing. The bass of the music. People were still here, drunk and laughing, beer and vodka spilling out of their cups. He saw a group of people he recognized stumble past him, laughing hard at something he couldn't understand. The light was green and blue, cutting sharp angles on their faces, turning them into hideous creatures. A lightbulb somewhere kept flickering like it was about to go out. Everything wavered in and out of focus. Maybe all the booze was what made it so hard to see straight. He looked away. Better go downstairs.

Before he could, though, he caught sight of someone he recognized. It was himself, junior year, laughing with a bunch of his friends. A girl was with him. As he looked on, his younger self filled up the girl's cup with another round of vodka, and she nearly dropped the whole cup as she leaned against the wall. Lillian Stephens. The memory looked different from this distant angle. He saw himself grab her arm when she tried to leave. He shouted something in her face while his friends jeered. Then he started dragging her toward a nearby closet.

She laughed with a wild, unsteady lilt, and she tried to pull her hand away. She was so drunk. She couldn't even walk well enough in the opposite direction. *Just shut up,* he remembered thinking that night. Then he opened the closet door, shoved her in, and locked them both inside the darkness.

Richard tried to recall exactly what happened afterward, but the memory was too hazy. There was her nervous laughter, and then some shouting. Someone clawing weakly at him. Wet streaks on her cheeks. His sudden, searing irritation with her. They were just having some fun. *Oh, come on,* he said. *Then you can go. Promise.* He remembered her fists pounding on the door. Her crying. He could barely hear her through the bass of the music.

Afterward, he staggered out and left her huddled in the corner of the closet. She looked like she wanted to sleep anyway.

He managed to make his way out of the house somehow, into the blur of his car, and onto the road. He shouted at the world to stop spinning so much. He'd almost made it home too, before he'd hit that damn deer and run himself straight into the lake. Shatter. Shards. A terrible screech. Then that green and blue light again, everywhere, and him struggling through the murky water to the police sirens above. Except, this time, he couldn't seem to reach the surface—

A loud clap of thunder jolted Richard out of the nightmare. He sucked in a terrible gasp of air. Sweat beaded his body. Outside, the wind was slapping the branches against his window again. Richard looked wildly around until he knew for sure he was back in his own room. Then he flopped his head back down on his pillow and let his breath out.

That stupid psychiatrist, planting memories back in his brain.

A faint tapping sound made him turn in bed. His eyes settled on the closet.

The door was wide open again, the doorknob tapping gently against the wall. Inside, it was blackness. The hairs rose on Richard's arms and neck. Suddenly the room seemed colder, the weight pressing again on his chest, the terrible feeling that something in here did not belong. On a strange compulsion, he rose from his bed and took a step toward the closet. Then another. Step by step, he made his way over to the closet until he stood right at the edge where the blackness began.

Inside the closet crouched the pale-haired girl without a face, her wrists and arms slashed with dozens of lines, blood smearing the wall behind her. She reached her scarlet hands out to him. He opened his mouth to scream.

Morning came.

Bright sunlight streamed into his room. Someone was pounding on his bedroom door. Richard went to the windows and pulled down all the blinds. He curled up in defense, then pushed himself into the corner of the bed. His bloodshot eyes stayed on the closet door. He couldn't remember when it had closed again, or whether or not it'd been closed the entire time, but he couldn't take his eyes off of it, and he couldn't stop trembling. His body felt sticky with sweat, and he was afraid to look down in case he saw blood smeared across his skin.

"Honey?" The pounding again. It sounded like Mom, but he couldn't be sure. "Are you all right?"

He didn't want to answer. *Go away.* What if it was the girl, trying to tempt him out of bed?

"*Honey.*" The voice sounded more urgent now. "Honey, the police called again. They said the neighbors saw you wandering around the middle of the street last night." She sounded frantic. "Richard? Did you hear me?"

I don't know. It wasn't me. Richard started shaking his head to himself. He looked down at his bed. Mud and grass stained the sheets, and his feet were dirty.

Ridiculous. He couldn't have gone anywhere last night—all he did was wander around in his nightmares, that damn party that just refused to go away. When he heard his father's voice join his mother's outside the door, he finally lifted his head. "Go away!" he yelled. "I'll come out. Just please *go away.*"

His mother gave some muffled reply through the door, how they were here to support him through whatever trouble he might be experiencing, that they were going to wait downstairs for him.

He didn't move until the sun had shifted into late afternoon. By then, his parents' voices had turned sweet and coaxing. *Sweetie, please come down. You should eat something.*

"I'll be there, goddamn it," he finally spat at the door. He stumbled out of bed and forced himself to the bathroom.

There, he let out a choked gasp.

He looked horrible. Worse than horrible. His eyes were so bloodshot that it looked like his irises swam in a red sea. Were his eyes *bleeding*? The veins on his hands and wrists stood out, swollen as if ready to pop. His skin looked ashen, a corpse-like gray.

Richard splashed water on his face, scrubbed it hard, and looked again. Then he started to cry. What was wrong with him? Why was he being punished like this? It wasn't his fault Lillian had taken it all so badly. After the night of that party, after the rumors had already spread like wildfire through school—Lillian, that slut, she gave herself away in a closet at a house party, she wanted it, that slut—the girl just shut down like a broken toy. Richard didn't see what the big deal was. How could she be so depressed over *nothing*? She'd been drinking as much as he had, maybe more. Besides, *he* was the one who got slapped with a DUI and destruction of property after the deer and the lake. His dad had to make a personal call to Harvard to explain that one.

They were all just fooling around.

Richard hadn't expected to go to school one day to hear that Lillian had been found dead in her closet, her wrists and arms slashed apart by a razor.

Then came the accusations against him from her parents, and the trial. A whirlwind, a nightmare. Sure, his parents had plenty of money and influence to fight it, and the charges were dropped—lack of evidence, and all—but the damage to him was done. His parents had to move across town and switch him into a new private academy. He'd fought to put the whole thing behind him.

Richard had a sudden urge to smash his mirror into pieces. *I don't deserve to be punished like this.* He stared at his reflection. His thoughts echoed back at him, filling his mind until it sounded like a different voice said the words.

The sun shifted again. Afternoon turned into sunset, and his room bled with red light. Darkness crept forward. His mom started calling for him again.

What would she say, once she saw how terrible he looked? Richard sighed and raked a hand through his hair. Finally, he went to his dresser and started pulling out some clothes. His movements turned feverish as he went. He pulled out more and more, until a pile of clothes lay on the floor. That was what he had to do. He had to get out of here, before the girl found him again.

A faint movement at his window distracted him. He paused in what he was doing and turned to look out at the street.

Except it wasn't his street any longer. Instead he saw a long, dark hallway stretching away from him, a hall covered in portraits,

its walls faded and charred as if burned by fire. It looked like a shadow of the home where the party had happened, its details eerie and inaccurate. The portraits' eyes were all closed, their brows all furrowed. The wallpaper, once cheery and yellow, was singed with dark streaks.

And standing in the middle of the hallway, framed by his window, was the girl. She had her back turned to him, and all he could see of her was her torn sweater and her long, pale hair. She turned her head slightly, so that he could see the outline of her cheek, and then slowly, excruciatingly, she turned all the way around. The deep, jagged lines carved into both of her arms were sharply visible, blood dripping in long streaks down her fingers and dotting the floorboards of his bedroom. Now he could make out the curve of her lip, the dark circles under her eyes. He ran over to the window, dragged his dresser away from his bed, and shoved it in front of the windowsill with a loud crash, blocking the opening halfway. Outside his bedroom door came the alarmed sound of his mother's voice, but she seemed so far away that he couldn't tell if she was there at all. Richard yanked the blankets off of his bed and piled them up on top of the fallen dresser, then dragged an armchair over to add to the barricade. He pulled his bed over. He picked up the floor-length mirror in the corner and stood it in front of the armchair. His breath came in short gasps.

Maybe that will keep her out.

His mother's fist continued pounding weakly on the door, but he was no longer listening.

Beyond the barricaded window, a thick darkness began seeping into the room. It crawled in along the edges of the walls, shutting out the light until a yawning black fog stretched across half the room, reaching for him. He stumbled backward with a cry. His bedroom door's knob jiggled. Richard's back hit the wall. When he stared at his reflection in the floor-length mirror, he saw that the whites of his eyes had turned completely red.

Then his reflection vanished, replaced by hers. Blood stained her arms.

Richard suddenly felt the grooves of the closet door behind him. He yanked on the door—it swung open without a sound. He scrambled into the safety of its small, enclosed space, and then he shut the door and locked himself in. *Go away,* he whispered into the darkness. Tears ran down his cheeks. *I didn't mean it. I'm sorry. Just go away and leave me alone, please leave me alone, please.*

Go away, Lillian.

For a moment, it seemed as if the world stilled. As if it listened to him. Richard's sobbing quieted—he straightened, listening for the sound of footsteps or a girl's voice, waiting for the weight to press down on his chest. Nothing. He kept waiting, until his legs grew cramped and the closet had started to feel stuffy. In his haste, he realized that he still had his shaving razor clenched tightly in one hand. Through the slit below the door, he could see a thin sliver of light. The world had gone quiet. Maybe she'd gone away. He'd imagined this whole insane scene in his head and now that he had shut himself away, he'd cleared his mind, and when he opened the door he would see his room all put back together. The girl would be gone.

Long minutes dragged by. Finally, he reached out and pushed the closet door.

It wouldn't open.

He pushed harder, then searched for a lock that didn't exist. His breathing grew labored; he jiggled the doorknob again, and when that didn't work, he shoved himself to his feet and slammed all his weight against the door, again and again. The door stayed as unmoving as a brick wall.

Maybe someone had accidentally locked himself in there, Dad had joked.

Richard started screaming for help. His fists pounded on the door. Somewhere, far away, he thought he could hear the frantic shouts of his mother. He pounded until his fists were bruised and raw.

His breath started to rise in clouds. When he paused long enough to look around the dark closet, he realized that he was not alone. The girl without a face was crouched in one corner of the closet. Richard scrambled away from the door and huddled into the closet's other corner. She kept staring with sightless eyes. With a whimper, Richard brought his hands up to block her from view.

"What do you want?" he whispered into the darkness. His voice trembled. "I'll do anything. Please."

When he opened his eyes again, the girl had crawled halfway to him, leaving red stains on the floor as she went. He curled tighter as she drew near. She lifted her bloody hands, then reached for him. Her hands touched his cheeks. He opened his mouth to scream, but no sound came out.

I want you to see me.

For a split second, the girl's face came into clear focus. It was a familiar face, one he'd seen in a closet and one he had worked for a long time to blur out. Small, thin lips still shiny with gloss. Skin so pale that little blue veins appeared along her temples and eyelids. Smudged black mascara that cut a sharp line across the top of her left cheek. Irises of piercing gray that surrounded dilated pupils, bloodshot eyes.

She looked down at the razor in his hand. She touched it—and at her touch, the razor crumbled into pieces, leaving behind only the blades. She held one of them up to his face, then brushed it across his arm.

Then you can go, she said.

Outside the closet, Richard's parents finally broke down the door to his bedroom. Two police officers followed behind them. They shouted frantically for their son, but no one answered. The room was dark, the dresser and mirror and blankets all piled haphazardly in front of his window. They turned on the light. The police searched the entire room. Finally, Richard's father yanked open the closet door.

Richard sat huddled against the closet wall. His face stayed turned down in concentration. Blood covered his arms. In his hand was a blade from his razor, and he was busy sawing deep, jagged lines into the flesh of his arms.

His mother screamed at the sight. His father lunged to snatch the razor out of his son's hand, but Richard shrieked at him to get away. It took his father and a police officer to drag Richard out of the closet and into the light, but even then, they could not pry the razor out of his hands.

"No," Richard gasped as they tried to restrict his arms. "You don't understand. She said I could go, if I did this. *She promised I could go.*"

Spring changed to summer, then to fall. The semester began at Harvard, and a new flock of freshmen filled its halls. Absent among them was Richard. In a hospital several miles from home, he sat against the soft wall of his room, struggling, as always, to free his hands from their bonds. In the corner, the girl without a face watched.

How frustrating, he thought, that no one would give him what he kept asking for. All he wanted was a blade. But it never came, so he struggled alone, trying, failing, to act on her words.

Finish. Then you can go.

Inspired by the 2000 film *What Lies Beneath* and the 2010 film *Los Ojos de Julia*

A Girl Who Dreamed of Snow

McCormick Templeman

Petals of snow fell on her shoulders as the girl hugged her mother good-bye. Jaw clenched, the woman looked down at her child with clear, dry eyes. There would be no weeping today. "It is time to go, Nara. Your father awaits and your duty calls. Your time is now."

"Don't go." A small hand wrapped itself in her skirts. Nara's sister stared up at her. Nara wanted to pull her close and tell her she would never leave. Instead, she kissed her softly on the head.

Turning, she looked out at the icy landscape, the soaring trees, branches dark and bitten blue with frost. And for a moment, she had something like a premonition, a feeling that something terrible was watching her, something hungry and sick. She could nearly hear it out there, panting between the trees, its breath ragged and spoiled.

Sins of a faraway people had sickened the earth, changing it. And now there were whispers of something coming, something catastrophic sweeping ever closer. Her people could hear it in the song of the birds and the creak of the ice. The earth held many secrets, some of them too terrible to tell.

× × ×

The first leg of her journey was to be the easiest, and yet Nara found herself queasy with fear. A shaman's daughter, she'd learned the ways of the wind and snow as others might learn to speak and crawl, and she thought on wild things and night creatures as her brothers. Even the wolves howling in the frozen stillness didn't frighten her. They sang their song, and she sang hers. But still, there was something in her bones that told her she was being followed. And as she fell asleep each night, hoping to see her father's face in her dreams, she saw only snow.

Nara had been walking for seven days when she came to an outcropping of trees at the foot of a tilted mountain. Hunger gnawed at her bones. She built a fire, curled up next to it, and settled in to sleep.

Behind her closed lids, she could see the dancing of the firelight.

"Father," she whispered. "Father, I'm coming."

She could see him there now in her mind's eye, tormented, broken, and her heart yearned to join him, to ease his pain. She recalled the shaman's song he had taught her, and with an aching heart, she began to sing. Her small voice rose like a sparrow's call, and as the night grew ever darker, the earth below her seemed to soften and receive.

Soon she drifted off. But had she not, she might have seen a change in the flames, an alteration in their trajectory as shadows gathered, as something cold and silent slipped out of the earth and circled her like the outward swelling of a maelstrom.

× × ×

Mowich stoked the fire and stared into the dark. She was out there somewhere. This girl his brother sought. The one he said would fetch them the highest price of all. Mowich didn't like it, never had. But who was he to fight it?

It was five years now since the plague had come. A pestilence brought back from a plundered land, it sickened the girls and killed the women, quickly devastating the countryside. At first the healers prescribed witchgrass. Born of ice and snow, it grew wild on the hillsides near the outer edge of the land. But when the witchgrass was depleted, the skies dried up, no moisture fell, and the land grew stingy and bare.

Mowich's mother had died soon after Izlette was born. He'd clung to the baby, to her sparkling eyes, to each sprout of chestnut hair on her newborn head. She'd shown no sign of the sickness until last spring, just before her fourth birthday. Then it came on fast and strong, sucking the flesh from her bones. It wouldn't be long now until it carried her to the grave. Without the witchgrass, there was nothing to do but watch the women-folk die, and to fetch fresh ones from territories up north where the women were hearty and strong.

It was only his first trip, and already so much had gone wrong. Whatever had happened to the girls they tried to take in the village by the river, he was sure it hadn't been wolves. Four girls, caged and ready to take back to market. Mowich had been sick in the snow over it. When dawn came, when he'd gone to check on them, to give them water and food, all four were laid out in the snow, their throats gouged, torn, their lifeless eyes staring up at the heavens.

"Night creatures," his oldest brother, Sain, had proclaimed, and the others had believed him, but Mowich knew better. Sain, though small, had always had a wicked way about him, and something in him was turning, warping for the worse. Terrible things had happened to those girls. Something had gotten to them, something worse than any creature that lurked in the woods. He knew that at last Sain's vile predilections had eclipsed even his greed.

It was the morning after that when Sain had his vision. He'd called them all together, all six of them—Mowich and his older brothers, fat-cheeked Ig and curly-haired Dairn, and the Fairlish twins, whose gold had procured the wagon, whose muscle drove the horses, and whose lack of brains made them useful as Sain's thugs.

Sain had gathered them at dawn with a strange, wild light in his eyes, and he'd told him he'd had a vision of a girl with hair like moonlight and eyes as dark as coal, her blood newly upon her. She'd fetch a price like none other, he'd sworn. After her, they'd need not make another trip north. Though for now they would need to travel farther than their countrymen were wont to do—high to the icelands, into the land of ancient things.

They all knew the stories about the things that lived up there, where long ago men had gone mad, driven to consume the flesh of their brothers.

But gold was gold, and so it was decided.

They'd traveled on through the snow, so foreign to their southern blood, and all the while, Mowich's heart had grown sicker and sicker. It had taken seven days to find her, to ferret out her camp, snug against the base of a tilted mountain, to find her sleeping by firelight. But when the time came to fetch her, Mowich was unable to move. He'd pleaded with his brothers, but to no avail. And so he'd stayed behind here at camp, earning Sain's wrath.

Mowich stoked the fire again and stared off into the hills. They must be upon her by now. And yet he heard no screams. Shivering, he turned suddenly, peering into the darkness, the trees like sentries standing cold and still. Behind them, something seemed to linger.

"Hello?" he called.

Silence answered back. And something behind it, a distant throbbing, deep and heavy as a heartbeat.

He tightened his grip on the stick and peered deeper into the darkness until it seemed his eyes played tricks, until night itself seemed to undulate and pulse.

A distant scream cut across the sky and the movement was gone. A trick of his mind after all. He turned and stared toward the slanted whiteness of the distant mountains. They had her now, he knew. He sighed, an ache in his chest as he thought of his own small sister, of Izlette's sunken cheeks, of the sharp demarcation of her wrist bone, of the monster eating her alive from within.

Another distant scream, muffled and strained, and he asked himself what he really knew of monsters.

The Hunter moved with lash-quick precision. The call had been sounded. The time was now. His quarry was on the move. He'd heard it in the earth, below the ice, that darkness unfurling. Most Hunters served a lifetime without answering such a call. How many could say they'd heard it twice in as many years?

Inside his hut, he examined his weapons. Hatchet, dagger, curved blade. He pulled each one down and wrapped it like a father might swaddle a newborn against the cold. The hunting knife he slung on his hip.

It was dusk when he set out, the smoke from his fire still ghosting behind him. His belly growled, and he tasted it: human sweat and fear. It hung in the evening air like a freshly gutted kill.

He walked with purpose, tall but swaybacked, faster than any normal man. And his eyes searched for one thing only. When he found it, there would be penance paid. When he found it, there would be blood.

Nara was sleeping, dreaming again of snow, calling it forth in signs and swirls, speaking the language of the ancients. She barely felt the bag slip over her head, but as soon as she was hoisted into the air by rough, groping hands, her scream burst from her chest, cutting through the callused burlap, echoing across the night.

She writhed and fought, but quick, heavy hands clamped around her neck. It would take no more than a snap, she knew. She quieted herself, though her heart beat wildly in her chest. In her mind, she saw her father. His gentle face. His smiling eyes. Soon she would be with him. Soon she would find him and give him the message. She had to hold that hope in her heart, or she would never make it.

They bore her away through the dark night, jostling her through the snow, laughing and congratulating one another on their catch. *Catch.* As if she were an ocean pike and they the hearty fishermen.

They walked—twice they skidded on the ice, nearly dropping her—and at last they reached their destination. With rough hands, she was dropped in the snow. A moment later, the sack was removed from her head. She knelt there, shivering in the cold. She didn't speak, just stared.

There were many, all boys, knee-deep in manhood. The two that looked alike—twins—had thick red beards and hands like meat. Then there were two who averted their eyes, one round of face, the other with locks curling down to his shoulders. Behind them there lingered a slim, dark-haired boy. He stared at her like he wanted to speak. In his eyes she could almost see an apology.

The one who concerned her, the one who could make things go

bad in an instant, was the smallest of the lot. Sharp and lithe with bright blue eyes and hair like wet hay, he smiled hungrily, his incisors grazing the soft flesh of his full lower lip. He held a cudgel in one hand, gently tapping it against his leg.

"What is your name, then?" he said, his eyes flashing with hunger. He took a step toward her. The dark-haired boy flinched. Instinctively, she withdrew.

"Do I frighten you?" Blue Eyes asked, his voice friendly but his lips drawn tight at the edges.

She shook her head.

He held out a hand to her. Not seeing any other option, she took it. His palm was icy, yet slick with sweat.

"Do you know where you're going?" he asked.

She nodded, doing her best to keep her eyes downcast.

"And where is that?"

"To your land."

"And what land is that?"

"Down south. Where the sun meets the moon and makes waves on the land."

"And do you know why you're going?"

She swallowed, blinking back tears. "Because your women are gone, and your girls, they are dying. The gods have turned your earth to stone, and your witchgrass won't grow. Without witchgrass your women die. Without women, your people are no more."

Looking up, she locked eyes with the dark-haired boy, and she was certain he was trying to tell her something.

"Look at me, girl," Blue Eyes said, squeezing her hand hard, his nails digging into her flesh. "Tell me why I took you."

She looked into his face, and she knew his kind at once. Her heart began to race.

"To sell me," she said. "You've taken me to sell me to a southern man that he might have a wife, that he might have sons, sons that can live without the witchgrass."

He narrowed his eyes. "You say that like it's a bad thing. Tell me your name."

"Nara," she whispered.

"I'm Sain," he said. "Remember that name. Always remember it. And that boy over there, the one you keep staring at. His name is Mowich, and he isn't your friend. He does what I tell him. Do you understand?"

"I understand," she said, and eyes still averted, she continued, "I understand that you've taken me that your sons might live and breed, but what of your daughters? Your daughters still die. Taking me won't save them." She glanced up quickly.

His eyes widened, and he licked his full lips. "I don't care about saving them." He shook his head, a terrible smile cutting his face. "And that isn't why I've taken you."

Nara stood, still small beside her captor, but she looked him in the eye, and when she spoke, her voice was certain. "Then why did you take me?"

His face went blank. Nara recognized the look. The Gray Woman of her village had worn it the day her husband died. Her kinfolk had tried to console her, but she'd been impervious, as if something inside her had simply taken flight. It was later that night that she'd taken her babies three out to the edge of the world and set them on an ice floe. After wrapping them up tight in a handsome blanket, she pushed them out to sea, watching as they drifted out to the open ocean and to certain death. They found her the next morning, her eyes empty, her face mad.

The boy pulled her close so that his lips were wet against her cheek, hot breath down her neck. "I took you . . . because I wanted to take you."

And then with lightning reflexes he pushed her to the ground and raised the cudgel high in the air.

"No!" someone screamed—then pain and a darkness deeper than death.

Across the ice, the Hunter stalked, metal case in his hand, sealskin bag slung over his shoulder. He was closing in now, the scent drawing him near. No sleep. Not yet. Not until it was over.

Somewhere up the hillside, an animal screeched as a wild thing's teeth sank into its flesh. The Hunter uttered a low growl. Last time, his quarry had nearly escaped him. He had the souvenir to prove his victory. Absently, he ran a finger over the string of teeth that hung from his waist like a belt. Each from a different hunt. Each one worthy prey. This time, though, things were different. This time it was darkness itself he hunted. This time there was no room for mistakes.

Mowich glared across the campfire at Sain. His brother stared coolly back. The girl was doing better now. She was breathing at least. Sleeping in her cage. But Mowich couldn't bear the sight of her. She was someone's daughter, someone's sister. Once, she might have been Izlette.

"She's a child!" he said.

"She's bled," Sain replied. "And I will do with her what I like."

"And we don't have a say?"

Laughing, Sain swept his eyes over the five of them. "Of course you have a say, but which of you doesn't want to bring home gold to your starving father? Which of you has enjoyed watching our way of life destroyed, watching our sisters die before our eyes?"

"There are other ways," said Mowich.

Dairn pushed a dark curl from his eyes and cleared his throat. "I think we need to stop arguing. We need to keep moving."

The others stared at him, and Sain cocked his head. "And where do you propose we go, brother? You want to travel through this terrain at night?"

"It's just that," Dairn said, looking away, "I've been hearing things. I think . . . I think someone might be following us."

Sain smirked. "No one's following us. We're in the middle of nowhere."

"Don't tell me you don't feel it too. In the darkness. In the trees. There's something out there. Something is watching us."

"Night creatures. And let me tell you, they die plenty quick if you've got a good blade in your hand. Let them try. They'll cook up nice and toasty on a spit." Sain laughed, but when he looked to his brothers for approval, he was met with dour expressions. "Oh please, not all of you."

"Dairn has a point," said Ig. Mowich nodded, but the Fairlish twins snorted and shook their heads.

"This land is full of ice magic," challenged Dairn. "They've got hungry spirits up here. Their kind can call them forth to kill a weary traveler just like that."

"Bedtime stories," one of the twins spat.

"Dairn knows what he says," said Ig, leaning forward. "The Five. The ones who stand still. Who's to say they're not out there now? Out there watching us?"

"That's what this is about?" Sain laughed. "Devils and magic?

Hungry spirits that can make man slaughter his brothers and eat up his children, picking their teeth with the bones?" One of the twins laughed and Sain slapped him on the back. "Perhaps we should call on a benevolent fairy to protect us. Or sing a magical song to take us to a land made of honey and gold."

Dairn lowered his eyes and shook his head. So they would stay put tonight. But in this tiny fracturing, Mowich began to see an opportunity.

The next day, they drove on through the snow, on through the cold, and Mowich noticed the little things. The hitch in Dairn's voice as he spoke to Sain. The fear in Ig's eyes as he scanned the trees. Even Sain seemed different. His brother held his shoulders a little higher, his lips a little tighter, and if Mowich wasn't mistaken, when dusk began to settle, he'd seen Sain flinch suddenly, his eyes flicking to the forest. There was something out there. How much longer could they deny it?

Soon dusk crested into night, and tempers flared. Dairn had taken the reins, forging ahead despite Sain's demands to stop that they might camp for the night.

"I said stop the cart," Sain growled through his teeth. But Dairn shook his head, his lips an angry white line.

"Do as he says," grunted one of the Fairlish twins. But Dairn refused.

"They're out there," he whispered. "They're watching."

"You're acting like a fool."

"We can't stop. We have to keep going."

"It's too dark!" shouted Sain. "Stop the cart."

"The moon is full. I can see just fine."

Sain grabbed his brother's arm, meaning to wrench the reins away, but Dairn was stronger and pushed back. Sain stumbled and fell against the front of the cart, spooking the horses. But it was more than that. More than horses spooked by ordinary commotion. Their muscles tensed in strange waves. In their throats, gurgling sounds. They surged forth as if driven by an unseen hand.

Sain, staggering, pulled himself to stand.

"Stop the cart!" he bellowed.

"I'm trying!"

Dairn pulled tightly at the reins, but it only vexed the horses more. They pushed harder, faster against the darkness. A jolt as the cart hit something hard. A wheel sprang free and the cart skidded on its side, careening through the trees and thundering across the ice, finally coming to a stop at the center of a moonlit clearing. Mowich had been thrown clear, some distance from the others. He sat, stunned, watching as chaos rained down. The horses reared up like harpies, crying and straining against the night. Sain struggled out from under the cart. One of the wheels had nearly crushed him. He was on Dairn in an instant, smashing his fist into his brother's face. Blood spurted from his nose in a magnificent spray. Furious, Dairn raised his own fist just as Sain pulled his blade from its hilt.

"Don't push me, brother," he said. "You've seen the things I can do."

Ig stepped in, bleeding from a cut on his forehead, and put a hand on Dairn's shoulder. He guided him away from Sain. "We don't need to turn on each other," he said, staring behind them and into the trees. "Let's get the cart fixed and be on our way."

That seemed to bring a measure of peace. The boys quietly dispersed and set to their tasks.

Mowich, still dazed, found himself staring at the moon. It was odd, that moon. Steel blue and so full, it seemed almost like it might split at the seams. Pushing himself up to stand, he took a few steps away from the group, trying to understand why it was he felt so uneasy. He noticed the trees, tall and angular, their branches like enormous thorny limbs, and for a moment he felt certain that they were about to consume him. He shook off the thought. *You're seeing monsters where there stand only trees.* He started to walk back to the others but stopped. It wasn't just those trees. With a slow panic, he came to realize that there were dozens more. He stood at the very center of a perfect circle of trees. The pines stood around him, predatory, as if waiting for some violence to delight them. He was reminded of his father's stories of long ago, when men were made to fight terrible beasts, as spectators watched from the seats of an enormous circular theater. He was imagining things. But what was this place? What had spooked the horses? What hand had brought them here only to drop them at the center of this gruesome stage?

Slowly he backed away. Now was his chance. He had to be quick, while the others were distracted. He would take the girl, run, escape.

He hurried over to the cage. It had been thrown a good ten feet from the wagon. She'd removed the sack from her head and had crawled out, the cage door apparently forced open in the accident. She was free, and yet she hadn't tried to run. She just sat there, dark eyes watching him, pale hair almost indistinguishable against the snow. He noticed blood on the ground.

"My god, you're hurt," he said, a break in his voice.

She raised a palm to show him a clean, half-moon slice. Blood seeped from it in lazy rivulets, its path slowed by the cold.

He offered his hand. She frowned, an uncertain look in her eyes. Then she nodded and gave him her unwounded hand.

Over by the wagon, Dairn was shouting something at Sain. Voices grew louder. Ig looked over at Mowich. He had been gathering up the supplies that had been dashed into the snow, but now he watched Mowich with a frightened eye.

"She's bleeding badly," Mowich called to him, trying to keep his voice from shaking. "I'll take her down to the stream to wash the wound. We don't want an infection."

Ig nodded quickly, shifting his eyes away.

Mowich helped Nara to her feet and then, with an awkward grasp around her waist, led her from the circle, down to a nearby stream.

They stood there a moment, Mowich listening. The rapids of the icy water beat the same pace as his heart.

"A fight is about to begin," he whispered. "When it does, we will run. Back to your people. Back to safety. We'll be gone before they realize it."

She turned to him with troubled eyes. "Why are you doing this?" she asked.

"To protect you," he said.

She reached a hand up toward his face. Instinctively, he grabbed it. He moved closer, but she brought her lips to his ear. "When I tell you to run," she whispered, "run as fast as you can and don't look back."

"What?" He frowned, pulling back. "What are you talking about?"

"I only need five," she said.

"Five what?"

"Five," she said, her eyes downcast. "To sate them. You are extra. You can go."

He started to laugh, but then he saw a figure move in the darkness behind her. Moonlight caught Sain's eyes. Mowich's heart surged with panic. He tried to wrap his arms around her just as Sain stepped into the light. His brother smiled, lifting his hand to reveal a hunting knife, twisting the handle to let the blade glint in the moonlight.

"You're not trying to take what's mine, are you, Mowich?"

"No," Mowich said.

Sain laughed, and with his free hand he grabbed Nara by the wrist, yanking her toward him.

"Let her go," Mowich said to his brother.

"From now on she stays with me," Sain said. "She—"

Nara slipped from his grasp and started running. But Sain, his face a grimace of rage, was on her heels. Mowich sprinted after them, but stopped just as suddenly. Nara ran not away but *toward* the others—toward her prison.

"Nara, no!" he called, scrambling up the slope to the clearing. But when she came into view again, he found himself struggling to take in the sight. Sain was a good distance from her, entranced by what could only be called a transformation. She stood at the very center of the ring of trees, and although she was still small, there issued from her an unmistakable power, strange and pulsating. She seemed capable of stirring the depths of earth with a movement of her hand.

"What's she doing?" one of the Fairlish twins called.

They all grew quiet, and as if pulled, started walking toward her.

"What are you doing, girl?" Sain called to her, his voice low and careful.

She closed her eyes and bent her head forward. She spoke quiet words in a foreign tongue, her lips moving, and then with a slow, graceful gesture, she raised her hands in a circle over her head.

"She's crazy," laughed one of the twins as he quickened his pace, closing in on her.

But Mowich knew better. It was a sacred tongue she spoke, a powerful tongue, and the song she sang was the shaman's song. This girl was no ordinary girl.

"Stay away from her," he tried to warn. But then something rose up behind the Fairlish twin, something dark and taller than any man. Mowich tried to call out again, but the words stuck in his throat. Whatever it was, this thing, it was made of shadow, made of night. It seemed to ache and swell as it rose up ever higher, its opacity splitting the moonlight like a knife. Mowich backed away. "Behind you!" he finally managed to call out. The twin sneered, but it was enough to make him look over his shoulder, and as he did and saw the darkness swelling up behind him, he went utterly still.

Mowich turned. He meant to warn Nara, but she stood staring down into the snow as if she could see the future there.

"Nara?" His voice broke.

Slowly, she raised her eyes to him.

"Run," she said. "Run now."

He didn't. He couldn't. He was unable to tear his eyes from the monstrous shadow come alive. Looking at it was like looking into the face of God.

It began to undulate, moving forward, fast now. It wrapped its inky darkness around the Fairlish boy until he seemed almost to vanish. There was a sound like tendons popping, a gurgled scream, and then nothing but blood puddled at the foot of the darkness, a crimson stain glinting in the swell of the moonlight, soaking the snow.

High above Mowich and the others, an icy wind screamed through the trees.

And then it started.

Four more shadows rising, five in all. The Five. The Ones Who

Stand Still. Called from deep inside the core of the earth. Called forth for the rite.

The others were screaming, suddenly stirred, but Sain was staring at Nara, his face blank. And then, ignoring the towering darkness descending upon him, he pulled out his knife. Raising it high above his head, he rushed at her, a terrible screech rising from his pitch-stained soul.

Nara did not flinch. She closed her eyes. Behind her lids, she saw snow falling on fields of green, saw the dream she'd held in her heart since birth.

But then the sound of a struggle.

She opened her eyes to see Sain on the ground, Mowich above him, the knife now in his hand. "No!" she screamed, too late. She watched Mowich slit Sain's throat with one clean stroke.

Mowich dropped the blade into the snow and struggled away from the body. He looked at her with haunted eyes, a brother's blood now upon his hands. "He was going to kill you," he said.

"No," she cried out as the shadows grew taller, grew closer. "You were supposed to run. I told you to run!"

Mowich looked at her, lost. And then he saw the five shadows. The one now sated, the puddle of blood at its feet, stood still. The four others moved in silence, closing in. Five shadows. Five boys. And as the shadow meant for Sain grew ever nearer, Mowich understood. He looked at her with terrified eyes.

She shook her head. "I'm sorry," she said. "There's nothing I can do. I'm sorry."

"Oh god," he gasped as the darkness enfolded him. Around him the others' screams rose in the air like smoke. Nara looked away as the creatures began to feed.

The Hunter found her at the center of the circle of blood. She was on her knees, face in her hands. The shadows, their offering accepted, stood still and tall, inert. He approached with his hunting knife.

"I don't want to fight you, old man," she said, her voice so calm and clear, it gave him pause. "You can put away your blade."

He stood still, his eyes trained on her. A shaman girl, able to sing out the darkness, to call it forth in dreams of snow and make it do her bidding. A forbidden rite, one her people had officially renounced long ago. It was the duty of the Hunter's people to see that hers kept their word. It was his job to rain down justice when they did not.

"You can come easy, or you can die right here in the snow," he said.

She nodded once. "What's done is done. I have no reason to fight. I will come with you. I will face the punishment."

"They were only boys," he said, looking around at the carnage, and then he spat. "Stalked them and killed them, you did. Offered them up like meat."

"They were no innocents. I made sure of that when I called them here, when I sent the vision. If their souls had been pure, they wouldn't have answered. Yes, I stalked and killed them, but what were they going to do to me?"

The Hunter grunted. "Blood sacrifice is blood sacrifice. Your people have been warned before."

She nodded. "There is no use in upbraiding me. It is done. The spirits have received their offering, and they've granted my prayer. The weeds will grow. The girls will live. Order is restored and bloodshed and war will not come to my people. I have protected them all as I was sworn at birth to do." She hesitated as if struggling past some difficult emotion. "And . . . and I can give my father the message. Our oath is completed and he can rest. We all can rest."

He knew her father. He'd had to spill the old shaman's blood the previous spring. The Hunter ran his finger along the row of smooth white teeth.

"You should know better, a girl like you. The darkness must stay hidden, must be kept separate. Your ancestors paid the price for mixing with those devils. Driven mad, driven to feast upon one another's flesh."

She nodded. "But you will take them now, won't you?" She looked up at him. "You will take them. Bury them deep in the ice so they can do no more harm?"

"Aye," he said. And then he looked around at the bloodshed, and shook his head. "And then I take you to your judgment."

Keeping the girl in his sights, he set his case on the ground and undid the latches. Next to the blades, five glass bottles, each stoppered with rough cork. He pulled on the heavy work gloves. Slowly, methodically, he did what he'd been trained to do. Carefully, he collected them, luring each into its bottle, careful not to look too deeply into their quicksilver eyes as they pulled in, shrank down, accepting their confines.

When he had finished his task, he latched the heavy metal box and removed his gloves. His blade in his hand, he looked at the shaman child. She would meet her punishment with chin held high. He shook his head and put his knife away, and offered her his hand. He had to admire her courage, if nothing else.

He helped her to her feet, his hands the last gentle ones she'd ever know. The hangman wore rough leather and smelled of pig sweat.

Arms crossed, head bowed, Nara walked slowly through the snow, and with greater purpose even than the Hunter, she took her first steps toward the edge of the world and the gallows awaiting her there.

Far to the south, Mowich's father awoke with a start. Something had changed. Something irreversible. And then he felt it deep in his bones. His boys. They were gone. All of them.

Crying out, he sprang from bed and ran down the hall to Izlette's room. The covers were pulled back; the bed was empty. A strange silence hung in the air.

A thrust to his gut and the fear swelled there again. Not her too. Not little Izlette. Not yet. Hands to his eyes, he cried out. What had they done? His boys. What had they done?

"Izzy!" he called out.

But there was no answer. Steadying himself, he started down the dark corridor, trying to prepare himself for whatever he might find. That was when he felt it—the cool breeze against his face. It brought an odor with it, strange and sweet. The kitchen door was open. He surged through it and out into the yard. He followed the smell to its source. He stood, stunned by what he saw. Not twenty yards from the house knelt Izlette, chest high in a sea of green reeds, her face bright, shining. But it wasn't Izzy. It couldn't be, for there was color in her cheeks. She was chewing on something.

"Look, Papa," she laughed, holding out her arms as if to receive a blessing.

Thunder groaned across the sky and a moment later, soft white powder began to drift down, dusting the green with brilliant white crystals. Snow. Snow like angels' wings. Izlette stuck out her tongue and caught an icy white flake. Closing her eyes, she smiled.

And then he understood. The green in the fields as far as the eye could see. Healing witchgrass stretching out into the distance, growing, soaring up toward the sky and out toward waters as if sown there by a magic hand. He couldn't have known the sacrifice that had brought it forth, couldn't have known how the shaman girl had given her own life to save a thousand others. Nor could he have known that the penance paid was the blood of his own sons. All he saw was his daughter's smile. All he saw was the gift of salvation, born of a sacred dream of snow.

STITCHES
A. G. HOWARD

Prologue

The first time the wrens sang at night was three years ago, when I used a rusty saw to cut off Pa's left foot. The birds drowned out his screams.

Wrens don't normally sing after sunset, but I wasn't surprised by it.

Birds are known as spirit carriers in mountain lore. When someone dies, birds of all kinds carry them back and forth between this world and the afterlife, so folk can keep watch over their living loved ones, even after they're gone. I figured these wrens heard how loud Pa was wailing, and gathered in expectation of a fresh delivery.

At least fifty of them sat under the eaves of the slanted garden shed—my makeshift operating room. Dark skies folded around our mountain like a boy's hand covering an anthill. Regular folk would assume that the storm had driven the birds to seek shelter, but there'd never been anything "regular" about me or mine.

My identical twin sister, Clover, and little brother, Oakley, weren't allowed to watch Pa's dismemberment. Even at age thirteen and a half, Clover was too squeamish, and Oakley, being seven years younger, was too tender. I'd left Clover in charge of things in our tiny cottage some ten yards away. Upon my last look, they hunched in the farthest corner, a quilt wrapped tight around their heads as they shivered at the thunder in the distance.

Pa didn't scream long before he passed out. He was strong that way. A rock, Ma used to say; a rock that needed his edges filed. She was the only one who could tame his temper. When she disappeared on my and Clover's thirteenth birthday, and Pa's drunken rampages spiraled out of control, it fell on me to file him down.

By the time I turned sixteen, my surgical instruments and abilities had improved. I'd taken Pa's other foot and his eyes. His tongue and ears, too.

I soon came to realize that rain always accompanied dismembering days, as did the wrens. I suspected they were tied somehow to The Collector, the boy who claimed the parts and gave us our cash. Seemed like both the weather and the birds knew when he was gonna pay a visit. Or maybe it was the other way around, and *they* told *him* when it was time. Whatever the case, at the scent of rain and the rustle of feathers, I made the first cut, because I knew he was on his way.

1: Hollow Bones

We first met The Collector when I was thirteen and a half, the day after Pa drank two bottles of tequila and popped Clover so hard, her front teeth fell into the chicken soup. When she fainted from shock and pain, I took over supper duty. I added some sage, the herb of my namesake, and boiled the broth on the stovetop without even fishing out Clover's incisors, letting the aroma of comfort and blood fill the air. There was a part of me that hoped those teeth might come to life in Pa's belly and eat him from the inside out. Oakley hadn't grown big enough to merit any beatings yet, but by the next year, he'd be the age Clover and I were when we first encountered Pa's wrath. So, while Pa guzzled a steaming bowlful, I imagined those incisors going to work on his innards.

Pa ate every bit of dinner, leaving us nothing. He always ate like he was starving, but couldn't gain a pound. He'd never been a very stout man, and had become even thinner over the months since Ma's absence, frail and hollow-boned like a bird. But he was still as mean as a feral bobcat when he drank.

He cussed at me till I handed off the keys. From the picture window, I watched him swerve down the dirt road in his Chevy truck, kicking up weeds and grass as the tires spun this way and that. Just before following the curve through the magnolia trees and vanishing from sight, he dipped his head out the window and spewed up his supper.

I remember thinking what a waste of food that was, and that my high hopes for Clover's teeth had been for nothing.

The sun set over the trees, bringing shadows to life. Pa was to be gone all night.

My sister did her best to entertain us, despite the gray bruise that swelled her mouth and chin until it looked like a rotten plum. She insisted on making treats and having a slumber party.

The inside of our cupboard and fridge had more cobwebs than food, but we always made do. Before our ma disappeared a few months earlier, she taught us how to make gingerbread without eggs, and homemade cocoa using chocolate bars and water.

I used to watch her hands as she stirred and folded and whipped, bending ingredients to her will. Those same hands that were rough from hours spent tending the garden, yet still had a soft touch when someone was hurt or sad. She always took off her bird-shaped wedding ring when she baked because she feared she'd get it dirty with the batter. I loved seeing the white imprint that her ring had rubbed onto her skin . . . like a dove tattooed above her knuckle.

I tried not to think of how I missed Ma as Clover heated the cocoa and I stirred gingerbread batter, then shaped it into perfect boys and girls to be baked. It was mid-summer, and the old black stove heated the cottage till the stench of our sweaty bodies overpowered any discomfort we felt at being home alone.

I forced down the gritty, spiced cookies and scalded my throat on overly sweet chocolate water without complaint. I figured by letting Clover ease our hurt, it could take the bite out of her throbbing lip and gums. With full bellies, we undressed to our skivvies and opened the windows to let in the cool evening scent of pines and mountain air.

When it came time to sleep, Clover and I stripped the beds, tossed quilts and pillows on the floor beneath the picture window, and snuggled Oakley atop the pile to tell him stories.

I started with Frankenstein. I'd always liked the idea of people giving up their parts to make a new person who could outshine them. Maybe I was too graphic about the blood and chopped limbs and cracking bones, because Clover got as green as the plant she's named after, and Oakley as stiff as a tree.

Me? I was ready for dreamland.

A shame my story scared Oakley so much. He moaned for more cocoa and a happy fairy tale before he would calm enough to count stars and go to sleep.

Clover—with the added charm of her fat-lipped lisp—told of a young princess who'd once been struck by lightning. She had auburn hair with a white-blond streak and blue eyes. This princess met a prince who swept her off her glass-slippered feet with a diamond ring shaped like a bird, and promises of a happy ever after. He rescued her from slaving in a bakery in a town infested with pastry-craving dragons, and carried her to the mountains, where they lived in a cottage-shaped castle. Together, they raised parakeets and fuzzy potbellied pigs to sell to pet stores.

Since Oakley was only six when Ma disappeared, I don't know if he picked up on the similarities, but the cotton-candy lies Clover wrapped around the truth made my mouth dry and my teeth ache as if I had cavities. In the fairy tale, the prince and princess lived forever without any woes. In the real version, the *prince* had tended to our animals while he was drunk out of his mind. He forgot to latch the chicken coops. Later that night—while he slept off his liquor—high winds rattled the coops till the gates fell open and all the hens escaped into the yard. An electrical storm scorched the sky and caught fire to the hog house. The hogs ran out in flames and trampled the chickens until they were singed, hollow-boned corpses.

When the princess ran out to open the gate so the hogs could escape the spreading fire, she was struck by lightning, giving her another streak in her auburn hair and breaking something in her mind. She came into the cottage, screamed at the prince in some indecipherable tongue that failed to wake him, then disappeared into the night. The heavens opened up a flood of rain that doused the fire, but it must've swallowed Ma too. For she was never to be seen again.

Hollow bones. They make a blood-curdling crunch when you step on them. Drops the soul right out of you, unless you like that sort of thing. And roasted pork doesn't smell nearly so appetizing when mixed with the funk of scorched feathers and beaks. Still, I dragged what was left of our hogs out of the bone pile and we ate them anyway. With Ma gone the next morning and Pa vanishing to look for her without coming home for two days thereafter, we couldn't turn our noses up at free ham and bacon, no matter what was used to spice it.

In Clover's fairy tale, the prince wouldn't have spiraled into even deeper rages after losing his princess and their one means of income. He would've found another way to make cash instead of taking odd jobs in town, then spending every penny on whiskey, tequila, and the occasional carton of eggs when a carton of cigarettes was too steep.

I fell asleep after the storytelling ended that night, listening as a snore whistled through Clover's empty tooth sockets, wishing the prince of her fairy tale could somehow, someday, be our pa.

In the years that followed, I came to understand why they say to be careful what you wish for.

2: The Collector

Pa showed up the morning after he punched Clover, as apologetic and humble as a dog caught in the act of peeing on his owner's rug. I'd like to think it was the sight of her bruised and swollen mouth that did him in. But why would it bother him any more than the busted cheeks and black eyes he'd given me and Clover in our past?

Whatever it was, I chose to be grateful, because something broke him good. I could've sworn I heard the sickening crunch of hollow bones as he knelt in the yard and begged us to forgive him. I wished *he* was cracking beneath my feet, like the skeletal corpses on that fated morning we found Ma disappeared.

After Pa's apology, I didn't remember much of the conversation. Only that he said he'd found an answer—to our finances and his soul sickness. He had made arrangements for us to meet our savior. Pa called him The Collector, and he was to arrive that afternoon.

When the sun was midway over the mountain, beaming in hot yellow streams, Clover and I took the dirt road to the forest and climbed some magnolia trees to watch for our mysterious guest. Barefoot in cutoffs and sleeveless shirts, we swung upside down from our perches.

In the months since Ma's disappearance, my favorite tree had become the one with a white split in the bark starting at the lowest branches and running all the way to the ground. That breach in the wood showed up the day after Ma left. The color of the split reminded me of the streaks in Ma's hair. I was convinced the same lightning storm that struck her also struck the tree, which somehow made them connected. This tree was still alive, so she had to be too. And one day, she'd come back to us.

As I swung in and out of the shade, beads of sweat crept through the top of my scalp like creepy-crawling ants. I braided my wavy, red hair without turning upright, tying off the end in a knot before dropping it so it hung like a noose from the network of branches. It shimmered in the sunlight, favoring a giant piece of cherry licorice that would be sweet and stick to my teeth. I grabbed my braid by the end and nibbled the dusty, brittle strands, almost surprised when it didn't taste of cherries at all.

"Sage," Clover hollered from another tree a few feet over. "Look . . . a motorbike."

There he was, as promised, coming up the dirt road wearing a modern suit, dress shirt, and tie that looked out of place atop the old-timey sidecar motorcycle. Not a stitch of skin showed under his grown-up clothes. He even wore mittens . . . the woolly, winter kind that only had space for your thumb and then a place where the other four fingers sat snug and cozy, like baby chicks under their ma's wing.

But even with all that, I could tell he wasn't much older than us . . . skinny and just starting to get his muscles. Dappled with sunshine and shade, he took on a funny green tint as his bike rumbled beneath our canopy of leaves. He roared past the trunks, looking up once, then down again before I could catch the reflection of my cherry licorice hair in his shiny black helmet.

A flock of wrens followed in his wake, blackening the sky. They drove me and Clover from the branches in their haste to find perches. By the time we scrambled down and followed the boy's tire tracks up the winding road, he was already parked next to Ma's dried-up vegetable garden and banging on the front door with a black, fisted mitten. He held the handle of a red-and-white ice chest in the other covered hand.

Pa opened the screen with a swing of creaking hinges, inviting The Collector across the threshold. Clover and I stepped in behind. The boy was taller than I originally thought, and leaner. We strode to the kitchen behind him, where Oakley sat with a plate of left-over gingerbread from the night before. A small electric fan blew crumbs and stagnant air around the room, its head revolving as if taking us all in.

Our visitor tugged his helmet free and laid it on the table. My tummy did a flip, fascinated and repelled by what I saw. Mainly because I couldn't see *anything*.

He wore a mask made from a soft tan cloth . . . like the shammy Pa used to dry his truck after a wash. The edges were gathered at the boy's neck under his shirt collar and secured with the tie. Two holes were cut, big enough to show soulful brown eyes and dark lashes. There were slits for his nostrils, which was the only way he could breathe, since there wasn't a hole for his mouth.

The Collector stared at Oakley, who had a half-eaten gingerbread boy's leg drooping from his lower lip. My brother's freckled face twitched, on the verge of either tears or hysterical laughter. When the gingerbread plopped into his cup of raspberry Kool-Aid and spattered the white-and-ivory-checked tablecloth with red droplets, Pa sent him out to play.

Oakley obliged, but not without grabbing the binoculars he'd made of empty toilet paper rolls, tape, and plastic wrap. He perched on a stump outside the kitchen window and stared in through the fake lenses.

Me, Clover, and Pa settled at the table. Ma's chair was left empty as always. None of us touched it anymore out of respect, or superstition.

The Collector sat where Oakley had been, his mittened thumb tracing one of the perfect gingerbread people on the plate, as if mesmerized by the shape. The cookie caught on the wool and he had to shake himself free.

Afterward, he pulled a piece of paper from his jacket pocket and pushed it into Pa's hands. I realized then why our guest didn't need a hole for his mouth. It appeared he wasn't much of one for words.

Pa didn't like to read aloud, so he slipped the paper to Clover, since she was the one who always volunteered when Ma used to teach us our lessons.

Clover cleared her throat and read, trying to conceal the lisp from her missing teeth: "In Matthew 5:29–30, it says: 'If your right eye makes you stumble, tear it out and throw it from you; for it is better for you to lose one of the parts of your body than for your whole body to be thrown into hell. If your right hand makes you stumble, cut it off and throw it from you; for it is better for you to lose one of the parts of your body, than for your whole body to be damned.'" Her hand shook, but she continued. "'If the foot leads you astray, remove temptation; see no evil, hear no evil, speak no evil. Feet, eyes, ears, tongue, and hands. That will be the order of dismemberment.

Payment to the amputee is ten thousand dollars per piece.'"

Clover's blue eyes fluttered and she looked up with a flushed face into Pa's watery gray gaze. "Amputee? It has your signature."

I could see the wooziness overtaking. I helped her into the faded petal-pink bedroom we shared, guiding her onto the bottom bunk.

When I returned to the kitchen, Pa told me everything. How he'd been arrested for drunk and disorderly behavior the night before. How The Collector—under the employ of a wealthy doctor who was rumored to have found religion and moved here from a big city to study folk medicine and its ties to the Bible—had brought a note that offered Pa bail. The condition was, Pa agreed to help the doctor prove his new theory: that godly qualities were transferable through skin and bones.

Supposedly, the doc could make Pa a better man by switching out a specified map of body parts with a "good person's" cadaver pieces. In keeping with the Bible verses Clover had read, there were five bodily sectors most inclined to sin. And if Pa were to trade out his offensive parts for better ones, he could be the kind of parent he wanted to be—a substitute for Ma and her productive, gentle ways. The only catch was the doc was a recluse, and refused to come out of his house to chop off any parts or stitch on cadaver pieces. No one was welcome to visit him, either. So that duty had to fall on someone else.

Pa had signed the contract in jail just to get back home to us. It was as good as done.

I bounced a glare from him to the masked visitor, who was preoccupied with Oakley's plate of gingerbread again. "So, you're going to do the amputations, then?"

Instead of answering me, The Collector lifted his dark brown eyes and held up his hands in the mittens, working them like lobster claws as he shook his head. Something told me it wasn't just his tongue that didn't work right, and I wondered how many other parts of him were broken.

I studied the contract again, staring at the dollar signs. Ten thousand per piece. I'd never seen that much money in my life. Lord knew we could use it.

"There's no guarantee," Pa said, his voice wavering. "I could die. But either way, we get paid. And you're the only one strong enough to help fulfill the donations, Sage."

I thought again of the pile of chicken bones out in the yard after the storm six months ago. How I wished Pa had been the one to run out into the lightning to save our livestock. Then maybe Ma would still be with us. Not a day went by when I didn't fantasize about how much better life would be without his drunken rampages. Without *him*.

That's all it took for me to nod and force my tongue to work. "I'll do it."

As if coming out of a trance, The Collector reached into his pocket and handed off a business card to me: *Cut clean through the bone and cauterize the raw edges.*

I frowned and looked up at him. His gaze stayed on mine for an instant and I thought I saw pity there. Or maybe regret.

Then he handed off another card, of which he seemed to have an endless supply. This one had post-surgical instructions, and a promise to return when the deed was done. It said we wouldn't need to contact him. He had ways of knowing.

The Collector stood and without our offering them, carefully wrapped the gingerbread people in a napkin and dropped them into his jacket pocket. Then he put on his helmet and left.

3: Gingerbread Man

Pa and I decided there was no better time than the present to earn our first payment. He grabbed the bottle of sedatives The Collector provided, along with a canning jar filled with moonshine. Clover and Oakley stayed in the house due to the storm clouds rolling in.

Pa and I walked together out to the shed. He even chose the saw.

It felt so strange, him handing me a weapon, after being one himself for so many years. It was like an offering. A penance. And I was ready and willing to take the payment.

I didn't have the proper tools. I didn't have the proper experience. What I did have was the ability to imagine myself in another time and place. Ma used to call me her fanciful girl, because I could pretend so intensely, I would lose myself and forget everything around me. It came in especially handy when she had to stitch something up . . . like the gash I got in my forehead when I was eight and Pa pushed me into the barbed-wire fence that surrounded the garden. My fault, for not doing the weeding right.

"You're just my little gingerbread girl," Ma chanted softly as I cried, then explained how the stitches were little scallops of white icing that would hold me together so I'd be in one piece and pretty.

After Pa drank half the moonshine to wash down two pills, I helped him climb onto his cleared-off workbench. He rolled up his pants leg, fingers slow and awkward from drowsiness, until his left ankle was exposed. Then I tied down his hands and feet, to keep him still . . . for his own good.

Saw in hand, I was no longer Sage Adams, looming over the prone form of my wretched, troubled pa. I was a French baker in Paris, slicing up a gingerbread man. The spurt of blood that slicked my fingers as the saw ground back and forth, the curling of flesh, and the cracking of bones became raspberry filling, marzipan coating, and cookie dough burned too crisp around the edges.

Once Pa passed out, and with only the swell of the wrens' songs and the storm brewing outside, nothing could distract me from my imaginary bakery. Not the sweat drizzling along my brow, not the coppery tang of fresh blood, not the ache in my hand, biceps, and forearm from sawing so long to get through the bone.

Only when his foot plopped onto the pillow of newspaper I'd arranged to catch it, did I drag myself back to reality. My stomach turned. I bent over and threw up, but was careful to aim away from the ten-thousand-dollar foot.

During the hot and cold sweats that followed, I cauterized his mutilated stump as the card had instructed. I used the hot iron . . . the one Clover pressed our clothes with and made her hair straight with so Oakley and Pa could tell us apart. The sizzle and stench of burned skin made me nauseous again. I chewed the lovage root The Collector had supplied. It eased my stomach before I spit the soggy clump from my mouth and packed it around the wound to prevent scar tissue from forming.

The room spun as I wrapped the amputated foot in a heavy plastic bag and placed it in the ice chest.

Wiping my bloody hands on a dust rag, I escaped, leaving Pa to sleep off the sedatives in the garden shed. I returned to the cottage carrying an ice chest worth more money than I'd ever seen, all for two hours' worth of labor. That is, unless you counted the lifetime it took for Pa to grow it.

At the sink, I washed my hands till the water no longer ran red, and gurgled salt water to rinse the taste of vomit and lovage root from my mouth. Clover and Oakley had fallen asleep. Thunder rumbled in the distance and the wrens had silenced.

Not many people realize the truth about wrens. They may be smaller than a kitten's head, but they're brave. Stare down their mortal enemy, beak to fangs, if their home or hatchlings are threatened.

Maybe Pa had been watching those birds since Ma had been gone. Because he'd finally stared down his enemy in a way most men would never have had brass enough to try.

That night, I dropped into bed and dreamed of life-sized gingerbread houses made of human legs and arms, held together by stitches of red licorice that were actually blood veins. Instead of gumdrops and jellied candies decorating the windows, there were organs: hearts, lungs, kidneys, all dripping and fresh from their corpses. The sidewalk leading to the house was made of hollow bones that rolled beneath my feet with a teeth-jarring crunch.

The Collector showed up the next day to pay us and trade the red-and-white ice chest for a blue one containing Pa's new piece. He also handed me a small tub of regenerative ointment. The handwritten label listed ground salamander hearts as the main ingredient, and claimed that by slathering it on the cadaver part's raw edges, it would regenerate Pa's skin and bones to the donor foot once it was stitched into place with the hemp thread provided.

I found that the stitching went easier than the cutting off. I only had to pretend I was piecing a broken cookie together with icing.

It took Pa three months to heal enough to use the foot, so we decided everything would have to come off one at a time. One foot, then the next after the replacement healed. One ear, then the other. One eyeball, one hand, and so on. There was also some adjusting, since his cadaver donor was two sizes smaller than Pa. But we accepted each new and improved body part along with the money without flinching, because the transplants were going to make him a better man. Like Ma had always said, beggars can't be choosers. And we would never be beggars again.

Over the next three years, The Collector's drop-offs and pickups became as ordinary an occurrence as doing laundry or mopping the floor.

The experiment was working. The donor's blue eyeballs that replaced Pa's gray ones helped him see without his reading glasses. With his new tongue, he spoke softer, kinder. And he never cursed. After the ear exchange, Pa listened closer to everything we'd say. Who cared if his ears were smaller? He never ignored us or forgot the important things. That's all that mattered.

That, and the money.

Pa had always loved Ma's cooking. I'd taken over kitchen duties, and in time, as Pa started changing, I started wanting to use her recipes. Maybe because it made him smile, and I'd forgotten what he looked like when he was happy.

Now that we had a steady income, I didn't lack for fresh ingredients. Once Clover and I were of driving age, we took the truck to town and did the shopping.

Pa rarely left the house. He was too self-conscious about the scars. There was no reason for him to leave anyway. We'd fixed up the house real pretty and had a proper stove. We'd even bought Oakley a swing set and fort for playing Cowboys and Indians.

Over time I started to notice that, quiet as he was, The Collector had a kind heart. He always stopped to play with Oakley in his fort when he came by. He also gave us gifts. Not the kinds that were expensive, but the kinds that meant something. He gave Oakley a real set of binoculars and showed him how to use them to scope out giant hawks from the roof of his fort. He gave Clover new eyeteeth on a dental fixture connected to a retainer. And me? I got an endless supply of cherry licorice. Any time I ran out, he'd bring more.

I started to make a habit of baking fresh gingerbread men on the days he was expected, because I'd grown fond of how his dark eyes shone bright each time I wrapped some up careful and insisted he take them home. I found myself talking to him a lot, even though he never talked back. Until finally, one day, he pulled out a memo pad and pen from his jacket, and began to respond through notes written awkwardly with his clawed mitten. It was almost like hearing his voice, reading that messy script.

My favorite thing to do was to tell him jokes. He'd always snort through his nostril holes, then write: *You have me in stitches.*

Later, I would come to see the irony in that statement.

4: Cadaver

Clover and I were sixteen and a half, and The Collector had become a man. He looked to be eighteen or nineteen, though I could only guess by the way his suits hung different on broader shoulders and thicker arms and legs. He still showed up each time in the mask that never revealed his face, and mittens that covered his hands.

Pa's final dismembering had been a success, bringing us to our last meeting with our strange friend and business partner.

I'd just laid out a batch of gingerbread men to cool so I could decorate them while we waited for his arrival. A brisk breeze blew through the half-opened picture window and the early sun slathered the room in an apricot haze. It was only Pa and me that day. Clover had taken Oakley out to bird-watch in the forest.

"Did you substitute brown sugar for the molasses in this batch?"

Pa asked after taking a bite. As a side effect of his tongue transplant, he could pick out spices and flavorings in the things I baked and he'd lost the taste for liquor completely. Hadn't touched a drop in over a year.

"I used both," I answered. "Just wanted to try something new."

Pa nodded. I could tell by the crimp between his eyebrows he was troubled. Today we would get his final puzzle piece. Blots of red dotted the bandage that covered his left wrist and fresh stump. The blood looked like birds flying across a horizon to some unexplored destination. Maybe to carry some dead soul between the real world and the afterlife.

Pa lifted his right hand to take another bite of the cookie. He had started favoring his right even before we removed the left. Apparently, his cadaver donor wasn't a southpaw like him.

His frown deepened as he chewed on the gingerbread man's head.

I pressed gumdrop buttons into the other cookies while I waited for him to say what was on his mind. Maybe he was going to miss The Collector as much as I was. Or maybe he was scared to see the money stop coming in.

There was no reason to worry. We'd managed to live off only a small percentage of the one hundred thousand dollars, and the rest was in savings. Clover had found a job in town at a local grocer, and Pa and Oakley had revived Ma's vegetable garden, providing us plenty of food with enough left over to sell to Clover's boss. I planned to get a job too, once Pa was finally put together for good. Although I wasn't sure what sort of job I was qualified for . . . other than baking things, or chopping parts off of people and sewing them back on pretty. I'd become good at making perfect stitches. Pa had been my guinea pig.

"There's something I need to give you," Pa said at last after swallowing a swig of milk. He reached under the table and dug in his pocket, pulling out a small box and offering it to me.

I opened the lid. Ma's bird-shaped diamond ring glittered from inside a nest of tissue paper.

My throat swelled up. "Where did you find this?" I asked. She'd had it on when she ran out the door into the storm that night. I saw it reflect the lightning in the darkness. Something inside me started to uncoil . . . something teetering between numb and potent, like a snake that had been dormant.

"This has to do with that magnolia tree you're so fond of," Pa answered, his gaze turned down. "The one with the gash in its side. Sage, it wasn't lightning that caused the wood to split. Something crashed into it. I had suspected that all along after seeing it the day after Ma went missing. The tree knows. It—" Pa couldn't finish. He started coughing, as if something had caught in his throat. He guzzled his glass of milk and studied me over the rim.

The sadness in his blue eyes scored me deep. There was more to this story, but it was as if his new tongue refused to work . . . as if it physically hurt him to recount it.

At last I understood. All those months after Ma left, he looked for her. That was why he refused to get a job. Why he'd go into town and stay away until he was skunk drunk. Because he could never find the answers he was seeking, and it was killing him not knowing. And he held it all inside himself.

But that changed the night he met The Collector.

Pa laid his right palm on the table and stretched his long, delicate fingers. "These replacements have given me peace. The doctor helped me find your ma again. And I finally did right by you kids."

His words were cryptic and smoky, as if secrets singed the edges of each one.

A. G. HOWARD

He took out the ring and dropped it in my palm, wrapping my fingers around it with his soft hand. "You keep this part of her. She'd want you to have it. You're the strongest of all of us. Remember that today, when you get the last cadaver piece."

I slid the ring on, wondering if one day I'd have a bird indention in the skin above my knuckle like hers. My chest twisted up tight. I'd always figured she'd come back. And now, the reality of that never happening felt like a knife sawing my heart, back and forth, until it snapped clean through.

I squeezed Pa's palm for the first time since he'd had the new hand. It felt so familiar, like when Ma would wrap her fingers through mine. Like when I first learned to walk. When I broke my elbow. When I had scarlet fever.

The flutter of wrens outside the window startled me. I pulled away.

The Collector's motorbike roared into our front yard and Pa looked at me as if in a daze, then stood and left the kitchen to let our guest in.

I put the finishing touches on the gingerbread men, drawing hair, faces, and tailored vests with icing. My hands trembled and Ma's ring sparkled on my finger in the soft light. I couldn't shake the feeling that I was missing something. Something I'd been missing all along.

Something Pa's new tongue just couldn't tell me.

The screen door opened and closed and I waited for The Collector to come in. But it was only Pa, holding the ice chest.

"He left," Pa said, handing me a note. "But this is for you."

I unfolded the paper and silently read the words: *Your family is together now. I hope at last we can all have the pieces we deserve.*

Pieces. In place of *peace.* I'd read enough of The Collector's notes to know he had perfect spelling. The pun was intentional.

"I'm going to sleep now," Pa said, taking the sedatives with him.

"Wake me when it's over." He started out the door for the shed but paused. "Don't judge the doctor or the boy. They tried to do right by us."

I stared at Pa's retreating shadow, then back at the note. My whole body quaked as I opened the ice chest's lid and carefully lifted the cadaver hand to the light. There, on the left ring finger, was the dove imprint worn into the skin.

I gasped and dropped the hand.

I clamped my jaw shut, swallowing the bile that climbed my throat.

The doctor helped me find your ma again, Pa had said.

Looking into his blue eyes, listening to that gentle tongue, it was as obvious as the scars upon his wrist, ankles, and ears. Both of my parents were inside the patchwork quilt of skin that had sat in the kitchen with me minutes ago, eating gingerbread.

The donor cadaver's identity was a mystery no more. And it was time to pay the reclusive doctor a visit.

5: Burying the Hatchet

That night, I stitched on Pa's final piece, but there was no pretending. I couldn't block out or forget that it was Ma's hand, but I also could never let Clover or Oakley know where it came from, either. I understood on some level that Pa was innocent. He only wanted to give us back our ma and give us a better life. He'd done that. He deserved to be complete and to never have any regrets. He also deserved to be perfect, all but one left ring finger, amputated just below the knuckle.

As he slept off the sedative, and Clover and Oakley dreamed the simple dreams I would never have again, I tossed an ax into the back of Pa's Chevy and headed for town. When I passed Ma's tree, I could finally see why Pa thought something violent happened there. The split no longer looked to me like a streak of white in auburn hair like it once did. It looked like a gash—an infected pus-filled wound.

The town looked different too. Lonely and looming. All the stores and cafes that usually pulsed with life stared back with dark windows, reflecting the truck's headlights. I took the same side road where I'd once caught sight of The Collector's motorbike turning and wove my way toward the outskirts of town where the doctor was rumored to live.

I hadn't let myself stop to think how The Collector was involved in all this. Somewhere in my heart, I couldn't imagine he'd been behind Ma's death. But if he was . . . he would warrant the same ending as his employer.

The three-story house, large and dark, looked like a black gaping maw in the moonlight. I parked the truck and wove my way through the hundreds of wrens pecking the ground. They didn't seem to notice or care that I was there. They just moved aside, busy with their routines. There were even more, some singing soft and haunting from the house's roof and eaves, high above, and others flapping their wings in the oak trees that surrounded the estate.

Spirit carriers.

My fingers tightened on the ax's handle. They'd be happy tonight. Soon they would have someone new to whisk away.

My climb up the creaky steps seemed to take forever, stretched out even longer by my realization that the windows were boarded up. The hair on my arms bristled as the wrens grew quiet and still, as if watching when I came to the front door. It had been left ajar and a flutter of yellow candlelight seeped out. I gulped hard and cinched my hand around the ax, prepared to swing without question, then I pushed it open.

The scent of cinnamon, vanilla, and something stale wafted over me. As my eyes focused on the flickering room, the air drained from my lungs. I was alone, but dioramas stretched from wall to wall on multi-tiered shelves. Little boxes with miniature, three-dimensional scenes numbered and played out in still life. Instead of clothespin dolls to represent the people, as one might expect, there were gingerbread men, boys, and girls. All the ones I'd given The Collector over the years. Their bodies were stiff and shellacked, tilted in place to play out strange, unsettling events.

Gripping my ax, I walked closer to the diorama marked number one, where a gingerbread girl stood on the roof of a building in a big city. Flames made of tissue paper spewed out from the windows. Diorama number two showed her in a pile of icing and crumbs on the sidewalk next to the burned-out building, where she'd jumped to escape the inferno. In the next, a man in a doctor's coat with a Bible in hand, and a young boy in a modern grown-up's suit, stood at a grave. The one after showed the boy with his shirt off, as the doctor pressed feathers into his skin. Miniature dead birds speckled the floor. In scene five, the man drove a black car up a familiar twisty mountain road, with the boy in the passenger side. A storm and lightning streaked the painted sky. Next, the car tilted on two tires, as if losing control. Scene seven: The car crushed up against a tree. Sandwiched between the bumper and tree trunk was a gingerbread girl with two white streaks in her reddish hair. Her top half tilted off-kilter. She'd been split in half at the waist.

Wooziness filled my head, but I couldn't stop staring. I stumbled along, my gaze trailing each diorama. The one where the doc had a gash in his head from the wreck as the boy drove him and the broken gingerbread girl back down the trail. The next, where the boy put my ma's dead body into the freezer, and tried to stitch up the doctor, who I now understood was his pa. When I came to the one where the boy sat across from a prisoner in jail and offered him a box, I knew. The night The Collector visited Pa, he gave him her ring and explained what happened. That's what broke Pa.

That's what changed him.

As if to verify this, next to the diorama was another contract, where The Collector offered Pa a way to fix our family . . . to save his hell-bent spirit, and at the same time save his own pa from going to prison. My pa had been so drunk and heartbroken, he waived his rights to take legal action for the doctor's involvement in the accident.

My throat burned, as if it had been hornet-stung from the inside. I didn't even have to see the next diorama, where The Collector was breaking off Ma's left foot. Because every other scene that remained, I'd lived it as we stitched my ma's pieces onto Pa.

In the final diorama, the gingerbread boy in the suit sat in a chair by a bed where the doctor lay, hooked up to an IV and other machines. The painted background showed it was a room on the top floor of the very house I stood in. The Collector had been putting these scenes together since the day he first came to our house, in preparation for me to come tonight.

He wanted me here. Now, to find out why.

The ax's handle was slick in my palm as I squeezed it on my walk up the stairs. The unsettling flutter of wrens gathering in the eaves outside scattered my nerves. They were waiting. And I wondered if it might be my spirit they'd be escorting away tonight.

There were five rooms on the top floor, but only one was open at the end of the long hall. Candlelight streamed out, painting dancing shadows on the wooden floor and walls. When I stepped inside, The

Collector was right where I expected, seated next to his pa's bedside.

My ears barely caught the sound of the beeping machines and the pumps filling the doctor with oxygen. I was too intent on his face. He looked younger than I'd have thought. A handsome man, in spite of the fact he'd been in a coma for three years. There was stubble on his chin and jaw, as if his son had tried to keep him shaved but given up recently.

"Was it your ma who died?" I asked The Collector, my pulse drumming below my jawline like a sledgehammer.

He nodded under his mask.

"And your pa, he heard about the bird folklore. He was trying to fix you so you could be a bird and fly to your ma. Be with her without dying." I looked at the doctor's arm where it was arranged atop the cover. "If it worked for you, he was going to fix himself too. Am I right?"

The Collector looked down, flinching in the mask's eyeholes.

"But I don't understand. There are birds everywhere on your lawn. You have enough feathers already. Why were you on my mountain that night?"

He slipped off his mask. Candlelight flickered across him, his face a tragic mishmash of stitches and feathers. He didn't have any lips. They'd been removed, and the skin sewn shut. I realized then what the extra IV in the room was for. It was how he'd been surviving.

I couldn't move, so stunned by the scarred, twisted image. His pa must've gone to the mountain in search of a bird with a bigger beak, like the hawks Oakley watched through his binoculars. A bird with a beak big enough to sew on The Collector's face in the place of a mouth.

I took a shaky breath and forced myself not to look away from the young man who'd been so kind to my family. Forced myself to see past the ugly, vile things that had been done to him through no fault of his own.

"You tried to give me my ma back," I said. "In the only way you knew how. And you fixed my pa."

He nodded.

"What *your* pa did to you. It was wrong. Do you understand that?"

He nodded again.

"So I'm gonna kill him now. It's the only way to make things right."

The moment I said it, The Collector stood and worked off his mittens. All his fingers were stitched together except his thumbs, as if to form a wing tip. Gray and black feathers sprouted where there should have been only skin.

Slowly, he drew a knife from his jacket lapel.

I tensed and raised the ax in self-defense, but he backed up and turned his mutilated hand over, laying the knife in his downy palm—a peace offering.

It looked similar to a paring knife. The kind you use to peel skin from fruit while leaving it intact to make pretty embellishments for special desserts.

Then I understood.

He'd been keeping his pa alive, just for this purpose. So he could become human again using his skin and limbs.

Even if The Collector's hands hadn't been damaged, he would've needed me. Not everyone has the ability to imagine themselves away. I'd had years of practice being Ma's fanciful girl, and had perfected it through Pa's reformation.

I set aside my ax and took the knife, squeezing The Collector's feathery hand for comfort. "I'll fix you good as new," I promised.

With a somber nod, he left the room.

In the flickering light, I took the doctor off his IV and the machines keeping him alive. Then, the moment his heart stopped, I slid the knife beneath the flesh at his ear, carefully cutting away his stubbled face while leaving it intact.

I was no longer Sage Adams, quiet country girl with tears streaming her face, thinking of the jar of formaldehyde hidden in the garden shed with a finger afloat inside, worn with the dove-shaped imprint of a ring. Instead, I was a chef in a renowned restaurant, peeling the skin off a kiwi for a gourmet fruit sorbet.

On the I-5
KENDARE BLAKE

EmmaRae Dickson sits in the booth nearest the kitchen of the Flying J Truck Stop just outside Lodi, California. It isn't much to look at, at nearly four in the afternoon, not that it would be at any other time. The red-brown pleather under her ass sticks to her thighs despite the A/C, and something else sticks her hands against the tabletop even though she hasn't ordered yet. She grabs a napkin from the dispenser and wipes her fingers, then pushes the ratty green duffel bag deeper into the booth. The metal buckles clang against the wall. Not her bag, but she'll make do. And it makes her look less out of place, anyway.

The diner isn't crowded, but there aren't that many free tables. Seems a solitary long-haul trucker can fill a booth as well as a family. Waitresses stand behind the counter, writing on their pads or bullshitting with guys in caps that maybe they've seen before. EmmaRae makes eye contact with the nearest waitress, and turns over the coffee cup in front of her. The woman, in her early forties with dishwater frizz hair pulled back in barrettes, frowns, annoyed, but she comes over, and grabs the coffeepot on the way.

"Sorry," she says, and hands EmmaRae a plastic menu. "Thought you were waiting for someone."

"No, ma'am." EmmaRae scans the diner's offerings: biscuits and gravy, a Denver omelet, a couple of grilled sandwiches. She feels the woman's eyes on her and for a second it makes her squirm. The woman is about her momma's age, and she recognizes the feel of the look she's getting.

"That accent. Sounds like you're a long way from home. Where are you coming from?"

"Just south of Batesville, Mississippi," says EmmaRae. She looks up from the menu and wishes the waitress really were her momma, that she'd slide into the booth on those long legs of hers, legs just like EmmaRae's, and kiss EmmaRae on the cheek. But the waitress is already scratching *coffee* onto her pad, and she doesn't look much like Momma anymore.

"I've never been there," the waitress offers. Her gold name tag says Tina. "I grew up in Spokane and came down here with my husband. Well. My fiancé, back then." Tina nods over her shoulder, toward the windows and through to the lot, where semi-trucks and trailers are lined up in massive rows. Most are parked and quiet, but a few sit idling, or pull through to refuel and get back onto the I-5. The constant hum of engines is audible even through the glass.

"Did you ride all the way out here with your daddy?" Tina asks.

"Yes, ma'am," EmmaRae lies. "But he's sleepin' now."

"Well, sit inside as long as you want, okay? And there's a shower in the women's restroom if you need one." Tina points her pen at the menu. "Do you want to order food now? Or wait?"

EmmaRae glances down. She isn't exactly hungry, but she's not unhungry either. As if wanting something as badly as she wants it has made her start to want everything, a little bit.

Something rumbles in the kitchen, the big Rubbermaid rumbling of a trash can, and a boy's voice calls that he's headed out back. It makes EmmaRae's whole body tingle.

"Can I, um . . ." she says quickly, "start with apple pie?"

Tina gives her a look, one eyebrow raised, but EmmaRae's always had one of those faces. The kind you can't say no to. Momma used to say it was the curse she'd passed on.

"Since your daddy's asleep."

"Thank you, ma'am."

And she means it. Tina doesn't look at her like she thinks she's trash, and she doesn't look at EmmaRae's budding chest either. She looks at her like what she is: a girl.

EmmaRae waits until Tina is back behind the counter before sliding out of the booth, her thighs coming unglued with a rubbery, tearing sound. She leaves the bag so they know she hasn't gone for good and slips quickly around the side of the building, to the dumpsters in the back.

She sees the kitchen boy right away, hard to miss in a grease-stained white apron and blue jeans, dragging a sack of trash near as big as he is.

"Hey there!" she calls.

The boy stops short. He even jumps a little, like he's scared of her, and that makes her like him, even if there are splotches of zits across his forehead.

"Hi," he says, and still sounds unsure. He's older than she is, but only a little, with dark brown hair and a square jaw that's going to make him look close to mean when he grows up. But for now, he's caught off guard, tongue-tied by the pretty girl with long chestnut hair and lean legs.

"You got a smoke?" she asks. "I'll help you with that trash if you do." She grabs the garbage bag and drags it away from the dumpster with the open lid, hauling it toward the one nearest the kitchen door. He helps her open it up, and they toss the bag in, EmmaRae putting on a good act of huffing and puffing, even though she could've tossed it with a pinky finger.

"How about that smoke?" she asks, and he fumbles in his pocket for one.

"My name's Jason," he says as he lights it.

"EmmaRae." She exhales. The smoke tastes different now, like everything tastes different, and it feels like she could smoke a million. It's an empty, unnatural feeling, and suddenly she wants nothing to do with the apple pie she ordered inside.

"You just passing through?" Jason asks.

"Yep."

He looks so disappointed, she's almost sorry. But it isn't her fault she can't stay, and he's none of her concern anymore, now that he's away from the open dumpster. Doesn't seem to be much point in flirting. *Don't you lead them on, EmmaRae Dickson. Men will follow you to the ends of the earth, so don't you lead them on.* As if it was her fault. As if she threw ropes around their necks.

"How old are you?" he asks.

"Fourteen."

"No way."

She is fourteen. An old fourteen, and for how many times she's heard that, she can almost believe it really was her fault. That maybe some girls really are nothing much more than meat on spits.

"I should probably take that cigarette back," he says.

She holds it out, and something in her eyes makes him stop smiling.

"Nah," he says. "It's all right. Just don't tell anyone. I'll see you around." He heads back into the kitchen, rubbing his hands on his apron like they're filthy. EmmaRae listens to the dishwasher running and plates and silverware clinking around. Then the door swings shut.

She whistles through her teeth in one long exhale.

"Close call," she says to the girl in the open dumpster behind her.

The girl says nothing. But EmmaRae knows she's in there. She felt that itch from forty miles down the freeway. EmmaRae takes another drag off the cigarette and walks slowly backward. She puffs and paces and kicks stones until she's close enough to the dumpster to stand on the overturned plastic crates stacked beside it and peer down inside.

It was a sloppy job, whoever did it. Good thing she'd come out and redirected the trash, or old Jason would have had the fright of his life. His hand would have probably rubbed right up against the murdered girl's calf.

EmmaRae reaches in and shoves aside the bags and garbage until she can see her face. She was pretty. Fine cheekbones and light brown hair, not unlike EmmaRae's own. There are bruises on most of her, and circular ones around her wrists where she was likely bound. No ring around the collar though, so she figures there are stab wounds somewhere she can't see. Or maybe she was smothered. The girl's eyes are half-open, and EmmaRae wants very much to reach out and close them.

"Not what you're here for," she says to herself, and takes another drag. Whoever the girl was, she hasn't been in the dumpster long. Not long enough for bugs to really make a meal of her, or take up residence in her hair, and EmmaRae is right grateful for that. She does stink, though, like rot and discard. Or maybe that's just the smell of the dumpster she's in.

EmmaRae leans in to inspect a spattering of cigarette burns on the girl's calf, small dark circles in a pattern that could be some sinister constellation. The burns are dull, without red rings or inflammation around them.

"I wonder if they did that to you when you were alive," EmmaRae whispers, "or if they just hated you so much, they did it even after you were dead." She thought it looked like the latter, but it wasn't like she was some kind of gardamn medical examiner.

That almost makes her smile. Even though it isn't the right time, she can't help it. Thinking of Gran shouting from some other room: *I don't know what you want me to do with this bankbook, Rebecca Jean! I ain't no gardamn financier!* And Momma looking at Emma-Rae, and them laughing while Gran goes right on shouting. Gran and Momma. She should have listened to them and stayed home. Now she'd probably never get to see them again.

EmmaRae tosses her cigarette onto the ground. Looking at the dead girl, a feeling of calm settles into her bones. She takes a breath, and carefully arranges the plastic bags over the top of her, doing a fine sight better than whoever dumped her there in the first place. Then she pats the trash softly and hops down off the crates.

It won't be long until dark, and then the two girls can really get started. Starting out fresh, and starting up finishing.

Time in the diner passes slowly. EmmaRae eats slices of pie that taste like nothing and listens for anyone in the kitchen going out the back doors, but no one does. She waits for the sun to go down and give her cover.

Tina leans over the table to warm up her coffee and slides a slip of paper across.

"Almost the end of my shift, sweetie," she says. "Have to close out my tickets."

"Sure," says EmmaRae. She digs cash out of her pockets and counts out what she hopes isn't a completely shitty tip. "I don't have to go, do I?"

Tina looks at her carefully.

"You've been here a long time," she says. "Your daddy must be a good sleeper."

EmmaRae looks right back, knowing that Tina suspects the truth: That there is no daddy, that none of those men in any of those trucks know anything about this girl from Mississippi, where she came from or why she's there. That suspicion will eat at Tina for weeks afterward. That maybe she should have helped that girl. Maybe she would have, if there hadn't been something so inexplicably off about her.

In the end, Tina shrugs and takes the cash. Someone with a new name tag will come over and tend to EmmaRae, or maybe she'll be gone by then.

The night has come on cool, and made the diner chilly; EmmaRae has put on a faded red zip-up sweatshirt. Again, not hers, but it will do. In fact, it makes her almost warm. It belonged to the beast, and feels a little like wearing skin. An oversized skin that smells of sweat and spilled whiskey.

The trucks are louder now as the night drivers get ready to head onto the interstate, and the diner picks up with orders for to-go sandwiches and coffee. The buzz of the dead girl out back in the trash vibrates through EmmaRae like a song. It's hard to wait for the night drivers to go. The urge grows in her chest until she wants to bite, wants to run fast as a colt, wants to scream up loud to the black heavens until she can't scream no more, no more screaming for EmmaRae Dickson, no thank you, no ma'am, she's had plenty of that. Time now to let her lie down and puff away like a stepped-on seedpod in the dirt.

She's so full of that urge, she doesn't notice the other, darker feeling until the door of the diner swings open. As soon as it does, as soon as he walks in, she lifts her head and sniffs like one of Randy's coonhounds and smells his smell clear as if it trailed green fog to her nose.

For a mad second she wonders if this is the one who did the girl in the dumpster. If he's come back now to double-check his work, or maybe try to slide the girl back out of the trash and leave her someplace better. Someplace with less people and more scavenging animals, or a nice hole with lime in the bottom. EmmaRae's fingernails gouge into the plastic-coated tabletop and rake back a quarter inch of the stuff. She's waited long enough for her dead girl, for the right dead girl, and she isn't interested in hanging around another diner or another muddy riverbank for the next one.

But the monster looks her way, and smiles, and EmmaRae relaxes. He isn't the one. Not the one who burned those cigarette marks into the dumpster girl's calf. He's just another one. A different monster, a different beast, walking the same walk and smelling of that same sour, sweaty reek. He even looks a little bit like her own beast, only older. She could almost believe it *is* him, that she's gone forward or back or sideways in time, if she weren't already wearing her beast's red, zip-up skin.

EmmaRae sips what's left of her coffee, room temp and turning bitter. She listens to the whisper of the dumpster girl and tries to ignore this new beast. She thinks to herself how he should mind his own. Mind his own and leave her alone, have some sense when she's got just this one last thing to do. She thinks that even as she wonders how another one has managed to find her, and wonders how many there are. How many terrors in the world, so many more than all the hundreds her momma and gran warned her about.

Leave me alone, she thinks again, as he puts his eyes on her. See that I ain't afraid. That I ain't got no needs, no wants from a man like you. Leave me alone. She's thought that before. Many times back in Mississippi. And not a man in her life has ever left her alone.

He slides into her booth and she imagines what it could be like, if she could reach out and slap him or show him the blood under her fingernails, show him the blood stuck in the underside of her hair, blood and rage he would see if only he'd get his eyes off her parts and back to where they should be. But those don't seem to be the rules, if there *are* any rules, and besides, if she's honest, the scent of him in her nose disgusts her and makes her mouth water at the same time.

He smiles and asks her name and she says, "EmmaRae." He's not from the I-5. He's gussied up in business clothes, driving a car instead of a semi, but that's not right, she thinks. He's no trucker, but he is from the I-5. He's driven up and down and through state lines, turning a stretch of road into a hunting ground. He's done it for years, and he's not hardly afraid anymore, of getting caught.

"Where are you from, EmmaRae?"

"Batesville, Mississippi."

"Is your daddy out there in one of those trucks?"

She chuckles a little and shakes her head.

"What's so funny?" he asks.

"People out here," she says. "They say 'daddy' on account of the way I talk. Because of where I'm from. Daddy, like that's what I'd call him, if I knew him at all. But I didn't. And if I did, I'd have called him Pa."

"I'm sorry," he says, and his face is a good face. Handsome and trustworthy, like her own beast's was when he picked her up on the side of the highway. Like he had a family, and friends, and a daughter or two of his own. She doesn't know why God gives those kinds of faces to these kinds of men.

"It's all right," she says. "Weren't his fault. Momma didn't know who he was, so she couldn't tell him. Weren't her fault neither."

"I'm still sorry. Is your momma gone now too?"

"Yes," she lies, and her face is an angel's face.

"Where are you on your way to, EmmaRae?" he asks.

"Los Angeles," she says, and listens while he tells her it isn't safe by herself on the road.

The girl in the dumpster is a buzz down her spine as the man called Charles drives EmmaRae away in his long gray sedan. *Hush,* Emma-Rae thinks. *Hush your dead ass right up, and I'll be back soon.* She doesn't think that the girl is telling her to stop, really. Only that she's afraid, and doesn't want EmmaRae to go so far away. But that's stupid. Fear isn't for dead girls in dumpsters. EmmaRae turns the radio on to drown her out. Of course it does no good.

"And what do you think you're going to do, down there in Los Angeles?" Charles asks, and she shrugs. "I mean, what brings you all the way out here, from Batesville, Missouri? Family? A boyfriend?"

"No boyfriend to speak of," EmmaRae says.

"I can't believe that. A pretty thing like you? You must have them falling over."

"I suppose I do, mister."

"Charles," he says, and smiles. "So what, then? One of those stars on the Hollywood Walk of Fame got your future name on it?"

There's something a little mean about that smile, a little mocking, and EmmaRae grinds her teeth. What nerve this beast has. Not that the mocking touches her personally. She had no designs on acting in movies or becoming America's Next Gardamn Top Model. It was just that home seemed so small and so close. Everything there she'd already seen, twice or more. All that Mississippi had to offer, the pretty and the not so pretty and all of it in between.

"I suppose I just wanted to get out of Batesville," says EmmaRae. "We weren't even in Batesville proper. We were south. In the country. Seemed like an easy thing, to get up to Memphis and ride the forty all the way." On the map it looked like a straight line, straight as an arrow. "But I never got there."

"Well, we'll get you there tonight."

"Sure we will, mister," she says in a way that seems to give him pause. But not enough to stop. Not enough to let her out of the car. This one never lets them out of the car. This one takes them to the woods or to the desert, and EmmaRae can still smell their fear, and their blood, and their decay all over the seats. It mixes in the air with his stink. Their bodies vibrate a little in her bones too, but they're gone, spread out far and wide, and sometimes in pieces, and she tells herself not to listen. Not when she's got a dead girl fresh and found back at the diner. A dead girl she's already promised. She watches the highway lines flicker by and vaguely recollects a poem she learned in school.

This is my last mile, she thinks. My last mile before I sleep.

When the car pulls off the I-5, she hears herself ask where they're going, just like she should, and listens to his answer, so thick with bullshit that it almost makes her laugh.

He drives a long way, down deserted roads, into the middle of nowhere. EmmaRae knows that even though no one would hear you scream out here, lots of girls have done it. She did it, not too long ago, in her own middle of nowhere.

"I don't know what I was thinkin'," she says to no one in particular. "Goin' by myself out there. Fourteen. What kind of job did I think I was goin' to get? What did I think I was goin' to do?"

"Don't sell yourself short, EmmaRae," says Charles, who thinks she was talking to him. "You're a very grown-up girl. A very grown-up fourteen."

The car is stopped now, and Charles's seat is pushed back from the steering wheel.

"I wasn't stupid," she says, and touches her face, surprised to find she can still cry. She wasn't stupid. She was just sad. And young. So full of life, she thought she could afford to lose some.

"You are so, so pretty," Charles says, as if he can't see her tears at all, and can't hear her words. Then he puts his hands on her.

"It won't be the same as my beast," she says. It won't be anywhere near as gratifying as it was to see her beast's face, that special face that only she could get him to make. Shock. Denial. Terror. A sweet mix of all three. It won't feel like it did when she walked into his house, and Charles's screams won't be the song that his screams were. She might not feel so white hot and almost alive when she slices through Charles, not quite so alive as she did when she felt that first coil of her beast's intestine give way under her fingers. When she pulled. His blood won't taste as good neither, but that's okay. Beast blood is the only thing that tastes like much of anything anymore, and after that depressing apple pie back at the Flying J, EmmaRae is ready for any kind of taste at all.

"It won't feel as good," she says, and Charles promises that it *will* feel good. He lets his mask slip just a little bit, and tells her that it *will* feel good, right up until it won't.

KENDARE BLAKE

It annoys EmmaRae that he still thinks she's talking to him, and she wonders if he's ever in his life just listened. If he's ever really seen.

But not even Charles can ignore how cold she's become as she slips the last of her living-girl mask, and when he touches her bare flesh, he pulls his hand back. When the cold spreads up his wrist, he starts to whine.

"What's wrong with you?" he asks. He tries to get away. He presses himself against his door. EmmaRae doesn't know how she looks now, but it must not be so pretty anymore, judging by the way his eyes bug out.

"Shut up," EmmaRae hisses. The swollen, black handprints return to her throat. She can feel them. They hurt. And it only makes her angrier. "You shut up and don't say things! Like it was my fault. Like I had it comin'."

Charles babbles about getting out of the car, her or him, she isn't sure which. It doesn't matter. He's still not listening. All that talking and all that looking, so he certainly has need of his eyes and mouth. But his ears EmmaRae figures are fair game, and she reaches up and rips them clean off the sides of his head. After that she doesn't talk anymore, because she at least knows what ears are for. Charles still talks, though. Talks and screams, while he can. Then he just sort of gurgles.

It doesn't feel as good as it did with her own beast, but she imagines all those girls spread out in the rivers and the deserts and the forests and the fields would say it's a fine day's work, and that, she guesses, is good enough for her.

EmmaRae pulls her arm out of his abdomen, red and slick to the elbow and looks at it. Such a skinny thing.

"You were right about one thing, mister," she says. "I am grown-up. As grown-up as I'm ever gonna get."

EmmaRae drag-walked the dead girl a long way, out of the dumpster and through the parking lot, traveling for miles beside the road, far enough from the lights to keep from being seen. They would look quite the pair, a bruised-up dead girl and EmmaRae, her arms coated with drying blood. There aren't many hours now before sunrise. She had to walk all the way back to the J, and then had to get the girl up and out of the trash all quiet like, and it took a while. Would have been nice to have driven Charles's car back, but she never learned how.

EmmaRae sets the girl down. They've made it. This little patch of land, this nothing strip of ground before dawn with not a thing to distinguish it from the rest. But it's right. EmmaRae kneels and leans forward to dig in the dirt. It's easy at first, and then harder; her fingernails rip on tricky bits of rock, but that doesn't matter. She can't feel it, and it's sort of a nice change from the ease of tearing into bellies and throats.

The night is cold on her shoulders as she digs. She left the beast's sweatshirt on the side of the road after taking care of Charles. It was soaked with Charles's blood, all sticky and sunken in deep, and it felt wrong to have the two beasts' blood mingling. Like they were commiserating. Like they were thick as thieves. If she'd had a lighter, she'd have burned the damn thing.

"But I s'pose I left you waitin' long enough," she says, and the dead girl watches as the hole in the dirt grows deeper and slowly forms a rough oval. "Wonder how they got you," she whispers. "If they grabbed you, or if you were dumb like me and just climbed on in." She wishes she knew the dead girl's name, and thinks that maybe she'll get to, afterward. That maybe there is a special heaven for murdered girls and she might meet her there, after both their tasks are done. She wonders if Momma and Gran might visit there one day too.

"In you go," says EmmaRae. She rolls the girl in with a shoe and makes sure she lies faceup. It doesn't seem right, booting her in, but EmmaRae's hands are torn fairly to bits from digging the hole in the first place. That's a good thing too, about her hands. One more clue, so the girl will know what she has to do, later on.

She pushes the dirt back in, and pats the mound smooth when she's done, like Momma used to do in the seedbed back home.

"Don't get too comfortable," she says. "You think this is for you, but it isn't." She taps the dirt. "We dig our own holes around here. And you better gardamn know that when you come out. You better not leave me to bake in the sun. It only takes a few minutes, to roll a person in and cover them up." But EmmaRae isn't really worried. When EmmaRae crawled out of the shallow ditch and saw the corpse of the girl who came before lying beside it, she'd shoved her in and buried her first thing. It was only afterward that she stopped and stared and wondered why she'd done it. The dumpster girl will do the same thing for EmmaRae.

EmmaRae plops down on the ground. She listens to the cars go by on the interstate and looks up at the stars. Nothing to do now but wait. And not a single cigarette to her name to smoke while she does it.

"Starting to get tired," she says, and tugs her knees up to her chest. "Do you think, dead girl, that there's a special place for girls like us? Do you think we always to go heaven, no matter what we done before?" The dirt doesn't move, and EmmaRae frowns. "Wish I'd buried you different. With your hand sticking out to hold. Somethin'.

"I think we do," she says. "I think we had our share of pain and scared. I think we're right with God. I think maybe we're his angels."

The girl will wake up soon. Night is almost over. And EmmaRae's bones ache to be finished.

"You won't be scared. Time for that's passed. And you'll know just what to do, and where to find him, like I did. The look on his face . . ." She giggled. "When I showed up, breathin', with no bruises. My beast. He couldn't believe it. Right up until all the blood ran outta him, he couldn't believe it. And your beast won't believe it neither."

EmmaRae lies down and stretches her body beside the mound of dirt. She doesn't put an arm over it protectively, even though she wants to. It doesn't feel quite polite, when she doesn't even know the girl's name.

Her gran always said that places like Los Angeles ate little girls alive. But Gran was wrong about that. The whole damn godforsaken world eats girls alive, and EmmaRae should be glad to leave it. To get away forever from bitter exhaust in her nose and people yelling and hating her and tired and ugly looks from girls and boys alike.

"Wish I hadn't gotten into that car," she says. "Wish I'd never left home at all."

The sky overhead turns pale and then paler. She doesn't suppose she'll be around to see the true sunrise, but in the dim pre-dawn she can see the land around her, and the smoothness of the dirt. All the vast heavens, and the wisps of clouds. Not such a bad place to spend forever, all things considered.

"Looked at another way, Momma," she whispers, "you could say I almost made it."

Beside her, the mound of dirt trembles, and the not-as-dead girl begins to push her way through to the morning. EmmaRae smiles, or at least she thinks she smiles, and even takes a breath to welcome the girl back, and maybe introduce herself. But before she can, Emma-Rae Dickson stops being EmmaRae Dickson, and goes back to being a corpse on the side of the highway.

Inspired by the 2007 film *Death Proof* and the 1986 film *The Hitcher*

About the Authors

STEFAN BACHMANN is the author of steampunk-faery-fantasies *The Peculiar* and *The Whatnot*, and the upcoming YA thriller *A Drop of Night*. He was born in Colorado, but spent most of his formative years in Switzerland, where he lives in a very old house and moonlights as a student of classical music at the Zürich University of Arts. Find him online at stefanbachmann.com and on Twitter @Stefan_Bachmann.

LEIGH BARDUGO is the *New York Times* and *USA Today* bestselling author of the Grisha Trilogy: *Shadow and Bone, Siege and Storm,* and *Ruin and Rising.* She was born in Jerusalem, grew up in Los Angeles, and graduated from Yale University, and has worked in advertising, journalism, and most recently, makeup and special effects. These days, she's lives and writes in Hollywood, where she can occasionally be heard singing with her band. Her new book, *Six of Crows*, arrives October 2015. You can find her at leighbardugo .com and on Twitter @LBardugo.

KENDARE BLAKE is the author of six novels, including *Anna Dressed in Blood, Antigoddess,* and most recently, *Ungodly.* Her work tends toward the dark, is sometimes humorous, and is always violent. Everything she writes turns to guts. Sort of like the Midas touch, only with viscera. Connect with her at kendareblake.com.

A. G. HOWARD was inspired to write *Splintered*, the first book in her bestselling Splintered series, while working at a school library. She had always wondered what would've happened had the subtle creepiness of *Alice's Adventures in Wonderland* taken center stage, and hopes her darker and funkier tribute to Carroll inspires readers to seek out the stories that won her heart as a child. You can learn more about her and her books at www.aghoward.com.

JAY KRISTOFF is an award-winning sci-fi/fantasy author. He is 6'7" and has approximately 13,220 days to live. He abides in Melbourne with his secret agent kung-fu assassin wife, and the world's laziest Jack Russell. His new series, ILLUMINAE (with Amie Kaufman), a YA sci-fi . . . thing, kicks off in 2015. He promises it's like nothing you've ever read before. Find Jay online at jaykristoff.com and on Twitter @misterkristoff. He does not believe in happy endings.

MARIE LU is the *New York Times* bestselling author of the Legend trilogy and *The Young Elites*. Before becoming a full-time writer, she worked as an art director in the video game industry. She currently lives in Los Angeles, where she spends her time writing, reading, drawing, playing games, and getting stuck in traffic. Visit Marie online at marielubooks.tumblr.com and on Twitter at @Marie_Lu.

JONATHAN MABERRY is a *New York Times* bestselling author, multiple Bram Stoker Award winner, and comic book writer. He writes in multiple genres, including thriller, horror, science fiction, fantasy, action, and steampunk, for adults and teens. His works include *Rot & Ruin*, *The Nightsiders*, *Patient Zero*, *V-Wars*, *Captain America*, and many others. Several of his works are in development for movies and TV. Find him online at jonathanmaberry.com and on Twitter @jonathanmaberry.

DANIELLE PAIGE is the *New York Times* bestselling author of *Dorothy Must Die* and its upcoming sequel, *The Wicked Will Rise*. In addition to writing young adult books, she works in the television industry, where she's received a Writers Guild of America Award and was nominated for several Daytime Emmys. She is a graduate of Columbia University and currently lives in New York City. You can find her on Twitter and Instagram, both @daniellempaige.

CARRIE RYAN is the *New York Times* bestselling author of the Forest of Hands and Teeth series, *Daughter of Deep Silence*, *Infinity Ring: Divide and Conquer,* as well as the Map to Everywhere series co-written with her husband, John Parke Davis. Her books have sold in more than twenty-two territories and her first book is in development as a major motion picture. A former litigator, Carrie now lives in Charlotte, NC. Visit her online at www.CarrieRyan. com or on Twitter at @CarrieRyan.

MEGAN SHEPHERD is the author of the Madman's Daughter and the Cage trilogies. She has lived all around the world, but now resides in a 125-year-old farmhouse in the Blue Ridge Mountains that is most definitely haunted. If you ask her nicely, she might tell you your fortune. Find out more about Megan at meganshepherd.com or @megan_shepherd.

NOVA REN SUMA is the author of the YA novels *The Walls Around Us, 17 & Gone,* and *Imaginary Girls.* She has an MFA in fiction from Columbia University and lives in New York City. Visit her online at novaren.com.

McCORMICK TEMPLEMAN is the author of *The Little Woods* and *The Glass Casket.* She lives and writes in Portland, Oregon. Visit her at mccormicktempleman.com.

APRIL GENEVIEVE TUCHOLKE's debut novel, *Between the Devil and the Deep Blue Sea,* was a 2014 YALSA Teens Top Ten nominee and received numerous starred reviews. Its sequel, *Between the Spark and the Burn,* was published in 2014. Her third novel, a stand-alone entitled *Wink Poppy Midnight,* will be released in 2016 from Dial/ Penguin. Tucholke has lived all over the world and currently resides in Oregon. Find April on Twitter @apriltucholke.

CAT WINTERS has been a fan of horror since she stumbled upon a book about real-life haunted houses in her elementary school's library. Her debut novel, *In the Shadow of Blackbirds,* was named a 2014 Morris Award Finalist, a *School Library Journal* Best Book of 2013, and a 2014 Best Fiction for Young Adults pick. Her other novels include *The Cure for Dreaming* and *The Uninvited.* She lives in Portland, Oregon. Visit her online at catwinters.com and on Twitter @catwinters.